JUSTIN RISHEL

Executioner's Lament

Book 2 of the Martin Aubrey Series

First published by Rowdy Dog Press 2020

First edition

ISBN: 978-1-7344133-4-2

This book was professionally typeset on Reedsy. Find out more at reedsy.com

For E, G, and T.
Makers, menders, learners.

Contents

II Part Two

III Part Three

Prologue

MARYLAND GENERAL ASSEMBLY
1982 Regular Session
To: Judiciary, Division A
By: Senator(s) Berman, Golec, Fackrell
Senate Bill 773256

AN ACT TO AMEND SECTION 97-3-19, MARYLAND CODE OF 1972, TO CREATE AN AGENCY OF THE JUDICIAL BRANCH THAT SHALL CARRY OUT TERMINAL SENTENCING OF PERSONS FOUND GUILTY OF A CRIME RESULTING IN THEIR IMPRISONMENT.

BE IT ENACTED BY THE GENERAL ASSEMBLY OF THE STATE OF MARYLAND:

SECTION 1.97-3-19, Maryland Code of 1972, is amended as follows:

(1) An agency of the Judicial Branch shall be created to carry out death penalty sentencing upon persons imprisoned in Maryland state prisons.

(2) The agency shall be charged with the execution of imprisoned persons judged to be unworthy of life.

(3) A person shall be unworthy of life who has been deemed incorrigible by the agency and no form of treatment nor time shall redeem the person from committing evil acts causing death or serious injury to others.

(4) The agency shall observe and assess imprisoned persons

in an objective and unbiased manner before judging and selecting said persons for death.
(5) The agency shall swiftly and without malice or unnecessary suffering, carry out the death penalty on imprisoned persons selected for death.
(6) The authority granted herein to the agency shall last no less than ninety-nine (99) years from the passage of this act.
(7) The agency hereby created shall be called Order of the Coppice.

I

Part One

1

The Tapper

Brother Rudolfo, Member of the Order of the Coppice, watched the three inmates from a small observation room not far from where they sat. He watched and listened to the conversations and interactions taking place between them.

The cameras looked down on the inmates wearing their normal white prison uniforms. Their black barcodes tattooed down the middle of their shaved heads, looking up at Rudolfo. They were taking advantage of regularly scheduled recreation time by enjoying a game of cards. For Rudolfo, it was an opportune moment to watch.

The rec room was set up precisely for these observations. While it did serve to alleviate some of the inmate population's profound boredom and its resultant bad behavior, the primary purpose of the room was for behavioral analysis—the type Rudolfo was conducting at that moment.

At first glance, any casual passerby would see the space as a standard rec room for a prison population. Stationed around the room were shelves of books and magazines, boxes with checkers sets, board games, stacks of playing cards, and in the corner a small TV playing the national news around the clock.

Casual observers in the Maryland Regional Corrections Center, also called the Coppice or the Keep, would not notice the half dozen cameras, sensors, and scanners hidden throughout it. Rudolfo watched on a video screen as the three men, inmates 5334, 8920, and 4557, sat in metal chairs around a plastic square table playing a game of cards he didn't recognize.

To the naked eye, their card game was civil and mundane, meant for the men to break up the monotony of the day and commiserate with others suffering the same plight.

"Good throw, man," inmate 5334 said, nodding his approval of 4557's expert play on the last hand.

"Yeah, where'd you learn to play, newbie?" 8920 asked.

4557 was pulling in small stacks of cards from the other two inmates. He raked them in with wide eyes and a Cheshire grin.

"Oh, I learnt here and thar. But I tell you whut—you boys gonna owe me somethin' awful if you don't find some luck. Maybe I'll pull this rabbit foot out my ass and let you borrow it!" He slapped the table, sending cards flying.

The three men laughed like old friends; it was difficult to see it any other way.

Rudolfo saw it differently. His training and the tools in front of him made it so. The frequent glances between 5334 and 8920, both men's rapid foot tapping, and the sweat forming on 8920's upper lip in spite of the fifty-eight-degree ambient temperature were all clues. The rest of the proof was on the monitors.

The machines made it clear that inmates 5334 and 8920

were being false—pulse spikes on the remote EKG, flushes of dark red on the biometrics sensors, blood vessel constrictions on the functional MRI.

Inmate 4557, on the other hand, showed no signs of stress or anxiety other than the slightly elevated levels one would expect from a game of chance with stakes on the line. 4557 had no idea the game was a ruse and that he was in danger.

Rudolfo decided he had seen enough. A guard was near the rec room, but the two attackers could do a great deal of harm in the two to three seconds it took the guard to intervene. Rudolfo had to stop it before it started.

He reached toward the small blue button to call the guard but stopped short of pressing it. In the room, the three men suddenly looked toward the door. As one, they rose and bolted from the room as if running from a fire.

Then, Rudolfo felt it. There was a vibration beneath his feet. An earthquake, he thought for a moment before realizing how ridiculous the notion was. Utilities or facilities maintenance was more likely. The men must have felt it, got frightened, and ran for safety, he decided.

From an inside pocket of his form-fitting black cassock, he removed a stylus pen. Leaning forward, he opened a leather-bound book on the desk. He would enter his observations onto the pages dedicated to 5334 and 8920.

Before putting pen to paper, he felt it again. The vibration in the floor was there, although when he thought about it, it had never left. It was rhythmic, like the beating of a drum. There was a sound, unintelligible, but it was there beating in time with the thrumming in the floor.

His ward of the prison complex was like all the others—loud outbursts were common, but the vibration in the floor accompanying it made him curious and more than a little concerned.

Rudolfo stood and walked to the door, pulling it open.

The crash of sound that pummeled his senses made him wonder if they weren't in fact in the middle of an earthquake. The rhythmic crashing sound was like a slow jackhammer beating the air on all sides.

The bright white hallway was unusually barren for this time of day. The cold, stale atmosphere continued to pulsate with the steady rhythmic pounding.

He stood there for a moment and began to recognize the sound not as machinery or seismic activity, but as voices. Voices chanting violently as one, but he couldn't understand what the voices were saying. It was so loud it seemed to come from everywhere, but he had a feeling he knew where to find its source.

With a snap, he pivoted right, heels clicking as he made his way to the North corridor. He was in passageway four, the outermost of a series of concentric circular hallways. Passageway four with its many offices was lightly trafficked by inmates and at the moment it was empty, even of guards.

He reached the North corridor, turned, and stopped cold. The chant reached him clear and crisp, coming fresh from its source.

"TAP! TAP! TAP! TAP! TAP!"

Fifty yards ahead, where the North Corridor terminated at the Great Atrium, he saw the backs of tightly packed inmates filling the corridor. The ones at the rear of the crowd were fighting to move forward, pushing and pulling the men in front of them. They were trying to get closer to the metal cage that lined the Great Atrium.

He made his way toward the commotion, passing the three concentric passageways lined with cells. With every step the chant grew louder, the pounding through the floor grew stronger; it pulsed through his feet and up his bones.

Nearing the crowd at the end of the corridor, he could not see beyond the group ahead of him. It was clear they were all staring in one direction—somewhere off to the right and above them. The throng in front of him undulated as each man jockeyed for a better view, standing on unknown objects only to be pulled down and replaced by a usurper. They climbed on backs and shoulders desperate for a better look.

Fists shook and bare hands slapped cinder block walls, but the most jarring sound came from the cage. The metal cage that lined the Great Atrium—that massive cylinder of open air that penetrated the full height of the forty-eight-story prison.

The inmates lining the cage slammed against it with closed fists or open palms, the whole time they chanted.

"TAP! TAP! TAP!"

They were using the slang term for the solemn duty that a Member of the Order performed. Most people inside and outside the prison referred to Members as Tappers, but never to their faces and never shouted with rage. To hear it shouted en masse laced with such acid was unnerving.

"Gentlemen," Rudolfo said. No one noticed him over the din.

"Gentlemen, please," he said again only slightly louder. For a moment, it appeared no one heard him. Then, the man nearest Rudolfo caught sight of him.

"Oh shit, sorry," he squealed, bending his head low to look

at the floor while he pulled on the shoulder of the inmates in front of him. They turned and had a similar reaction.

The process repeated man after man until the respect given to Members of the Order parted the sea of bodies in front of Rudolfo. He walked forward through the deferential inmates and onto the grated catwalk.

Immediately, he noticed the crowding wasn't limited to his floor. The Great Atrium's cage was packed tight with shouting prisoners half-a-dozen floors above and below.

Incarcerated men and women screamed in unison, "TAP! TAP! TAP! TAP!"

From his place on the catwalk, he could see what they were all looking at. Every eye was focused on a single person standing on a shallow maintenance platform two stories up. The Member of the Order was easy to spot. He was the only black spot in a sea of white jumpsuits.

It was clear to Rudolfo why the mob of prisoners was so fervent. Members of the Order were the incorruptible, uncompromising selectors that filled death's coffers. Now here was one of them about to select himself to take his place among the many he himself sent into the void.

Suicide was not encouraged at the Coppice, but it certainly wasn't discouraged. If an inmate decided that the world would be better off without him, the powers that be allowed him to take that step. The maintenance platforms were the only access to the inside of the atrium's cage, and they were secured with nothing but a simple gate that was never locked. Inmates jumped so often that most of the others wouldn't leave their bunks to watch. Those who happened to be on the catwalk when someone jumped would break their conversation as the poor man or woman fluttered past, but they paid no more mind to it than that.

This situation was much different. Brother Wilcott had been a Member of the Order of the Coppice for thirty-eight years. He had been responsible for the executions of an untold number of inmates. Because of the mystery surrounding them, Members of the Order received unquestioned respect, if not awe, from everyone around them, especially the inmates. When a Member showed weakness and vulnerability, the inmates fed on it like starving animals.

Hands pounded against the rusty cage in rhythm with the chant.

"TAP! TAP! TAP! TAP!"

It was a visceral impassioned plea for death.

Rudolfo quickly scanned the levels within view. Corrections officers and other Members of the Order stood out here and there, inky splotches against a backdrop of white.

He looked back at Brother Wilcott. The chant as steady as a metronome resounding from a half dozen levels above and below Rudolfo. "TAP! TAP! TAP!" Metal pounded metal, driven by angry flesh.

Rudolfo watched Brother Wilcott who stared straight ahead. His short white hair was combed neatly to the side, his face smooth with a fresh shave. His eyes tired.

Wilcott shot a look directly at Rudolfo. They gazed at one another for several seconds. There was something behind Wilcott's look, as if he were waiting for Rudolfo. Then, the older Member resumed his forward stare and raised his hands to his chest.

It looked as if he was about to pray, which would have been exceedingly odd—Members of the Order were not religious or spiritual for a very good reason.

Wilcott was not praying. He pulled off the black glove on his left hand, held it out for a moment and let it fall. Then he started removing the right glove.

Rudolfo held his breath; he had no idea how the inmates would react.

Brother Wilcott removed the right glove with care; the prisoners surrounding the Great Atrium quieted. When he dropped the glove, most of the inmates looked confused. To them, it must have looked as if he was still wearing the glove. Gradually, the mob realized that it was not a glove at all; it was the man's bare skin stained a deep purplish-black—the result of decades of serving out the Sacred Task beset upon the Members of the Order. It was the result of countless lives ended.

Wilcott was a death dealer and the poison used for the Task had marked him, as it marked all Members. His skin bore permanent witness to his deeds.

Seeing his polluted hand made the inmates go silent, but only for a moment. Once it sank in what the black hand meant, when it was clear the one rumor about Members of the Order was true—that a bare finger was dipped in poison to dispatch the selected—the inmates grew more ravenous than ever before. The chant and the banging resumed with heightened ferocity.

"TAPTAPTAPTAPTAP!"

The words melted into one another until the noise became a discordant racket.

No inmate appeared willing to push Wilcott off the platform, even after seeing his hand. It seemed they dared not touch the Member for fear of being inadvertently executed. They simply screamed and banged and spat and shook.

Rudolfo watched the glove tumble like a leaf through the air, then scanned the crowd once more. When he looked back at Wilcott, it was only to find the old Member staring back at him. The same blank face. The same tired eyes. Just staring.

Brother Rudolfo grew less calm. His breathing grew heavier and the heat around his neck became more evident.

Wilcott looked away. He reached to his chest again and began unbuttoning the top of his cassock. He continued unfastening the large shiny buttons until the tight woolen cloak was completely undone and his pale flesh shone through.

He pulled the cassock off his shoulders. Underneath he wore nothing but white underwear and his mark; the dark stain, stretched from the fingertips of his right hand to his chest.

The prison fell silent. The breadth of the stain was a surprise to everyone, even Rudolfo, who knew from personal experience how the stains grew. He would never be in a position to see any stain other than his own, however.

Wilcott's entire arm and part of his shoulder were completely covered in inky blackness. A kind of cruel tattoo. The mark continued past his shoulder in several long tendrils which stretched like tentacles across his chest, the longest crossing directly over his heart.

Rudolfo didn't know if it was the size of the stain that made the throngs grow quiet, silently guessing at the number of executions required to create such a mark. Or if it was the symbolism behind it, the magnitude of his role in death and life at the Coppice.

Wilcott held out the cassock and removed a small item

from a pocket before releasing the garment, letting it flutter through space like a piece of paper on the wind. He clutched the item in his left hand and inserted his blackened right index finger into the opposite fist. As Brother Wilcott withdrew it, light glinted off his fingertip.

"No," Rudolfo whispered.

From such a distance, he couldn't see exactly what coated Wilcott's finger, but he knew in his heart it now shimmered with the Solution. Incomprehensible mutterings drifted through the throng of onlookers around the Great Atrium. Rudolfo couldn't hear them clearly, he only vaguely registered voices around him. His mind fixed completely on Wilcott's right index finger. A secret, tightly held for generations, glimmered there from Wilcott's first knuckle down to the tip of the nail for all those present to see. But did they understand it, he wondered. The inmates wouldn't fully comprehend everything unless Wilcott did the unthinkable.

Surely not, Rudolfo thought.

Then, as if in response to Rudolfo's inner questions, Brother Wilcott lifted his right hand to the back of his neck. Bowing his head low, placing chin to chest, he touched a spot at the base of his skull.

The world paused.

Rudolfo's breath trapped in his chest.

Instantly, Wilcott's body went limp, folding over on itself. He collapsed into open air, gravity flipping him end over end as his corpse plummeted twenty-six stories. Already dead from the self-inflicted tap to the neck, the fall for Wilcott would be peaceful.

The initial excitement of the spectacle seemed to wear off as the hundreds of witnesses turned in still relative silence to go back to their day-to-day business.

With his mind reeling from what he had just witnessed and attempting to organize his thoughts, Rudolfo turned to leave. As he did, an inmate standing ten feet in front of him in the emptying corridor looked straight at him with sunken, jaundiced eyes. This was strange, as Members of the Order held an almost mystical aura with the inmates and were rarely stared at for too long. Those in their right minds seldom made eye contact.

"Room for one more up there," the pale, pockmarked inmate said. Disdain and malice dripped with every syllable he uttered, his mouth upturned in a self-satisfied grin.

Rudolfo stared back, unmoved. He made a mental note of the incident and strode past the man.

2

Signs

Nicholas Fox, inmate number 6484, felt his breath quicken with excitement. With his arms folded in front of him, he leaned against a bulkhead on the twenty-fourth floor of the Keep.

He had watched from behind a thick crowd of prisoners while the Tapper offed himself. He'd marveled while his fellow inmates pounded their fists against the thin steel cage that separated them from oblivion. He watched as his fellow inmates found courage. He watched them find themselves. He watched them wake up.

Fox fully comprehended the irony that the impetus of this awakening was the man who'd fallen from the maintenance platform, the man in black. That face of death, that taker of life would ultimately resurrect the prison.

"What do you think about all this, Professor?" said Warren, a short, fat man to his right.

Fox had forgotten years ago why they called him the Professor. Something to do with the fact that he'd finished college, but so had many of the inmates in the Keep. Or maybe something to do with how he carried himself. He didn't know and he didn't care.

He stood two heads higher than his tiny confidant Warren. He squinted at the man over a long nose and rolled his bony shoulders. He knew exactly what this was: a sign. A sign he had been looking for. A sign that it was time to begin.

Several weeks ago, he received an impossibly cryptic message from an old friend. Even with exceptionally high mental acuity, it took Fox several days to decipher it. Once he knew his friend's plan, he had looked desperately for the right time to begin. It must happen organically, he'd thought. There must be a unique and profound call to action.

Here it was. And Fox could not have orchestrated it more perfectly.

The Tapper had removed his gloves, then his long coat. His skin was solid black from his right fingertip to his shoulder; long branches stretched across the upper half of his body.

Fox had heard the rumors, but he had chalked them up to overzealous storytelling. They had been wrong on some counts—the Tapper's skin was not scaly and peeling and the arm itself was not withered and dying. The skin was certainly blackened, however, and if it indicated the man's tenure in his position, as some speculated, he had been on the job for quite some time.

How the stain grew and how it started, Fox could guess. It was probably a side effect of whatever poison the Tappers used to execute those unlucky birds who'd ended up on the wrong side of their ledger. The same toxin he and hundreds of other inmates had just watched the Tapper use on himself.

One thing was certain: what they'd witnessed was unique and profound. Exactly what he needed.

The Tapper had made a show of it, Fox thought. He'd wanted everyone to see. Fox didn't know why he'd do such a thing and he didn't care. The spectacle would serve his purposes and that was all he needed.

Fox had seen other Tappers on his level and on those above and below him. Around each executioner, there had been a radius of several feet of space clear of inmates. As ever, the Tappers carried a mystique that generated superstition and fear.

Perhaps that is changing, Fox thought.

Moments passed and the levels cleared. Talk was high-spirited, the stories already being exaggerated.

Fox felt something. There was something different in the air now. Something had changed.

"Warren, I'll tell you what I think. I think it's time." Fox unfolded his arms and sauntered away toward his cell; Warren close behind. It was indeed time, he thought, but first, sacrifices were needed.

3

The Apprentice

"Hey, new guy," a gravelly voice crackled in Ken Holt's tiny ear piece.

It was his first day on the job, but he felt certain he'd always be the "new guy" around the other train attendants. The shortest tenure among the others was eight years.

"Go to the back and tell the senior officer that we will be making an unscheduled stop in a few minutes," said Armen Muntz, Ken's trainer for the day.

Ken looked across the brightly lit train car toward his much older, much grumpier coworker. Compared to Ken in his newly pressed uniform still in mint condition, the older train attendant staring back at him looked downright shabby. His faded red uniform jacket and black slacks had the wear of twenty-three years on them with stains to match. Other than the two of them, there was a third attendant in the tenth and final car. The engineer sat in a cozy booth in the train's nose to Ken's left as he stood near the front entry doors.

"How do I know which one is the senior officer?" Ken asked into his lapel mic.

"Look, just find someone back there that isn't shackled to their goddamn seat and tell them. Jesus."

Ken's so-called trainer had hated him from the start. A train attendant job on the prison transport line was a government job and highly sought after for its stability, benefits, and low stress. Ken, at his age and by all rules of fairness, had no business in his position, but having a grandfather in an influential position in the city government had its perks.

The high-speed rail line stretched one-hundred-fifty miles from New Aberdeen, Maryland to the massive Regional Correction Center prison complex, unofficially referred to as the Keep. The rail line stood a good deal higher than the surrounding forest of tall longleaf pines. The vast grove of trees, much like the train's operation and routine, were orderly and set, standing tall and neat in long straight rows.

Gliding along at an effortless five hundred miles per hour, the gleaming white transport was making the twenty-minute trip for the first of many times that day. The fifty passengers in the first car sat comfortably, six to a row on their way to the morning shift at the Keep.

Two-thirds of the passengers wore the standard issue two-tone blue uniforms of corrections officers; the rest were in civilian attire—administrators, IT workers, and maintenance personnel. All of them sat quietly. Ken imagined they were mentally preparing for a long day.

Ken nodded his compliance to the grizzled veteran attendant and made his way to the rear of the car. He continued through sliding doors into a small sealed compartment then into the next car. Though he knew what he would find in the second car, he was on edge. The chill hit him first, then the smell. The air was cold even through his woolen attendant's jacket. His nose stung from the intense odor of sanitation solution.

The sliding doors hissed closed behind Ken and he looked around for the senior officer. The scene was dramatically different from the one he just left.

The last nine cars of the train were reserved for the Keep's primary import: prisoners. Each of the nine cars was identical to the one which Ken found himself. Down the center of the car ran rows of metal benches where four prisoners sat locked and clamped into place with magnetic restraints. They were all clad in fresh prison whites, their skin showing raw and reddened from the sanitation process, their bald heads ready for the tattooed stamp of their prison identification number.

Looking around, Ken noticed one armed guard standing at the front of the car on the opposite side of the benches from him. Another stood toward the rear of the car with two more pacing up and down the outer aisles. To reach the nearest guard he'd have to walk in front of a row of four surly looking prisoners. Even with restraints securely in place, Ken felt uneasy at this idea; he felt it was best to avoid going near them at all if possible. The guard at the front hadn't looked in his direction anyway, so Ken proceeded down the bulkhead aisle toward the officer pacing that area.

Risking a glance to the left, Ken considered the prisoners; their faces wore the look of either resignation or pure insanity. He wondered what each of them must have done to end up here. What violence had they caused, he wondered. Were those bombers from a few weeks ago here in this car? No, he answered himself; they were all killed in that shootout with police.

Ken's grandfather, being a man of some standing in the government, knew a fair amount about the prison system and shared most of what he knew with Ken just yesterday. Ken knew all the unfortunate souls in this car and the others already at the Keep would serve an unknown amount of time there.

No one on this train knew how long they'd be in prison.

They would be judged by a mysterious group officially referred to as the Order of the Coppice, but unofficially known as Tappers. They would allow a few inmates to leave while others would only be worthy to live out their natural lives in prison. Most, however, would be found unfit to share the world with the rest of humankind; their lives would be taken from them while they slept.

The justice system, as Ken knew it, was straightforward. If you found yourself convicted of a crime worthy of prison time, you were sent to the Keep. No judge or jury delivered your sentence; that was determined after you arrived at the Keep. The courts decided if you were guilty. Tappers decided how to punish you.

Ken approached the guard, who was facing away from him and walking in the opposite direction. Ken chose not to call out to the officer, not wanting to draw the attention of the soon-to-be inmates. In fact, Ken thought if he stayed close enough to the gray bulkhead, he might just blend in, avoiding detection altogether.

His plan failed.

"Hey, boyo," called a prisoner with a cheese grater for a voice.

Instinctively, Ken turned and immediately regretted the

decision.

"Come sit on mama's lap and let her make you a man." She flicked her tongue through a large gap where her top four teeth should have been.

"S-sorry, ma'am," Ken stuttered. "I c-can't do that. I just need to ..."

"Ohhh, don't be sorry, baby," she said. "Why don't you let mama pop your cherry, boyo?" With a thumb and forefinger, she made a circle and, with the other hand, she stuck a finger through it. "I'll go slow."

The prisoners around her burst out laughing. Men and women alike began catcalling in a similar vein. Ken was told he'd be their special boy, that he'd be treated right, that wifey at home couldn't "make it happen" like they could.

He didn't know what to do. He turned in place several times, initially thinking he should go back to the first car then deciding he had to pass on the message they gave him. But at the moment he struggled to remember what the message even was. Something about stopping soon, he thought. The guard approached.

"Shut the fuck up!" he bellowed, raising his baton threateningly. "Want a cracked skull on your first day? Want to get tapped on your first night? I'm in good with the Tappers and all it takes is a word." He said this in almost a whisper which was all he needed. At the word "tapped," every voice fell silent.

The guard pulled a stunned Ken to the bulkhead. "What is it, new guy?"

"I ... um, oh yeah, we're making a stop soon, but only for a few minutes." Immense relief passed over Ken as the memory of the message finally came back to him.

"All right, I'll pass it on to the commanding officer. And listen kid, don't talk to the prisoners ... ever. Got it?"

Ken nodded. "Hey, how did you know I was new?"

The guard chuckled and shook his head. "First, no one who knows his ass from a hole in the ground talks to these animals. Second, they always send the new guy back here with messages. They could just call us." He pointed to his earpiece. "Instead, they decide to fuck with you. Next time, tell them to use the radio."

Ken nodded, feeling sheepish. The guard resumed his patrol.

Ken moved as quickly as he could to get out of the second car without running. Catcalls complimenting his rear-end followed him until he passed gratefully through the pair of sliding doors and into the comparatively luxurious and warm passenger car.

Nearly stumbling into the car, he immediately looked for Muntz. He saw him still stationed behind the engineer's booth. Muntz could barely contain himself with laughter; his entire body convulsed as he gasped for breath.

"Did they like you, kid?" he said when Ken came near. "Did they? What did they say, huh?"

Muntz was bent nearly double, slapping his thighs with his hands.

"Fuck you, Muntz," Ken said. "Next time use the radio ... you ... crusty old buffoon."

Ken turned and quickly resumed his prior station by the front doors. He ruminated on his choice of insult, not his best. Staring out of the large windows in the front entry doors, he let the moment pass like the stalwart trees below them.

The prison transport would make twenty-four trips during Ken's shift. It would make another twenty-four during the next shift, after which Ken would be back to resume his post as a dutiful attendant.

Several moments passed and Armen Muntz joined him at the entry doors. He said nothing for a short while as he watched the endless forest of trees go by.

"See that one there," Muntz said, pointing at a random longleaf pine, tracking it with his finger as it flew past. "That one is my favorite."

Ken appreciated the attempt at a peace offering and gave Muntz's joke a sincere but suppressed chuckle.

"Today is your lucky day, Ken," Muntz said with a sideways glance at Ken. "I've been working this train for twenty-three years and I've only seen what you're about to see five times."

"What? Does it have something to do with the unscheduled stop?" Ken craned his neck to look down the track, but the curve ahead made it impossible to see anything but the green tops of more trees.

"You'll see, kid. Don't worry, you'll know exactly what it is when you see it. And a word of advice, don't make a spectacle of yourself when you do."

Muntz turned and walked back to his side of the train just as Ken was about to ask another question. More hazing, Ken thought. It was probably just more bullshit to make the new guy look like an idiot.

* * *

Francesca stared up at the bright, late morning sky wondering when she'd see it again. Bold blue stood behind impossibly white clouds that skittered past. She did her best to be in the moment, tracing the outer curves of the fluffy white puffs as if she could commit each one to memory.

She stood on a high square platform above the trees, waiting for her train. The track stretched beyond the horizon in both directions allowing the bullet train to surf over the treetops. After she boarded, free moments like these would be precious few.

She closed her eyes and inhaled deeply. The piney scent of the woods below her filled her nose. The musty smell of the damp forest floor left her moments ago as she ascended the many flights of stairs to reach the top of the platform. The wind caressed her face, threatening to pull loose ends of her hair from the tight platinum braid hanging between her shoulder blades.

The fourteen-mile trek to the platform was compulsory, as it had been for all Apprentice Members of the Order. She turned her head, scanning the forest in search of the path she knew was down there somewhere. It eluded her. The trees were too tall, the canopies too broad. She had walked that path once before, but away from the train, not toward it. That had been eighteen years ago when she was just a child leaving a life at the orphanage behind to start a new one at the Pupil's School of the Order.

Her legs burned from climbing the stairs and her back ached from the hike. The walk exhausted her, but she also felt the weight of the responsibilities that awaited her at her new home, the Coppice. Would she be capable of performing the Sacred Task? Was she mentally skilled enough to clear her mind and judge with wisdom and without bias?

Earlier that day, as Francesca set out in the still dark

morning, one of her teachers had seen her off.

"As you know, I cannot go with you," the auburn-haired master said. "A Member's life is one of solitude, willingly accepted. Your decisions, your judgments are your own, as they should be. Your journey to the train platform is symbolic of your taking these steps on your own and ultimately accepting what this life will bring you."

"Thank you for your wisdom." She looked at the ground and adjusted her duffel bag hanging from her shoulder. "I know the rules, but I hope..."

"We will not." He shook his head. "We will not see each other again. Mine is simply to prepare Apprentice Members for the next phase of their journey. The first phase, now complete, was merely education. Now you must experience. True learning has not yet occurred."

He bowed his head as a final goodbye, and they parted company.

On the platform, the breeze paused. The heat of the day broke through her black cassock for the first time, baking her under the thick cloth. She opened her eyes and looked down at the duffel bag at her feet. Everything she owned was in the bag—some books, spare clothing, a few morsels of food leftover from her hike through the forest. She bent down, unzipped the bag, and removed a book. The cloth cover was worn from years of use, its edges frayed, the gold on the embossed lettering now a dull yellow. She ran her fingers over the title—*Order of the Coppice, A Brief History*. It had been the first thing she'd received when she arrived at the Pupil's School. It was meant to give her a background of her new life, to bring her some peace when she thought of the past. She preferred to think of it as her locomotion into the future. It gave her a base of understanding about who she was and what she'd ultimately become.

She turned to the first page.

Coppicing is an ancient practice used to manage woodlands. It takes advantage of a tree's natural capacity to grow shoots from a cleanly cut stump. Felling a tree at or near ground level encourages the tree to start anew with several infant shoots growing from the stump. These new shoots exploit the original tree's well-established root system.

In this manner, forest harvesters grow many trees from one. The mother tree is sacrificed to bear her sons and daughters who will grow quicker and straighter to fill the space she left behind. The shoots, when ready, are harvested like their mother to make room for more of their brothers and sisters. On and on the cycle goes.

In 1982, the wisest and most prominent leaders of the time created the Order of the Coppice. They tasked the Order with practicing this ancient art in a new setting and with new subjects. Society itself became the mother tree. Her people became the shoots. The Order became the harvesters.

What began as a social, legal, and political experiment of sorts, the Order has blossomed into an institution without which our society could not function. Economies have flourished, crime rates plummeted, culture has been enriched. Studies show that without the Order ...

Movement in Francesca's peripheral vision caught her attention. Squinting down the length of rail to her right she saw it. Sunlight glanced off the windshield of the train, still miles away but moving fast. For a moment, she forgot to breathe. Her heart beat noticeably harder.

As the train coasted silently toward Francesca, she thought

about what these next steps of her journey meant. She was trading one life for another. The first life had been intended to prepare her for the next one. But had it?

The train slid to a stop with a quiet bump followed by a low hiss. In front of Francesca, the doors opened. Thus began her apprenticeship, after which she would transition to the third and final phase of her life as a full Member of the Order of the Coppice; the phase that would end in her mandatory, self-inflicted death.

* * *

The prison train's boarding doors, inches from Ken's nose, came abreast of the small square platform outside. His stomach twisted as awareness of who was on the platform hit him like a punch in the gut.

Watching the platform come into view several minutes ago, he assumed they were picking up or dropping off a maintenance crew. As the lone figure materialized, clearly a woman whose blonde hair shone bright in the harsh sun, he grew confused. Was she a crew of one out here working on the track alone, out here in the wilderness?

When the train stopped, he knew exactly who she was. Rather, he knew what she was.

He had never seen a Tapper up close. As the train halted with a silent hitch, she was a foot away from him, just on the other side of the glass. The woman's dark eyes were warm but hard and didn't flinch as Ken stared into them with bewilderment. He felt them bore into him, slicing him up into his essential parts, dissecting him, examining, and judging him.

Ken stood wide-eyed as the doors gave a quiet ding and slid open. He didn't move. He couldn't move. Too much had happened to him today, too many new things shocked his system and now this.

A death bringer here, right in front of him. Panic bloomed in his guts and spread down every vein until it enveloped him. His mind spun. Was she here to execute someone on the train? Did they kill in public? Was she here for him? What if she touched him? Could they kill with a single touch? Of course, they could, he thought, that's why they called them Tappers.

"Excuse me," she said.

The Tapper spoke in a low, calm voice. Unnervingly calm. So much so, Ken's senses snapped back to him in a flash. He jumped aside to let her pass. Without another word, she entered and took an empty seat near the front.

The doors hissed closed once more, and the train sped off toward its only other stop—the Keep.

Ken's eyes found Muntz across the car standing at his normal station. Muntz stared back. He wasn't laughing this time and his face had lost a little of its color. With a knowing nod to Ken, Muntz turned to walk the aisle and converse with the passengers.

4

The Mentor

The train crested a small rise and made a long, sweeping turn above the sprawling forest of trees. Several minutes had passed since she'd taken her seat near the window and Francesca could still feel the eyes of the other passengers watching her. Sideways glances, incognito peering over the edges of tablets, outright glaring. One turn of her head toward the onlookers seemed to extinguish most of the rubber-necking. She appreciated their curiosity. Most prison workers who weren't guards would rarely glimpse a Member of the Order, but she would not allow herself to be gawked at like an animal at the zoo.

She gazed out the window into nothingness. So much was behind her now. So much in front of her. The train was the bridge and she was likely never to board it again on anything other than Order business.

From some distance away, Francesca saw the dark monolith break the horizon and grow steadily in size as they sped toward it. After a life spent in the austere Pupil's School of the Order tucked away in an unreachable part of the forest, the prison looked enormous, larger than anything she could imagine. She knew it was not as large as most of the skyscrapers in the cities, but its significance far outstripped the physical space it occupied.

The Regional Corrections Center, known to the Order as the Coppice, known to most others as the Keep, had an ash gray shell almost totally featureless. Only two things marked its exterior. Around its top rim, a single row of identical square windows circled the building like crown jewels atop a faceless head. And where the dark exterior met the earth, a bright archway, two stories high, appeared like an open maw.

From the archway, the maglev rail stretched toward them and beyond to the city as the only physical connection between the two. Francesca and the other passengers were heading into the archway, into the prison's one and only exit.

The maw swallowed the train and its riders as they coasted silently into the Coppice's depths.

Francesca thought it was fitting as most of the people on this train would never leave their new home, herself included. They were swallowed, digested, and metabolized; their energy reallocated.

Just before entering the maw, Francesca craned her neck to look up at the Coppice. It was hard to guess at its true size, but she knew its specifications by heart. Learning about the physical structure had been almost as important as learning her purpose within it.

"An artist," her teachers had told her, "must know the brush, the paint, the canvas as well as they know the strokes they will make and the beauty they will produce. They are extensions of the artist, not tools.

"This is true for you, too," the teacher continued. "The Coppice is as much a part of you, as you are of it. It is a living, breathing animal. Its physical nature must be known and intimately understood if you are to properly perform your function within it."

The layout of the building and all its floors, the intricacies of the mechanical and electrical systems, and all the general processes and procedures for its inmates had been objects of her studies for years. She would not be where she is now had she not committed all of it to memory long ago.

The train began to slow while she pondered on the word so often used by her teachers to describe her new life as an Apprentice Member: function. Her teachers had always used that word coupled with others like "sacred" and "honored" and "noble" to describe what Members of the Order did. It was equal parts spiritual and mechanical.

The Coppice was a body ridding itself of diseased, dying, or useless cells, but also a world where the chosen few ushered its unworthy inhabitants into the beyond. Selection and judgment had been reserved for those who stood higher than the rest.

Was she higher than the rest? After all, she was chosen so young, how could they possibly know she was special? And when was she ever given the option?

The bright white lights of the depot poured into her car and she shook her head sharply; the doubts and questions were gone. Her mind was as clear as it had been before boarding the train this morning. The next phase in her life had already begun and it would not benefit anyone to look back into the past and ask questions. Forward was her path now.

Her car slid past a large, empty platform packed with

guards in tactical gray uniforms wielding non-lethal batons. The floor of the massive inmate debarkation area was painted with wide black lines crossing the width of the floor; a guard on each end. Doors on the far side, she knew, led to processing—identification tattoos, uniforms, and chip implants. This is also where the new inmates would have their cerebral signatures recorded and logged, assisting with round the clock tracking and identification.

Everything about the prisoner debarkation area was foreboding—the ceiling was low, the lights were bright white, almost blue, flickering intermittently to the point that looking directly at them was disorienting. Other than the black stripes on the floor, every surface was painted gray and appeared not quite clean. A cold feeling passed over her as she and the other passengers in the first car passed the large room.

Just as a wide concrete barrier flew past the nose of the train separating prisoner debarkation from the visitor's platform, she glimpsed at least five Members stationed around the prisoner debarkation area.

Dressed in the traditional black cassock, the Members gave the impression of being casual observers but exuded a presence of strength and purpose easy for her to feel even on the train. She had always been told, "be a part and apart." But she had never quite understood until now.

Seeing the men and women of the Order standing around that huge, brightly lit room, she finally, truly understood what it meant. They were unmistakable. You couldn't not see them, but you would walk right past them and not think twice about it. This she realized was the only way for them to effectively perform their function. They observe their charges in all aspects of prison life. This must be done on an intimate level and therefore, the only way was to be a part and apart. Otherwise, she knew, their judgment would be inaccurate and unfocused.

Their purpose was to judge the individual as a whole. Only then could a Member properly determine the inmate's fate. Only then could they grant life or take it.

The barrier passed. In a moment the inmates would be welcomed to their new home.

The train stopped and the passengers in Francesca's car began to disembark. She stayed in her seat wanting to be the last one off the train. She wanted to watch.

She knew her Mentor would be here and she wanted to see him before he saw her. The workers crowded on the platform for a moment, naturally forming into three lines to pass through the Coppice's secure entry points leaving the platform, beyond which a large bank of elevators would take them to their duty stations.

The lines crossed the platform intermingling with new passengers waiting to board the now departing train, their shift just ended.

Through the crowd, against the far wall, she saw him. There was no doubt who he was or why he was here. No other Members were on the platform. They rarely were, she assumed.

He stood stock still, more like a fixture than a sentient being. Hands behind his back and his head cocked slightly to one side, he stared at her through the crowd. She stared back with equal intensity, although for different reasons.

With a snap of the mind and body, she stood and exited the train.

She traversed the wide platform with long steps and approached the man that was to be her Mentor. He stared unmoving, as she came nearer.

He was assessing her even now, she thought.

He had black hair with well-formed tear-drop shaped gray spots on his temples, the points stretching toward the back of his head. Francesca thought they could easily be mistaken for an extra set of eyes.

His face, drawn, waxy, and clean shaven, held light eyes containing an energy that would have given the impression of vigor and youth, had they not been sunken in proud sockets, surrounded by deeply etched wrinkles, and topped with a furrowed brow.

She stopped in front of him.

"Francesca?" he asked, parting his lips only enough to let the air carrying the words past them.

"Yes."

"I am Brother Rudolfo. I am to be your Mentor." He spoke evenly, completely neutral and robotic.

"It is a pleasure to meet you, Brother Rudolfo," she said bowing her head slightly. "I'm honored to ..."

"The Member Principal would like to meet you. We should be on our way."

Brother Rudolfo turned and walked toward a nondescript gray door in a wall to their right. Francesca followed, half-jogging to keep up with his long strides.

5

Martin Aubrey

May 5, 2043

Martin Aubrey woke from a long nap, his second of the day. Rubbing his eyes and scratching at his temples, he tried to revive his groggy brain. Cracking his eyelids, he turned away from the sun pouring in through the cheap blinds. Beeps behind him, the constant low hum from the vents overhead, and the sterile air all reminded him where he was. Still in the hospital. For one sweet moment, just after his mind awoke from its slumber, he thought he'd fallen asleep at home.

No such luck, he thought. Still here.

Many patients at the hospital had to adjust to life in the waking world; he had to remember what it was like to sleep again. Added to that, he'd never been much of a napper. But his doctors at the hospital wouldn't allow him his daily dose of Zentransa, so sleep assaulted him with a vengeance.

"For a man in your condition, you need real sleep," the doctor had told him.

He had to admit to himself that he had been in particularly bad shape when he first arrived at the Metropolitan

Memorial Hospital. He'd been shot, beaten, and blown up by a group of terrorists guilty of killing scores of innocent people in the city of New Aberdeen, Maryland. In the end, he'd gotten the better of them; they were dead and he was alive. But days of recovery later he still felt terrible. Aches and soreness plagued his body. The spot where the bullet entered his leg was tender and burned and itched twenty-four hours a day thanks to the implant that was now healing him. His head pounded from the blast that killed the leader of the terrorists; the blast that detonated a few feet from his own head.

Aubrey knew full well that his doctor regularly worked seventy-two-hour shifts with no sleep all thanks to that tiny pink pill he now refused to give Aubrey. All the doctors and nurses were on Z. Sickness didn't sleep and neither would they; Zentransa was just another perk of the job. Eliminate sleep with the Z pill and doctors treat more people, save more lives, bill more patients, bring in more revenue.

Aubrey could overlook the doctor's hypocrisy, however, if becoming a sleeper again meant he could leave the hospital sooner rather than later.

Between no Z pill and the plethora of medications they were giving him, he had slipped into the bad habit of napping twice a day on top of a full night's sleep every night. He felt like all he had done was sleep since he woke up in his hospital bed four days ago. It had been seven days since the firefight that put him down and nearly killed him.

The anti-anxiety meds and mood stabilizers they pumped into him helped him sleep by keeping most of the nightmares at bay—one benefit of never sleeping was the convenient lack of nightmares that haunted someone like Aubrey. Years of fighting overseas with the Marines and battling criminals on the streets as a cop stuck with you, in a bad way. Worst of all were the mistakes that cost others their lives. One mistake, the one that resulted in Aubrey leaving the police, tortured him most frequently. The meds worked mostly but the dreams came now and then—faceless enemies running around him, his legs immobile, his weapon unusable, the faces from his past—and he'd find himself sitting upright in bed drenched in sweat.

Before the firefight that landed him in the hospital, he'd helped the Metro PD find the terrorists he'd fought and, if it wasn't for Aubrey, the bad guys would have detonated a small mountain of explosives adding hundreds more to the death toll. The police would never admit to his being there. The Chief of Police made sure everyone knew that her men and women, the full-time cops, were responsible and no one else.

Aubrey was working for the police on a volunteer basis only after giving the investigative team their first real lead, which impressed a senior officer on the force. The fact that Aubrey had once been a cop himself had helped as well. The terrorists, who went by the moniker One Front for the People or OFP, had claimed responsibility for seven deadly bombings and a string of child poisonings. The poisonings, dubbed Boarding School Syndrome, or BSS, left at least four children in a perpetual state of sleep. No one knew how OFP was making the kids sick, all anyone knew was why they were doing it. The victims were children of prominent citizens with connections to Ventana, Inc., the makers of Zentransa. OFP's goal was the eradication of the Zentransa pill, anyone associated with its propagation, and anyone who used it. The Z pill, according to them, was a destabilizing wedge in society, a disease which had to be snuffed out.

Aubrey's employer, OWG Insurance Inc., was naturally upset at the Chief's reluctance to recognize Aubrey's contributions. They did after all, continue to pay Aubrey and provide him benefits while he was working for the police under the assumption that the company would be recognized for going above and beyond in the city's war on terror.

It was Aubrey, OWG's employee, who used his investigative skills and the company's proprietary technology and resources to find the bombers and put an end to the weeks of carnage.

The Chief reminded OWG's Board that Aubrey had no business engaging in any violent confrontations and the only reason he wasn't on his way to the Keep instead of recovering comfortably in a hospital bed was the fact that he saved the lives of several officers. She made it clear that her sweeping the incident under the rug and erasing Aubrey's presence at the firefight from the official record was thanks enough.

Eventually the two parties reached a compromise: the Chief thanked OWG for contributing a "consultant" to the investigation and for the technology that led in part to the raid that killed the terrorists.

No mention of Aubrey's name would ever be in the press. His part in the firefight that saved hundreds of lives and ended the worst reign of terror in memory would never be told.

All of that was fine with Martin Aubrey. He cared little about receiving credit because, in his mind, the brutal fight that sent one cop, eight terrorists, and a would-be suicide bomber to their graves plus a half dozen more cops to the hospital was only the beginning of the story.

Key players in the whole mess were still unaccounted for. Although OFP claimed credit for the havoc wrought on the city, Aubrey had his doubts. He had good reason to believe the terrorists he fought and killed had nothing to do with OFP at all. He believed they hijacked the OFP mantle to hide the real puppet master behind all the killings and BSS. Prior to the bombings, OFP had been vandals and protestors who never once engaged in any violent acts against the public.

And then there were the scientists. Four former Ventana scientists had been arrested and sent to prison for financial crimes unconnected to the bombings. While at the Keep, the four of them were put to death by the state sanctioned group of executioners called the Order of the Coppice for reasons unknown. Their executions came a day after Aubrey and his partners, Liz Reynolds and Ryan Grant, made an unheard of visit to the Keep to question the scientists on their possible connections to OFP, the bombings, and BSS. Before their execution, Aubrey saw the four scientists as having an obvious vendetta against their former employer, Ventana, Inc., and its CEO James Sarazin.

Aubrey had discovered that the scientists, led by Dr. Leo Alkorn, had once been the chief minds behind the Zentransa pill and had worked for Sarazin for nearly three decades. Then, mere weeks before bombs began exploding throughout the city and children were struck down with Boarding School Syndrome, police arrested Alkorn and his team. Shortly after, the courts found them guilty and they were sent to prison. They had motive, opportunity, and expertise.

The Ventana four, as Aubrey called them, were the world's

foremost experts on sleep and, without question, the Zentransa pill. Aubrey felt they must have known how to re-engineer the properties of the pill in order to weaponise it in the form of BSS and administer it to the children of Ventana's most powerful players. As they were also chemists, Aubrey didn't feel it was much of a stretch to assume they would have had a hand in the bombings.

Shortly after Aubrey interviewed Ventana four, however, they'd been executed. Someone had ordered them killed. Anyone who could force the Order to murder four people had vast reach and innumerable resources. This made them formidable beyond measure.

After Aubrey's firefight, police discovered a burner phone at the scene with dozens of incoming calls from a single caller. The caller, the voice, was the one behind it all, he felt certain. Whoever called that phone was his man. He just had to find him. He hoped the now dead scientists could lead Aubrey there.

A knock at the door interrupted his thoughts. His brain still foggy, he sat up as the door swung open and Detective Ryan Grant rolled in on a wheelchair pushed by Deputy Inspector Liz Reynolds who had one injured arm wrapped in a sling.

"He's awake," Grant said. "Look at that Liz, he's part of the land of the living again."

The three of them laughed and exchanged greetings as Grant and Liz settled in on either side of Aubrey's bed. Both wore hospital gowns with sweat pants underneath. Liz had her straight dark hair pulled back while Grant had allowed his blonde buzz cut to grow a tad shabby over his hospital stay.

It had always amazed Aubrey how quickly people could bond when put in extreme circumstances. The three of them had only known each other for a few weeks while investigating Boarding School Syndrome and the connected bombings. The day he walked into the Command Center at Police Headquarters and met his new partners felt so long ago.

Spending every waking hour with people had that affect, he thought. Then, there was the firefight. Bloodshed and extreme danger tended to compound the swiftness of the bonding time. Moments before Aubrey jumped into the fray at the firefight, Liz and Grant had both been wounded in action.

"How's your belly?" Aubrey asked, pointing at Grant's midsection.

"Not shitting in a bag anymore." He shrugged. "So, there's that. They're letting me go home tomorrow."

"They're letting you go home tomorrow?" Liz looked confused. "Why are you still in a wheelchair?"

Grant smiled sheepishly. "I don't exactly need it, but you offered to push me all the way here, so ..."

A tissue box flew over Aubrey, catching Grant in the forehead. He yelped.

"I felt sorry for you, ass." Liz smiled and Aubrey smiled with her.

Both of his former partners seemed more upbeat than usual. Laughing and good-hearted pranks weren't commonplace when the three of them were working in the Metro PD Headquarters.

The heaviness of Aubrey's frustrations subsided for a moment. The three of them together was a distraction, to be sure, but more than that, they were friends. He'd developed real affection for Grant and Liz, who were both excellent detectives and good, honest people.

He sincerely hoped he'd get to work with them again.

"How long are you two on light duty?" Aubrey asked.

"Six more weeks for me, at least," Grant explained. "They have to make sure all my insides stay sewn up. Liz here is about the same."

She nodded. "Whenever I can move this thing normally." She raised her right arm about shoulder height, like a chicken wing. "Then, it's back to work."

Grant gave Aubrey a half-smile. Aubrey knew what it meant, and he felt the same way. He'd give nearly anything to go back to work with them.

"Speaking of ..." Grant leaned in toward Aubrey and spoke in a low voice. "We saw Lewis yesterday. You really don't think it's over?"

"No, I don't." Aaron Lewis was Aubrey's longtime friend and former partner. The two of them had come up in the police together since their academy days. Aaron helped lead the investigation into OFP, the bombings, and Boarding School Syndrome. At the battle seven days ago, Lewis had been the first one in and got wounded in the melee. During his hospital stay, he'd kept Aubrey up to speed on developments as the case wrapped up.

"You'll keep it going, then? Where are you going to start? What can we do?" Reynolds said, leaning in now.

He had been afraid this would happen. His old partners would want to help him, and he'd have to tell them no. As far as the Metro PD was concerned, the case was solved and closed with the deaths of the terrorists who carried out the bombings. Aubrey knew what it felt like to lose his badge and he wasn't about to let Liz and Grant take a similar path.

He held up a hand to slow them down. "Listen, I know you want to help. I know you want to see this through as much as I do, but I can't be responsible for you getting into trouble with the Chief."

Reynolds and Grant both leaned back, looking deflated.

"Told you," Grant said, looking across at Reynolds.

"You knew I'd say no?"

"Of course," Liz said as she leaned in and rested a hand on Aubrey's forearm. "But we thought we'd ask anyway. I know you don't want us to get in trouble or get fired, but seriously, if you need anything, don't hesitate to ask."

* * *

If it hadn't been for a throwaway comment from Aaron Lewis, Aubrey wouldn't have known where to start digging on Alkorn and the rest of the Ventana four.

The day before Grant and Liz's visit, on his last day in the hospital, Lewis came by Aubrey's room to visit. They two men were watching the news on the television when a story came on covering the latest celebrity scandal. An actor called Shaul Waters had recently been hacked and every detail of his life online scattered to the four winds. Shaul also had a major motion picture releasing in the coming weeks.

"I swear they do this shit on purpose," Lewis had said. "Personal cyber security is so cheap these days and even the free stuff out there is damn good. No one with that kind of money should ever get hacked."

"Hackers are good too," Aubrey replied with no real stake

in the argument.

Lewis turned toward Aubrey. "Do you remember that guy years ago ... what was his name?" He rubbed his chin and glanced at the ceiling. "The guy who swindled all those old people out of millions and would have got away with it, but he killed that one lady's dog. Remember?"

Aubrey thought briefly, then said, "Yeah, I do." He could picture the man, tall and gaunt, wire-frame glasses and a pencil-thin mustache. "Uniforms were called in about the dog, then found a bunch of evidence connecting him with the fraud cases."

Lewis snapped his fingers. "Crowder. That was his name. Anyway, they found enough to connect him with at least one of the fraud cases, but we thought he had to be connected to more. We got a warrant to search his cloud drive and do you remember what happened?"

"No."

"Every damn cyber security geek at police headquarters tried to break into that drive and they got nowhere. And it was just basic security on his account—nothing special." Lewis shook his head. "My point is nowadays if you don't want to get hacked, you can avoid it easily. Someone has to be damned determined to break into even the simplest security."

Aubrey thought about it. An individual's entire life was online which meant everything was out there all the time. He'd lived with it for his entire life, so he had no real thoughts of paranoia. The way he saw it, everyone was in the same boat.

"What did you do to get into Crowder's drive?" Aubrey asked.

"You'll like this. We hired a consultant."

Aubrey felt a smile cross his face. "Except, unlike me, I bet you paid them."

"We did," Lewis said. "Brought her in and she cracked that cloud drive like a damn coconut with a sledgehammer. Only took her two hours using some programs of her own design. And she hunted down a half dozen other accounts of his that linked him to about ten more victims."

"I remember her." Aubrey shifted in his chair, picturing a small woman, mousy haired, somewhere near his own age. "She got caught for that whole thing with the last mayor, all those documents that got leaked. Wait, didn't you and she have a thing?"

Lewis looked at him with a slight grin threatening to go full Cheshire. "Yeah, we did for a while. We met on that case, actually, and ... well the details aren't important. Let's just say it didn't last."

Aubrey noticed a distinct faraway look in Lewis's eyes and guessed he was recounting some tryst the two of them had.

"You're right about her record. She leaked a bunch of stuff on Mayor Cosroy and exposed his long history of duplicitous behavior. Cost him re-election. Only she wasn't caught by us, someone turned on her and snitched. She only avoided prison time by working with us on a couple of cases, including the dog killer one. A few high-ranking people at PD headquarters with ties to the mayor didn't like it, but we needed her." Lewis rested his chin on his fist and closed his eyes. "She was damn good."

"I bet."

Lewis opened his eyes and in an obvious attempt to look innocent, he said, "At the black hat stuff, I mean."

"Sure."

"Like I said, it's hard to get hacked these days, but she's one of the few that can do it. I mean it. If she's after you, good luck because you can't hide anything from her. She'll find you and expose all your skeletons. That's the other thing about her, she's righteous. She hates evil people, which is why she took down our thoroughly corrupted mayor."

Aubrey's interest piqued, an idea forming in his brain like two storm fronts colliding. "What's her name again?"

"Her name is Malina. Malina Maddox."

6

Malina Maddox

May 7, 2043

Martin Aubrey left the hospital dressed in gray sweatpants, white t-shirt, and flip flops courtesy of the hospital. In his hand he carried a plastic bag containing a small hygiene kit and a new mobile phone, his having been destroyed in the raid on April 28. The clothes he wore to the hospital nine days ago were cut from his body in a hurry as doctors and nurses worked to patch his wounds. Looking back on that day, he doubted that he would have wanted the blood-soaked, scorched rags back.

Jogging down the front steps of Metro General, Aubrey found his hired car waiting at the curb. The street was busy with vehicles whirring on their way under the benevolent control of the Metropolitan Traffic System. Like a multicolored river of water where the surface never broke, it flowed along gracefully with every stop, turn, and merge dictated by an artificial intelligence that knew where everyone was going and got them there quickly and safely.

He slid into the back seat, the only seat in the driverless

vehicle, and the car swept into the flow of traffic.

Aubrey was on his way home, but he wouldn't stay there long. He needed to change clothes, take a hot shower, and refill his pill case with a fresh supply of Zentransa. Then, he had to get to work.

He pulled his phone out of the plastic bag and sent a text message to Aaron Lewis.

Need a favor, he typed.

While Aubrey waited for Lewis's reply, he thought about the long road ahead. He had no idea where this investigation would lead, no idea how long it would take, no idea how wide his net would have to spread. He only knew the next step and that, at least, was comforting. He needed to find out as much as he could about Dr. Alkorn and the other scientists from Ventana. For that he needed someone who could dredge the deepest parts of the internet to uncover what the official case files had not.

He needed Malina Maddox.

Aubrey knew that if she couldn't or wouldn't help him, she'd point him in the right direction of someone who could. She was a do-gooder like him, he knew that. Do-gooders couldn't help themselves.

Aubrey's phone vibrated in his hand.

Anything you need, brother, Lewis replied.

I need to find Malina Maddox.

Aubrey stared at the phone, waiting. No reply came.

He yawned and rubbed his temples. Leaving the hospital had been almost as painful as the wounds that landed him there. Paperwork, last minute checks by every doctor he'd seen plus their nurses took nearly all day. Passing the traumatic brain injury protocol had been more difficult than he thought it would be.

But the mental therapy was the worst of it. Post-traumatic stress disorder was best treated before it occurred which meant directly after the causal incident. For Aubrey, this meant reliving the worst parts of the raid, the various dust ups he encountered as a cop in the last few years, and scraping what was left of his memory of his action overseas in the Marine Corps.

He understood their tenacity. If he left the hospital only to freak out and gun down a crowd of innocent people at the grocery store, they could be held liable.

Aubrey wasn't too optimistic about Lewis knowing Malina's whereabouts. Someone who made a living digging up dirt on people would not be easy to track down.

* * *

Malina Maddox sat at the bar by the front window of *Le Grind*, a busy coffee shop in what was considered the fashion district of New Aberdeen. People bustled in and out to get a coffee from a human barista, one of the few establishments in the city where one could get it. The shop was long and narrow with a counter that stretched almost its entire length. The quiet, jazzy music could barely be heard over the conversations around her and the baristas shouting for coffee owners.

She assumed most of the customers in the shop were, like herself, taking Zentransa daily. She always found it ironic that even a person living a sleepless life couldn't do away with their love for caffeine. The Z pill made sleep unnecessary, but it couldn't give you the jolt of energy needed to get to your next pill. Much like a sleeping person grew physically tired hours before they actually slept, a zoner grew tired hours before taking the pill. Hence, the omnipresent need for stimulants like coffee.

"Small decaf cappuccino for Joe, Joe Banks," yelled one barista three feet behind her.

She pretended not to hear the din through her oversized headphones and green hoodie pulled over short, spiky hair dyed dark brown. She moved her head to a nonexistent beat. Her work put her in the precarious position of being on many powerful people's shit lists, so she made every effort to stay vigilant while appearing the opposite to onlookers.

Her client had five minutes before she bolted. She didn't like waiting and the information she was sitting on was the type that could take her from shit list to hit list. She wanted rid of it. Her days of fighting the good fight were behind her, but the money for this job was too good for her not to take it.

Her coffee had gone cold ten minutes ago, along with her patience. Standing up to leave, she spotted the client pushing his way through the lunch hour foot traffic outside on the sidewalk.

Most people would not recognize Desmond Varela in person, but his name in print would have caught their attention. The winner of several awards for investigative journalism, Varela had made a name for himself over the last several years for exposing dirt on corrupt politicians and other prominent citizens.

"You're late," Malina said as Varela lifted her red canvas shoulder bag off the stool next to her and sat down.

"I'm always late," Varela replied, placing her bag on the bar in front of her. “And you always wait. Why do we have to have this discussion every time?”

“Well, this is the last time I’m telling you. Maybe you’ll be more polite to your next gopher.”

“We’ll see,” Varela said, unconvinced. He pulled his leather jacket off and laid it across his lap, smiling at Malina. “I don’t know why you act so put out. This is a good thing we’re doing.”

She reached inside the bag and pulled out a small clear plastic case the size and shape of a business card but a quarter of an inch thick. Varela laid an open hand on the bar, palm up.

“Payment,” Malina said. It was clearly a statement and not a question. Varela did not move his hand nor take his eyes off Malina.

“This too? We have to do this every time too?” Varela shook his head, feigning disappointment. “Check the account.”

Malina pulled her phone out of a jacket pocket to check her bank account, one of many under an alias. A quick glance told her the money was there—several months’ work in one shot. She couldn’t help but feel satisfied with herself.

“I’m serious, you know.” Varela still had his hand out. “You really should feel good about this. We’re going to take down some bad people who are doing bad things.”

“Bad people that do bad things usually don’t take it very well when the world finds out about it. They’re sort of known for being unforgiving.” Malina opened the small case; it was full of tiny memory cards, some sticks of gum, and a scrap of paper.

“My name is going to be on this article,” he said. “I wouldn’t write it if I thought it was going to get me killed. And you’re safe because I don't even know who you are."

She pulled out the scrap of paper and placed it in his hand. Varela looked at the paper and read it several times, committing its contents to memory, and handed it back to her.

"Everything in there? Everything we talked about?"

Malina shot him a look in response to his question.

"Just asking. Take it easy." Varela held up his hands in supplication.

Transaction complete, she hopped down from the high stool and was reaching for her bag when Varela grabbed her arm.

"Listen, you do great work. It'd be a shame if you ... went into retirement."

Malina said nothing but tossed the scrap of paper into her cold coffee; within seconds, the paper dissolved.

She turned away from Varela and pushed through the small crowd queueing near the coffee shop's door and stepped onto the sidewalk. Her five-foot-six-inch frame melted into the throng.

7

Strangers

Aubrey returned home to his empty apartment, happy to see that it was exactly as he'd left it seven days ago. The air was cool but reeked of rotten food. The austere furnishings added to the chill; everything was made of wood and metal, the floor bare concrete.

From pure habit after a week in the hospital, he walked to the living room and turned on the TV. Something about the background noise made him feel more comfortable. He turned on the news on the off-chance that they may discuss the OFP or BSS cases.

Moving toward the bedroom, he stopped when he heard the voice coming from the speakers of the sound system. He turned back to the TV to see the CEO of Ventana, Inc., James Sarazin with his arm resting on the handle of a shovel jammed into the ground.

"... here at the site of the Charlie Lattimore Convalescent Home for Childhood Diseases." Sarazin was speaking to a group of reporters. The sleeves of his white oxford were rolled back, his tie hung loose, and his black hair was tussled.

The man was only a head taller than the shovel. The text at the bottom of the screen read *Ventana CEO Donates Land and Personal Capital for Hospital.* "There will be room here for 1,500 kids with diseases or disorders that require round the clock care. There will also be space enough for families to stay with their children long term. The idea is to make this place as much like home as possible."

"When do you expect the facility to be complete?" a reporter called out from the crowd.

"We fully expect for it to be operational and welcoming new patients by next spring," Sarazin replied.

"Charlie Lattimore was a victim of Boarding School Syndrome. Are you doing this in honor of the other victims as well?" another reporter asked.

Sarazin looked at his feet for a moment before replying. "The Lattimores are close friends of mine and it devastated me when I heard the news about Charlie. The," he cleared his throat, "terrorists who I won't name, targeted them specifically because of his affiliation with me and my company. I felt the least I could do was give Charlie and the other victims a place to convalesce that provided not just top-notch care but also some peace. But this facility is not limited to BSS cases, only inspired by them."

A reporter in the front of the crowd over-shouted the others with her question. "Is Ventana still contributing to the bombing victims support fund?"

Sarazin nodded and stuck a hand in his pocket. "We are one of many contributors, but yes we are providing a substantial amount to the fund. We're also one of several contributors to the first-responders support fund. We mustn't forget about the police, fireman, and medical workers affected by the recent terror attacks."

The news stations cut away to an anchor in studio and Aubrey resumed his walk to the bedroom to get cleaned up. After a long, hot shower, he put on fresh clothes and packed a small bag with a spare laptop and several other tools of his trade. He was hungry, so he grabbed a quick snack from the fridge. Feeling properly sated, he went to his bathroom and removed a small pill bottle from beneath the sink. He opened it. Inside was his spare stash of Zentransa; it was only a few days' worth, but it bought him time enough to get a new supply.

Aubrey was reaching inside the bottle to extract a Z pill, his first in eight days, when his phone vibrated. He twisted the cap back on the bottle and exchanged it for the phone in his pocket. A message from Aaron Lewis appeared on the screen.

Okay. I have it.

Aubrey was about to reply when another message came through.

Don't you dare tell her you got it from me.

A final buzz on his phone indicated the contact information had been sent.

I owe you a beer, replied Aubrey.

Many beers, Marty. Many, many beers.

Aubrey rushed out of the apartment and summoned his car from the elevator. Before he stepped out onto the lobby floor, he mapped the address Lewis had just sent. Confused, he stared at the pin on the map.

"Who the hell would live there?"

* * *

The ride to Malina Maddox's residence took longer than he expected, nearly half an hour, which was a long time for a traffic system that was by all measures perfect in its execution of delivering people to their destinations. The fact that she lived in an industrial area not known for habitation and its location on the very outskirts of the city contributed to the travel time.

The car traveled east, toward the Chesapeake. On the way, Aubrey contemplated sending a message to his employer, OWG Insurance, to tell them he was out of the hospital but decided against it. Technically, he was only discharged from the hospital that day and the doctors had told him to take it easy for a while. In addition, he felt that winning his company a good deal of fame through its assistance with the bombing investigation had also won him some time off.

Thirty minutes after setting out, his car parked itself in front of a tall, gray windowless building. Its façade held one distinction: a set of large silver doors resembling a freight elevator.

Stepping out of the car and craning to see the building in its entirety, Aubrey thought there must be some sort of mistake. He looked at his phone at the address Lewis sent him—315 East Third Street—double checking it against the navigation system in his car. It checked out. In the lower right corner of the building's front were large numbers—315.

He was in the right place.

Aubrey looked at the rest of the address—unit 542. Looking back to the building, he thought it must be the strangest apartment building he'd ever seen.

Shrugging, he walked to the elevator.

Searching the wide bezel around the doors, he could find

no buttons, only a small oval thumb pad to the right about waist high. Glancing around the nearly deserted sidewalk and deciding he was in no great danger of being observed, he reached into the bag hanging from his shoulder. From it he pulled a small aerosol can and a flat plastic case, both courtesy of his employer OWG Insurance.

Two wires extended from the sides of the case with a purple sphere at one end and a clear flexible pad at the end of the other. Pressing the rubber pad firmly onto the elevator's thumb reader, he the then released a cloud of clear mist from the aerosol can. As the mist cleared, its residue clung to the wall revealing dozens of fingerprints.

Finding a print that he thought looked good, he held the wire with the purple sphere up to it and pressed a button on the plastic box in his other hand. A beam of violet light lit the fingerprint in a phosphorescent glow. At the same time the rubber pad at the other end of the wire flashed blue and began replicating the fingerprint on its surface.

The swirly, broken lines materialized onto the pad. Once the print was complete, the thumbprint reader scanned it.

The reader flashed red. The doors did not open. He repeated the process several more times until he found a print that was both complete enough and belonged to a person with access to this building.

On his fourth try, the reader flashed green and the doors slid open. As he stepped in and pressed the number five on the keypad, Aubrey wondered what someone who lived here would do if they had visitors. There was no intercom system that he could see.

Aubrey stepped off the elevator into a long hallway stretching laterally across the width of the building. Lights above him came to life as he moved. Looking left and right, he counted a dozen halls branching off this main one running the length of the building. Much like the outside, everything was gray.

At the end of each block of rooms were sets of numbers. He found one that read 525-555. He walked down this hallway, passing a series of corrugated metal doors—the style that rolled up into the ceiling.

The hallways weren't hallways at all, they were aisles. The blocks didn't hold rooms, they held units. Storage units. That explained the absence of an intercom system. People were not supposed to live in storage units.

Proceeding down the aisle, he found 542 to be rather longer than the others; the distance to the next door down was two to three times that of the ones previous.

Not knowing what else to do, he knocked. The metal door clanged loudly against its cradle, echoing up and down the aisle. No response from inside. He scanned the door and the frame around it. The only security he could see was a locking mechanism at the bottom with a thumb reader like the one outside. Using the same device and the same technique as before, he quickly had it flashing green.

Aubrey bent to roll the door up and stopped himself. Reaching into his bag once more, he pulled out a long, thin device made of a pliable segmented material. On one end was a handle with a small red button; on the other was a glass sphere similar to the one on the fingerprint replicator.

Raising the door slightly, he gripped the handle on the scrambling device and slid the end under the door. He pressed the button on the handle and slowly maneuvered the device so it pointed in every possible angle. By doing so,

Aubrey made any biometrics sensors, motion sensors, and all video cameras inoperable. The device sent out powerful ultraviolet flashes that fried electronic sensors and video equipment. Anyone watching on the other end would see nothing but a white screen when he was finished. The technology was bleeding edge, courtesy of his employer OWG Insurance, and virtually unknown to the public, so he felt comfortable that even someone like Malina wouldn't expect it.

Sabotaging Malina Maddox's security system could backfire. He didn't want to scare her when she arrived home, but he also felt sure she wouldn't come home at all if she saw a stranger sitting on her couch. He hoped that he could at least make his case to her in the brief span before she either attacked him or ran away.

Aubrey gripped the handle at the base of the door and slid it up along its greasy track. The metal clattered lightly as it rolled into itself above the door frame. He clicked on his flashlight and shone it around the space in front of him.

What he saw was not what he expected. This was, in fact, a living space. Several rugs softened the concrete floor. A sofa ran half the length of the far wall. String lights hung from the ceiling, stretching crisscrossed from corner to corner of the long rectangular space.

Pulling out the slim scrambling device once more, he activated it and pointed it into all the blind spots he thought he'd missed from a moment ago. He leaned forward beyond the door frame and looked around. A single cabinet, large silver bowl, and a hotplate dominated the corner to his right. A makeshift kitchen, he thought. To his left was what looked like the command center: a large desk stretched from corner to corner topped with enormous monitors, several keyboards and many other devices whose purpose he could only guess at.

He yawned, a normal occurrence since he entered the hospital over a week ago, and stepped into the storage unit turned living quarters. Closing the door behind him, it was then he noticed the wall opposite the sofa. Against the wall was a large stack of books, actual books. The stack was higher than his waist and formed a rough triangle over ten feet wide at its base.

With the print industry virtually extinct, it was a rare sight to see so many paper books outside of a collection house. He scanned the titles—*Brave New World, 1984, A Brief History of Time, Pale Blue Dot*. Impressed by the size and variety of her collection of books he decided to sit down.

His body was tired. His head was tired.

He fell into the couch like it was the arms of an old friend. He would wait for her. His only hope was to convince her he meant no harm and make his case before she reacted.

He yawned again and looked around the one room home taking it in, trying to figure out who she was by what she owned. This was difficult as the room was sparsely appointed. The most revealing objects were the books, though he imagined her life existed on the computers to his right. Imagining the complex security she must have built into accessing the system, he yawned again, longer and deeper than before.

One thing Martin Aubrey had forgotten was how long it takes to discipline oneself against the brain's demand for sleep after abstaining from it for so long on Zentransa. The demand came on him like a storm, raging against every cell of his body.

The sofa was soft; it enveloped him. His eyes were heavy. Didn't he take his Z before he left his apartment?

Exhausted, he didn't care to think too hard about it.

Just a little tired, he thought. He decided he would rest his eyes for just a few minutes.

* * *

Malina Maddox walked home from her meeting with Varela. It took much longer to walk than to hire a car, but something about the exchange she just had made her feel like walking.

The exchange of information for money always made her feel dirty. Working on her own to expose the corrupt was one thing, her payoff was the satisfaction of knowing the bad guys were going down by her hand. Her work for the police never felt wrong either. The pay was next to nothing and the evidence she uncovered went to actually prosecute and imprison wrongdoers.

On the other hand, the transaction with Varela was simply to expose assholes for being assholes. They were criminals, but in the end the whole story was about embarrassing rich people—exposing extramarital affairs, stealing from partners, defrauding stakeholders. It was a case of wealthy assholes hurting other wealthy assholes.

But those assholes had means and motive to come after her if they found out about her.

The money she'd been paid would afford her the luxury of working on projects from which she derived real satisfaction. She equated it to stealing bread to feed the poor. She'd put the money to good use.

Having grown up in small conservative town part of a wealthy family, she'd always been the black sheep. For their part, her puritanical parents only briefly tried to force her to be anything other than she wanted to be. In Malina's middle school years, they tried and failed to get her to wear more paisley colors, grow her hair long and adorn it with bows and glittery clips, and to join organizations more fitting of her station like the equine or sailing clubs.

Once they realized she'd never be who they preferred and that a dark room with a powerful computer was where she belonged, they relented.

Her parents were gone now. She and her two sisters split the family fortune, which Malina never touched. She was saving it for the very real possibility that she might have to one day disappear for good.

The phone in her pocket dinged. The tone was that of her security system alerting her it had detected something in her unit. Unalarmed, she pulled the phone out. This happened often due to the abundance of rodents in the building and the fact that hers was the only unit in the building that contained food of any type.

She looked, shocked by what she saw. The alert wasn't for movement inside the unit, it was alerting her that all her cameras and sensors were down. She checked the feeds. Nothing there.

With a few quick taps on the phone to check other systems inside the unit, she confirmed she still had power. What could have taken down all those sensors and cameras if not a power outage, she thought. And if it were an outage, she had backup power packs for her security.

The only explanation was a local failure of some type—rats

chewing through her cables perhaps. She needed to hurry home to figure it out, but first she wanted to check something.

She opened an app on her phone she'd created, a reporting tool that received a feed from the building's only entrance: the front elevators. Opening the app, she checked the activity log. Someone had entered the building by scanning their thumbprint less than half an hour ago.

Running a cross-reference search, she discovered that the thumbprint belonged to the owner of a unit on the second floor who visited every few months. It had been three months since their last entry and it was the only activity all day. One of the perks of living in a storage unit was the infrequency of people coming and going.

She breathed a sigh of relief. Her apparent security outage was not connected to the person entering the building thirty minutes ago. If the information she'd just handed over had gone public already, she would have been more worried, but for now she felt secure.

It took another hour to walk the rest of the way home. Physical exercise was a treat for someone who spent three-quarters of their life staring at a monitor. She walked fast and took the steepest hills along the way. By the time she turned the corner and saw her huge, gray box of a building her legs were stiff and her heart beating hard.

Something strange caught her eye as she called the elevator—a strange purple residue, like a mist, around the biometric reader. Vagrants. Vandalizing the property was nothing new and the cleaner bots would be around soon. She had no idea what the substance could be but forgot about it when the doors to the elevator opened.

By the time she stepped in front of her unit's door, she saw it again—the purple mist. In front of her, near her door's thumbprint reader was a small smear of it.

Coincidences be damned. She bolted down the aisle and stopped at the end of the block, panting against the wall.

Had the targets of her investigation already found her? Impossible. No one knew where she lived. No one even knew *who* she was. Not no one, she argued with herself. Some people did. People she thought she could trust.

If only she could see inside her unit, she thought. Then she remembered the Arlo.

A paranoid former owner of her unit had installed a simple, low tech camera in one corner. The Arlo dated back to the early 2030s. Malina had never removed it because it still worked, but also because it was an antique according to tech standards. She respected antiques.

She whipped out her phone and found an app that she had used to test the Arlo soon after finding it. Tapping a few commands, she powered it on. Her screen turned a dull gray. Confused for a moment, she remembered the camera had been pointed at the wall. Using the in-app controls, she panned the little camera away from the wall.

A light hanging directly in front of the lens obscured the view for a moment until she panned a bit more and zoomed out to get the widest view of her unit.

There, on the sofa, sat a man. And without a doubt, he was asleep. His head tossed back, mouth agape, breathing steady and deep. She tapped a button on the app for the audio; he snored. Panning and zooming a bit more confirmed he was alone.

She shook her head in disbelief. She hesitated, undecided

on what to do. He could have backup she didn't know about. He could be fake sleeping, but then he'd either have to know she was looking at him or he had been like that for over an hour waiting for her. Neither seemed likely.

Malina reached into her bag and removed a short, thick black rod. Swinging the collapsed baton in a short, quick motion it shot out, extending to four times its former length. She pushed a button on the baton's grip and blue sparks arced between two terminals in its tip.

She pushed her hood back and unshouldered her bag; she'd come back for it.

Malina held the baton tightly in her fist and walked with long steps toward the door of her unit.

* * *

Martin Aubrey's eyes slammed open. Every muscle in his body convulsed until he thought his teeth would crack against each other and grind to dust. His arms were contracted against his chest and he couldn't move.

Bright blue light blinded him. His vision cleared and he could see blue sparks blooming from the end of a black rod. It was a baton. Near him, the arcs of blue shot between two silver posts; at the other end stood a small woman with short hair. She raised the baton over her head ready to strike down Aubrey.

"*Who* the fuck are you, and *how* the fuck did you find me?" she shouted.

Aubrey curled, doubled over in pain on the strange woman's couch. White hot pain shot through his back as she hit him with the baton again. His entire body contracted as if trying to collapse in on itself.

The woman stood over him shouting over and over again. The haze from his nap had vanished. He could fend her off, but she was furious and he didn't want to make the situation worse. He did, however, want her to stop sending thousands of volts through his body.

She shouted into his ear, "I said, who the fuck are you and how the fuck did you find me here?"

Aubrey rolled back into a half-seated position and put his hands up in surrender as she thrusted with the baton toward his chest. In one motion, he batted the baton away and grabbed her wrist, pulling her toward him while raising his feet into a spring position. With her weight on the bottoms of his feet he shot them outward, sending her flying.

She crashed into the stack of books, scattering them in all directions.

Malina scrambled to her feet and dashed toward the open door.

"Wait, please, just wait," Aubrey shouted, throwing the baton aside.

Malina didn't leave the unit; instead she lunged for the kitchen cabinet. Flinging the cabinet door open, she reached inside.

Aubrey got to his feet. She spun around in a seated position, her legs spread wide in front of her, holding a small pistol. Her hood was down and her face dark with rage. She would shoot him, he had no doubt.

"Answer my fucking question." She was panting, but focused.

Hands in the air, he said, "My name is Martin Aubrey. I'm a friend of Aaron Lewis. He told me where to find you." He lowered his hands to the side, palms facing her. He tried to sound calm and unaggressive.

"You're a cop?" she shouted.

"No … well, it's complicated."

"As complicated as breaking into my house to ambush me?"

"You were the one with the lightning rod, lady. And would you really call this a house? I mean …" Aubrey said, looking around with his hands still raised.

"Don't get smart with me, mother fucker. I'll blow your …"

"I worked with Lewis for a while," he said, cutting her off after realizing the joke was a bad idea. "We worked on the Boarding School Syndrome case and the OFP bombings."

"How did you break in here and how did you disable my security system and why the hell are you here?" Her voice was quieter with these questions, but still very angry.

"I can explain how I got in here. I'll even share my gear with you, but we need to talk first."

"Talk about what?"

"About BSS and the bombings. About One Front for the People."

"What is there to talk about?" she said, getting more upset now as if this were another joke. "They caught the guys. It's all over."

"That's why I'm here. It's not over." Aubrey locked eyes with Malina. Hers were large and dark, the lights reflecting off them. "I need your help, or more people are going to get hurt."

* * *

Half a mile from the gray building, Jacira Barretto sat in the backseat of a large black sedan. The windows were darkened to the point of matching the car's paint job, but it was necessary. Surveillance required privacy. She could adjust the level of tint on the glass at any time with the touch of a button, which she would do if she saw any cops.

An expensive car parked on a street like this with windows as dark as hers screamed that a nefarious exchange of money for bodily fluids was taking place. She didn't need the attention.

The backseat was her mobile operations center. The backs of both front seats held small monitors showing different angles of the view outside the strange building Martin Aubrey had entered not long ago. She worked on a laptop and three tablets. The cameras were mounted to the bellies of two micro drones perched on ledges of adjacent buildings.

She checked the power levels for each and was satisfied to see they each had several more hours of life left. She hoped it was enough to catch Aubrey when he left, if he left. The drone had been tracking Aubrey since he left the hospital with Jacira first watching from the comfort of her plush apartment, then from the car.

If Aubrey was mobile, she needed to be mobile as well.

She'd been on Aubrey's tail ever since he left the hospital a few hours ago. Having only been on the job for a little over a week, this was her first opportunity to do anything other than wait for Aubrey to leave the hospital.

When Aubrey entered this building using his fancy toys, Jacira grew excited. Who goes to a storage unit other than to store something or remove something? Either way, she knew the unit wasn't Aubrey's or else he wouldn't have to break in.

She had no idea what this case was about. She had no idea what this Aubrey person had done to piss off her employer, and she had no idea what the information she was gathering would be used for, but such was the case for most of her jobs.

She did what she was paid to do and asked only the questions that would enable her to do so. She observed and reported, as instructed, though she had a hunch that she would be asked to do more in the end. Surveillance was the first of her two special skills. Most of her jobs began with surveillance and led to her employer asking for her other skill. Very few asked for it up front even though most wanted the latter more than the former.

Jacira watched for a while longer, making a mental note to get inside the building and figure out what unit Aubrey was visiting when she saw a small-ish woman approach the elevator doors at the front of the building. The woman hesitated for a moment, bending close to examine the area around the print pad, apparently noticing the leftovers from Aubrey's spray bottle.

Jacira saw Aubrey wipe the area down thoroughly, which meant this woman was incredibly observant. It didn't stop her from entering, however. It also didn't mean the two of them were connected as there were hundreds of units in the building.

Nothing happened for over an hour. When it did, it confirmed two things for Jacira.

Aubrey looked worse for wear coming out. In general, he was more disheveled than before and his shirt had scorch marks in several places on his chest. For Jacira, this confirmed that Aubrey and the woman were connected.

Second, it confirmed the encounter had not gone so well for Aubrey. She knew of only a handful of things that could cause those marks on Aubrey's shirt and the only one the woman could have carried in a bag was some type of stun gun.

Of course, it could all be a coincidence. Aubrey could have entered the building to retrieve an old lamp from his dead mother's storage unit, tested it to see if it still worked, and it blew up in his face causing the burn marks.

Coincidences were for cops, though. She worked on hunches and hearsay more than anything else most of the time. For this situation, her hunch was that these two were connected and more than that, they were working together.

She tapped a tablet and set one micro-drone to track Aubrey. The other she left to watch the building. If and when the woman left, Jacira would track her too.

Watching one screen change as the drone took off to hover high above while following Aubrey, she decided she'd better report in to her employer.

She picked up her phone and pulled up her contacts. Scrolling down the list, she found the name Mr. V. She tapped it and the phone started dialing.

Over the car speakers she heard the phone ringing. A man's voice answered.

"Yes?"

"I have a report, sir."

8

Ryan Grant

Detective Ryan Grant, still on light duty status and walking on carbon fiber braces, knew something was wrong the moment he opened the door to his apartment.

His building would not be considered luxurious by even the most liberal use of the word, but as a single man living on a police officer's salary, he considered it nice enough.

The ten-year-old building was clean, close to the office, and occupied with people mostly his age. His actual apartment was a one bedroom that had no business being referred to as such—his room was more of a glorified closet which he used for storage. He slept on the couch most nights.

The building lacked decent security—no doorman, no facial recognition, and had only token cameras with enough blind spots to make them useless. The main entrance used a keypad for entry with a physical key for backup. Being a cop, Grant had cared little about the security situation. The other tenants welcomed him, and his gun, with open arms.

As lackluster as the security measures in the building were, he'd never known it to be non-functional. Which is why he found it odd to receive an email from building management that afternoon. The email stated that the main entry's keypad was down, all tenants would have to use their physical keys, and the cameras throughout the building were inoperable. The management company was working on repairs and should have everything working before close of business the next day.

The news about the door and the cameras hadn't bothered Grant until he opened the door to his home and found it dark. His lights were programmed to illuminate the second the front door opened and had never failed him.

He paused at the threshold. Just paranoid, he thought. Maybe it was just a bug affecting the entire building—the door, cameras, and now his lights.

He took a half step into the apartment and looked to the left, toward the kitchen. He saw the glow of his small grow light and the reflection of blue off the leaves of herbs in their square pots. The power to the apartment was on.

The faint glow from the kitchen painted the apartment in its eerie light. Basic shapes of things were distinguishable, but the place was dark otherwise.

"Lights," he said, commanding his home's AI.

Nothing happened.

"Glitchy ass apartment," he said as he slid his pistol from its holster.

Stepping further in, he nudged the door with his elbow and waited for the sharp thud of the knob connecting with the wall. It didn't come. Only a soft bump. Something soft behind the door.

In one motion, he whipped around the door, flinging it away, and drew his pistol, activating its light as he leveled it on the spot behind the door.

Nothing there. The white circle of light shined on the beige wall, reflecting off the nooks and crannies of the concrete blocks.

He lowered the pistol to the base of the wall. A shoe lay there, its toe curled from the door. It was one of his. He didn't remember leaving it there, but no one had ever accused him of being tidy. Feeling foolish and overly paranoid, he holstered his pistol and slammed the door shut.

As he turned his back on the door, he saw a shape charging from the darkness. He reached for his holster, but there was no time; he threw his hands up and twisted. The assailant made a swift movement. The silver glint of a blade slashed through the air at him.

He threw up an arm, deflected the blow. An impact like the kick of a horse hit him in the upper thigh, collapsing his brace. Then another impact in the belly, doubling him over.

The darkness made it impossible to see the blows before they came. The rough outline of the attacker was all he could make out; the attacker moved with impossible speed.

The kicks came again, two more to his side and chest. The attacker was so fast, every time Grant reached for his pistol, he was hit, losing his grip.

Then he felt it. The sting in his side. He'd been stabbed before. He knew what it felt like.

Arms up, he jumped back, preparing for more knife slashes. And again, going for his pistol. He had it this time, withdrew it.

No more kicks came. No more punches. The shape of the attacker drifted backward into deep shadow.

"Quitter," Grant yelled.

The shape laughed.

Coldness swept Grant's body. A deep chill flowed through him, freezing him to his bones. It was followed by a feverish heat radiating from the inside out. His skin prickled, sweat formed under his clothes.

He leveled his pistol on the shape, but his hands shook. He couldn't aim, couldn't squeeze the trigger. His body quaked and then his fingers would no longer obey him. The pistol fell to the floor.

Grant's back stiffened and contracted, throwing his head back in a violent swing. Flopping to the floor, Ryan Grant's chest made a desperate rattling sound as he inhaled his last breath.

* * *

Balthazar Rhegus stood in the dark, watching the target writhe for a moment before falling still. He stared at the small man, cocking his head to the side. What had this poor man done, he wondered.

Shaking off the thought, Balthazar turned his hulking form toward the kitchen. He searched for a few seconds before finding what he needed.

He set the small dish on the counter then reached a gloved hand into his pants pocket. He withdrew a soft square of cloth and used it to wipe the end of his knife, ensuring he removed any residue of fluids from its surface.

Holding up the cloth square by one corner he turned to the stovetop. He clicked on a burner and touched the dangling end of the cloth to the flame. With a *whoosh* it caught fire.

Placing the burning rag onto the dish, the familiar smell

filled his nose. Could the smoke itself be deadly? he wondered. He shrugged while he ran the blade in and out of the flame. He had to be sure all of the residue was burned away. An accidental slip could be deadly otherwise.

Still holding the knife in the flames, Balthazar pulled his phone from his pocket. He logged into the secure digital dead drop and left a note for his employer informing him the job was finished.

9

Sacrifice

"You would be helping to usher in a new era here," Fox said in a low tone.

"Find someone else. My killing days are behind me," Truck whispered. Fox, or the Professor as he was called, was the closest thing to a friend that Truck had known for a long time, which is why Truck was still listening to him. He was someone Truck could trust, as far as you could trust anyone in the Keep.

"There is no one else. They're all too young and too stupid."

The Professor paused while Truck adjusted himself. He sat on the floor of his cell with his mattress folded under him; he thumbed through an old paperback. The raucous noise of the card game being played next to them masked their conversation.

"You saw what happened yesterday. You saw how the other inmates reacted. Have you ever seen anything like it? Have you ever seen our brothers and sisters so brave?"

"Brothers and sisters?" Truck growled. "I don't care nothing for them birds. I've been in here most of my life and no I haven't seen anything like it, but who cares? It'll pass and everything'll go back to normal soon enough. This ain't no movement like you're saying."

"That's right, it probably will pass. Which is why we must act now to harness it. I know you don't care about anyone here. But I know something else too; I know you hate the Tappers as much as anyone, maybe more. You're the oldest bird in our ward. You had friends here at one time and they're all gone now. Who killed them, Truck?"

"That Tapper killed 'em. You know that." Truck stared at the Professor with hard eyes. Even with seventy-six years behind him, he could still strike fear in most men. He did it now; the Professor turned his head only looking back at Truck through the corners of his eyes.

"I do. I do." The Professor looked away out the cell door. The rest of the ward was just getting up for the day. He looked back at Truck. "I know something else. I know you're tired. And I know you're sick."

Truck eyed him, wondering how he could know. It would have been easy for his own cell mates to notice of course. They could have told the Professor. Then again, how many more times could Truck wander the ward totally confused and unaware without someone noticing. It was bound to happen.

And the Professor was right, Truck was tired. He was tired all the time.

Truck's gaze fell to the floor. "Doctors gave me some time. I've still got time."

"Sure, you do. But do you want that time to be spent as a confused old invalid who can't feed himself or wipe his own ass? I'm giving you a way to go out on your own terms, and

I promise you this: I'll kill that son-of-a-bitch Tapper after it all starts."

Truck felt something he hadn't felt in years: relief. Relief that it could all be over soon. The Professor had just put into words the thoughts that had been clouding his mind for months. He could go the same way that Tapper did yesterday. Tapping was rumored to be painless and it happened in your sleep, so it could be a peaceful way to go. Better than the shit-your-pants terror the jumpers must feel before they went splat at the bottom of the Atrium.

He'd been thinking about a way out for quite a while, but the fear crippled him. Here it was, however: the courage to do it coupled with the satisfaction that he would get his revenge in the end even if he wasn't around to see it happen.

"You promise you'll do that? You'll kill him?"

"I do. I'll see to it myself."

"How you going to do that without getting wasted yourself first? Besides, you ain't no killer," Truck scoffed.

"I think I could surprise you." The Professor raised an eyebrow. "And after it all starts, it'll be quite a bit easier to get the jump on the Tapper than it is now."

Truck groaned. "So, what? I whack somebody, Tapper comes for me, and then what? What happens next?"

The Professor glanced around, then continued quietly, "There's something I need to do. I can only do it if I know the Tapper is coming for someone."

"Why don't you just wait?" Truck asked. "Bound to happen anyway, someone getting Tapped, sooner or later."

"I'm in a bit of a time crunch. I can't afford to take the chance that it might take weeks for someone to get selected. And a murder is the only way I know to guarantee someone gets Tapped."

He knew there must be more to all this. More than what the Professor was letting on, but Truck was too tired to care.

"When did you have in mind for me to do it?"

"Today. Then the Tapper will come tonight."

The Professor held out a hand. Something protruded from the cuff of his sleeve, the tip of an object wrapped in black electrical tape. Truck took the handle of the shiv, hiding the exchange under the guise of a handshake as the Professor stood to leave. He hid the weapon in the folds of his mattress.

"Pretty quick timing," Truck said.

"Has to be."

"Anyone in particular you want it to be?"

"Anyone you want. There must be someone in here you wouldn't mind seeing dead."

The Professor looked down at Truck for a moment, then left without another word.

Truck sat staring at his book. He thought there was one or two people who would be good candidates. It all depended who was in the shower when he got there.

Still sitting he reached to his bed, the bottom of the stack, and grabbed his towel. Tucking the shiv in his towel, he stood.

"Where you going, Truck?" said one of his cell mates, breaking from his card game.

"Going to get cleaned up. See you boys in a bit."

* * *

Stetson Vans, known as Truck due to a clever play on his last name, entered the shower room without incident. The guards only searched inmates at random and Truck had never given them reason to be suspicious. He walked right past them into the changing room where he would usually undress and lay his clothes on the long wooden bench.

He kept them on today, walking past the stalls full of men noisily passing their bowels and into the shower room. He looked around as he always did. This time, however, he didn't look for an empty showerhead, he looked for a sacrifice.

Naked men stood around ten tall stanchions which held six showerheads each. The room was crowded today, some inmates were doubled up under sputtering streams of water. Suds ran across the slick white tiles into a central drain. The sound of water filled the space along with laughter and banter of a general sort.

In a corner across the large round room, Truck saw a man who he knew had once instigated a fight that left a man dead. Truck hadn't known the dead man too well, but he knew of him as being decent. Roy was his name and he hadn't deserved being killed like that.

Deciding there were no better candidates, Truck walked toward his sacrifice. His shoes splashed in the shallow rivers of water, soaking his socks.

"Hey, Truck, what's up man? You forgot to undress," said a voice near him.

"He's alright, let him be," said another voice.

Ignoring them, he walked on, keeping his eyes on the sacrifice. Ten feet away, a tall dark man stepped in front of Truck.

Head cocked to the side, the man said, "Yo, dummy, this raintree is full. Wait for another one."

Truck looked at him for a moment, then peered around

him at his intended victim.

"You deaf, too, old timer? Get the fuck outta here," the man said, pointing to the exit.

Truck looked up at the tall man.

"I guess you'll have to do."

He dropped the towel to the floor and plunged the jagged blade deep into the man's abdomen. His eyes bulged in surprise and pain. He gripped Truck's wrist in both hands, attempting to pull the blade free, but the rough edge only caused him more pain as it moved.

Truck obliged the man and pulled it out himself, then pushed it in again in a different spot. Then again. Then again.

The man fell with a wet slap, eyes still open, clutching his belly. Water ran pale red into the drain. As Truck looked around the shower, it was empty now. In the entrance, guards were running at him. He dropped the blade and held out his empty hands.

10

The Member Principal

Brother Rudolfo's thoughts on his new apprentice were simple—he had no thoughts. He felt unaffected and unimpressed by her, which he concluded was a good thing in and of itself. Being unremarkable to a casual observer was a strength in the role of a Member.

Although rather plain looking, there was a time and a place when he would have said she was an attractive woman. That part of his life was far behind him. He saw a young Caucasian woman of average height and blonde hair. Obviously physically fit and, if the academy's reports were accurate, she was highly intelligent and an exceptional observer.

Rudolfo and Francesca exited the train platform through an inconspicuous door at the far end and into an empty hallway.

Brother Rudolfo led the way. He could hear Francesca following close behind. The rustle of her cassock, her loud breathing, and the swish of her duffel bag against her leg were all things he took mental note of as he lengthened the list of things they would need to address over the next several months. She did not, however, speak a word as they walked—a good sign.

Flashes of black stains and white uniforms, of pale naked flesh falling dozens of stories past hundreds of screaming and taunting inmates occupied his mind.

Rudolfo passed several heavy metal doors without labels.

"What is behind these doors?" he asked. He waited several seconds for the answer and was on the verge of turning around to inquire about her hearing and whether they would need to get her fitted with an implant when she spoke.

"Maintenance rooms. Electrical, heating, ventilation, and air conditioning. Also, plumbing stacks and communications." Her voice sounded confident, but breathy.

Rudolfo did not reply, satisfied with her answer. Understanding the physical structure and utilities of the building in which they served was a vital part of their education. He had expected nothing less.

Turning a corner, the mentor and his apprentice came to a small group of Members—two men and a woman huddled in a tight circle. Rudolfo slowed.

"Brother Rudolfo," said one of the men. "Good day to you."

"Brothers, Sister." Rudolfo glowered at the young man and gave a small nod. He had no doubt the three of them had been exchanging third-hand accounts of Wilcott's self-selection.

"I wonder if I may bother you for a chat later," said the man.

"Yes. But if it is gossip you're looking for, search elsewhere, Brother." Rudolfo clasped his hands behind his back. The other Members exchanged glances.

"Your new apprentice?" the woman spoke now, nodding

in Francesca's direction.

"Yes," said Rudolfo. From the corner of his eye, he saw Francesca look in his direction. She said nothing. Rudolfo approved.

"Ah. Well, good day to you, Brother Rudolfo. And future Sister." The man nodded to the Apprentice, then to the Mentor.

Without a word, Rudolfo set out again. Francesca's steps sounding behind him once more.

After turning several more corners, they came to an open elevator. Rudolfo entered first, followed by Francesca. He pressed the topmost button which caused a short, low tone to emit from the control panel. A small, round scanner on the panel near the door blinked red.

As it blinked, he turned to her and said, "Only Members have access to this elevator. No one else."

He waved the back of his left hand in front of the scanner. It turned from blinking red to solid green. The elevator door closed and the lift jolted to life, beginning its long ascent to the top level.

"You will be given access when your apprenticeship draws to a close." Rudolfo stared ahead in silence, relieved that Francesca did the same.

* * *

Francesca's impression of Rudolfo was incomplete, but she felt she had made a small but fundamental measure of him. He spoke little and thought much, carefully calculated his actions, and exhibited purposefulness. Whether he intended to or not, his interactions with her that morning had left her with profound curiosity.

The elevator slowed then stopped. The doors slid open and Francesca was momentarily blinded by an attack of bright light.

Several seconds passed while her eyes adjusted. Once she could see again, what she saw took her aback. In front of her was a round space almost as wide as the prison's exterior. In it, every vertical surface shined in high-gloss white paint. She looked up; sunlight blazed through a ceiling made of glass above her. The light reflected off every surface, filling the space and making her feel like she had not just risen forty-eight stories, but had somehow traveled several light-minutes closer to the sun itself.

Squinting at the glare coming at her from all sides, she walked several paces from the elevator before she noticed the floor.

In front of her, the floor was made of glass. Like the ceiling above it, it was a massive skylight. A thirty-foot wide path ringed the circle of glass. A smaller version of the one above her, the floor skylight sat directly over the Great Atrium below, that cylinder of air that penetrated the center of the prison from top to bottom.

It was plain to see that it was the same diameter as the Great Atrium—thirty feet—designed to spill natural light down into the prison. Francesca estimated that if she measured from the center of the glass to the outer edge of the path, it would equal about one quarter of the prison's total diameter.

She moved along the outer path, to where Rudolfo waited for her. They walked. Looking down through the floor, she could see into the levels below. Many prisoners walked along the catwalks. Some exercised, others merely congregated.

One small group of six inmates appeared to be attending a sermon of some sort, watching one man with a small book gesturing toward the sky.

As they walked, she noticed that, other than the elevator and what appeared to be a stairwell exit, there were several other doors off the circular path.

She looked up out of the skylight above and then down through the one below. More than anything, she wanted to walk out to the center of floor and look down into the Great Atrium. She thought of an image from her childhood—a picture of a train tunnel in the side of a mountain. It stretched away and away until it became a tiny speck of light in the distance.

She imagined the view from the center of the glass floor as another endless tunnel descending into nothingness. Each circular floor growing smaller and smaller until they blurred and disappeared, not to a speck of light, but to a cold, black pit.

Francesca and her Mentor continued circumventing the glass floor. She assumed it was strong enough to hold their weight, but Brother Rudolfo appeared to give the clear space a degree of reverence, avoiding it. She got the sense that he saw it as more than she did.

"This … room," said Francesca, struggling with the correct word for the space they were in, "it was not in any of my studies."

"Nor should it be," said Rudolfo. "It does not serve a function necessary for you to perform your function."

* * *

They stopped in front of a door across the floor from the elevator. Before entering, Rudolfo thought about the conversation he was about to have with the Member Principal. He had already decided to include Francesca as it was now her prerogative to know exactly what he knew. He turned to face her.

"I have business here other than your introduction," said Rudolfo. "Albeit important for the Principal to meet a new Apprentice, a ... significant event occurred today." He inclined his head, gazing through the familiar skylight as he spoke. "Since, you are now my apprentice, I feel it is something you should hear us discuss. Later, you will have questions and I will answer them ... later."

"I ... understand," said Francesca.

"No. No, you do not," he said shaking his head. "But let's hope you come to comprehend the meaning of it, if nothing else."

Without knocking, he opened the door leaving the sunlit round room behind to enter a much more compact one with several chairs around a small table. There was a door on each side of the room and after a moment the one to their left opened and Member Principal Jacobi stepped through. Dressed in standard Member garb he had gray hair, almost white, and stood taller than Rudolfo.

"Ah, Brother," the Member Principal said, grinning at the two of them.

Rudolfo met his eyes before the Principal turned his attention to Francesca. Rudolfo watched as he stared at her before turning his eyes back to his old friend.

"Our meeting has become dual-purpose, has it?" the Principal asked.

"It has, Brother Jacobi," replied Rudolfo. "As you know, Francesca has come to us from the Pupil's School this morning. She is now my Apprentice."

"Of course, of course," said Jacobi, turning again to Francesca. "How was your walk to the train? Uneventful, I hope."

"Yes, Wise Brother Jacobi. Uneventful."

"Good. Good. Unfortunately, Francesca dear, recent events have," Jacobi's gaze shifted to a spot on the wall and he smoothed the front of his cassock, "diverted my attention and I'm afraid a more substantial meeting between us will have to wait a little while."

Jacobi turned his attention back to Rudolfo. His look of concern was obvious to Rudolfo and he wished Jacobi wasn't so out of practice at managing his emotions.

"Rudie, let us talk. Much to discuss. In private, I'm afraid," Jacobi said with a sideways glance at Francesca. "You'll wait here, but we won't be long."

Rudolfo cringed at Jacobi's use of the term of endearment. "Actually, Wise Brother, she will be joining us. I believe we will begin our relationship with transparency."

"Transparency," repeated Jacobi, nodding. His eyes bounced between the two of them. "Yes. Apprentice Francesca, you may join us. But please try to remain," he looked at Rudolfo, "transparent." Jacobi turned and left through the door he had just entered.

* * *

Following the two elder Members, Francesca entered a sunlit room, almost as bright as the large round space they'd just left. Long and narrow, the room followed the curvature of the prison's shell and its contents shocked her. The room was a library or a well-stocked reading room. Books dominated the space followed closely by art, and antique furniture. The walls were packed with volumes on shelves fit to burst.

The spine of every book had been pulled to the edge of its shelf to make a uniform, flawless plain. Most striking was the choice of how the plethora of titles was organized.

Turning around, she saw the wall through which she had just walked was covered in large, dark-brown books that gave her the feeling of being imposed upon. Flowing to the wall opposite the windows and around the room clockwise, the colors became lighter. The large books sat on higher shelves and shrank in size toward the bottom. From brown and to orange and red and yellow and finally into blues on the last of the shelves on the outer wall under the windows. By the floor sat pale blue books no wider than a pencil.

The books flowed around the room like a gaudy wave. They washed the walls of the library in an evolution of emotion. Foreboding and dark to fiery anger to light and happy, and finally terminating in low melancholy.

The floor was covered in a patchwork of thick rugs of a middle eastern color palate and design. Several tall lamps stood around the room and a low, squat globe dominated the far corner by the window. High-backed leather chairs were placed at odd locations; two of them near her sat around a low wooden table. Natural light bathed the floor through small square windows that she now realized were the same she saw around the top rim of the prison.

To her, the atmosphere of the room and its design seemed off. It seemed to contradict some belief she did not know she had about the preferences of the Member Principal of the Order of the Coppice. It reminded her of the jolt one felt when a step was one inch too high or too low—the mind expects one thing and gets something else that is not quite right.

She wasn't sure what she had expected to see as she was unaware of this level's existence until moment ago. Additionally, interior decorating habits of Member Principals had never come up in her studies.

She knew one thing: this space was out of focus; it was more important than it should be.

Neither of the men noticed her gazing as they sat nearby in the two high-backed chairs.

Jacobi sat in the far chair, profiled against the light in the windows, his hands folded across his legs. For a silent moment, he stared at Rudolfo opposite Jacobi, his back to Francesca.

"You saw it?" Jacobi said.

"I did."

Jacobi let out an audible sigh and turned his head toward the windows. He rested his chin on a fist.

"Very disturbing," Jacobi said.

"Is it?"

Jacobi did not respond, but continued staring at the windows.

"Our purpose is to select," said Rudolfo. "Assess and select. If one a Member ..."

"Our purpose," Jacobi said without looking back to Rudolfo. "Our purpose. Our function. What of our purpose now? A dead Member is useless to fulfill their purpose. And what of us that remain now that so much has been exposed? Do you feel we can still fulfill our purpose?"

Rudolfo was silent until Jacobi turned back to face him.

"I do." Rudolfo adjusted the folds in his cossack and brushed lint from one knee. "As I was saying, if a Member chooses to assess and select themselves, it is their right to do so." Now, Rudolfo was staring at the windows. "It is not forbidden. Nor is it uncommon. Frowned upon maybe, but has his commitment not been fulfilled? He did not abandon his duty, as others have."

Francesca saw the slightest turn of Rudolfo's head toward her. He checked himself before saying the word "others". Jacobi appeared uncomfortable, rearranging his cassock behind him and between his legs. Francesca wondered if Rudolfo would have spoken openly if she were not in the room.

Transparency, it seemed, did not mean total.

"Brother Wilcott's reputation was one of consistency and diligence," continued Rudolfo. "If asked my opinion ..."

"You may assume you have been asked," said Jacobi.

"I think Wilcott was near the end," Rudolfo continued. He looked back at Jacobi, inclining his head. "I saw his mark. It was considerable. I believe he felt he had fulfilled his commitment. Purpose being served, his respite was to self-select and prevent nature from taking its cruel and painful course."

"By god, Rudie," said Jacobi.

He was now more animated and agitated than before. His brow creased and fists clenched in his lap.

"It is not the fact that he self-selected. You think I care about that?" He smoothed the front of his cassock. "That is to say, I do. I always wonder if a Member has self-selected too early on purpose. And I obviously care if one of our brethren dies, regardless of how." He waved a hand, brushing the idea away. "But that is beside the point! Self-selecting is one thing, but to do it as Wilcott did! You know of what I speak, Rudolfo." Jacobi leaned in toward Rudolfo. "Since our founding, our methods have been kept secret. And he goes and makes a show of it! Makes a goddamn spectacle of it, Rudie!"

The man was flush. Red splotches creeped up his neck onto his pale face. He inhaled deep in an apparent attempt to calm himself.

"I agree," said Rudolfo.

Rudolfo's demeanor had remained placid. She knew he wanted to bring Jacobi's mood down, so he brought his own down to a point that his voice was close to a whisper.

"The choice of method and venue was curious. But I believe he simply wanted it to be painless."

"Did he really disrobe, Rudie?" Jacobi placed one gloved hand on his chest.

"Yes."

"So, they saw all of him? They saw his mark as you did?" asked Jacobi.

"Yes."

"And what did they make of the mark and the method?"

She listened as Rudolfo went into detail about the reaction of the inmate population upon first seeing Wilcott's hand, then his arm and torso. How they were struck dumb for a moment, but soon became more fervent for Wilcott to jump.

The Member Principal sat quietly for several seconds tracing his jawline with the back of one hand. "We must be careful, Rudolfo." His voice had sank low, his eyes locked on the floor. "We must be careful that this incident doesn't affect our position with the inmate population. This could jeopardize our very perilous hold on them."

Rudolfo paused before continuing. "I understand. Shall I return with a more thorough assessment of the situation?"

Jacobi turned his head toward the window again. There was another long pause before either of them spoke.

"Wise Brother?" said Rudolfo.

"Yes?" replied Jacobi, appearing to snap out of his thoughts as he turned back to Rudolfo.

"Shall I return with an assessment?" Rudolfo asked.

"No, no, don't bother yourself with such things. I've been around long enough to know this will get sorted," Jacobi said, waving a hand at Rudolfo. He returned his gaze back to the window as Rudolfo stood to leave. "Just tend to your duties as per usual. They require you full attention."

11

The Sacred Task

The Apprentice and her Mentor entered the elevator after a silent walk around the bright, circular space. She watched as he reached out to the keypad and pressed the number twenty-four, waving the back of his hand in front of the scanner once more. She watched as he stood facing the elevator doors. She watched him expecting some indication that it was okay for her to ask questions.

As if reading her thoughts, Rudolfo gave her a sideways glance. "You have questions."

"I do."

"I told you I would be transparent. Ask your questions."

"What happened to Brother Wilcott?" she asked.

Rudolfo continued to face the elevator doors, his hands behind his back. "If you can't tell me what happened through simple observation and the context of the conversation you just witnessed, our time together will be difficult for you."

"Wilcott self-selected." She turned to face him and raised her chin.

"Correct."

"And they saw his mark. The inmates saw his mark."

"Correct."

"He performed the Sacred Task on himself and the prisoners saw that too."

"Correct."

She understood the rest of the story—Wilcott was older, near the end, and self-selected to choose the time and place of his end. The question, in her mind, was what impact the Member Principal feared the incident would have on Members' standing with the prison population.

She continued, "The Member Principal is afraid the inmates will not fear or respect us as they have before? Now that they have seen the actual Task performed."

"I think the Member Principal is mistaken. Rumors have been mostly correct about the Task anyway. I think if anything it might make them more fearful, however I believe he is right about one thing. It has changed the way they will perceive us."

His words were stiff; she could feel them. His tone had not changed, but his breath weighed heavy in the air.

"Why?" she asked. "Why will they perceive us differently?"

"Before now, the Sacred Task was only a story, almost an old wives' tale. Now, they know the truth. They may be more fearful, but they know exactly what to fear."

"We're not the bogeyman anymore." The words left her lips before she could think to stifle them. Rudolfo snapped his head toward her and grimaced then slowly turned back to his forward gaze.

"I suppose not," he said.

She looked aside before continuing, trying to answer the question before she asked it. Failing, she asked, "How did they see his mark?"

The mark, or the stain that signified the lives taken by a Member, was known only to those in the Order. Rumors among the inmates abounded about its existence, meaning, and origin. Now, it seemed, some of the rumors had been confirmed for an unknown number of men and women in the Coppice. Soon, the entire prison would have an idea of what it was and what it meant.

"He removed his cassock. When he fell he was all but nude." Rudolfo looked at her. His eyes told her nothing of his emotions, they were lifeless.

The elevator slowed, nearing the twenty-fourth floor.

"Today was not typical for a new Apprentice of the Order," he said. He turned and stared ahead again. "Tonight, however, will be. Tonight, you will witness the Sacred Task."

The elevator doors slinked open. Rudolfo stepped off the elevator leaving Francesca speechless and alone.

Tonight, she would watch someone die.

* * *

Francesca's introduction to her new home was unceremonious. She hurried off the elevator after Rudolfo. Her lack of emotion surprised her; she had just stepped into a world which she would call home for the rest of her life, yet she felt little.

She forced herself to consider her new world.

Striding down the empty hallway with Rudolfo several steps ahead, the first thing that struck her was the emptiness of it all. The outermost passageway, number four, which stretched ahead of her into the distance as a gentle curve, stood devoid of other people. Nothing could be heard, just her footsteps echoing off the walls, Rudolfo's in the near distance, and a low hum hanging in the air.

In stark contrast to the Member Principal's quarters, which blazed bright with the sun's rays, artificial blue light bathed the east ward of the twenty-fourth floor, and it looked as cold as it felt. The air felt moist and heavy, and smelled of harsh cleaners. Endless tubes of light ran along the corners where the ceiling met the wall in an interminable loop throughout the ward. Floors, walls, and ceiling all bore the same pale gray paint designed to calm the inmate population.

She caught up to Rudolfo and the two of them continued down the outer passageway around its slow arc passing rooms on their left and right.

"This passageway," Rudolfo explained, "is filled, for the most part, with rooms meant for education and entertainment. Recreation, you might call it."

All of this Francesca knew but she did not interrupt her mentor.

"Ours is the west ward. Our quarters are also here along with some administrative offices." He gestured to several such offices as they passed them.

"Our ward is male?" she asked.

"Correct."

There was a strict segregation of genders at the Coppice. Male and female inmates comingled on working parties, but prison wards were designated male or female based on gender identification.

Rudolfo resumed his description of the outer passageway. "What the prison population does not know is that these recreation rooms serve only one purpose: observation. We stage these rooms to encourage interaction, the exchange of humanity so that we may observe and assess. We observe, assess, and we judge. If needed, we select."

She listened as he went on to describe his ward, which made up the western half of the twenty-fourth floor, and how his small section of the prison worked, now her new home for the foreseeable future.

Rudolfo and one other Member of the Order had responsibility for the observation, judgment, and selection of every prisoner on this floor—sixteen hundred inmates in total, eight hundred quartered in eighty cells. Prison guards patrolled for the general protection of the prisoners and staff. Rumors and gossip kept Members safe for the most part he pointed out.

Reaching the central corridor, they turned left and straight ahead she could clearly see bright sunlight spilling in from the Great Atrium. It was midday, the sun was at its apex, and its rays spilled down the atrium like a waterfall.

A metal cage lined its interior, keeping inmates from falling into its emptiness. It glimmered reflective crimson in some places, but the majority of it was dull with rust.

Off the main corridor they entered the third passageway. It was empty of prisoners and guards here too. Rudolfo explained how the inmates were in various parts of the prison on work details—maintenance, reconstruction, and refurbishment assignments—while others were taken in parties to the nearby timber harvesting operation. The prison sold the lumber on its property as a source of revenue. Free labor made it a profitable business.

The passageways held the inmates' quarters. She knew the cells' dimensions by heart—each was a ten-foot cube—but seeing them in person was another shock she hadn't expected.

The prisoners' beds hung from the ceiling in what the inmates called a stack. Each cell contained two stacks at right angles to each other. Five beds in each stack were fastened to the ceiling and floor via stout cables welded to two corners and had the long edge of each bed bolted to the wall. The ten-foot-high ceiling gave less than two feet of space between each bed when accounting for the small gap between the last bed and the floor plus the thickness of each mattress and frame.

Reaching the end of passageway three they followed the corridor to enter passageway two. It was here that Francesca had her first face-to-face encounter with an inmate, one of Rudolfo's charges.

The man was tall, towering over Francesca who was herself of above average height. When she and Rudolfo entered the passageway, the inmate saw them and whirled around to cower against the block wall of the passageway. He bent his head low and shut his eyes tight. His head shook back and forth; his shoulders quaked. Muffled whimpers escaped his lips.

She stared at the pale man as they walked by. Scars covered every visible patch of skin. It was obvious, he had led a brutal life. His white uniform hung loosely on his frame, dust on his bald dry scalp, no shoes on his feet.

The inmate's visceral reaction to their presence took her aback. She found the fear a Member inspired to be profound, beyond what she'd imagined.

Francesca and Rudolfo left the man behind and only then did she realize that her Mentor had maintained his detailed description of the prisoners' quarters and, as far as she could tell, did not give any notice to the whimpering man now behind them.

After seeing her first inmate in the passageway, several more appeared in random places around the ward—alone in a cell, staring into the atrium, meandering about. Rudolfo explained that these inmates were excused from work detail either because they had worked a night shift, were injured, or sick.

Their reactions mirrored the first. These prisoners only saw impending death when the black cassock came their way; they necessarily avoided it. With one exception.

One inmate stared through deep-set, sallow eyes saying nothing, exhibiting no emotion when Francesca and Rudolfo approached. She felt the severity, the purposefulness, of the prisoner's non-reaction, but once again, Rudolfo appeared to have taken no notice.

She followed her Mentor up the north corridor, back to passageway four. He walked a short way, stopped outside a door not far from the elevator, then turned to face her.

"Your quarters."

She opened the door to be greeted by a room similar to that of a prisoner's cell—a perfect cube, ten feet long on every side. Along the left wall stood a narrow bed with a green wool blanket folded neatly atop white linens. In the wall past the foot of the bed was a narrow door, which stood open revealing a small bathroom complete with a shower stall. One corner held a squat set of bookshelves. The rest of the room was barren, painted in the same dull gray as the rest of the ward. Standing in the doorway, she felt her mentor waiting behind her. Francesca took a step inside the room, dropped her bag onto her bed, and returned to the hallway.

Francesca nodded her thanks just as Rudolfo turned to lead her further along the passageway, past the central corridor to another room. This one was deeper, narrower than hers and outfitted with five monitors on a long table, a control console covered in buttons and knobs, and in the center a small table with two chairs.

"Sit here." He pointed to the table. "I will return in a few moments,"

Francesca did as she was told. While she waited, her eyes drifted to the screens on the long table.

Each displayed a video feed from a different part of the ward. Two were in passageways, she wasn't sure which ones; one was in the recreation room, judging by the appearance of books and games; one was a view of what she assumed was their side of the catwalk around the Great Atrium; and the last showed the inside of a cell. In the cell, two inmates sat talking. A number in the corner read 24E52. She easily deciphered the designator—twenty-fourth floor, east ward, cell number fifty-two.

She was alone with her thoughts for the first time since she arrived at the Coppice. The Sacred Task was not something she expected to witness on her first night as an Apprentice. Thoughts of who it could be and why they were sent to the Coppice swirled in her mind like leaves in a storm.

She would need to witness a dozen before performing the Sacred Task herself, and each Member had total control over how many Tasks they performed and how often. There were no quotas; Members demonstrated their commitment to the Order and its purpose in their own way, on their own time.

Some Apprentices waited months to perform the Sacred

Task on their own; others, and she had assumed she would fall in this group, waited mere weeks. Rudolfo's reputation was one of diligence and efficiency. It was said he performed an above average number of Sacred Tasks because he took his role so seriously. But it was also said that he performed the Task only when he had to. Francesca took Rudolfo's above average number of Tasks as a sign of his relentless commitment to his duties.

Rumors at the Pupil's School held that several Apprentices in years past had performed the Sacred Task within days of arriving. She cringed at the thought of this; it cheapened and befouled the sanctity of the Task.

Rudolfo returned with a large, leather-bound book several inches thick, under his arm. He sat down across from her at the small table and opened the book. She heard its spine creak, watched him turn the yellow pages densely packed with tiny black writing.

He looked up and met her eyes. "This book contains a record of every inmate that has passed through my ward whilst I've served as a Member of the Order."

He had opened the book to a small blank section of pages toward the end of the book, then worked his way back through handwritten ones in different states of completion. The pages were thick and heavy, each time one fell she felt a light puff of air. She watched his eyes search the pages, looking toward the top of each until he stopped.

Rudolfo spun the book around and slid it across the table. "Read my observations. Give me your assessment." He pointed to the page on her left.

She scanned the page, absorbing the purpose of this book. Each page was an inmate's life here at the Coppice. The top line of each page held a number. The page Rudolfo pointed to read 0882, followed by a brief description of the inmate—brown eyes, olive complexion, spiderweb tattoos on both elbows, left hand dominant.

The rest of the page was covered in miniscule script written in a close, looping style of hand. Each line stretched across the page from the outer edge to the junction of the spine, top to bottom—detailed descriptions of incidents and observations taken by Rudolfo. She bent close to read the tight scrawl.

Participated in fight with four other inmates on a working party—he was not the instigator, but easily goaded into violence by the others. Stole food in cafeteria. Watched during card game with other inmates, cheated, then lied. Actively trading protection for sexual favors. Not following through on protection after exchange. Physically intimidates newcomers—arranged beating of one who refused to pay for protection. Three shivs found in cell.

She read to the bottom of the page finding the same offenses repeated—violence, theft, thievery, instigation of violence.

The last line ended abruptly in the middle of a sentence. Confused, she looked to the next page only to find that it started with an entirely new inmate like every page did. She was about to ask if there was more when her left thumb grazed the edge of the page and the text moved, scrolling upward. She could now see new lines at the bottom of the page. Touching the edge of the page with her thumb again she swiped upward and the text scrolled to reveal more and more lines.

Francesca looked up in surprise at Rudolfo. This book was not made of paper, although it appeared strikingly similar. The pages were capacitive film, scrollable and editable like any tablet. The technology wasn't new, having been invented two decades ago and becoming mainstream in many industries ten years later. To see it here used by this man was a juxtaposition that made her wonder what other surprises he may be hiding.

Rudolfo stared back at her. An almost imperceptible nod at the book told her to get back to her assignment.

Francesca scrolled and read until she reached the end of inmate 0882's profile, which ended with his fate.

0882 selected for the Sacred Task.

She read this last line several times before looking up. When she did, Rudolfo spoke.

"Do you agree in my selecting 0882 for the Sacred Task?"

"What was his crime? Why was he sent here?" she asked.

"His crime is irrelevant."

"His crime is what brought him here."

Rudolfo raised his eyebrows at this. He seemed to be considering her for a moment before pulling the book back across the table. She assumed the lesson had ended, but he turned to another page, one much further back toward the beginning. Spinning the book around once more, he slid it to her.

"Read this," he said pointing to a page on the right side of the book this time.

She read the page. It didn't take her long as the incidents and observations barely covered half the page and many of them exhibited positive behavior on the inmate's part.

Shared food with newcomer. Educated foreign born inmate to speak English. Sits quietly most days, avoiding the other inmates. Four inmates attempted to start violent confrontations with 9898, he resisted and was beaten as a result.

She read the last line before looking up.

Inmate 9898 selected for release.

"Do you agree with this assessment?" Rudolfo asked.

"I do. He is clearly not a threat to anyone."

Rudolfo pointed at the table holding the four monitors. He gestured to the one on the far right.

"Go to that computer and look up inmate 9898. Tell me what his crime was that brought him here."

She stood and walked to the computer he had indicated. She found the icon for the prison's intranet, opened the app, and found a search function under a tab labeled "Inmate Records." She keyed in 9898.

The profile was standard. A large picture appeared at the top followed by personal identifying information: name, prior address, identification number. Several rows down, below height, weight, eye color, tattoos and other markings, was the line for "Conviction." She stared at what it read.

"Well?" said Rudolfo.

"Triple murder. Wife, her lover, and an innocent woman with the lover when 9898 caught up with him."

"How did he kill them?"

"With a hammer," she said with as much impassivity that she could muster. "How long was he here?"

"Now look up 0882."

After a brief search, she said, "Drug trafficking and armed robbery."

"Now, do you see?" he asked.

Francesca returned to her seat across from Rudolfo. She thought for a moment before responding. Each Member was bound to serve out the Sacred Task and none was given strict guidelines on how to deal it out, to whom to deal it, or how often. One of the most commonly held understandings among them, however, was that consideration of the inmate's crime was paramount. Her Mentor was now telling her a charge's crime was irrelevant.

"We are not to consider our charges' crimes when assessing them?"

"No."

"But we were taught that ..."

"Yes, you were," he said. "I'm asking you to think about it in a new way. Many do not agree with me, but each Member of the Order is free to choose their own methods of assessing and selecting."

"How are we supposed to punish them, if ..."

"Please do not use the word punishment when speaking of a Member's duty." He raised his voice and for the first time she saw real emotion in his eyes. His fist clenched tight on the table top. "Being separated from society and sent to this facility is punishment enough, in itself. We must have faith that the justice system sent them here for good reason after using wisdom and thorough science to convict them." He took a deep breath. "Our duty is to decide the fate of the man or woman as they are now," he jabbed a gloved finger into the table, "not as they were."

"I'm sorry, Brother Rudolfo. I didn't mean to question your philosophy." She bowed her head. "I seek to understand. This is simply a different way to look at things than we were taught at the Pupil's School."

She sensed that this eased his temper.

"I showed you those two men for a reason, Francesca. One committed a horrendous crime, stayed here for ten years and over that time exhibited zero indications that he was, at heart, a violent person." He waved a hand to each side of the table as he spoke as if the two inmates were standing next to them at that moment.

"The other committed what most would consider low-level crimes, but arrived here and began showing signs of duplicitousness, bloodlust, and murderous behavior if not murder itself. It was my assessment that 9898 could be released back into society posing almost no threat, while 0882 would almost certainly take a life if he was back out on the streets. Now do you see?"

"We judge who they are," she said.

"Not who they were." He finished her thought.

At the Pupil's School of the Order, they were taught to look at all parts of a person, most especially their crimes. They'd also been taught to look up old criminal cases from the years before the Order had formed for comparison and precedent. These things were meant to give them a holistic view so as to be more fair in their assessments. She'd assumed, coming to the Coppice to start her Apprenticeship, that assessing and judging the inmates would be more transactional. If you did x number of bad things, you were bad. You got selected for the Task. What Rudolfo was doing required a philosophical approach. There was wisdom in it. Wisdom that she appreciated and wanted to learn more about.

They sat in silence for many minutes. She attempted to absorb the lesson. It was difficult to push aside much of what she was taught in the academy and Rudolfo's ideas, on their face, seemed wrong, but they intrigued her.

A new door had opened in her mind and she wondered how many more doors Rudolfo would open for her. She also wondered how many other Members agreed with him.

"Can you show me who we'll be performing the Sacred Task on tonight?" she asked, breaking the silence.

He nodded, turned the book so he could read it, and turned many pages toward the front of the book. Then, he returned it to her and pointed to the page on her right.

She read the list of incidents, offenses, and observations for inmate 0505. What she saw was an inmate who had lived at the prison for twenty-eight years and had committed a series of only minor violent offenses until the second to last line.

Murdered inmate 7423 in shower room. Inmate 0505 has been selected for the Sacred Task.

"I don't understand. He didn't seem to be murderous until very recently."

"Until this morning." Rudolfo scratched his chin. "This man is in his late seventies. He has never been well-behaved enough to be granted release, yet never violent enough for the Task. It is my belief that he has grown tired of life here and killed that poor man in the shower to seal his own fate. Maybe he couldn't do the deed himself, so he chose suicide by Tapper, knowing the outcome for murder is a guarantee."

Rudolfo's use of the slang term for Members of the Order caught her off guard. It was taboo to use the word Tapper among Members, especially when referring directly to the Sacred Task.

"I see," she said.

He nodded. "Yes, I think you do. The inmates will be back from work parties soon. It will be a good opportunity for you to observe them as they return."

* * *

Hours passed while she observed the inmate population from various points in the ward. Her black cassock had the same effect as before.

In the mess hall, at evening meal time, she stood against a bulkhead watching the inmates queue up. Rows of tables sat in front of her, the food line on the other side of them. Hundreds of men passed, not one looking in her direction. She wondered if being a part and apart was made easier when the inmates refused to look at her. How many knew she was here at all? Had they grown so accustomed to blocking them out that it happened naturally?

Individuals who came near her diverted course as if an invisible bubble deflected them. Rudolfo, on the opposite wall, had the same effect. The overall mood seemed low. She'd expected chatter and laughing, lighthearted banter or vicious bullying. What she witnessed now could be described as robotic; men going through the motions of acquiring sustenance.

In the passageways and corridors, she experienced the same avoidance of gazes and physical space.

The afternoon and evening passed without incident. How was she supposed to observe inmate behavior if it was altered with their presence? She posed this question to Rudolfo as they walked one of the corridors.

"Most valuable observation is done via the camera feeds or eyewitness accounts from the guards." He spread his arms wide. "Our physical presence here is more of a reminder. Although, I've witnessed plenty first-hand."

The lights around them dimmed, leaving a dusk-like

glow throughout the ward. They made their way back to passageway four and stopped outside her quarters.

"Wait here a moment," he said.

When he returned, he handed her a thick book, identical to his own but not as worn.

"This is for you. Begin logging your observations and thoughts in here." He clasped his hands behind his back and inclined his head. "You will get another one when you graduate to full Member. For now, use this as a journal of our lessons in addition to inmate assessments."

She rubbed the smooth leather on the front cover and turned the book over in her hands. Opening it, she saw that it contained the same capacitive film pages as Rudolfo's.

He gestured to her door. "Go. I will fetch you in a few hours for tonight's Task."

* * *

Francesca recorded the events of the day but could not bring herself to be more creative than scrawl a simple hour by hour description. Her thoughts were a bundle of twine, its beginning indistinguishable from its end.

In the academy, she'd attempted to absorb all they taught her. Philosophy, history, sociology, anthropology, chemistry, mathematics, legal studies. Her grasp of these subjects was why she was beginning her Apprenticeship now and not someone else; she had shown great promise. There was no age limit for a Pupil to end her or his studies and move on to be an Apprentice. One started an Apprenticeship when one was ready.

She'd especially excelled in legal studies and philosophy,

proving to her instructors that she was capable of the complex comprehensive thought required to judge someone and sentence them to death.

Now, her Mentor forced her to question the very threads in the fabric of the Order. Those threads were tethered to the very crime that put an individual in prison. But he was asking her to judge a person for who they are and not who they were, to be agnostic of past deeds. She refused to believe the simplicity of it but also could not help but see the wisdom in it.

Was the Coppice's purpose to punish in order to prevent future actions by the guilty or was it a device meant to separate civil society from those who'd disrupt it? Punish the deed, quarantine the person, or remove the unwanted? All three perhaps.

The hours passed and she scribbled away in her new ledger, describing all she had seen, heard, and learned that day. She attempted to add as much substance to as she could manage with what she felt was little success.

A knock at the door shook her. Slamming the cover shut on the thick book, she sprung to her feet and opened the door.

Looking more impassive than she thought possible, Rudolfo stood several feet from her door, his hands behind his back.

Without a word, he turned to his right and walked toward the central corridor. She followed him down the corridor and past passageway three. They turned into passageway two and down it to its center. The lights were dim, the tube lighting array at only one-third its usual brightness. In the empty passageway, Francesca could hear chatter from the cells up and down the passageway. No one, it seemed, was asleep. Nor did it sound like they were close to being so.

Rudolfo stopped in front of an empty space on the wall between cell doors. Francesca stood watching him with bated breath, wondering how he would perform the Task with so many lively inmates inside.

She knew how the Task was performed, how the poison was administered, the way it interacted with the nervous system extinguishing all life functions almost instantly. But the details of ensuring a sleeping recipient was something she had always been told she would learn from her Mentor.

She watched Rudolfo wave the back of his left hand in front of a plain brick in the wall. For a moment, she wondered if the poison he had administered so many times had found its way to his brain.

Rudolfo moved his hand up and down, then stepped back staring at the brick. Nothing happened for several seconds, then a soft *clunk* came from somewhere inside the wall. The brick disappeared into the wall, sucked back behind its neighbors.

Sensing from Rudolfo it was okay to do so, she stepped forward to see what was inside the small cavity.

A keypad and a round dial rested on an inclined shelf. Rudolfo reached in and typed a long series of numbers into the keypad. While he did so, a red light flashed above his hand then turned green and went out.

"There are necessarily a series of security barriers to this," he said as he typed with his left hand, the same he'd used to open the brick. "A twelve-digit code and two scans of my implant. The first scan opens the control box, but only scans my implant to be sure I am me and that I am alive. The second scan is performed while I type the code."

He finished typing the code and removed his hand, pointing at the cavity. "This reads my implant, but also my biologic data to ensure that I am not under duress. If my pulse, respirations, temperature, or any other bodily functions indicate that I am under great stress or otherwise fearful it would terminate my access."

"What are you about to do?"

Without answering her, he reached inside the control box once more. He gripped the black dial between his forefinger and thumb, spinning it counterclockwise a full turn until it stopped. At once, the banter and light conversations in the cells began dying down. After a few seconds, the noise ceased altogether.

Just before all went quiet, a voice cried out, "Good luck, boys!" She heard a soft thud in the cell nearest her.

She looked to Rudolfo, expecting an explanation that never came.

"This way." He walked further down the passageway, stopping outside the second to last door. Francesca joined him at his side. Staying silent, he stepped forward and passed his left hand once more over a sensor, this time on a small metal box just outside the cell door. A green light flashed and a soft *clunk* told her the door was now unlocked.

Rudolfo reached forward and pulled the door open. They entered the quiet cell.

Eight men lay slumped in their beds, unconscious. Two more men lay in a heap on the floor, caught unawares in an apparent lovers' embrace. The state of their clothes told her of their amorous intent interrupted by tonight's business.

"The gas works quickly and has a residual effect of at least one hour for the average sized man, one hour twenty minutes for a woman."

It seemed so ingenious now that she saw the process in action. Of course, a Member would not just waltz into a cell filled with awake and dangerous inmates to perform the Task on one of them. Putting them to sleep with gas was simple but effective.

"The entire passageway is unconscious then?" she asked.

"Yes. Easier and less disruptive this way."

She watched as his eyes searched the tiny cell until they landed on a man on the bottom bunk to their right. He was rolled on his side facing the wall. With the limited space between beds, he was wedged between his and the one above.

Rudolfo went to one knee and reached in to roll the man onto his back. He then pulled a small rectangle device from the pocket of his cassock. Pushing a button on the device, he pointed it at the man's head where a long red laser flashed on the man's bald scalp. He ran the red laser over the bar code tattooed there and looked back to the device. Satisfied, Rudolfo replaced the device in his pocket.

"I've known this man for years, but we must verify for certain each time." Rudolfo reached under the man's shoulders and began rolling him onto his stomach. "The device will read his bar code, but more importantly it scans his cerebral signature and matches it with the one I uploaded to it this evening."

Stunned once more at the technology used by the veteran Member, Francesca made a mental note to ask about the device and how it worked. Her education at the academy taught her nothing of such a thing.

Rudolfo finished rolling the man gently to his stomach and

gingerly placed his forehead on the pillow so his neck arched upward.

Rudolfo stood and pulled a vial from his pocket. The glass tube had a wide blue band around its middle and a metal cap on top.

"You know what this is?" He held the vial out in front of her. The amber liquid inside reflected and bent the light in the room creating a rainbow sheen on its surface. She peered at it.

"That is the Oil."

"And you know why we use it?"

"It protects your flesh from the Solution. But not completely."

"Correct on both counts." He held the vial by its rounded bottom. "This container is programmed to only open for me. As is its twin holding the Solution."

He held out his left hand. "I've forgotten to remove my glove. Please ..." She gripped the glove by the tips of the fingers and pulled as he extracted his hand.

Rudolfo wrapped his bare hand around the small glass tube and after a brief pause the metal lid slid open.

Without looking at her, he held out his right still gloved hand to her, palm up. She stared at it, uncertain.

"Remove it please."

She reached both of her hands to his hand and pinched the tips of the forefinger and pinky, pulling while he removed his hand. She fully expected what she saw next, but it sickened her, nonetheless.

The blackened flesh of his hand looked as if it had been charred by magical fire that didn't burn but discolored. Hints of purple in the black and the dim light shimmering from his fingernails were the only things distinguishing the hand from the black leather gloves she now held.

He seemed not to notice her reaction to the sight of his hand.

"Why don't we use gloves to perform the Sacred Task?" he asked.

The question caught her off guard as her mind still tried to process the stained flesh of Rudolfo's right hand and arm.

"Um," she hesitated. The answer was on the tip of her tongue; it had been drilled into her since she was a child and first discovered what it was she would become. "We take life." Three words was all she could get out.

"Yes. And?"

"In order to take a life, we must give a bit of ourselves each time. Eventually, our life is taken by the very thing we devote ourselves to: our duty as Members." She took a breath, grateful the answer came when it did. She went on, "It is a great honor to be a Member. To be of such great service to society. This honor requires sacrifice. Much like a priest who pledges a life of poverty and abstention of marriage and sex for the honor of serving their god."

Rudolfo's eyebrows raised and he nodded subtly. "True enough. I, unlike most Members, however, view it differently." He motioned to the sleeping inmates. "This thing we do, this Task, is terrible. Necessary and important, but terrible, nonetheless. Each time we dip our finger into the second vial, preparing to end a life, we take a small dose of the Solution as a penance. Understand?"

"Yes." Once again, Francesca had never heard anyone speak of a Member's duties and responsibilities in such a way. As contradictory as they were to the lessons she learned at the

Pupil's School, they were just as enlightening.

"And why do we use this?" Rudolfo held up the vial of Oil.

"To slow the effect of the Solution on the Member's body."

"Yes, but why?" he asked. "If it is a Member's fate to die by the Solution, why use any protection at all?"

"Um," she hesitated. Had they covered that in their studies at the Pupil's School? She couldn't remember the topic ever coming up. And now that she thought about it, how could she have never thought to ask?

Rudolfo didn't wait for her answer. "As you said earlier, the Oil protects a Member from the Solution but not completely. We extend the Member's life by using it for two reasons. First, the practical: if a Member used the Solution with absolutely no protection, with only the bare skin of their finger, they may only be able to accomplish a handful of Sacred Tasks before they expired. So, the Oil allows them to perform almost an entire lifetime's worth of Tasks." He held the vial of Oil up to the light and turned it.

"And the other reason?" Francesca was curious to know more.

"The other reason goes back to what I was saying about penance. We must pay our penance for the Tasks we perform. As you know, the Oil allows some of the Solution to enter our system. Thereby, it allows us to live a longer life while paying our penance over time. Each time we perform the Task, we place a grain of sand on a scale. Eventually, it tips and our time in this realm is over." He turned to her. "You understand?"

"Yes." She nodded. Her response was sincere. It seemed every time Rudolfo spoke he taught her a new lesson that both challenged and reinforced what she'd learned at the

Pupil's School.

Rudolfo dipped his stained right index finger into the Oil up to the second knuckle and kept it there for several seconds then withdrew it. He held his finger above the vial allowing the excess to drip back in. Holding his oiled finger at chest height, he used his left hand to close the lid to the Oil. He replaced it in his pocket, then reached into another pocket and removed a second vial.

He held it out for her to see.

Francesca's breath was missing from her chest. She didn't recall exhaling, but all the same it wasn't there. Her eyelids refused to close. She swallowed, hoping Rudolfo hadn't noticed.

In the vial he now held floated a liquid that looked impossibly black. It seemed to absorb all the light around it creating a tiny singularity. For an instant, her instinct was to slap it from his hand and bury it deep beneath the earth. After a pause in which she found her breath, she came back to the moment and to herself. Rudolfo cocked his head in expectation.

"That," she cleared her throat, "that is the Solution."

"Correct. The Grim Reaper carries a scythe, we carry this strange, colorless concoction." He spoke in a whisper as if he were afraid to wake the men in the cell. Or was it reverence? "Many people compare us to death itself, oblivion personified. But unlike death, we do not act indiscriminately. We act methodically. We judge. We choose. And those that we choose do not come to us lightly. They earn their place here."

Unable to speak, she feebly nodded her understanding. Her eyes felt dry, her throat tightened.

Rudolfo knelt and turned toward the man lying face down.

He held the Solution in his left hand. His right forefinger glistened with its thin coating of Oil. He sat on the backs of his heels, closed his eyes, and bent his head. Only a second passed before he looked up again.

Rudolfo dipped his oiled finger into the vial holding the Solution, held it there for a moment, then removed it. The blackness engulfed the tip of his finger, which he kept pointed down. The black colorless liquid shimmered and appeared to move of its own accord while it clung to him not dripping to the floor. The Solution was darker than his stained skin, deeper and richer in color; the source of his mark more intense, more concentrated.

Francesca watched from the side, several feet away. Rudolfo extended his right arm and touched the back of the inmate's neck, at the point where the brainstem met the spinal cord.

The Solution slid off Rudolfo's finger like a liquid magnet suddenly in contact with a chunk of iron. It made a tiny pool on the man's skin and as Rudolfo pulled away, Francesca thought she saw it swirl. Then, it sparkled and shined in the scant light, vanishing as it absorbed into the inmate's skin leaving behind a tiny circle of color exactly matching the stain on Rudolfo's arm.

Inmate 0505 inhaled a shuddering, deep breath. He held it for a moment before exhaling in a quiet groan.

She'd just watched someone die for the third time in her life. This was the first she'd seen taken by another human.

The man, inmate 0505, had expired. He'd gone.

Still in the ritual, Rudolfo pulled a white rag from a pocket and wiped his killing finger several times. He set the rag down and touched it with a small silver device. It burst into flames, flaring green for an instant before smoldering into ash and black smoke. She turned her head as the acrid smell reached her.

Her Mentor swept the ashes into a square of paper which he folded and placed in his pocket. He stood slowly, seeming to waver as he did so. She followed him as he stepped toward the door. Uniformed guards waited outside. She assumed they'd been alerted by Rudolfo's activating the gas.

Out in the passageway, Rudolfo stopped and leaned against the wall. He held himself up with his left hand on the wall, his right clutched his chest.

He took several deep breaths. His reaction to the event surprised her. She had no idea how many times he had performed the Sacred Task but assumed by now he would not be so emotionally affected by it.

Soon, she realized her mistake. Watching her Mentor's shaken breathing, the shudder in his limbs, and the glassy state of his eyes, she understood that this was not an emotional reaction. It was physical.

At the Pupil's School, they taught her about the after effects of the Solution on Members. Apprentices referred to it as the Taint.

The Solution would attack the body of the Member for several hours, sometimes days, after performing the Task. The Taint would do its worst, though the Member would recover every time. Except for one. The Solution would build up in the body so that each time the Task was performed, the Taint worsened. Until it killed.

The Oil kept the Taint at bay, kept it from invading the body at full force, but it did not stop it entirely.

Rudolfo's hand slipped on the wall and Francesca lunged

to catch him. She strained under his weight.

"It is acting much faster this evening," Rudolfo whispered between breaths. "You must get me to my quarters."

"Is it the Taint?" Inwardly, she chastised herself for asking the question. She knew full well what was happening. Rudolfo squinted his disapproval at her question.

"This is my penance. The more lives I take, the greater the penance must be—the greater the mark grows, the more intense and prolonged the aftermath becomes." He shook violently for a heartbeat, then said, "Get me to my quarters. Now!"

12

Aftermath

Supporting his weight as best she could, Francesca ushered Rudolfo toward his quarters in passageway four. They walked in tandem, his arm slung across her shoulders, her arm wrapped around his back. She looked up at him as they turned the corner to enter the last passageway. Even in the half-darkness, she could see the color drained from his face. His weight pressed down on her more with every step.

Rudolfo's right hand, now gloved again, clutched at the collar of his cassock. His steps were slowing and she could feel the heat radiating off him. His weight grew heavier.

They arrived at the door to his room where Francesca reached for the latch. Rudolfo grunted something inaudible. She stopped and he swung his left arm off her shoulders, waving his hand in front of a spot just above the latch. A *clink* sounded and she flung the door open still holding onto her Mentor.

They shuffled across the threshold, then he stopped.

With his eyes closed, he said, "Tomorrow, I must rest. You will watch the ward from the observation room. Record your thoughts." He took a deep breath and shivered before finishing. "You are not to go into the ward without me. Observe and write in … your journal." He slumped in her arms, nearly bringing them both to their knees.

She scanned the darkened room for a bed, finding it in the farthest corner. With one last exertion, she managed the last few steps and flung his shaking, sweating body onto the bed. He lay across it, heels grazing the floor.

He mumbled incoherently, in a whisper at first, then louder as he stared at something on the ceiling. In a flash, he lifted his head and locked his eyes on her standing at the bedside.

"Go now. This will pass." His eyes closed. "Go."

His head fell back again onto the thin, hard mattress. Sweat beaded on his face, running down into his hair in thick rivulets. He began mumbling again, thrashing his head from side to side. The mumbling grew louder.

"Get him …" he said. "Get him out. Someone …" His voice faded as his entire body contracted, his knees crashing into his chest and arms. He writhed from side to side, rolling and twisting in pain.

Francesca stood transfixed in horror. She couldn't imagine what it must be like to be in his head. She had heard the Taint could be brutal, but this seemed like a living nightmare.

After what felt like several minutes, his body relaxed once more and he lay still. After a pause, when she thought the worst was past, he began pulling at the collar of his cassock with one then both hands, tugging on it with weakened hands.

"Burning … I'm burning alive," he whispered, his eyes clamped shut. "So hot. So hot. Am I going to die?" His voice came out like a pleading child. "Someone … get him out … please. Pull!" His demands came out as whimpers, at the same time far away and right there on the bed.

A part of her wanted to run, to leave her Mentor here in this state like he had asked her to. But his voice sounded so helpless, like a small boy.

She leaned over him, one knee on the bed, and began unbuttoning his cassock. Reaching the last button, Francesca whipped it open to reveal the loose white undershirt beneath.

He flailed, trying to be rid of the thick coat, screaming now. "So hot. Make it stop. Please help."

"I'm trying. I will help," she said. Rolling him onto his side she pulled the left arm from the cassock. Rolling him back the other way, she pulled the right arm out.

Rudolfo now lay flat on his back quite still, arms sprawled out to the sides. His breathing had grown steady. His undershirt lay unbuttoned to the middle of his chest and in all the rolling and twisting to remove his heavy cassock the sleeves on both arms had been pushed up to the shoulder.

The Solution's mark stood out harshly against his pale skin. The bulk of it rose to well above the crook of his elbow to the midpoint of his bicep. Short, thin branches of it snaked up Rudolfo's upper arm to the shoulder. The longest dark tendril twisted its way into his armpit.

Francesca didn't know how long she stood there staring, only that she knew it had been far too long. Her fate was there on his arm, etched into his skin like a diseased roadmap showing her inevitable destination. The path would pave itself differently for her, of that she was certain, but it would be paved nonetheless.

Her time for this kind of suffering would come. When it did, she would have earned it, deserved it. Each life taken by her would be a debt borrowed against her own healthy body and it would come to collect from her in the end. Like it did for every Member.

Satisfied that her Mentor was finally settled and as comfortable as she could make him, she left for her room, for her journal.

* * *

After a sleepless night, Francesca rose early the next day. The events of the evening before kept her busy writing in her journal well into the early morning hours and as she lay in bed afterward, staring at the ceiling, the night replayed itself relentlessly in her mind.

Her thoughts often wandered to the well-being of her Mentor. She assumed he would heal quickly and that he had many more Tasks in him before the Taint finally laid claim to his body.

Perhaps, she thought, last night's effect from the Taint was worse than usual. Perhaps some other variable exacerbated the impact.

Wiping sleep from her eyes, she wondered when her Mentor would allow her to take Zentransa. Full Members were allowed and encouraged to take the sleep eliminating pill, but it was the Mentor's choice whether to allow an Apprentice to do the same. She knew that some full Members abstained, but it was extremely rare. Most used the pill for the extra time it gave them to write in their journals or study. Francesca had never taken the pill and questioned if she would find the loss of sleep to be a positive addition to her life. She enjoyed the cleansing effect of sleep. She enjoyed the feel of a warm bed and a soft pillow. Maybe after her apprenticeship, she would be one of the few Members that abstained from the Z pill.

Standing, she stretched for several minutes. Her Mentor's last order had been for her to spend her day making observations. Tempted to check on Rudolfo though she was, she resisted the urge to go see him. Instead she showered, donned clean clothes, and ate some food from her duffel bag—an apple and some bread with nuts and dried fruit baked into it. With her journal tucked under her arm she left and made her way to the observation room.

It didn't take long for her to figure out how to toggle between cameras on each of the five monitors. She played with the viewpoints until settling on two that covered common areas and two that bounced from cell to cell.

It was early in the morning, 6:30 am, and most of the prisoners were not awake yet. Some, however, began milling about outside their cells the minute the automatic locking doors sprung open at 6:00 am. Guards stood by in every corner and she felt there must be many more watching from cameras like her.

Breakfast in the mess hall started at 7:00 am and the prisoners had until 8:00 am to finish eating. Then they would be herded into the massive freight elevators to be ferried down to their working parties. In the early evening, 6:00 pm, all work would stop and they would be returned to the ward to eat dinner and have some free time, with lights out at 10:00 pm.

They would repeat this routine six days a week with every Sunday reserved for rest, relaxation, and religion.

She sat and observed the ward in the hours before the

inmates left for their working parties, carefully watching every interaction for anything worth noting. There was nothing.

She toggled cameras non-stop, zooming in and listening to scene after scene, but nothing stood out. At breakfast, with most of the ward in the mess hall at one time and with her and Rudolfo physically absent, she expected to see or hear something substantial. Other than curse words shouted in jest here and there, the entire morning passed without incident.

At 8:00 am sharp, she watched the prisoners line up in several columns just outside the freight elevators. This was a well-practiced routine, each inmate knowing where to be. Some were cajoled and prodded into place, but most were compliant. Soon, neat lines of white-clad men were packed into human rectangles of a hundred inmates, ready for work.

The working parties were their only break from the monotony of the Coppice; most looked forward to it, especially the ones who got to work outside. It took four trips for their entire ward to be transported to various floors of the prison or down to the train platform. Each team of inmates was escorted to their duty stations by a guard.

Using a surveillance map Rudolfo had shown her earlier, she was able to find which cameras showed the part of the prison she wanted to view. This included the elevators and working party locations. Outdoors was more difficult, but she could also tap into the guards' bodycams, giving her a somewhat comprehensive if shaky vista of the prisoner's activities.

She could use the cameras stationed on the prison's perimeter and those mounted on transport vehicles. Using the inmates' bar code tattoos, she was able to program the video feeds to highlight those from her ward with a yellow halo.

Working parties were integrated with prisoners from different wards. Larger ones, like the tree harvesting crews, were made up of men and women from nearly every ward.

She watched for hours and was relieved to find that the intermixing with the other wards incited several incidents and exchanges worth noting. She had no desire to see these men and women do bad things, but she wanted to test her own skills of observation in real time.

Before lunch, inmates from her ward were involved in a fight that broke out in a scullery, two were caught in a sexual exchange in a maintenance shed, and one was discovered with a shiv hidden in his clothing. All were punished on the spot by the guards and/or isolated for the day.

She noted everything including the other inmates' reactions to the violators, which could be just as important.

Shortly before midday, Francesca watched the tree harvesting crew from one of the vehicle-mounted cameras. She noticed a prisoner, tall and thin, haloed in yellow, talking to a small group. He leaned on a long shovel stuck into the ground and appeared to be in light conversation, but the other inmates looked at him with stares that looked too intense for casual chatting.

The group hung on every word and it was clear to her that whatever the skinny man was saying held great weight with them. He spoke to them for several minutes and despite her efforts, she could not get the vehicle's camera or any nearby to zoom in close enough to hear what he was saying.

As she watched, the speaking man gave a sideways glance to an approaching guard and the group broke up. As they dispersed, the man with the shovel, whose words so interested the rest of the group, walked toward her camera. A minute later, he passed in front of it.

She recognized him at once as the man from the day before, the only one who would look directly at her and Rudolfo, the only one who dared make eye contact with them.

Taking notes on what she saw, she decided she would highlight this when she spoke with Rudolfo later that day or the next, whenever he felt up to it.

Suddenly, she felt hungry and, thinking of Rudolfo, realized he must not have had anything to eat that day since he couldn't leave his room. Springing to her feet, she rushed back to her room, gathered what food remained from her duffel bag and marched to her Mentor's room.

* * *

Nicholas Fox left the group of promising recruits and strolled past the large orange mulching truck with its six tall wheels. The guard had cut short his impromptu speech, but Fox had made his point. When the time came, those men would be willing participants, ready to contribute.

Truck's contribution to his plan had worked perfectly. He couldn't have asked for more. Truck had followed through with his dirty deed and right now his body was being vaporized in the prison crematorium. Soon, he'd be added back to the earth, as they all would be.

Truck's sacrifice gave Fox the conditions he needed to conduct his experiment. Fox had to see if it were possible to remain conscious during a Tapping. He now knew that he could, even as gas filled the cell.

Inmates had dabbled in the trickery for years—using all manner of homemade breathing devices from long tubes connected to canisters and bags of air—with varying degrees of success.

The gas released during a Tapping permeated every crack, crevice, and fold; it penetrated every fabric, which made it more complicated than simply hiding under a blanket or breathing from a tube connected to a plastic bag.

Fox had long guessed that the cells were pressurized and during the gas's release the pressure was manipulated to ensure it traveled into every available space. He also guessed their blankets and clothes were made from overly porous material to allow the gas to pass through them with ease.

Fox himself had tried it once or twice, but the trick to it was to be prepared. One had to know exactly when to use the alternative breather before the gas started and knowing when a Tapping was going to occur was akin to playing the lottery. Sometimes one week bore witness to several Tappings, while at other times months might pass between them.

Even a very small amount of the gas would, in short order, put a full-grown man on his back. And then there was always the question of why do it in the first place. Many inmates openly enjoyed the gas and the dreamless sleep it provided. Sleeping well in prison was exceedingly difficult. Plus, there was the added benefit of not knowing if it was you who was not going to wake up; passing ignorantly into the void was preferred to seeing it coming.

Therefore, the breather was easy to procure. Fox went for his normal work detail on the tree harvesting crew and approached his usual supplier of strange goods. Later in the day, they both feigned injury and were returned to their cells.

Fox only had to wait patiently in his cell for his supplier to turn up with the breather, which he did just after lunch.

It wasn't complicated—a rubber mouthpiece with a thin hose running from it to a cylinder about as long as Fox's forearm—but guaranteed by its maker to work. He claimed to have used it himself a number of times. Fox still marveled at how easy it was to get his hands on an item like this. All the technology inside the Keep and they still couldn't prevent people from being devious and clever.

He began breathing from it the moment the lights went out the night following Truck's murder. The breather's maker told him he had several hours of breathable air, but he had to be careful to keep his nose closed.

That night, in his bunk, he laid on his side to conceal the device under his blanket and began breathing through the mouthpiece while holding his nose closed.

As the noise in the passageway died away, he made doubly sure his lips made a tight seal around the mouthpiece and squeezed his nose ever tighter. From one cell over, an inmate yelled, "Good luck, boys!" then all fell quiet—the only sign that the colorless, odorless gas had been released.

A thud on the floor told him someone's ill-timed ascent to their bunk went awry. Deep breathing above and below him signaled the sleep had come for everyone else in his cell.

Fox continued breathing through the tube for what felt like an hour. The stomp of the guards' boots outside the cell told him it was close to being over. More sounds in the passageway were, he assumed, the guards removing the body of his willing sacrifice Truck.

A short while later, life returned to his cell. Inmates stirred while others slept on.

Fox, on the other hand, had made it through the entire Tapping wide awake.

Now, he would need one more volunteer in order to get his plan moving.

* * *

At Rudolfo's door Francesca knocked. A brief pause, a beep, and she heard the door lock click. Taking this as a sign of welcome, she pushed the door open and entered.

Laying on his bed, Rudolfo lay reclined on a few sad looking pillows. A worn paperback book lay on his lap. He looked up at Francesca as she entered. His eyes were soft and welcoming for a moment, then hardened as they settled on her.

"I thought you were someone else." He rolled his head and continued reading. His chest rattled with labored breathing, his skin still appeared pale and gray.

Uneaten food lay on his bedside table and his cassock lay neatly folded over a nearby chair. He wore a long sleeve undershirt, buttoned and clean; overall, he looked quite tidy as did his room. It was the same size as hers with not much more in the way of possessions. His bookshelf had more books than hers, which held exactly zero at the moment.

He did not wear gloves, but his hand was the only stained part of him exposed, the rest hiding under his long shirt sleeve.

"I brought some food for you," she said, holding up the small parcel.

"As you can see, I already have food." Not looking up from his book, he waved a shaky hand toward his nightstand.

"Yes, I see. Is there anything I can do for you?"

"You can follow my instructions," he said, now glaring at her. "I believe I told you to observe the ward from the observation room today. Last night was a blur for the most part, but I do remember that."

She straightened and lifted her chin. She knew he must be in a great deal of pain in addition to being tired and weak. His tone stung, but she wouldn't let him know that.

"Yes. Quite right. I will return to my station." She turned to leave when his words cut off her escape.

"Or have you come here hoping to get a glimpse of what is underneath my clothing—to have another look at my mark?" The words hit her like poison gas.

Francesca had been morbidly curious about Rudolfo's mark even before last night. She still was, but the accusation was clear.

"I told you to leave me. I told you to let me be." He pointed the paperback at the chair holding his cassock. "And yet, I wake to find myself disrobed, which I could not have done myself."

"You were suffering," she said, staring at the wall above his head. She would not push back but she would not be a weakling either. "You said you were hot, so I …"

"I was hallucinating! Do you have any idea what years of doling out the Task will do to you?" Splotches of red appeared on his neck and cheeks. "The toll that hundreds of them will have on the mind?"

"Yes, but …"

"Then you should have known better!" He tried to raise himself but could only manage to lean on one elbow, pointing at her with the book in the other hand. "Or, did you do it just to see? Just to ogle at my arm?"

"No, of course not."

"A Member's path is their own to take." He coughed and wheezed, forcing him to roll further onto his side. Francesca lunged to him, afraid he would roll off his bed but he threw out a hand stopping her. "This burden is mine." He was staring over the edge of the bed at the floor, his breathing harsher now than before. His voice came out in a graveled whisper. "This is my path to take. I will not be a spectacle for your sick curiosity."

Rudolfo took several deep ragged breaths and with some effort flopped onto his back. His eyes on the ceiling once more, the two of them stared in silence for a moment.

"Twice you've disobeyed me." He spoke without looking at her. "Do not let there be a third time."

"Of course. Next time ..."

"Next time?" he interrupted. A deep breath gargled in his chest, then he finished his thought. "If there is a next time, I'll Tap you myself."

The words were a blow, more bruising by far than the vitriol with which they were delivered. Using the slang term for their essential function reduced her to something lowly, something unworthy. It was as if he were suggesting they perform the Sacred Task on a slug.

She stood stock still, but her mind sank. She barely registered a sound at the door—someone knocking. She turned as a young man, not much older than her, walked in. He had a well-defined face, his hair close cropped. He wore a guard's uniform—light blue shirt and dark gray trousers.

The guard's eyes grew wide, as if not expecting to see her in the room with Rudolfo. She looked to the guard's side where he held a large book under his arm. The book looked strikingly similar to her Mentor's. The guard held a Member's logbook, she had no doubt.

The new visitor didn't say anything but looked at Rudolfo who continued lying on his back.

The Member raised a hand and made a shooing motion. "Return to your duties. You are done here."

There was no mistaking whom he directed this toward.

13

Partners

June 7, 2043

"To Ryan Grant." Deputy Inspector Liz Reynolds held her half-empty mug of amber colored beer high over the table in a back corner of Winky's Bar. A dozen hands gripping identical mugs, brown bottles, and cocktail glasses swung in to meet hers in a din of *clinks.* Murmurs of support, "Cheers," and, "To Ryan," followed.

Aubrey lowered his glass and took a long, deep pull from the warm swill inside. She pushed through the crowd to stand next to him and they exchanged a somber nod. He resisted the urge to ask how she was doing. The glaze in her eye told Aubrey all he needed to know.

He set his mug down next to ten other empties on the table. All around him were cops in and out of uniform there to honor their fallen brother. Aubrey was the only civilian among them, but since he had once carried a badge coupled with his work on the OFP and BSS cases from weeks prior, they all treated him as if he were one of their own.

"Have you spoken to his family?" Aubrey asked. Despite

being four beers into what looked to become a long night, Liz still wore her blazer and her shirt was neatly tucked into her slacks.

She downed the last of her beer and wiped the moisture from her lips as she stared down into the empty glass. "He only had a sister left. His parents were pretty old when he was born and they both passed a few years back." Liz shook her head. "She took the news as you'd expect. I told her we'd be here for her. You know, all the usual stuff, because I had no fucking idea what to say."

Aubrey regarded the others in the room. Drawn faces, untucked shirts and loose ties, some laughing heartily at unheard jokes. Each man and woman dealing with the loss in their own way based on their own built-in coping mechanisms.

Aubrey never knew how to act or what to think when he lost a friend. It took time for him to cope properly and allow himself to come to terms with the person's absence in his life. He'd remember Ryan Grant as a brave, funny, and intelligent person and a fine detective. He assumed the others would as well.

Aaron Lewis approached the two of them with three bottles in his hands. Sweat gleamed off the brown glass.

"It looked like you two could use a fresh one," he said.

"Was it really just a random break-in?" Aubrey asked the two of them.

The details of the case were strange— death by a single stab wound. No toxins had been found in Grant's system and other than a few bumps and bruises, the stab wound was the only injury. Aubrey's natural paranoia led him to theorize on all the possibilities, all the connections.

Lewis scoffed. "Doubt it. We all have enemies out there. You know that as well as I do."

Aubrey sipped from the bottle; not his brand, but it would do. "Who has the case?"

"Yentley, Homicide. She's damn good. She'll figure it out." Lewis cleared his throat. "How about you? How's your thing going?"

At this, Liz raised an eyebrow.

Aubrey had to be careful with his words amongst all the other cops.

"Our mutual friend and I are working on it. I should hear something from her very soon."

* * *

Four weeks had passed since Martin Aubrey had left Malina Maddox's storage-unit-turned-domicile. She promised to get started on her part of the investigation right away and would call him if she found anything worth talking about.

He'd reached out to her several times to check on her progress only to be greeted the same way each time.

"Leave me alone," she'd tell him. "I'll contact you when I have something."

Aubrey felt confident she was working in earnest. She was like him; bad guys were going around doing bad things and she just couldn't stand it.

Their first meeting had not gone quite like he'd planned. After she had calmed down and realized he was not there to harm her, they talked for a while. He explained everything—the mercenaries, the lack of substantial connection between them and OFP, BSS, or the pill plus the timing of the attacks and the mysterious caller on the lead mercenary's phone.

She admitted the connections were compelling and could possibly lead to something. She wasn't keen on getting involved in another case that could lead to threats on her life. The tipping point for her decision came when she asked him a follow up question.

"Why don't you just go talk to the scientists? Or their cellmates or something." She sat in the aged black chair at her computer desk.

"Good question. I actually did," he said.

"And?"

"And they didn't tell me anything and within a day, they were dead."

He'd paused to let the words sink in. If his assumptions were correct, she'd loathe murderers and corruption equally. Combining the two were intolerable.

"I'm pretty sure they were killed because I went out there. Because I was getting close to some answers." Aubrey recalled watching Malina from her couch, waiting for any sign of that do-gooder gene rearing its head. It only took a few seconds to see it; her eyebrows pinched together and her lips tightened.

"How were they killed?" she asked, her eyes staring into space.

"Executed, Tapped, selected. Whatever you want to call it. A Tapper or multiple Tappers killed them."

"Hmmm," she groaned and spun in her chair, round and around for a moment, apparently lost in thought.

He'd guessed it wasn't the fact that they were dead that bothered her so much, they were key suspects behind a great deal of violence after all. More so the idea that someone had them killed. The fact that there was a "someone" was the clincher. That "someone" was capable of great evil and, as Aubrey suggested, capable of much more. Murder plus corruption.

She looked at her computer as if she were wondering if it was worth calling it into service. She could have been a gunslinger sizing up her old steed. Could it take another ride?

"But you got the bombers." She'd rubbed the desk with one hand while she spoke, her legs curled up under her.

"Yes, we did. We got the guys actually making and deploying the bombs, but not the person telling them what to do. And it won't be the last of the violence. And I can all but guarantee kids are going to keep getting sick." He stood on instinct. His passion for the case boiled. "Despite what the police say, we found zero evidence that the bombers had anything to do with BSS."

"And where would you suggest I start?"

"Where do you usually start?"

"Usually there is a crime or some nefarious activity. An event or a victim." She spun toward him and stood also. "I start there and work my way back to the perpetrator."

"Start with the scientists stealing from Ventana." Aubrey began pacing as he spoke. Game-planning required pacing. "Any messages that went between them that references Ventana, Sarazin, money, anything. They all had cloud drives and the normal digital footprint. Anything that links the four of them, where the four of them interact as a group. I'd start there."

As he left her home that day, she had already started

typing and clicking away on her computer. She'd become so engrossed she hardly noticed when he left.

Later that day, he sent her a link to a shared cloud drive containing everything he had managed to take with him from his recent, and brief, stint with the police. She agreed to dig into whatever rabbit holes she could find on the four Ventana scientists. He wanted to know everything he could about them. Were there any details the police may have missed regarding their embezzlement from Ventana? Did the scientists leave any communication trails online alluding to their plans to act out against Sarazin or Ventana? What links, if any, were there between them and One Front for the People and, as a correlation, the bombings and BSS?

Since he'd last seen her, Aubrey had resumed working his actual job. His boss at OWG Insurance had sent him several fraud cases. They were all straightforward and unexciting for Aubrey, whose mind was occupied with the job no one had asked him to do.

While Malina was busy dissecting the scientists' lives they'd left behind online, Aubrey hit the streets to interview as many former colleagues of Alkorn and his team as he could. He avoided anyone still working at Ventana, Inc. Unsanctioned by the authorities, he preferred to keep attention away from his work as long as he could.

Eliminating Alkorn's Ventana associates limited the number of people that could have solid intel. Of those people, the number was cut even further by those that were willing to talk to him. As Alkorn was a well-known miserable curmudgeon, albeit a brilliant one, the people willing to talk with Aubrey did so only to further tarnish the scientist's memory.

Aubrey spoke to a dozen people who had known Alkorn. No one had anything useful to say. They all agreed on one thing however—Alkorn was a bastard but not capable of killing. That was to be determined, Aubrey thought.

Poring over the case files from the Ventana theft again and again turned up nothing as well. As days passed, Aubrey kept hoping that the next interview might uncover some kernel of evidence. It never did.

He hoped Malina was having better luck.

He watched the news obsessively waiting for the next BSS case or another bombing. Nothing happened. That didn't surprise him. If he were the puppet master behind all the violence, he would lay low too. He'd wait until everyone felt safe again, then strike.

Or the villain made his point already. Maybe the danger was over. Doubtful, he thought. The bombs, BSS, the scientists, it was all related. All connected. If there was another attack, he'd at least have new clues to analyze.

While scanning the news channels from his sofa, his phone buzzed. He looked at it; it was Malina calling.

When he answered, he could hear typing and loud rock music in the background. "I found something," she said, close to shouting. "Come by as soon as you can." She hung up.

* * *

An hour later, Malina surprised Aubrey by waiting for him on the sidewalk outside the storage facility.

"I thought I'd save you the trouble of breaking in again."

She wore a dark green sweatshirt with the hood drawn halfway over her head. In the bright afternoon light, her pale, pallid face bore the marks of many days and nights in front of a computer monitor—sunken cheeks, bloodshot eyes, skin tinted gray. She squinted against the sunlight, looking down.

"Plus, I needed to see the sun at least once this week." With closed eyes she angled her face at the sun and pulled back her hood. Five seconds passed. "Okay, that's enough. Let's go."

Inside her unit, Aubrey seated himself on the couch while Malina sat on the swivel chair in front of the large stack of books. They'd been neatly piled in the pyramid shape once more.

She settled into her chair and took a deep audible breath. Rock music played low from an invisible speaker. Overall, her disposition toward him was in stark contrast to their first encounter. She seemed excited about the work, downright cheerful. Aubrey knew it was the do-gooder in her, pumping her full of a serotonin.

"So, against my better judgment, I took your advice," Malina said. "I searched for anything online that the four scientists—Leo Alkorn, Rajesh Imanpor, Natalie Shoeman, and Stanley Winthorpe—were mixed-up in together."

Aubrey nodded.

"Naturally, several things came up—research projects, science and medical journal articles, speaking engagements, et cetera, et cetera. You get the idea."

He nodded again. "No surprises there."

"Right. I looked everywhere for communications between them—social media, email, even darkweb forums. I couldn't find anything." She held up a finger. "I should clarify. I couldn't find anything useful."

"Aren't some of those places, like the darkweb forums,

anonymous? How would you know they were there?"

Malina looked at him like he'd just asked her the color of the sky.

"There are ways." She gestured to her monitors and laptop. "If they were there, especially the four of them all visiting the same site, I would have found them. These aren't black hat hackers we're talking about, Martin."

Aubrey nodded and held up his hands in surrender. "Okay. So, you couldn't find anything useful there. Go on."

"Anyway," she said, looking away as if collecting her thoughts, "there was nothing out there that raised any suspicions. For three weeks, I used every trick, every tool, every algo I have and came up empty." She shrugged, looking defeated. After a pregnant pause, she continued. "Then, I started poking around Ventana's intranet." A faint smile crossed her face.

"Jesus. You broke into Ventana's system?"

"Yes. Please don't interrupt, I'm getting to the good part."

She spun in her chair, pulled a tablet off her workstation, and held it out for Aubrey to see. The screen showed a game board with lettered tiles arranged to form words crisscrossing the board. At the bottom of the screen was a bank of unused letters. Aubrey felt like he was missing something. Malina didn't notice or didn't care for his confusion.

She continued. "I used all my tricks on Ventana's servers only to come up with the same results as before—bupkis. There was plenty there—emails, internal memos, announcements, departmental meetings—but nothing out of the ordinary. Nothing criminal anyway."

"What am I looking at here?" Aubrey asked, gesturing to

the game.

She pointed an emphatic finger at the tablet. "That is what I found." She paused. "It's a game developed for employees at Ventana. There's a bunch of them actually. They all live on the Ventana intranet." She counted on her fingers. "There's a treasure hunt, an action adventure and then your simpler ones like sudoku and our little word game here. They're meant to encourage friendly competition, employee engagement, intellectual stimulation. What some people refer to as fun."

"Fun. Right."

"That's right. It's not for everyone, especially not our scientist friends. Most Ventana employees were regular players of at least a handful of the games, but not Alkorn and the gang. See, he ran a tough ship. Their schedules were insane. The pace and volume of their work was mind-blowing. Honestly, I'm surprised they didn't rob the place blind sooner. Really, I'm surprised the crew didn't mutiny on Alkorn and string the guy up." Malina leaned back in her chair, rubbed her chin for a moment. "Anyway, our people didn't play all the games. They only played one. And they only played with each other."

"This word-game?" Aubrey looked down at the tablet again and saw the game's title in large block letters stylized to appear carved into wood blocks. "*A Word With You*? That's what they called it?"

"That's right. Alkorn and team started playing that game regularly in January of this year. And that's all they played, all four of them in a group match."

"I get the feeling you're getting to something," Aubrey said.

"Most Ventana people who play this have games that last

two, three days tops. They're very competitive and some of their scores are pretty impressive, there're some smart people working there." Malina leaned forward, elbows on her knees. "But these four, arguably some of the smartest people at that company, totally sucked at this game. They were absolute shit. Their scores were abysmal and they didn't even finish a match. They only played one, as a team, for eight days."

Aubrey didn't say anything. Instead, he sat back and waited for the bomb to drop.

"In fact," she continued, "when I looked at the backend data for the game, their playing times were really strange. Again, most people at Ventana who played this game open the app and, within a minute or two, they make a move." She became animated. She threw a hand out as if showcasing something invisible. "But these bozos would just open the game and do nothing, sometimes for hours. No moves made at all."

"So, what? They open it and forget about it. Leave their phone sitting somewhere and walk away."

"No, the phone would time out and the game would show them as idle. No, they were active in the game. They just weren't playing." She leaned far forward, on the edge of the seat and her heels tapping the floor.

"Please tell me you know what they were doing."

"Oh yeah, I do." A satisfied grin filled her face. "There was a messaging system in the game. Most people would trash talk and that sort of thing, couple of times a game. Maybe more sometimes but not by much. Our science pals weren't playing the game, not really, but they were using the message system."

Now, Aubrey leaned forward, perched on the edge of the

sofa. His heart thumped. A flutter shot across his stomach.

"What were they saying to each other, Malina?"

She smiled even wider and shook her head. "I have no idea."

* * *

Jacira Barretto squinted at the news article on her tablet as if she needed to see it more clearly. The headline for Monday, June 8 read *Metro Cop Found Dead from Knife Wound.* The headline had caught her attention, but the first paragraph piqued her interest further.

An unidentified Metropolitan Police Officer was found murdered in his uptown apartment Friday morning. The officer appears to have engaged in a struggle with his assailant, but the death has been attributed to a knife wound.

"We're not sure what happened exactly, but we can rule out excessive bleeding or trauma to the head or major organs," the medical examiner on the scene stated.

What is certain is there was no signs of a break-in leading police to speculate that the attacker was someone the victim knew.

She recognized the handiwork. Her mind ticked through the possibilities when movement caught her eye. She pushed the tablet to the edge of her desk.

One of the three large screens on her desk showed Martin Aubrey and the woman entering the building. She watched them walk down the narrow hallway on a second monitor. On the third she watched a biologics readout, which showed red and green shapes enter a blue and violet rectangle then position themselves across from each other.

Aubrey, the larger one, was on the couch, while the smaller

woman sat near the desk in the corner of the unit glowing red with heat on the readout.

After weeks of trying, Jacira had been unable to identify the woman Aubrey was working with. Fingerprints, DNA, facial recognition turned up nothing. The woman was so completely off the grid, she didn't exist. Jacira saw it as a testament to the woman's skill that she was able to accomplish that feat. It was clear why Aubrey sought her out.

Having once made herself disappear, she recognized the work of a pro.

Jacira's recording equipment and sensors were installed in the unit above the woman's. She listened closely as the two of them talked.

When the conversation ended and Aubrey left, she sent her employer an encrypted, detailed report of what she heard.

After several minutes, her tablet pinged. The encrypted message showed Mr. V's reply.

Take next steps, as discussed.

Understood, she replied. *Question for you.*

What is it?

Do you have others working for you?

Others?

Like me, she typed.

I have many people who work for me. Some are like you. I have to go. No more questions.

So, the answer was yes. He did have others like her working for him and judging by the story of the murdered cop, they were much like her.

Jacira looked back at the reply from Mr. V.

Take next steps, as discussed.

She would now get to use her other set of skills, the skills that everyone asked for in the end.

* * *

"No idea?" It took a moment for Aubrey to respond. She must be kidding, he thought. He dropped his face into his hand, questioning whether this partnership was a good idea after all.

"Nope. No idea." Malina reached out and took the tablet away from Aubrey. "At least, not yet." She tapped and swiped a few times, then handed the tablet back to Aubrey. "All their messages were sent in code."

He pulled his hand away. What he saw were several screen-captures from the match the team had played against each other.

She was right, Aubrey thought, the messages were a jumble of numbers, a code. The first he read showed no pattern or discernible system:

04080151623402

The rest of them were similar. Each screen-capture held several messages. They appeared to be conversations in a group chat. Most of the messages were from Alkorn with short replies from the others. All of them were written in the same garbled mess of numbers.

"Okay. Why no mention of this in all the case files of their arrest and conviction? Can we really be the only ones who know about this?"

"My guess is no one thought to look. And if they did, maybe they just saw it as a glitch in the game or something."

She smoothed her short hair back. The exhaustion on her

face was more apparent now under the false light. Aubrey could tell she'd put in many hours to dig up this clue.

"Could be they saw it, knew it was encrypted and couldn't break it? I don't know, but it was pretty clever. They couldn't talk at work, any of their conversations could be recorded. They wouldn't be foolish enough to send anything over text or email. So, this is kind of an elegant solution and it all happened right under the nose of company security on a Ventana owned program." She shrugged and smiled. "Have to say, I'm pretty impressed."

Aubrey scanned the encoded messages, not seeing any patterns whatsoever. "Why not send their messages via some secure application? Why use the game at all?"

Malina leaned back in her chair. "I think the simplicity of it worked in their favor. See, if they used some kind of application on their phones or on a computer, it could be found. They would have known that the moment they were caught, all of their stuff would be torn apart and dissected. If all four of them had the app on their devices, there is a greater chance of their messages being discovered."

"So, what kind of code is this? What kind of encryption is it?"

"I think it's a book cipher." Her eyes went wide with apparent excitement and she leaned forward again.

Aubrey had heard of book ciphers before, mostly from novels he read as a kid. The criminals he'd investigated used more sophisticated forms of encryption. He found it difficult to believe that highly educated scientists such as these would use something so simplistic.

Then again, he thought, the reason he knew about criminals who used high-end encryption devices was because they were eventually caught.

Malina continued. "Think about it, they're nearly impossible to crack without the key book, so even if Ventana finds the messages, which I don't think they did, they would need to know the exact book used to create the cipher and not just the book but the page the cipher starts on. And with all the technology at their disposal, who would suspect a simple book cipher?"

Aubrey saw the elegance in it, but something bothered him. "Why couldn't it be just a simple code they all decided on? A cipher they created themselves. Why are you so convinced it was a book cipher?"

"The codes are so complex and varied that if they had a homemade cipher it would have been impossible to memorize, so they would have to keep it somewhere, which can be found. Same problem they'd have with an encrypted messaging application."

"How does it work? Walk me through it."

"In keeping with the simplicity of the cipher, someone walks in one day and secretly communicates what the title of the book is and the page number, or the page number could be built into the code itself. I'm not sure about that one yet." She stood up and began pacing back and forth. "Alkorn comes into the lab and may say, 'Hey, did you guys read that section about gene-splicing in *Science World Almanac*?' That tells the others the name of the book cipher key and the page number. They find the first page that mentions gene-splicing. Thereafter the numbers in the code indicate the words on the page. The first letters of the words are used to spell messages."

Her skills were impressive. The way she thought about

the problem and went on to develop unique solutions made Aubrey wish he'd known her sooner. Still, he thought, even after uncovering this sizeable piece of the puzzle, it made no difference if it didn't lead to results.

"Okay, so how do we break the codes and figure out what they were up to? How do we use this to lead us back to the ring leader?"

She shrugged. "I'm working on it; been working on it for a while with Ted."

"Ted?" Aubrey sat up straight, stunned that she would bring in someone else without him knowing.

"Yeah, Ted. He's the codebreaker program I built after I discovered the encrypted messages."

She shot a finger at her workstation. Relieved, Aubrey relaxed. For the first time, he gave her desk more than a cursory glance.

The three monitors were large and thin. Pretty standard stuff, he thought. There was a stack of laptops and tablets off to the side, a large keyboard with a multitude of extra keys he didn't recognize, a touchpad, and a random assortment of objects he had never seen.

Malina hadn't gestured to any of those items. She'd pointed to a small blue box roughly four inches square and a half-an-inch tall sitting in the far-right corner of the desk. A quiet whirring emitted from it.

"That's Ted?" Aubrey asked.

"No, that's my computer. Ted is inside it."

"Isn't most computing done in the cloud these days? Why do you need a desktop?"

Malina looked at him the way one looks at a toddler who just asked if chocolate milk comes from brown cows.

"They call it the cloud because it's out there." She waved her hands in the air in wide arcs. "And if it's out there, anyone can get to it. This," she pointed at the box then to the ground, "is only here. No one can get to it but me. All my equipment is tethered to it. I have layers of security making it impossible to breach. I take privacy very seriously."

Aubrey refrained from reminding her that he had managed to break into her domicile with relative ease. "Got it. So, Ted is working on it. What's your approach?"

Malina explained. She loaded all the coded messages into Ted then had the program use the codes to search all the books owned by the four scientists, both collectively and individually. She made no assumptions about which book or type of book it might be so she included anything over a hundred pages on any topic, non-fiction or fiction.

"Ted runs each coded message against the text in each book by first assuming the code includes an indicator block identifying the page number. Then, Ted will run it again assuming the indicator block is not included."

Malina glanced over at the small blue box humming away on her desk.

"Finally, it analyzes the results as it goes and if any words pop up that make sense in standard English usage, it gives me a ping. It's probably going to take a while. I started the program last night and ..."

One monitor on her desk came to life. A small dialog box appeared in the lower right corner.

"I can't believe it." She rolled her chair to the desk.

Aubrey stood and walked toward her; his eyes glued to the screen.

She clicked the dialog box and a window popped up filled

with white text on a black background. On the left were the scientists' names in all caps, to the right were their messages.

He leaned in close. In dismay, he stood straight again. The messages were illegible, now encrypted with letters instead of numbers. Nothing made sense.

"What are we looking at?" He gave a half-hearted wave toward the computer.

"Ted thinks it uncovered the key, but it just turned up this gibberish. I don't get it."

He sighed. "Maybe there's something wrong with Ted."

"Ted is fine." Her hand shot up. "Just give me a minute to figure this out."

Aubrey turned back to the sofa and sat. "Listen, I think we should meet again in a couple of days. When you've …"

Malina slapped her desk. "Son of a bitch." She turned to face Aubrey with a grin stretching from ear to ear.

"What do you have?" he said.

"Ted did find something. He thought he had a cipher that worked so he used it for all of the messages." She gestured with both hands at the computer. "The problem is they must have used multiple ciphers, multiple books. He figured out one cipher and tried to apply it to the rest."

"What do you mean he found one that worked? Did Ted decode something?" Aubrey walked back to the desk and stood behind her again, a hand on the back of her chair. Malina leaned in close to the screen, squinting at the small white text.

"Yes. Ted decoded three messages. Alkorn to Shoeman. And it looks like these were the only messages sent that day." She looked back at Aubrey. "I wonder if they used a different book each day."

Aubrey eyed her for a moment. "Maybe. Blow it up, let me see." He read the deciphered words.

ALKORN L: He knows

SHOEMAN N: Jorgetson

ALKORN L: Yes now we wait

14

Index Cases

"'He knows.'"

Aubrey had repeated the three lines to himself a dozen times while he paced back and forth in Malina's unit.

"'Jorgetson. Yes. Now we wait.'" He turned toward Malina. "Anything on Jorgetson yet?"

"Yes."

Bouncing between two monitors, she scrolled through several websites with information on Jorgetson. On a third, she had several windows showing personal accounts—bank, email, cloud drives, work history.

"The Jorgetsons are very wealthy. They come from old hotel money from back in the late twentieth century and early aughts."

She went on to explain that the elder Jorgetson had held several positions at high tech pharma firms including Ventana, Incorporated where he was Chief Operations Officer under James Sarazin. Jorgetson had been COO during the launch of Zentransa. Since then, he'd bounced around from board to board until recently going into semi-retirement.

Aubrey renewed his pacing, hands in his pockets, head down. He counted his steps before each turn, careful to land each step in the same spot as the last lap.

Malina read from one website. "'*Mandel Jorgetson served an integral role in Ventana's strategy to launch and market Zentransa to the public. It was his brilliant execution of James Sarazin's vision that drove Zentransa to become a staple in the economy, synonymous with progress, and Ventana's balance sheet through the stratosphere.*' Some bio."

Aubrey scratched his chin, squinting. "Alkorn must have meant that Mandel Jorgetson knew about the money he and his team were stealing from Ventana." Aubrey stopped pacing and looked to Malina for input.

"Maybe. But why not just turn them in? Nothing I've found indicates that they were friends or anything. If Jorgetson knew, then why wouldn't he just have them arrested?" She looked back at her screens and clicked the touchpad several times to bring up the decoded message. "Says here this message was sent on January 20th of this year. When were they arrested?"

Aubrey raised his eyebrows. "Right around then." He pulled out his phone and began searching his case notes when Malina stopped him.

"Got it. They were arrested on January 24th. Four days after this message was sent." She pointed to a monitor. "Which means, assuming Alkorn sent the message the same day he knew that Jorgetson knew, it took four days to have them arrested." She spun in her chair and grimaced at Aubrey. "Why wait so long?"

"Maybe Jorgetson tried blackmailing them."

"No, I don't think so," she said. Aubrey agreed. Everything they'd learned about Mandel Jorgetson showed them he was basically a Boy Scout. "I don't think he had it in him. And he was super rich already, so he wouldn't need the money."

Aubrey shrugged, still pacing with his head bent low. The problem with big breaks in a case was the hornet's nest effect. One good lead and investigators tended to release a multitude of potential theories that buzzed around and sent everyone into a tizzy. Only after the facts settled to give a clearer picture could one draw any intelligent conclusions. A skilled investigator abstained from jumping to conclusions.

"Maybe it took him that long to gather the evidence he needed to bring it to Sarazin. He probably felt the proof had to be overwhelming, since Sarazin and Alkorn were close." Aubrey sat down and rubbed his chin. "Either way I think we need to go see Jorgetson."

Malina raised her raised her eyebrows and pointed her chin at Aubrey. "Umm, you should go see him. I'm not a field operative and even if I was, I can serve you better from here."

It took Malina two minutes to find an address. Jorgetson had been mostly off the grid for several months and owned many homes around the globe, but she narrowed down his most likely whereabouts to an estate home twenty miles north of New Aberdeen in a wealthy neighborhood. The term neighborhood was putting it loosely, Aubrey thought. It was more of a region, with each estate covering tens of acres.

Before he left, Malina gave him an untraceable burner phone that he was to use when communicating with her.

"Never know who's listening," she said.

* * *

Jacira Baretto watched Martin Aubrey pull away in a black sedan four-door car from the woman's building. With a few taps on her keyboard, she commanded a drone on a nearby roof to mark and follow the car.

On the computer's monitor, she saw the viewscreen center on the car then pull back as if she were zooming out on a satellite image. The drone reached the programmed altitude of twenty-five hundred feet. Its size, roughly that of a softball, made it impossible to spot at that height.

The laser on board the drone bathed the car in invisible light, optically tagging it. At the same time, scanners memorized every characteristic of the vehicle in case line of sight was broken.

Satisfied that the drone would do its job and not in any sort of rush, she got up from her desk. Not knowing what the day would bring, she decided to loosen up with some stretching and light exercise. Afterward, she went to the to her oversized bedroom closet and picked an appropriate outfit—something black, breathable, and form fitting. She also selected proper footwear—a pair of black trail shoes that were tough but allowed for good agility and traction.

Crossing the bedroom, she entered another closet, smaller than the first. She pushed the hanging clothes to one side and after sliding her thumb down the left edge of the rear wall of the closet, the false back slid away.

She examined the array of tools in front of her hanging from pegs and laying on shallow shelves. Thinking about the possible sequence of events over the next several hours, she decided long range was best. Just to be safe, she decided on something that could cover medium, and short ranges also.

Standing at the end of her bed, she visually inspecting her gear lying on top of the white linens. She mentally checked off the list in her head.

Confident she had everything she would need, she packed it all into a large duffel bag and left her apartment.

* * *

Aubrey reviewed his notes on the Jorgetsons as his car sped down on autopilot down the two-lane highway. He'd left the city and its suburbs behind fifteen minutes ago, entering what most would refer to as the countryside.

When the road wasn't flanked by huge oak and maple tree forests with their thick canopies stretching across the road, the view became vast estates—rolling green hills, symmetrical hedgerows—crowned by a manor home high on some distant rise. The truly wealthy lived out here, he thought. Not some nouveau riche pretenders who struck it rich with overnight success; these estates held generational wealth going back a century or more.

He'd just passed under an arboreal archway of sugar maples when the car emitted a low tone.

"Thirty seconds to destination."

"Thank you," Aubrey said. "Approach slowly after we exit the road."

The car confirmed the command and seconds later, decreased speed to take the turn off the main road. For the first hundred feet, Aubrey's car drove down a paved lane between two walls of dark green hedgerows neatly trimmed with perfectly flat edges.

Ahead the driveway turned slightly, blocking the view. All he could see on three sides was green with a bright blue sky above.

The car made the turn, the hedgerows ended and before him, two hundred feet ahead, the house loomed the way a manor style home should—like an opulent yet understated crown atop a royal's head. It was imposing and welcoming all at once. The lane wound gently through a manicured lawn to a circle drive in front of the three-story home clad in gray stone. The main section of the home stood taller than the wings on either side which angled forward encasing the driveway and its fountain.

Aubrey ordered the car to stop as it rounded the circle drive. He stepped out onto crushed gravel and looked around at the impeccable landscaping; flowers in front of the house were in full bloom, bursting with color while the lawns looked pristinely trimmed. Aubrey crossed to the front door, the small pebbles crunching under his feet.

As he stepped up the wide stone steps, he noticed all the curtains were drawn in the windows. He knocked, waited several seconds, then rang the doorbell.

After a moment, the door opened. A woman answered, heavyset with short cropped blonde hair just starting to go gray. Aubrey expected this. These families had many people on as full-time staff.

Unsure of what to say, Aubrey paused. The woman stared at him with dubious eyes. On the verge of introducing himself, the woman broke the silence.

"I knew you'd come eventually." She spoke with a southern drawl. "Come on, he's this way." She turned and led him into the home. Before he could even speak, she continued.

"I knew who you were the minute I saw your car pullin' up. Hell, I knew you were coming months ago, probably before you knew you were coming."

He couldn't fathom what she must mean or how she knew him. Best to just go with it, he thought. Following the woman in silence, he took in his surroundings. He assumed she was taking him to see Mr. Jorgetson, but he sensed this was one of those times when saying nothing might prove to be the best course.

The woman led him through the foyer and into the front parlor, not turning to face him as she spoke.

The interior of the home impressed him as much as the exterior. High coffered ceilings loomed overhead. The foyer danced in reflected light from a crystal chandelier. Dark wood furniture, thick exotic rugs, and tall vases dominated the living spaces. Artwork of all types—sculptures, paintings, and giant framed photographs—occupied every corner and wall space.

The woman led him across the parlor, her shoes softly squelching against the glossy wood floors. She approached a wide staircase that descended from a catwalk spanning the entire width of the main house from one wing to the other.

"He's up here." She began climbing the stairs. "You know that car of yours isn't easy to miss," she said over her shoulder. "And even in civvies I knew you were a cop."

Aubrey didn't correct her. "What's your name?"

"Wanda Beasley. I'm the nanny."

Wanda reached the top of the stairs and started down a hallway to the left. She didn't speak again until she reached a doorway on their right where she turned to face him.

Light spilled out from the open door. Aubrey heard a soft

beeping. It reminded him of something, but he couldn't place it.

"In here," Wanda said, motioning into the room.

Aubrey entered the room. He did not find Mr. Jorgetson inside.

Shades of blue covered the walls of the large room. The wood floor was clean. A large rug in the center of the room with low bookshelves, trunks, and stuffed animals along the walls. A bed in the far corner, surrounded by play things.

The room belonged to a child. It was a little boy's room.

Everything was neat and tidy, arranged just so.

Confused, Aubrey looked back at Wanda. She wrinkled her forehead, then pointed toward the bed.

He'd took in the bed once more. At first glance he took the objects surrounding it for toy castles and towers. Looking more closely he realized the objects had only been decorated as such. The tubes and wires trailing from them, accompanied by the soft beeping betrayed their true purpose.

The bed was surrounded by medical devices—monitors, IV hangers, and sensors. The bed itself was in fact a hospital bed.

The high sides of the bed blocked its occupant from view. Aubrey had a hunch of what he would find, wishing he was wrong.

He stepped toward the bed and as he neared, he confirmed his fear. A boy, no older than ten, no younger than seven, lay in the bed sleeping.

It was Boarding School Syndrome.

At that moment, Aubrey realized that in all his investigations of BSS, this was only the second time he'd been this close to one of the victims. The boy had clean brown hair brushed to the side. He'd been well cared for by the woman behind Aubrey.

The tubes, Aubrey guessed, fed the boy nutrients to keep him alive. The wires ran to cuffs around his arms and legs, which periodically made his fingers and toes twitch. Stimulators to keep the boy's muscles from atrophying.

Over the boy's head, large wooden letters hanging at playful angles spelled a name: Owen.

Aubrey's heart sank as he leaned on the rails of the bed. Staring at the name on the wall, he asked, "Where are his parents?"

"All over. Don't stay in one spot for more than a few weeks. I think it helps keep their mind off Owen."

"How long has he been like this?" Aubrey's eyes settled on the boy, breathing gently, tucked in tight beneath his covers.

"Months."

"How long?" Aubrey's voice shook. "When did you find him like this?"

After a moment, Wanda replied in a quiet voice. "January 1st. New Year's Day. Ms. Jorgetson found him that morning. We thought he was sleeping in because they let him stay up late the night before to celebrate. Around noon, they got worried, called in the family doctor. She came and ran some tests."

"No hospital?" Aubrey asked, knowing the answer before she responded. Medical technology allowed most tests and treatments to be performed on the spot, allowing many patients who could afford it to remain in the home.

"No. She thought maybe the boy had a stroke, or an aneurysm, but it was strange because otherwise he was healthy." Wanda sniffled. Aubrey heard her footsteps coming closer. "Couple days went by while they monitored him, the doctor was in and out. One day, I left to run some errands. When I came back, Mr. Jorgetson sat me down and told me how we were going to care for the boy. He said we'd do this until they found a cure. There were some very smart people working on it, he said."

Wanda joined Aubrey at the side of Owen's hospital bed. She crossed her arms, then touched her lip trying to hide its quiver.

"When did the Jorgetsons leave town?"

"Couple months ago. Late April."

Aubrey's mind spun like a dervish. He could be staring at the first victim of BSS. The boy could have been the first attack. The fact that OFP didn't take credit for poisoning Owen puzzled him, but the boy could have been a test to see if the poison worked. Maybe it was something else entirely, like revenge.

His mind kept coming back to the voice on the other end of the mercenary's phone, the only inbound caller. That voice pulled all the strings. Those strings were becoming an intricate web Aubrey would have to unravel.

Aubrey looked at the woman. He sympathized with her. She clearly cared about the boy, had taken care of him on her own for months. But he needed answers.

"Why didn't they call the police? Didn't they realize what this was after the other BSS cases started?"

"They left before all that started." She wiped a tear only to have it replaced with several more.

"And?"

"They called one day to check in and ... I brought it up." She looked at her hands, pulled some tissues from her pocket.

"They assured me it wasn't connected. Said they spoke to the doctor and ..."

"You could have called the police. You could have called for help."

Wanda looked at him aghast, insulted, with blood shot eyes. Her cheeks had bloomed with purple splotches. "They're family. I may be in their employ but they're family to me. Do you have a family?"

"You're really going to give me that family bullshit?" He pointed a finger at Owen. "What's that boy to you? He isn't family enough for you to call for help?"

She covered her face, sobbing behind her hands. "Mandel said they'd have a cure soon. That he'd be okay before we knew it." She fell to her knees, rocking back and forth.

Aubrey tried to calm himself. This woman had answers he needed. "Why aren't they here? Why did they leave?"

She shook her head. "I didn't understand it. The Jorgetsons and the other family met here one day." She pulled her hands away looking more composed than a moment ago. "Patricia muttered something to me afterward about how these things are best handled among their own kind." Wanda wiped more tears away. "Anyway, they stayed for a while, looking after him. Then, then one day ... they left. I think it was Patricia. She just couldn't stand being here anymore. Wasn't herself. It was her idea to leave."

"Who was the other family?"

"I didn't know them. Never saw them before. I wasn't introduced and I never saw them again."

"What did they talk about when they met?" he asked.

Wanda took a deep, stuttering breath. "I'm not sure. I wasn't in the room but I could hear them from the other room. They mentioned the kids several times. They kept saying something about what was best for them. One of the men shouted a lot. He sounded angry."

"Why was he so mad?" Aubrey bent low to get on her level. "Did the other family have a kid like Owen? With BSS?"

She sobbed into her hands for a moment longer. "I have no idea, but it definitely seemed like they were all in the same situation and agreed," she shrugged, "on how to handle it or something."

Still reeling, Aubrey stood and walked past the woman. Were the super wealthy really so insular that they'd avoid the police altogether? Had they been threatened to keep quiet?

"Where are you going?" Wanda shouted.

Aubrey turned back to face her. "I'm going to call the police. You stay here and tell them everything you just told me."

Wanda stared up at him with wide eyes, clearly confused. "Wait. You're not the police?"

"No."

* * *

Outside the mansion, in the circle drive, Aubrey used the phone Malina gave him to call Aaron Lewis and relay everything he had just learned.

Before he ended the call, he said, "I want my anonymity protected. Consider me a confidential informant. I won't be here when you arrive."

Next, he called Malina.

"How is the decryption going on the other messages?"

"Slowly. Nothing new yet. What did you find at the Jorgetsons'?"

After briefing her on his discovery, he made a request.

"Check to see if anyone connected to the Jorgetsons left town in the last few months. Check to see if anyone left unexpectedly like last minute extended vacations, unexpected retirements, anything like that."

Malina didn't say anything. For a second, he thought he lost the connection.

"Hello, Malina? Did you get that?"

"Yeah, ... I uh. Yeah, I got it. I just ... I didn't expect kids." Her voice faded.

"I know. Listen, that's why we're doing this. If there's more of these kids out there or if there are more coming, we need to know. And we're the only ones working on this."

She responded with a sharp and steady voice. "Right. I got it. Let me do some digging."

After he hung up the phone, he placed his hands in his pockets and looked at the sky. Clouds formed overhead. He closed his eyes and attempted to put the pieces together. The other family Wanda mentioned was probably another case of BSS. Maybe the second ever. Both children stricken around the same time with both going unclaimed by OFP.

It didn't make sense. Why would OFP and Alkorn test the poison on two kids and not claim the attacks after they succeeded? The bombings may have been their larger objective with the poisonings secondary to them.

The child poisonings could have been a pet project of Alkorn's that he later offered to OFP as a weapon to create fear.

His brain knotted with theories and questions.

His phone rang. He looked and saw Malina's number on the display. He answered.

"Hey, Martin," she said. "I don't know if it's what you're looking for exactly, but I have something."

"Tell me."

"One woman with ties to the Jorgetsons on an extended business trip, starting around mid-April."

"That isn't much to go on. Just her, no spouse, no one else with her?" Aubrey kicked the rocks in the driveway. He hadn't expected much from her so quickly, but he had hope.

"Doesn't look like it, but there's something else. She and her husband have an eight-year-old daughter who hasn't been in school since December. Went home for the holidays and never returned."

A chill passed over him. Another child. He closed his eyes and took a breath, hoping once again that he was wrong. "Okay. Worth checking out. Send me the address."

The house was located ten minutes away, in the same general area as the Jorgetson's manor. The estate belonged to the Binns-Lourdes and as Aubrey pulled up the long driveway, he saw it stood just as large and impressive as the Jorgetsons'.

Along with the address, Malina sent a short bio on the family. Dory Binns worked as a venture capitalist whose family had grown to prominence as leaders in the airline industry. After graduating from business school, Dory married a well-known artist named Gregory Lourdes. The couple had one child, a daughter named Polly, who attended an all-girls academy in upstate Maryland.

Like the Jorgetsons', the Binns-Lourdes's home had a long winding lane leading to the main house that ended in a circle drive. Unlike the Jorgetsons', this home had no fountain inside the circle drive, only a small flower garden overgrown with weeds. The home itself was red brick with tall white columns across the front in the Victorian style.

Stepping out of the car, Aubrey surveyed the lawn and what he could see of the house. The grass stood knee high and unkempt; the shrubs bordering the lane had grown misshapen with long wisps of limbs jutting out at random places. Grass grew from cracks in the smooth concrete of the driveway and steps leading up to the house. The blinds in most of the windows were open, but Aubrey saw no movement in the house; no lights were on.

He stepped toward the door, then stopped, listening. He heard crying coming from somewhere on an upper floor. He looked up and saw an open window on the second floor to his right. Striding with long steps to the door, he raised his hand to knock. Before his knuckle made contact, he stopped again.

The sound of breaking glass pierced the still air. Then a gunshot.

* * *

Gregory Lourdes stood in his bathrobe next to Polly's bed, holding her tiny hand. So small, he thought. Polly, his little poppy-seed.

He brushed the golden blonde hair covering her closed eyes, touched the freckles on her nose that had been earned during many hours of exploring outside. He thought about the last time they'd been out there together, catching bugs and placing them in small jars for further examination. A budding scientist, always so curious about the world.

Now, she would see none of it, stuck in an endless

nightmare, never to awake.

He wouldn't let her suffer like this. He had no idea what she was feeling, what she saw behind those eyes, but he knew it was worse than death. Hanging on to an entire life spent asleep. He couldn't let her languish any longer.

Stumbling around to the opposite side of the bed, he set the bottle of gin on the nightstand. He began pulling the tubes and wires from her body, lifting the blanket to reveal pale skin beneath. He detached the cuffs of the muscle stimulators from her limbs and removed all the monitors from her chest, neck, and head.

Looking down at her, swaying as he stood, she looked almost normal—lying there breathing gently in her favorite unicorn pajamas.

His breath caught. He clutched his chest with one hand. Tears streamed down his face as he sobbed. He held her hand, caressing her knuckles with his thumb.

"I'm so sorry, poppy. I'm so sorry."

He reached down and pulled the pillow from under her head.

"We should have been better. I'm so sorry."

Grasping the pillow in both hands, he steeled himself as best he could.

"I'm sorry. Mommy and I love you so much, poppy. So much."

He extended his shaking arms. His limbs moved as if through sand, not wanting to obey. The tears poured from his eyes; snot flowed from his nose.

He couldn't breathe.

His heart pounded.

The pillow was an inch from Polly's face when he stopped.

His arms shook uncontrollably.

Gregory threw the pillow aside and collapsed to the floor, sobbing hysterically. He sucked in great gasps of air, wailing. He covered his head with his hands and arms. He pulled his hair.

He couldn't do it. This wasn't the way.

Coward, he thought. She doesn't deserve this. She deserves better.

After a few minutes, still weeping, he got to his feet and staggered to the master bedroom down the hall. When he returned, he held a small pistol, no larger than his palm. It had been a gift from his father-in-law, a family heirloom from the early twentieth century.

He examined the chrome finish and pearl handle. The old gun was spotless, probably never used. He had no idea if it still worked, but he had hope. He just needed something quick.

In his other hand he held a small bullet as thick as a pencil. How did something so small take a life? He'd never fired a gun, had never been remotely interested. But they wouldn't make a gun that couldn't kill someone, he reasoned. It'll work.

Gregory pulled back the silver slide on top of the pistol until it clicked and locked in place. He dropped the round in the chamber, like his father-in-law had shown him, then flicked the lever that sent the slide home.

Pulling the slide back had also readied the hammer. He pushed the safety button through the trigger guard until it showed red.

He walked back to his daughter's bedside, bent down, and kissed her on the forehead. His lips lingered there while another fit of sobbing overtook him. He pressed his face against hers, knowing this would be the last time he felt her alive. His tears covered the side of her face, but she took no notice, still in her eternal sleep.

After several minutes of crying fits, his resolve restored itself and he straightened. Reaching for the bottle on the nightstand, he lifted it to his mouth and downed as much as he could before choking on the bitter harshness of the liquor.

He flung the bottle to the side onto the floor. It landed with a shattering crash, breaking into a thousand pieces.

Gregory lifted the pistol to his own temple and pulled the trigger.

* * *

The shot echoed across the property. Aubrey tried the door; it was locked. He took a step back and kicked it. The door flew open and he ran.

Finding the staircase, he dashed up the steps two at a time. Turning right at the top of the stairs, he ran ahead, knowing the gunshot came from somewhere toward the end of the hallway on this floor.

A door stood open but he nearly slid past it as he tried to stop.

Inside the room, the scene confused Aubrey. A child in a bed, water on the floor, machines against the wall identical to those in Owen Jorgetson's bedroom.

Aubrey was about to check the next room for the source of the shot when he saw the hand. It stuck out past the end of the bed on the side nearest the window.

He rushed to the other side of the room and rounded the bed. The body was that of a middle-aged male, dressed in a dirty purple bathrobe. He lay crumpled on his side. Blood pooled under his head but not much. He still clutched the gun in his right hand; his left arm stretched out past his head, beyond the foot of the bed.

Aubrey bent down and placed two fingers on the man's pulse. He felt it. It thudded against the pads of his fingers.

He rolled the man's head. Blood ran from a small hole near his temple.

Aubrey sprung to his feet, pulling his phone from his pocket. After dialing 911 and requesting medical drones and an ambulance, he dialed Aaron Lewis for the second time that day.

His eyes fell on the small girl in the bed while he waited for Lewis to answer. He watched her chest rise and fall. She was alive. Examining the machines along the walls more closely, he knew what he was looking at.

She had BSS.

"This is Lewis."

"Aaron, are you at the Jorgetsons'?"

"Uniforms are on the scene. I'm on my way. Why? What's up?"

"I'm sending you another address." The pit in Aubrey's stomach grew colder. He couldn't take his eyes off the little girl. "Come here first."

15

The Hunter

Jacira Barretto took up a position atop a low wooded knoll with perfect line of sight down the two-lane highway. The air smelled of warm, moist earth. A stream babbled nearby.

She lay on her back, amongst the brambles and high grass watching the live drone footage on her tablet. She watched the bird's eye view of Martin Aubrey's car speeding along the curvy country road. She was lucky. Aubrey had selected a rarely trafficked road for the route back to the city. Perhaps he enjoyed the views or just felt like taking a long drive. Either way, it made her job much easier.

She zoomed out on the tablet far enough to find her own position, tapped the small hill where she lay, then tapped the target vehicle. A dotted line appeared from her location to the car displaying the distance between them in a small square along the edge of the screen. The numbers rapidly decreased as she watched.

Rolling onto her belly she lifted the buttstock of the rifle and seated it against her shoulder. The barrel of the long gray weapon sat on a bipod, the suppressor protruding six inches beyond it.

Peering through the rifle's scope, she ignored the inclination and declination markers on the outer edges of the reticle, and the temperature and wind readouts. It was all bells and whistles to her. She cared only for the small oval in the middle of the reticle with its black X in the center.

Panning the road below, she found the short bridge that spanned the creek, four hundred meters away, then the convenient crack in the bridge's joint where she placed the small but powerful explosive. From the crack in the bridge she panned up the road until she found the tiny pink dot she'd painted on the pavement, where the proximity sensors would trigger the explosive.

She wanted to place her shot through Aubrey's windshield several feet before he reached that point. Just shooting Aubrey wasn't enough, she would need to stop the autonomous car as well so she could make sure the job was done.

Centering the X on the pink spot, she pressed a button on the side of the scope. The X turned red, marking the location. As she moved the scope further up the road, the red X moved from the center of the reticle, floating toward the bottom then out of the reticle altogether.

An orange X replaced the red one in the reticle. She panned the scope back toward the pink spot and the red X appeared again, hovering over the pink dot on the pavement.

The scope would do all the work for her—calculate distance, the car's speed, how much to lead the target, wind speed. It would even account for tremors in her hands. All she had to do was keep the orange X on Aubrey until it met the red X, then pull the trigger.

She waited. Her heart rate was steady, her breathing even. If she had biologics monitors on her right now, she knew what they'd tell her—she might as well be asleep.

This kind of work had never bothered her. It might have been the years spent in her former life where her job sanctioned killing. And every bit of it was legal. Maybe, she thought, all her training and experience in that life made killing easy. Or maybe she always had a knack for it. Or maybe she was a sociopath.

Being okay with killing people made the transition into her new life an easy one. She'd had a lot to learn; killing angry, disagreeable targets was not so easy. Her new training had been intense and necessarily secret, but required. Finding work, to her surprise, had been easy. Plenty of people wanted other people dead.

It never started off that way. The client always just wanted to watch and see what their target was up to. So, she'd play detective for a while, find what they were looking for, and deliver her findings knowing what they'd ultimately decide.

If, on occasion, she had to fudge the findings to persuade them a bit, so what. One thing her new life and her old one had in common was the steadfast belief that some people just needed to die. And she stood by that belief now as much as she did then.

Glancing at her tablet, she saw Aubrey's car coming into range. She readied herself.

Staring into the scope, she positioned it so she could catch the car as it came over the ridge in the near distance.

The car rose over the ridge. She sighted the target placing the orange X on the windshield. The glass was darkened against the midday sun, making it impossible to see Aubrey inside. She tapped a button on the handguard of the rifle several times to find the optics display she wanted—biologics.

She now saw the world in gray tones with the exception of Aubrey's red and pink body sitting on the front seat of the car. A dark red mass pumped in the center of his chest.

A small readout at the top of the reticle counted down the distance to the sweet spot. The meters closed fast.

She followed her target as it coasted down the straightaway.

The countdown passed under two-hundred meters.

Her breathing steady. She brushed her thumb against the trigger guard, verifying the safety was off.

Under one-hundred meters to the sweet spot. Birds overhead chirped excitedly. The creek gurgled, unaware that a body would soon be dumped into it.

Under fifty meters.

All thought left her mind. She became a machine, made for a single purpose.

Under twenty-five meters. Her finger fell to the trigger.

Under ten. She tensed her finger.

A pause. She squeezed.

* * *

Martin Aubrey typed furiously on his laptop, recording everything he saw in the two homes that morning. His notes, his thoughts, his theories—he wrote down everything.

He saw the two children in those homes as turning points in the entire investigation. They were the first cases of BSS; they were index cases, patients zero and one.

He needed time to think, time to put the puzzle pieces together. He needed to talk it over with Malina as she had proven herself to not only be an incomparable hacker, but also a skilled investigator. Aubrey was immensely grateful to have her on his side.

Back at the Binns-Lourdes residence, once the police had verified through the home's surveillance footage that Aubrey had not shot Mr. Lourdes, they'd agreed to let him go, albeit with some reluctance.

They'd correctly assumed he was the confidential informant leading them to the Jorgetson home, but when Aubrey refused to give up his own sources, they grew frustrated and angry. Aaron Lewis intervened and after a few minutes of haranguing, they dismissed Aubrey.

The car cruised down a gentle rise and Aubrey scanned his notes, ensuring he left nothing out.

The words forced him to replay the discoveries at both houses. Two families afflicted by the same tragedy. The scientists, now dead, were responsible. And some hidden figure pulled all the strings.

He looked up from his laptop, staring absentmindedly out the car's windshield, noticing the stream ahead. Getting his thoughts down in his notes helped calm his mind.

He closed his eyes to think, when a freight train slammed into his shoulder.

Half-a-second later, a bright flash of light and the front of his car lifted off the ground and slammed back hard onto the pavement.

* * *

Jacira slapped a release on the side of the rifle and jerked down on the pistol grip. A short 9mm pistol slid from the bottom of the rifle, which she left lying on the ground as she dashed down the small hill toward the fiery car.

She neared the vehicle, its front end now flat on the ground, tires deflated and the wheels canted to the side ninety degrees to the car. The onboard fire suppressant kicked in, dousing the fire.

A hole the size of her middle finger sat in the middle of the windshield. She rounded the car's front and moved to the driver-side; she raised her pistol.

* * *

On instinct, Aubrey threw himself flat on the seat of the car. He held his left shoulder, warm blood pouring through his fingers, soaking his shirt and jacket. His ears rang from the blast, but he heard the whoosh of the fire-suppressant canisters dousing the flames under the hood. The operating system must still be functional, he thought. It made sense as the car's "brain" was in the rear.

He glanced at the windshield, saw the hole there and said a silent "thank you" to his company for purchasing police grade ballistic glass for his car. It had done its job the best it could, but Aubrey guessed the bullet was too fast and too powerful to be stopped entirely. Instead, the glass had slowed the projectile and deflected it. His shoulder was in agony, but on the plus side he wasn't dead.

Knowing his attacker would be coming to ensure the wet work was complete, he said aloud to his car, "Tint windows. Maximum setting."

Instantly, the inside of the car went dark. Bright light poured in from the hole in the windshield like a flashlight, but dark otherwise.

Aubrey sat up until he could see outside. He saw a woman running toward his side of the car. She had a sidearm at the ready.

Aubrey, as a licensed investigator and a former cop, stayed armed when he left the house. But he wanted to question the woman. He needed her alive.

* * *

Jacira creeped closer to the driver-side door. She couldn't see anything through the pitch-black windows. Keeping her pistol trained on the window, she extended her left hand toward the door's handle.

It burst open toward her. The very edge of the door connected with the gun and sent it flying. It clattered across the pavement. A flash from inside the car. Her leg screamed in pain, sending her to one knee.

A thought occurred to her— Aubrey wasn't trying to kill her.

She would use that.

* * *

Aubrey held his pistol on the woman as he shimmied out of the car's front seat. He stood a few feet from her, circling to more open ground. Her black hair was pulled back into a tight bun. Her olive skin glistened with sweat.

"Hands behind your head and lie on your stomach." Aubrey

spoke in a quiet tone, hoping to calm her, but knowing she was a professional and would not comply.

The woman held her thigh for a moment, then her hands lifted toward her head, surprising Aubrey for a moment. He should have seen the ruse for what it was.

Like a catapult, she sprung from the ground slapping Aubrey's good arm away with one hand. She produced a knife from thin air with the other.

He threw his body back, bending at the waist to avoid the blade as it slashed through the air across his belly. She missed. The force behind the swing of the knife left her shoulder exposed for a split second as her body turned.

Aubrey, unsteady as he was, kicked; his foot planted hard on her shoulder blade.

He brought his pistol down, leveling it on the woman. Just as he did, she used the momentum of his kick to do a full spin, coming around with an outstretched foot.

Her kick connected with Aubrey's gun, dislodging it. He didn't have time to watch where it landed. Her vicious backhand with the blade nearly spilled his bowels.

She missed again, but this time she prevented her own momentum from betraying her. Still crouched, she looked like some sort of scorpion—legs bent like a tensioned spring and the knife gripped in a wickedly fast hand ready to sting.

In one motion, she pounced and lunged with the knife. Aubrey leapt backward in retreat. She jumped to her feet and kicked him in the chest.

With an inhuman quickness, she turned for a roundhouse kick. Aubrey caught the leg, holding it high to throw her off balance, but her flexibility wouldn't allow it. She slashed and jabbed the knife at his arms and hands, seemingly unconcerned with cutting her own leg.

Aubrey couldn't match her speed and skill. He could only hope to overpower her. He had to go to the ground and hope to get his gun back.

With a vicious leg sweep, he took her down, landing on top of her. He managed to secure her knife hand in an iron grip and wedged an elbow under her chin. Scanning the area, Aubrey spotted the gun—five feet away near the mangled front of the car.

She punched with her free hand again and again, but Aubrey didn't dare loosen his grip on her knife hand.

Her legs wrapped around him, squeezing his ribs like a python. Her head slammed into his. He saw stars. She was too close for him to effectively strike, so he used his weight, applying all of it into his elbow, raking it across her face. She squeezed tighter, punched him several more times in the head.

He worked her knife hand and slammed it into the hot pavement, but she held fast. He maneuvered his hand around to get a reverse grip on her wrist and twisted backward until he felt a pop.

She screamed in pain and the knife came loose. He reached for it, then felt a clamping, sharp pressure on his forearm. She bit him; her teeth sank deep. He groaned with pain and anger.

Taking a page from her book, he threw his head back and slammed it forward into her face. She relented.

The blow left her dazed and Aubrey took the opportunity to go for his pistol. From his knees he lunged for it, but his feet slipped and he came up short by a foot.

Expecting his attacker to be on him any second, he rolled

to his back and braced himself. She was there, but she didn't pounce, she stood there holding her own gun. She had recovered hers first and pointed it straight at his heart. Aubrey wore no body armor.

A crooked smile crossed the woman's face under a bruised and battered eye.

A shot and Aubrey jerked, but he felt nothing. Instead, the woman tumbled to the side, landing on her shoulder.

From her side, she fired down the street in the direction Aubrey had come. He rolled and caught sight of a vehicle parked catty-corner across the road. Someone fired over the car's hood at the assassin, feet from Aubrey, rounds creating pockmarks in the pavement.

She rose to a kneeling position, unleashing controlled fire on the car. Standing, she began walking backwards around the front of Aubrey's car maintaining steady fire as she went.

Aubrey crawled the two feet to his gun, secured it, aimed and fired. She buckled sideways and spun on Aubrey. He fired again, she flinched backward, but remained standing.

Body armor.

She ran, holding her side and firing at Aubrey and the other car. She crossed the bridge, making for the woods nearby.

Aubrey rose to his knees, inhaled a deep, slow breath and fired a carefully aimed shot.

She spasmed, arching her back and stumbled into the metal guardrail on the bridge. She bent over it, hanging there for a moment while Aubrey got to his feet.

A familiar voice shouted behind him.

"Marty."

Aubrey didn't turn. He kept his eyes on the assassin.

"Don't move," he shouted.

They had her. She could lead them to the source of everything.

With his weapon trained on her, he took a step closer. She was fifteen feet away, bent over the guardrail. She stared down into the rushing water. Was that defeat on her face?

"Don't move," Aubrey said again. "There's no getting out of here. More cops are on the way." He took another step toward her.

She glanced at Aubrey then back at the water. She leaned further over the guardrail and with a feeble kick of her legs, she fell headfirst into the rushing creek below.

Aubrey ran to the guardrail. He reached it and frantically searched the water below for any sign of her.

He couldn't see a thing. The trees were so overgrown and the creek was so deep and so fast, she'd disappeared.

Footsteps behind him grew louder. Aaron Lewis joined him on the bridge.

"We'll get the drones out," he panted. "Don't worry, buddy. We'll find her."

No, Aubrey thought, they'd never find her. But he had a feeling they'd meet again.

II

Part Two

16

Rewards

Dion Hill felt special. The Professor had come to him for this mission when he could have asked anyone. Dion wouldn't let him down. All he had to do was lie in his bed real still, use the breather machine the Professor had given him, and, when the time came, kill a man. Not a big deal for him.

"No problem," Dion had said.

The Professor didn't have to ask twice after he told Dion he'd get his hands on that black-handed bastard of a murderer. And, like most people in their ward, he trusted the Professor. If he said the breather would work, then it would work. If he said Dion was helping the other prisoners, then it was true.

There was also the other thing Dion had to do.

"Get his hand," the Professor said. They spoke in the shower room that morning under the intermittent spray from the rain tree. Dion leaned in close to hear. "His left hand. As in, the one that isn't blackened all to hell. Understand? We need that hand or none of this is going to work."

The Professor gave Dion the shiv, which must have been made special for this job. Like him: special.

Under his blanket before lights out, Dion ran his thumb along the five-inch serrated edge. It was jagged and would make for a rough cut, but it wasn't his arm he'd be cutting off, so he didn't much care. He'd done more with less.

Killing that son-of-a-bitch in the mess hall was nothing for Dion. If not for a guaranteed Tapping, he'd have done it a long time ago, for fun. This way, at least, he got a prize out of it—eliminating that slimy scumbag of a Tapper.

And all the rest—protecting his friends, helping the Professor start the revolution—all of that was a fat fucking cherry on top of an already delicious sundae.

The main lights went out with a flick, leaving the cell dim. Dion rolled to his side facing the wall and pulled the rubber hose from under his blanket. He shoved the awkward mouthpiece in between his teeth, made sure he had a good seal and did his best to breathe normally. He pinched his nose just to be sure.

The cell echoed with the sounds of his cell mates laughing and joking into the night. The excitement of what was to come wore off after what must have been two hours.

His eyes grew heavy. Maybe there was something in the breather making him drowsy. He'd have to tell the Professor about it. Maybe they wouldn't come tonight. Maybe they'd wait one more day.

No. They never waited that long after a killing.

Then, the voices around him went quiet. Soft thuds as heads hit pillows. Louder thumps as bodies hit the floor. He didn't feel sleepy at all. He didn't feel that familiar, irresistible pull on his brain tugging him towards sleep.

He couldn't believe it. The breather worked just like the Professor said it would.

This was it. He'd be here soon.

Minutes passed. A *clunk* at the door and a soft wind rustled the hair on his neck. Someone had opened the cell door. His heart pumped like a mule trying to kick its way out of his chest.

This was it. He'd get that son-of-a-bitch.

Voices behind him. Two voices. A man and a woman. That woman Tapper; she was here too. No concern there. It would be two for the price of one.

And she'd be a nice little treat for him after he'd finished the job. He'd deserve a sweet reward for his work.

And with everyone knocked out but him, there would be no interruptions. He could take his time.

* * *

In the days since observing the Sacred Task, Francesca resumed training with her Mentor and there'd been no mention of the harsh exchange during Rudolfo's recovery. Despite his promise of transparency, she asked no questions about the logbook she witnessed being delivered nor the guard who accompanied it.

She concluded if the information were necessary for her training, Rudolfo would have disclosed it. She held no ill feelings for her Mentor for the way he acted. She had been presumptuous and naïve. She'd been given a direct order and she disobeyed. She had meant it when she said it wouldn't happen again.

Rudolfo recovered swiftly. The day after she visited his

room and had witnessed the strange delivery of the logbook, he turned up fully healed.

She thought the nature of the solution must be to hit the body hard and then retreat, or Brother Rudolfo must have taken some form of treatment. She doubted the latter. Every Member embraced the burden the role put upon them.

Once he had returned to full duty, Rudolfo began mentoring her as if he had never stopped. When he was with her, they rarely used the video monitoring room unless an incident occurred for which they were not present. They watched the inmates in real time, as personal as they could make it.

They spent mornings observing the inmates in the showers, mess hall, and along the corridors. Every day he'd give her a specific inmate to observe and request input before she went to bed.

One evening, she broached the subject of Zentransa.

"Do you sleep, Brother Rudolfo?" she'd asked when he was skimming her logbook entries for the day. "I mean, do you take the Zentransa pill like most Members?"

His only reaction was a minute twitch in the corners of his eyes. Without looking up, Rudolfo said, "You should have noticed by now that I do not do anything as most Members do. That includes the pill. And while you are my Apprentice, you shall not either."

During the day, the two of them would follow the inmates on their working parties, mingling among them as they dug with shovels, repaired leaking pipes, and laundered clothing. It was important, Rudolfo insisted, to watch and listen in every aspect of their daily lives.

"If you only watch them when they eat or work, you're only

seeing part of the picture," he told her. "It's just as important to watch them walk the corridors, during transportation to work, while they're in line in the mess hall. Mundane interactions are often the most substantial."

Occasionally, Rudolfo would stage an interaction for the purposes of observation.

"Sometimes, there is the question of circumstances," he told her. "We see them in this situation or that and they act as they do, but is that truly the person they are? The routines of the prison are naturally constraining in the variety of situations we can find them. How would a spider behave if he was in a glass tank forevermore? You may conclude that this spider is kind and harmless. Place a cricket in the tank with him and you will find his true nature. Alas, we can only assess their true nature."

One afternoon, five inmates received notice that their good behavior was going to be rewarded with extra time in the rec room. They were escorted from their working parties to the ward by guards and deposited in the rec room. As the guards left, they locked the door behind them.

One inmate sat in the corner on a hard, plastic chair and read an old paperback book. Two sat in front of the wall-mounted television. The last two found a deck of cards and sat down at a table.

Rudolfo and Francesca watched them from the monitoring room down the passageway. Ten minutes into their ninety minutes of extra free time, all five inmates were in good spirits, playing nicely together or politely ignoring each other.

Rudolfo reached forward and tapped a few keys on the computer. Francesca noticed a number in the corner of the screen start to climb. He had turned on the heat in the room.

Other than some rolling up of sleeves, the inmates seemed not to notice. Five more minutes passed and when nothing more happened, Rudolfo keyed in another command. The lights in the room began to flicker—subtle at first, then steadily more intense.

One of the inmates at the card table grumbled something about the "cheap ass warden and his broke ass prison" but nothing more occurred.

For a third time, Rudolfo reached forward and typed a command. The television went out.

The two men watching it cursed and slapped the control panel on the wall. For five minutes, they struggled to make it work again. Failing to resurrect the television, they stood and made their way to the card table and sat next to the two men already playing.

The newcomers were dealt in peacefully enough, but after a few hands, an argument broke out. One man claimed he knew a better game to play. Another retorted that they were playing the first game, the one they'd started and that was that. An agreement was made between them and the game continued.

The remainder of the time passed without incident. As the inmates left to meet their wardmates at dinner, Francesca turned to Rudolfo.

"Nothing happened."

"Did you want something to happen?" he asked.

She did want something to happen. Deep down, she wanted to witness something significant so she could make an assessment—one that would prove she would be a worthy Member.

"I don't know," she said. "I think I assumed something would happen as you applied pressure on them with the heat and the rest."

Rudolfo leaned back and crossed his arms. "That is why we observe. Our assumptions about who these inmates are is immaterial. We can only assess actual behavior in their present state. It is essential that you understand this." He squinted at her.

"What if it would have turned bad? What if there had been violence and one of them killed?"

"Then the perpetrator would be selected for the Task." He gestured to the screen showing the mess hall and the inmates gathered there for evening chow. "One who would murder another inside this prison cannot be permitted to live amongst the others."

"But," she stopped herself for a moment, then decided she must continue, "you would have been responsible. They would not have been in the situation to kill if you hadn't put them there." She avoided his eyes and did her best to keep her voice steady.

"True." He nodded. To Francesca's relief, his voice remained calm. "But a killer would have been exposed. And a killer is a killer."

He lifted his chin, rubbed it then massaged the back of his neck. Perhaps the Taint was still with him, she thought. "Whether we expose him now or he exposes himself later is irrelevant. We created the situation, but we didn't drive his hand. This is something else you must understand: we observe behaviors to assess the true nature of a person. We don't influence the nature of him. We measure it."

"It's a test."

"All of this is a test," he said, waving his arms to the side and overhead. "What part of life isn't a test? Even if you spent your entire existence locked away in a room apart from every other person, that is, in itself, a test."

During their observations, no matter the situation or the place, Francesca was cognizant of the prisoners' feigned lack of awareness of them. With few exceptions, she and Rudolfo may have been ghosts.

Some would quiver as the two of them passed, while others went stiff. A few talked aloud, narrating their actions as if illustrating they were behaving and doing as they were told. They would speak to no one in particular, just loud enough to be heard by the Member and his Apprentice.

"Just boiling this here water on the stove now. Going to put the corn in here when it's bubblin'. Then, I'm going to take it to the pot man, so he can dole it out."

One morning found them outside, observing a work crew fell a tall pine tree. She and Rudolfo were on the edge of what was once a dense forest of conifers. Stumps, cut clean inches from the ground, were spread all around them like stepping stones perfectly spaced and lined up in rows like a well-disciplined marching band.

Francesca watched the team use long saws—some manual, some electric—to clear the fallen tree's trunk of its limbs while another team removed the debris with metal rakes. A third team began the process of dragging the bare log to an enormous machine whose purpose eluded Francesca.

It looked to be a gigantic tin can laying on its side and propped up on wheels as tall as her. A crane sat atop it like a long-necked bird of prey. A newly felled tree would go in one end of the can, hoisted by the crane's massive jaws and come out the other end totally smooth, free of bark, the nubs of its limbs completely gone. Where the logs went from there, she did not know.

She and Rudolfo walked on past the field of stumps to a clearing where a collection of guards and inmates watched another tree come down, ready to pounce on it with their tools. The two of them observed the inmates performing their various duties.

"The equipment they're using is deadly." She stated it as a point of fact, knowing the reply before it came.

"Certainly. It has been a point of contention between the Order and prison administrators for a long time." He stood with his hands behind his back, the bright sun beat against his black cassock. "The Order's position is what I explained to you earlier: our purpose is to observe true nature. If one's true nature is to pick up a rake and drive it through a skull, then that person will necessarily have to be removed from the population."

"Then, you're waiting to see what happens." She looked up at him, squinting against the sun behind him.

He shook his head, still watching the tree crews. "I'm not waiting for anything. If something happens, it happens. If nothing happens, nothing happens. When something does happen, we observe and assess."

* * *

Nicholas Fox walked at the tail of the tree hooker crew with his face angled toward the sun, letting it bake his pale skin. He felt pleased with himself. So far, his plan was playing out as intended. If tomorrow went the way he thought it should, things in the Keep would soon be very different. And he would be at the helm of the revolution.

The team of tree hookers passed near a lone guard watching them. Fox's long, metal tipped tree hook hung lazily across his shoulders as he altered his path to come within feet of the guard.

As Fox came abreast of the short, stocky man in light blue, he suddenly realized his shoe needed retying. He stopped and bent down, laying his tree hook on the ground. His team of tree hookers kept walking leaving him and the guard alone.

Nicholas stood with his hook, leaning on it and looking high into the trees surrounding them.

"Birds are out." Fox continued looking at the bows high overhead.

The guard didn't speak. He only grunted his acknowledgement.

"Migration season is coming soon, I think."

"Mmm, hmm." The guard looked to be more interested in a group of cutters nearby. He didn't look at Fox.

"Yes, I think the birds will be leaving soon." Fox turned his gaze to the guard, waiting for confirmation.

The guard gave him the slightest of sideways glances before returning his gaze to the group of cutters.

"When do you think that'll be?" His deep voice rumbled in his chest. Fox had always been jealous of men with naturally deep voices. Himself, he'd been cursed with a high tenor.

"Couple of days, I think. Could be as soon as tomorrow night," Nicholas said, returning his eyes to search the tops of the trees.

Another grunt, a short pause, and the guard gave Nicholas

an angry look. "Move along, inmate. Your working party is waiting."

Nicholas Fox bowed his head, lifted his tree hook, and headed off toward his group.

* * *

The next morning, Francesca and Rudolfo stood in the mess hall during the inmates' morning chow. Many were already seated, but most of them waited in line to receive their food served out on paper trays. The line snaked down one long wall and when it reached the door the guards broke it into two.

Francesca walked down a wide aisle between two of the three columns of tables. She looked left and right, watching the inmates eat, listening to the talk. The conversations were what she expected for first thing in the morning—mostly grumblings about how they slept the night before or the temperature of the food.

Rudolfo stood near the head of the line for several minutes before moving into the kitchens, out of Francesca's line of sight. She was passing the fourth row of tables when a commotion to the left caught her attention.

A short, broad shouldered man sat alone on the end of the table opposite Francesca. Another inmate had just left the line with his tray and passed the seated man.

"Hey, son, freshen my cup for me," said the seated man, pointing to a plastic cup in front of him. The other inmate kept walking, shook his head, and muttered something Francesca couldn't hear.

The seated man jumped to his feet the second the other

man passed him. With both hands, he grabbed the man's head, digging his fingers deep into his eyes. The inmate dropped his tray and screamed like a wounded animal.

The guards rushed in from all sides, but it was too late. In one swift motion, the first inmate twisted and flung the other's head into the table with a force Francesca would not have thought possible.

A dull clang rang when the inmate's head collided with the corner of the steel table.

He had refused to get the other man a cup of coffee. Now he lay dead on the mess hall floor.

* * *

That evening, Francesca and her Mentor sat in the observation room. Rudolfo wrote in his logbook while Francesca scanned the video feeds.

"Inmate 3916 is back in his cell."

Rudolfo did not respond, but continued writing. His stylus smoothly scratching on the digital paper.

"It hadn't occurred to me to ask before the last Sacred Task, but 3916 has nothing to lose now." She turned to face Rudolfo. "He must know that his hours are numbered. Isn't he a danger to his cellmates?"

He did not look up from his writing. "His true nature has been revealed, so they will take measures to ensure he does not harm anyone else."

"Measures?"

"Yes." He looked up from the book and pointed with his stylus at the computer monitor. If you look closely, you'll notice a small bulge around his ankle. 3916 will be closely monitored for the rest of the evening. If he poses a threat, he will be given a debilitating shock."

This puzzled her. "Why not just sequester 3916 in a room by himself? Now that his true nature has come to light, the threat to the others seems unnecessary."

Rudolfo looked up. He seemed to be considering her for a moment, then said, "I'm glad you are thinking of these things, but you must remember that everyone has a role to play."

"Even a man whose death is imminent?" she asked.

"Especially him."

She stared at the wall, thinking of the roles everyone in this place must play. It occurred to her that the prison was an ecosystem where the contributions of each individual contributed to the overall balance. In nature, that balance was created to support lifecycles. Here, that balance was created to support death.

"They must see him," she said, turning back to the screen to watch 3916 enter his cell. The other inmates gave him space. "The others must be reminded of the cycle."

"The cycle?" His face contorted into a pensive frown. "Yes, I suppose you could put it that way. But as I mentioned when you first arrived, it is not about consequences or punishment. He is left in his cell tonight to remind the others of death, but also of life." He bent back to his book and continued writing.

When she saw 3916 murder the other man in the mess hall, she knew the Sacred Task would be performed tonight. The killer belonged to Rudolfo's ward and was therefore their responsibility. She wondered how badly the Taint would affect Rudolfo tonight, so soon since the last Task. This thought brought another question to her mind.

"Are killings, or murders, this frequent in the ward?"

"No. They are usually much further apart." He continued writing, his brow creased in concentration.

"Does the frequency of these last two concern you?" She watched him write. He didn't seem to miss a beat, his quick scrawl never pausing.

"Not yet," he said.

* * *

Late that evening, well past lights out for the inmates, Francesca and Rudolfo met in the outermost passageway and walked to the central corridor. At passageway three, they turned left. The next few minutes passed in the same way as the last Sacred Task Francesca witnessed—Rudolfo opened a hidden compartment in the wall, inserted his hand and a moment later the chatter in the passageway fell silent.

Three doors further down the passageway, Rudolfo stopped. He waved the back of his left hand over a spot on the wall, she heard a *clunk*, and watched as Rudolfo pushed the door open.

This cell was identical to the last one she had been in. The exception was the floor here was clear of inmates—everyone had made it to a bed. She assumed the late hour accounted for that difference.

Rudolfo found the subject of the night's Task in a bunk second from the top, straight ahead of them. Her Mentor scanned and confirmed he had the right person.

After removing his gloves, he reached into his pocket and pulled out the vial of Oil. He dipped his right index finger into the glass vessel, extracted it, and replaced the Oil in his pocket.

Next, he removed the Solution from another pocket. For the second time, Francesca was struck by the total blackness of it, absorbing all light that touched it. And the way it moved in the glass tube. Once again, to her, it appeared alive.

With his left hand, Rudolfo gripped the vial, disarmed the secure lid, and slid it open. He carefully inserted his finger into the dark liquid, covering his skin up to the first knuckle then withdrew it.

Sliding the lid closed, he turned to the inmate in the bed and reached out with his stained hand.

In a flash, there was movement and the shimmer of metal flying through the air. With surprising speed, Rudolfo leapt backward.

The blade missed him but struck the vial still in his left hand. With a tink, it flew end over end and landed on the concrete floor.

The inmate flew out of his bunk, spinning and jumping to the ground. He charged at Rudolfo with the force of a rhino. In the process, his heavy foot landed on the vial shattering it, the contents oozed out onto the floor.

The inmate pinned Rudolfo against the wall, a forearm pressed hard against his face. The inmate's other hand held the blade. Rudolfo held 3916's wrist, struggling to hold it at bay. The inmate gained ground, and Rudolfo's strength was not up to the task.

In seconds, the blade would be buried in the Mentor's stomach.

Francesca stood shocked, at a loss for what to do. She had to do something.

She took a step to leap onto the inmate's back when she saw the puddle. The small black puddle, now a perfect circle of colorless liquid on the floor between her and them.

As she advanced, she bent and dragged her right index finger through the puddle. She stood, took another step, and pressed her fingertip to the back of the inmate's neck, just below the skull.

A brief pause and he froze. His back arched violently against itself, the blade clattered to the floor.

With a great, wailing gasp the inmate collapsed to the floor dead. Open, blank eyes stared back at her.

Rudolfo's now empty arms shook. With wide eyes he peered down at the dead man, then to Francesca, then to her blackened finger.

He locked eyes with her and muttered, "Foolish." Then, he was on her. A rag flew from his pocket and he wiped her finger, furiously twisting and pulling on it.

"No oil," he said. "Foolish. It will hit you full force."

Whether it was the shock of what she knew was coming, or the Solution taking its toll, she didn't know, but suddenly her legs felt weak. They could no longer hold her weight and buckled. She fell to her knees then fell back. Faint sounds of footsteps outside the cell came to her. Her finger turned to ice.

"He was going to kill you," she whispered.

"Foolish. The guards would have—"

His voice faded; it sounded like she was under water. The coldness in her finger traveled to her core. Ice formed in her belly. At the same time, her skin heated up. The fever radiated inward from her flesh to her organs.

She could have been in a furnace. She had to get free from whatever was smothering her body with this heat.

As if answering her wish, the heat seemed to dissipate. As

it did, she felt herself falling, melting into a void like a pillow graciously swallowing her.

Sounds of rain came to her, the heat left her. She opened her eyes. She stood at a window. She was small, low to the floor. Her tiny hands pressed against the cold glass in front of her.

The window faded as darkness crept inward from her peripheries.

The heat returned, engulfing her in invisible flames.

Pink light pierced her eyelids. She opened them. She was in a dimly lit, gray room on her back. A man stood over her. She didn't know this man.

She tore at her clothes, pulling and tearing at whatever this man had covered her with.

Darkness again. The heat faded.

She felt cool. Opening her eyes, she was at the window again.

She stared out a window at a lawn drenched in rain. It poured from the heavens, puddles forming in the short grass. The sky had opened like a sieve, pounding every surface. It ran like sheets from the edge of the porch's roof beyond the window. The farmhouse around her thrummed with the beating of the water. The tin roof sang out in a harsh cacophony like an endless tide of sound.

Thunder clapped and she jumped, startled.

"You okay, hon?" A tall woman to her left had appeared out of nowhere. She wore a flat periwinkle cotton dress printed with deep purple flowers. Her hair hung loose and wild from a low pony tail, but her face was kind and pleasant.

Francesca knew this woman.

"Yes, mama."

Her mother bent low to look out the window with her.

"Really coming down out there, huh, Frannie?"

"Yes, mama."

Her mother squinted and with a sly grin, she said, "Let's do something crazy."

She stood and pulled Frannie behind her, past the row of windows, through the dining room to the front door.

A second more and they were on the porch. The cool air stuck to Frannie's skin. Her mother looked down at her.

"Ready?"

"For what, mama?"

Without another word, her mother bounded off the porch nearly jerking Frannie to the ground.

She caught her footing and ran by her mother's side, splashing with bare feet through the puddles. Her nightgown soaked up water from the puddles while the rain ran down her hair and shoulders. The two fronts of water chilled her to the bone.

The two of them ran, Frannie taking three steps to every one of her mother's. The exertion warmed her up—that and the feeling of elation out here with her mother.

Her mother's zeal for life had always warmed her.

"It's a tempest!" her mother cried, spreading her arms wide as they went. They ran across the wide front lawn, into a field of short wheat grass. The ground was softer here, so they slowed.

A moment later, her mother stopped. She threw back her head and spread her arms palms up. She let the rain beat her skin. The water clung to her, pressing her dress tight to her body, plastering it over every contour of her narrow frame.

A flash of lightning over the nearby forest and a thunderclap brought Frannie out of the glorious moment. She huddled into herself, pulling her arms in tight against her chest, suddenly very aware of the cold. She pulled at her mother's dress.

"Mama, I'm scared," she shouted.

This snapped her mother out of her reverie. She looked at her daughter. She smiled with soft eyes. Water dripped down her face into her eyes and mouth, but she didn't wipe any of it away nor did she shield herself from the downpour. Strands of hair stuck, pasted to her cheeks.

She bent a knee to be eye level with Frannie. She gripped her daughter by the shoulders.

"Good," she said. "Fear is good. You won't know who you really are until something scares you out of your wits."

The darkness came again. Once more, the void engulfed her, emptiness pressed on all sides.

Frannie found herself in the woods, walking along a narrow lane. Old growth forest grew on either side of her. The ground rose steeply to her left and fell just as steeply to her right.

She stood further from the ground now. She was older. She walked behind a man. He wore a thick canvas coat and high boots. He looked back at Frannie and smiled.

"How's your brother?" he said.

Frannie looked back. Her little brother Hank sat in a homemade wooden wagon. He slapped his thighs in delight and babbled in the incoherent language only a toddler understood. Occasionally, he looked into the trees to find the source of some strange noise. Frannie pulled him, careful to make the ride as smooth as possible.

"He's fine." She smiled back at her dad.

It was just the three of them now; her mother had died almost a year ago. The sick irony was that Hank's birthday would also mark the anniversary of her death.

Frannie threw her braid of bright blonde hair behind her shoulder. They were on one of their frequent "walkabouts" as her father called them. They'd taken more of them in the months since her mother passed, but Frannie enjoyed them. It took all their minds off the hurt for a while.

The sounds of the forest and the smell of the earth made her feel small but also whole. There were larger things happening in the world, but she was a part of them. That made her feel good.

Her father stopped dead in the path ahead. Frannie slowed. He looked up into the forest on the high side of the path, up toward the ridge. He turned his head like he was listening for something. A second later, she heard it too—a rumbling high up on the hill.

It grew louder in the seconds since she first heard it.

Her dad ran back to her and Hank, lifted the baby from the wagon, grabbed Frannie by the wrist and pulled her down the path. They didn't run down the hill but across the path of whatever came toward them.

She ran hard next to her dad. She gasped for breath in the cold air. She could barely keep up with him, but he pulled her along, his iron grip ensuring she wouldn't fall behind.

Two seconds later, she could see it in the distance to their left. A brown mass amongst the trees slid down the hill, shaking the trees, pushing everything in front of it like a bulldozer.

The mudslide was fifty feet from them when her father threw his free arm around her waist and lifted her bodily off the ground. She bounced under his arm against his hips that dug into her.

He darted into the forest to their right, downhill. A thick maple tree stood there, its branches bent and twisted wide from the trunk. Nothing grew under it.

He threw her onto a limb, the lowest the tree had to offer, but he stretched just to reach it. Looking down from the branch she could see the first trickles of water and mud swirling around her father's feet.

Looking up the hill on the other side of the path, the ground churned. Trees quivered.

The earth itself looked alive—marching toward them in a boiling brown wave.

He handed Hank to her and she hugged the baby boy for dear life.

"Climb, Frannie! Now! Get as high as you can."

She couldn't move, she sat clutching her little brother, frozen to the limb and shaking.

Her father held onto the limb and tried to swing his leg up and over the branch. On his second attempt the wall of mud and debris came. A tidal wave of brown muck knocked his legs out from under him.

He dangled there for a moment, staring up at his children. His fingers desperately clutched the limb. Frannie reached out with one hand and tried to get a grip on his wrist.

In another instant, his fingers slipped. The dark tide swept him away like he was just another twig.

Frannie watched in disbelief as her father bobbed weakly in the dark sheet of liquid mud.

His shoulders and chest were sucked under then, a second later, his head. His hand lingered above the muck briefly before it too was swallowed up.

The tree under her trembled but held strong through the passing waves of destruction. It kept her and her brother safe.

Hank cried. She patted his leg.

"It's okay, bud. It's okay." She said the words over and over. In a way, she hoped the words would sink into her own mind and eventually she'd believe them too.

The world around her dissolved into nothingness. The void overcame her.

Moments passed and the heat returned. With it, came an ache, a soreness in every inch of her body.

She opened her eyes. A gray ceiling overhead, no sounds other than the rustling of pages nearby.

Francesca lifted her head. Her Mentor sat at a small table turning the pages of a large book. Her head fell back into the pillow; the energy required to lift it was too much right now.

"How long?" she whispered.

"Two days." His voice scraped her eardrums. Her body was oversensitive to every stimulant.

A chair made a scraping on the floor, splitting her head. She heard soft footsteps nearby.

"Foolish thing you did." She couldn't open her eyes, but she felt his presence. "Brave, but foolish." A pause. "Rest. We'll talk more about this later."

Francesca followed his order and allowed herself to sink, not into the void this time, but into sleep.

17

Liz Reynolds

Deputy Inspector Liz Reynolds of the New Aberdeen Metropolitan Police sweated through her shorts and shirt in the hot, humid summer heat. Her feet pounded the pavement in quick succession as she checked and rechecked her pace on her watch. Her skin reflected the city lights, bright and numerous enough to simulate dusk even now in the middle of the night. Her brown hair, pulled back in a tight ponytail, bounced against her neck.

She loved running at midnight. The streets were clearer; the air was cooler. She felt more alone, which she liked.

Liz pushed herself along her usual route—south from her apartment building, then east toward the docks and away from the false lights of the city's commercial center.

As she traveled east, through a heavy residential district, it still looked like dusk around her. She would have to reach the warehouses to experience anything close to real darkness.

She ran especially hard tonight. Her muscles and lungs protesting from the very start, but she didn't pay them any mind. Her thoughts were occupied with Ryan Grant, murdered in his home. She couldn't shake the feeling that his death wasn't some random break-in or someone he'd arrested just out for revenge.

As she thought about it, her mind drifted to the same nagging feeling she'd had for weeks—that they'd left something undone in the OFP case. Could Grant and the case be connected was a question she'd been asking herself. She prayed it wasn't.

The investigation into One Front for the People, Boarding School Syndrome, and the bombings had yielded results—the killing of the men behind both, or so it appeared. But the thought that those men were merely part of something else, as Martin Aubrey suggested, that someone far more dangerous orchestrated the entire thing left her uneasy.

She knew Aubrey continued the investigation on his own after being unceremoniously dismissed from his volunteer duty with the police. She also knew Aaron Lewis helped him. To what extent remained a mystery.

She thought back to the day Aubrey burst through the door of the bombers' apartment, when the terrorists had everyone pinned down and she was trying to drag a severely injured Ryan Grant from the chaos. Aubrey helped them turn the tide; without him they'd all have been killed.

As if on cue, her left shoulder sent a dull throb down her arm. She rotated her arm as she ran, working the joint. Its scar tissue and implanted hardware was a remnant of the battle.

She ran harder, hoping the exertion would work out some of the pain. Her breath came faster, with it the smell of salt from the nearing docks.

Up ahead she saw the first of the warehouses looming in

the half-darkness just outside the halo of the city's simulated dusk. Three more blocks and she would turn left for the marina and more warehouses.

How far had Aubrey come, she thought. What answers had he dug up and how much closer to the truth was he?

The recent discovery of the two children with BSS had rattled her. There was a new team investigating the Jorgetson and Binns-Lourdes kids, the detectives handpicked by the Chief herself. Reynolds suspected they wouldn't find anything new, they'd only confirm that the children were residual cases from the original attacks.

That was the Chief's line of thinking and the team would echo it.

No one mentioned the person who called in the discovery of the kids. The individual was being treated as a confidential informant. Rumors were that it was Aubrey. Aaron Lewis refused to say, but she thought it had to be him. No one else was looking into the case anymore, much less discovering new victims.

For once in her career, she considered leaving the police force to join Aubrey. Ironically, she would have to quit the police to continue the police work she wanted to do.

Reynolds turned left around a corner and the smell of the docks assaulted her. It was the same as it always was—sea air mixed with diesel and the earthy aroma of sludge—and she loved it. Everything at the docks felt foreign against the backdrop of the city's polished and gleaming façade.

It transported her away for those brief moments as she dashed through the yellow lights, past the long storage facilities and under massive H-frame cranes stretched out overhead. The Colossus of Rhodes stood guard over commerce.

The yellow flood lights cast dull circles on the concrete. Buildings to her left, water to her right, she considered this the home stretch of her runs. A mile and a half of this and then she'd take another left to make her way back home.

Artificial intelligence automated the loading and offloading, and the scant number of people who actually worked at the docks were mostly security. Solitude was the main reason she liked it there.

So, when she saw the person ahead, she knew something was wrong. The figure lay on the ground a quarter of a mile ahead, only partially visible—half in a circle of light and half in shadow.

She grew nearer and realized the person lay on their side, their back facing her. Long red hair spilled out the top of a black coat. The hair and shape of the body under the coat looked like a woman's.

Reynolds could have called it in on her watch, but she decided to check it out first. Could just be a drunk or someone overdosed on Z.

Ten feet from the body of the woman, she slowed her pace to a walk. A dark black patch of blood matted the red hair on the back of the woman's head. Reynolds rushed in.

"Hello," Reynolds said, "I'm here to help."

* * *

Oona Hobbs leaned against the exterior of the metal building watching the drone footage on her small tablet. The target rounded the corner to enter the docks. Why this woman chose to run down here three times a week, Oona couldn't fathom, but she didn't care. It just made her job easier.

She pulled the small pistol from the holster under her coat and chambered a round. Then she bent down to unclip the knife strapped to her ankle. The microsecond it took to undo it in combat could be the difference between being a victor or a victim. She chose to be the former.

Oona ambled from the darkness to the perimeter of the orb of yellow light on the ground. Checking her tablet again, she estimated sixty seconds until she made contact with the target.

"Almost forgot," she said. She pulled a small red gel pack from her pocket and smashed it on the back of her head. She ruffled her hair, ensuring it was considerably disheveled, then lay on the ground along the edge of the light.

Laying on her right side, she maneuvered the pistol so it was pointing back and up under her coat.

She sighed and wished she didn't have to put herself in the open like this. But this had to be clean and it had to be successful. Her employer made that clear. There was no room for a missed shot at long range.

Footsteps behind her and a voice.

"Hello," the woman said. "I'm here to help."

* * *

The woman did not respond. Reynolds skirted the long hair which had cast a considerable halo around the woman's head. She knelt down and reached with two fingers toward her neck.

The woman's head turned; deep green eyes glared at her. Her hands flew from under the coat; one held a gun.

Reynolds threw herself back in an awkward leap, throwing her hands up to protect her face. Heat lanced through her left palm.

On her back, Reynolds kicked at the hand with the gun, knocking it back. She lifted her leg high and brought her heel down on the side of the woman's head and neck.

The gun began to come around again. Reynolds spun herself into a crouching position and pounced. Pinning the gun hand into the concrete, grinding it against the bits of gravel. She punched with her other hand. The woman blocked nearly every blow.

The world flipped. Reynolds fell on her back, doing her best to fend off the woman's hammer-like punches. The punches came with a speed and ferocity Reynolds hadn't seen before.

Long loose hair dangled in her face. Her left hand still held tight to the gun and the attacker's wrist, but her strength waned. Reynolds's arm bent against her will. The woman was stronger than her and the run had drained Reynolds.

The woman punched her in the head once more, then landed one square on her left shoulder sending shockwaves through her arm and chest.

Reynolds howled in pain. More blows found her shoulder and soon her arm and hand felt numb from the abuse. She twisted and punched at the woman's torso but only found the familiar feeling of body armor beneath clothes.

Her left arm throbbed. The woman bent it at the elbow. The gun would be at her head soon.

Frantically, she punched and squeezed anything soft she could get her right hand on. Nothing worked. The woman was too powerful.

Reynolds's hand found something—a long thin object attached to the woman's leg. A knife. She pulled at it, attempting to unsheathe it.

The woman's left hand flew to her ankle to stop Reynolds. In that instant, Reynolds felt the pressure come off her left arm. With a well-placed knee to the woman's groin, she pushed her off balance.

In the space of a heartbeat, Reynolds had both hands on the gun. By the time the woman realized what had happened, Reynolds had bent the pistol and the woman's hand backward, the barrel pointed at her chest. Reynolds found the trigger and squeezed down on the woman's own finger.

The gun fired, deafening at such close proximity. The bullet met the body armor in a smoky flash.

The woman fell back, but held tight to the gun and Reynolds's two hands. She held them straight up. Reynolds had leverage now and sat up, breathing into the woman's face. Their four arms stuck straight up, held high over their heads, each woman struggling to bring the pistol back down to bear on the other.

"Hey!" A shout from the darkness. They both looked. A burly-looking man in a security guard's uniform ran toward them.

The woman looked into Reynolds's eyes and bared her teeth, snarling. She threw her head back, then slammed it forward into Reynolds's face. Her nose popped and crunched.

The attacker let go of the pistol with her right hand and swung a vicious right hook that smashed into Reynolds's cheek bone; she felt another pop in her face. She fell onto her back once more, the gun no longer in her control.

A shot cracked in the air. Not close, from some ways off. The guard's gun.

Reynolds cracked a puffy eye to see a figure in black running into the dark street opposite the guard. The light caught the long red hair, waving in a flurry behind her as she sprinted away.

18

Trails

Jacira Barretto's sneakers squelched on the highly polished floors as she walked with feigned purpose and intensity. The nurse's uniform was loose and billowy, not her style, but required for the day's objective. The dark blue scrubs matched those of the nurses in the ICU ward where she was headed.

Infiltrating a hospital was simpler than most people might think. The trick was to act like you belonged there—walk fast, appear focused, don't get distracted, and never get lost. Don't avoid eye contact, but don't let it get excessive.

Hacking the hospital's security and uploading your own cerebral signature and facial identification helped too; she had spent the better part of the morning accomplishing that feat. As a result, every entryway she wanted to pass through welcomed her like an old friend, the doors swinging open like they were expecting her the whole time.

Her pace slowed with the soreness in her back and a pronounced limp—products from the encounter with Martin Aubrey. Her recovery had been brief, hastened by the right narcotics. Still, the bandages and splints made her stiff. The bullets floating around inside her made her uneasy.

She marched down the mauve and seafoam hallways with their sickeningly pleasant artwork of seascapes and sand dunes. Easy listening adult contemporary music filtered through the ceiling tiles. She glanced at one of the pieces of so-called art and saw her reflection in the glass. She liked herself as a blonde.

She held a tablet in one hand and kept the other buried in the pocket of her scrubs' top where she rolled a half-inch long gel capsule between her fingers.

Door after door flung itself open for her until she finally reached the ICU. She had the layout of the ward memorized—a central nurse's station from which four hallways branched off with four rooms in each.

She passed through the ICU ward's doors and down one hallway toward the nurse's station. The room she headed to was in the hallway directly across the station from where she entered. Four nurses sat inside the circular station; their heads bent to their work. No one walked the hallways at the moment.

She breezed past the station without incident. One nurse looked up, gave a polite smile, then went back to her work. Jacira returned the smile with a curt nod. She continued into the hallway straight ahead of her. She stopped outside the open door of the last room on the left. A digital plaquette to the left of the door read Lourdes, G.

She entered the room.

Gregory Lourdes lay on his back in the bed. Tubes and wires ran to machines on the walls behind his head.

Jacira left the door open. A closed door in the ICU would

raise suspicion. The nurses would have monitors in the central station displaying patient information plus video feeds from all the rooms—Jacira would have to be quick.

Three long strides and she was at his bedside. She laid the tablet on his bed and pulled a chemical proof glove from her left pocket and slipped it on her right hand. With the gloved hand she withdrew the gel capsule from her other pocket. It was small, the liquid inside it perfectly clear. Synthesized and refined from a formula used in her former life, she deployed it in a number of ways always with satisfactory results.

This particular concoction would give her the time she needed.

In one motion, she grabbed a thicket of Gregory's hair and pulled his chin to his chest, exposing the back of his neck.

In her gloved hand she crushed the capsule and allowed the liquid to ooze out onto her middle and index fingertips. She reached out and rubbed her two fingers, slick with the clear substance, on the base of the man's skull. She had to ensure good distribution across and down the brain stem. Her refined concoction gave her the time she needed, but it was also less potent than its concentrated state.

She opened her left hand and let Gregory's head hit the pillow. She removed the glove on her right hand, ensured not a drop of it touched her skin and slid the used glove into a plastic tube which she placed in her pocket.

No one stopped her as she left the ward. Not a head turned as she left the hospital altogether. As she walked through the main entrance and onto the street, she pulled her phone from her pocket and tapped several commands. Instantly, her cerebral signature upload and facial recognition identification were deleted from the hospital's servers.

* * *

In the ICU, just as Jacira Barretto was stepping into her car, an alarm buzzed on the patient monitors inside the nurses' station. It identified the patient in need as Gregory Lourdes room 442. The charge nurse barked orders and she and the other nurses leapt into action.

In spite of their efforts, there was nothing they could do for Mr. Lourdes. The attending physician determined the cause of death to be complications stemming from a self-inflicted gunshot wound to the head.

* * *

June 10, 2043

"We believe the two children found yesterday are infected with what is popularly known as Boarding School Syndrome." The newly minted Chief of Police, Chevelle Long, stood at a dais surrounded by men in suits addressing the press. Media drones aimed toward the Chief buzzed over the heads of the group of reporters. The news station's call sign branded the bottom of the television screen—WMNN. *"The children were infected some time ago, and out of respect for the parents' wishes, we will not be divulging any more information. Thank you."*

Tall and lithe, the ebony woman stepped from the dais.

"Were they infected by OFP?" a reporter shouted.

She turned back to the audience of reporters with a cold, hard expression.

"One Front for the People is dead. My officers eradicated them months ago. It is possible that these children were infected during

their reign of terror and the parents were conflicted about going public due to the stigma associated with it. They're very private people, so that would be understandable. But let me make this clear," she pointed a finger at the small crowd, *"OFP is gone. If this is their work, it's the last we'll ever see of them."*

Martin Aubrey made a cutting motion with his hand and the television winked off. He leaned back on the cheap faux leather sofa and turned toward Malina Maddox. She sat at a desk in the corner of the hotel room.

"Anything good on?" she said, typing furiously on the keyboard unrolled in front of her.

"No. And Aaron told me the Chief is chalking these two kids up to OFP attacks from months ago. She's calling it old news."

He rocked his head from side to side and focused on taking calming breaths to allay his exasperation.

He continued. "Which begs the question: why didn't they take credit for those two? By the looks of it, these kids have been sick for a long time. So, what if the parents wanted to keep it private? OFP doesn't care about their privacy."

"Makes your theory look more plausible. That OFP had nothing to do with it really." She looked over her shoulder as she spoke but kept typing. "They were a front for the real killer or killers. Still think it was Alkorn and his crew?"

"Yes. The rest of their messages will prove me right." He pointed at the air as he spoke, as if trying to convince someone of his theory. "I think he was the only one capable of making whatever is causing BSS. He had a motive—a clear vendetta against Sarazin and anyone who had anything to do with him."

He stood and paced around the living area of the hotel

room. The mottled blue carpet beneath his feet had the distinct trademark look of a cheap hotel. The beige, textured wallpaper hid whatever stains existed there, but the bathroom appeared clean and the couch was comfortable.

After the attempt on his life, Aubrey felt certain they were in danger. He forced Malina to leave her storage unit hovel and set up camp in a hotel. She hesitated, convinced she could take care of herself better on her own.

He explained in great detail how the assassin ambushed him on the road, describing to Malina the equipment and expertise it required. This convinced her. A foe as formidable as theirs was not to be taken lightly. Better safe than sorry.

Malina brought her computer block and a few other necessary items which allowed her to continue working on deciphering the coded messages sent between the four Ventana scientists. She also brought along fake identification and untraceable cash cards for them to use. Malina proved herself to be extremely resourceful and a good partner.

Malina chose the Silk Princess Hotel situated in a less than desirable area of the city. Their security was non-existent which, she explained, meant their enemy wouldn't be able to use it against them. The hotel also lacked a certain thoroughness when it came to checking identification. Malina had insisted to him that her fakes were perfect, but just in case it was best not to deal with anyone overly diligent and upright.

Aubrey walked to the lone window next to the desk where Malina sat. He peered through the gap between the curtain looking at nothing in particular.

Things had become infinitely more complicated. He had the sickening feeling that a ticking clock was counting down and that something big and terrible would happen if they didn't solve it soon. Now, the clock had turned deadly, for him and Malina.

The voice behind all the terror now had a hired gun with deadly skill. Had Aaron Lewis not come when he did, Aubrey would have been the voice's latest victim.

In spite of Aaron's assurances, Aubrey knew the woman was still alive. She fell from the bridge by choice, knowing it was the quickest way out. It had probably been her plan the whole time. If things went south, take a swim. She'd probably placed a bug-out bag downstream somewhere. He had no idea who she was, but he knew he didn't want to see her again.

He massaged his left shoulder and rotated his arm in wide arcs to ease the soreness. He was lucky, the bullet didn't go too deep after having been slowed by the ballistic windshield. Nevertheless, having a foreign object gouge its way into a very important and often used joint hurt like hell regardless of how quickly it was removed afterward.

He looked down at his forearms. Bite marks were still visible on one arm and bandages covered slash marks on the other. Thirty seconds of fighting and he'd need weeks to fully recover from it.

The medics from the Binns-Lourdes estate had come quickly to patch up Aubrey, but he had refused a trip to the hospital. The hospital had a computer system connected to the cloud and an internal networked database, all of which could be infiltrated. He could be found. He preferred to be on his own in situations like these.

With Malina's help, they were off the grid, a difficult task in this world and he wanted to keep it that way.

His thoughts drifted to the two children—Polly Binns-Lourdes and Owen Jorgetson. Both stricken with Boarding School Syndrome, stuck in an unwakeable sleep state, for at least the last six months. Both sets of parents treated their children but refused to report the cases. Why?

Malina's searches of hospital records and patient databases failed to turn up either child. No official channels had been used to log their conditions or treatments. Medical records had not been not pulled or updated. Someone treated them, that was clear. Someone who made house calls and was willing to keep everything off the books.

"We need to find out who was treating those kids," he said aloud, more to himself but also for Malina's benefit.

"I was thinking the same thing."

She turned to face him. Since they'd arrived at the hotel, she had made herself comfortable, which meant a white tank top, soccer shorts and oversized fuzzy slippers. The spikey hair on top of her small frame made her look like something out of a manga comic book.

"It must have been someone both families knew." He ran a hand through his hair and sighed. "Both homes had the same devices hooked up to the kids. They have to be connected somehow. The two families met and talked about how to handle it."

"Other than the fact that both families were hugely wealthy and had kids around the same age," she shrugged and spread her hands palms up, "I could only find social connections and pretty casual ones at that. They were invited to a lot of the same parties, joined a few of the same clubs, but I can't find any indication that they spent a whole lot of time together."

She picked up a tablet from the table and swiped her finger

upward on the screen.

"Gregory Lourdes is an artist of some notoriety in the city and his wife Dory Binns is a venture capitalist. She comes from money." She scrolled further on the tablet. "The Jorgetsons come from money too. Mandel's family did well in the hospitality industry and Patricia's family made their millions in real estate. She was a stay at home mom and Mandel bounced around from C-suite to C-suite."

"Including Ventana." Aubrey rubbed his chin and looked at Malina. "We know why Dr. Alkorn would go after Jorgetson, but why Binns-Lourdes?" He moved to the couch and sat heavily. Resting his head in his hands, he spoke through his fingers. "See if Binns's investment firm had anything to do with Ventana."

Malina's chair creaked as she spun to face her impromptu work station. He heard keys tapping and Malina humming to herself. It only took her a moment to find out.

"Actually, yeah, they did."

Aubrey looked up.

"Binns's firm, Binn Capital, was an early investor in Ventana and a minority stakeholder with one and a half percent ownership. No seat on the board, but still influential."

That's a relief, Aubrey thought. The MO was intact, all the victims were connected to Ventana.

"Okay, so Alkorn and OFP had a motive to target them too," Alkorn said. "The question of claiming responsibility still lingers, though."

"Maybe they didn't have OFP on board yet. Maybe they were just testing the toxin or chemical or whatever. This would have been before they were arrested, so it couldn't have been out of revenge like the others."

Aubrey shook his head. "Or Alkorn simply knew he and the team were going to be arrested. The arrest records showed the plot to steal from Ventana went back months. These people are exceptionally smart. They would have planned ahead."

He shook his head again. They were getting off track. They needed to refocus on the two families and the kids. Somehow, the unknown doctor was key. "Do you have financial records for the Binns-Lourdes and the Jorgetsons? And by that, I mean personal financial records."

She spun to face him and nodded. "Of course."

"See if there are any common payments both families made to a person or company. Let's see if anything stands out."

Malina nodded again and reached for a large tablet lying on the desk. She handed it to Aubrey, then tapped a few commands on her own tablet.

"Okay. Now you should have what I have." She pointed at him, still staring down at her tablet. "Everyone they made mutual payments to in the last six months is highlighted."

Aubrey looked down the spreadsheet. It had two columns, one for each family. There was a mix of bank account draft payments, credit cards, and other electronic payments.

He tapped the menu and filtered the lists to show only the highlighted cells. There were dozens of payments made to same companies or vendors, but nothing stood out. The Binns-Lourdes and Jorgetson families both used the same utilities provider, landscaper, and grocery delivery service. The rest were a mix of party planners, tutors, coaches, and decorators.

No company or individual appeared to be obviously medical.

"Unless I'm missing something ..." Malina began.

"You're not. Nothing here looks like a doctor's office or any medical service of any kind."

Aubrey threw the tablet across the couch. He hated the feeling like they were so close to an answer but couldn't see it. He didn't understand how so much medical equipment could just show up at those homes. The parents had to pay for it somehow, especially if they didn't report the BSS to a hospital.

Someone had to pay for it, he thought.

He sat up straight. Someone had to pay for the treatment.

"Here's something," Malina said, breaking his chain of thought.

"What," he said, distracted.

"Looks like a payment to Nebular Medical Group. For five thousand dollars and some change."

Aubrey reached across the sofa and picked up the tablet again, scanning for the entry.

"I don't see it." He scanned the lists several times but didn't see anything for Nebular Medical.

"It's only on the Binns-Lourdes list, but it might be something."

He turned off the spreadsheet's filter and saw the transaction. "What do Nebular Medical do?"

Malina turned in her chair and began typing. After a moment, she said, "Nebular Medical Group designs and manufactures neuromuscular electrical stimulation devices. Whatever that is."

He watched her scan the screen. Apparently, she was a speed reader too. "Nebular's devices use finely tuned electrical signals to stimulate muscular tissue. They're used mostly for physical therapy for accident and stroke victims. Coma patients use them also to prevent atrophy."

Aubrey stood and walked to Malina's side. He squinted at the screen and motioned for her to scroll up the page. Then, he saw it. A photo of a device he had seen not long ago at the Jorgetsons' home, then later that day at the Binns-Lourdes'.

"I've seen that before." He pointed at the device on the screen. In the photo, a small cream-colored box sat mounted to a wall with six cables running to six black cuffs floating in mid-air. "Yesterday. Both kids were hooked up to one of those. The exact same one."

"That's the Stimuthera 700. You're sure it's that exact one?"

"Positive. That's it."

She clicked the menu on the website and searched for a moment more. "Prices match up. That must be what that expense is for. But why did the one family have it on their statement and not the other? They'd both need it."

"I was just thinking about that." Aubrey paced. "I'm not sure that the families were paying for the treatment. I think someone else was paying and maybe the Binns-Lourdes needed a replacement stimulator. Theirs broke down and they ordered it on their own without going through the other source—whoever was paying."

He stopped pacing and looked toward Malina. With a deeply furrowed brow, she looked puzzled.

"Why would someone else pay for the kids' treatment?"

"I don't know yet." He bent his head in thought and resumed pacing. "Can you get into the Nebular Medical database and see if there were other invoices for that device? We need to find out if there was one ordered for the Jorgetsons as well. Then, maybe we can find out who ordered them."

As she turned to begin working to infiltrate the Nebular Medical database, Aubrey's phone buzzed. He looked at it and saw a text message from Aaron Lewis.

Let's talk. In person.

"Who is that?" Malina said, without looking at him.

"Aaron. He wants to talk."

"About what?"

Aubrey shrugged. "I don't know. Probably just a follow up on the attack at the bridge."

"Okay, well, I'm going to need some time to work on this. Let me know what he says."

As Aubrey was typing his reply, his phone buzzed again. This time it was a notification from his news streaming app.

BREAKING NEWS, the notification pop up read. He tapped the alert and the article almost made him drop his phone.

Another BSS Case Discovered, City Shocked, Police in Denial

After the shocking discovery yesterday of two children stricken with BSS, a third child is believed to also be afflicted with the mysterious illness. Found by his mother this morning, the mother …

Aubrey's vision blurred. The text dissolved in front of him as the news sank in. Another child with BSS and it looked like a fresh case.

"What is it?" Malina stared at him. He hadn't noticed she'd turned around. He also hadn't noticed how long he had been staring at his phone.

"They found another one," he said, not looking up. "Another BSS case."

"You just mean one of the two kids from yesterday. Right?"

"No, it's a new one. The attacks are still happening." He

looked up at her with cold eyes. "I'm going to see Aaron Lewis and find out what the hell is happening. You find out what you can at Nebular Medical." He grabbed his coat and holstered his pistol. He stopped short of the door and went back to the bedroom where he doffed his shirt and donned body armor before replacing his shirt.

On his way out the door, he stopped again. "Tell Ted to hurry the hell up on those messages."

"He's a computer, I can't just …" she said as Aubrey slammed the door shut behind him.

* * *

Winky's Bar was surprisingly well-lit. Sunlight poured in from the filthy windows at the bar's narrow front. Looking around at the dingy interior, Aubrey decided he liked it better in the dark. Ignorance was bliss in a place like Winky's.

He passed the long, battered bar with its equally battered bartender and walked straight to the back where Aaron Lewis sat at a high-top table. A sweaty glass of water sat in front of him.

Aubrey dropped his phone on the table in front of Aaron, the screen showing the news article about the BSS case.

"This what you wanted to talk about?" Aubrey asked.

"Partly."

"What can you tell me?" Aubrey took a seat across from Aaron.

"It's a new one. Not like the two you found. The mother swears she just found him like that this morning."

Aaron Lewis's eyebrows drew together over eyes with dark circles below them. The discoveries of the two children the day before and the BSS bombshell that morning had taken their toll on Aubrey's old friend. They dredged up the feeling of hopelessness they all felt during the OFP investigation weeks ago.

"Can you give me their name?"

"Laverno," Aaron said, staring with glassy eyes at the wall behind Aubrey.

Aubrey texted the name to Malina with the question: *Ventana connection?*

"Anything else on the kid or the family?"

"Nothing much," Aaron said, pursing his lips and shaking his head. "Went to school here in the city, seven years old. Same as the others." He shrugged and took a sip of water. His hands shook. "No ideas on how or when it happened. Just that it happened." He set the glass down with a dull thud.

"What is Chief Long's take on it?" Aubrey asked, knowing the answer before it came.

"Same as the other two you found. Residual poison left over from One Front for the People's reign of terror." Aaron sipped from an empty glass but didn't seem to notice. "In private, she speculates it's a copycat. They can't say that in public because it's just as bad to have a copycat killer as it is to have the original. People would freak out."

Aubrey nodded and continued typing notes into his phone. He looked up to see Aaron Lewis looking at him.

"Marty, if you find something. You have to let me know."

"Just you?"

"Well, tell me first, at least. I'll take it from there and make sure it … gets the attention it deserves."

Aubrey nodded. Then, he remembered something.

"You had something else you wanted to discuss?" Aubrey

suddenly felt thirsty and scanned the bar searching for the bartender.

"Gregory Lourdes is dead."

Aubrey forgot about his thirst. He felt his jaw drop.

"When? How? I thought that .22 round didn't penetrate his skull."

"This morning. And it didn't penetrate his skull. They don't know how it happened. All of his vitals just … crashed." Aaron leaned back in his seat with such force he almost toppled over.

Aubrey stared at his friend in disbelief. The police hadn't guarded Lourdes, he knew, because they didn't see him as having any value; he was just a distraught father deeply saddened by his child's illness.

A promising lead was gone. Aubrey had been attacked just as he uncovered crucial information. They were linked, had to be.

"It was her. The woman from the bridge, she did this," Aubrey said.

Aaron didn't answer, he only shrugged.

"Any more bad news?"

"Yes." Aaron Lewis's shoulders fell. "Liz Reynolds was attacked."

* * *

Malina sat with the lights off and curtains drawn. The only break in the darkness came from the glow of her computer monitors. She preferred working in the dark. Back at her storage unit, she rarely turned on her one lamp. The computer screen and a single strand of Christmas lights were plenty.

Her hands flew across the keys of her portable keyboard roll. She scoured the once secure financial documents of Nebular Medical Group. Page after page she pulled down from their internal server, scrolling and searching every record for the Stimuthera 700.

She soon discovered that Stimuthera was a popular item sold by Nebular hundreds of times in the past six months and used in facilities all over the city. Invoices showed the quantity ordered and the requesting physician or, in the case of hospital orders, the name of a procurement officer.

Patient names accompanied most of the invoices for individual physicians, but not for the hospitals who, she assumed, were ordering in bulk. She ran the hundreds of invoices through a search tool of her own making to look for the Jorgetsons and Binns-Lourdes.

The invoice for the order placed by the Binns-Lourdes surfaced which matched the date and the amount paid in their personal file. Since the Binns-Lourdes ordered directly from Nebular, there was no doctor name associated with the order. She was not surprised when the Jorgetsons's name didn't turn up. Why would they, she thought. If someone else was paying for their care, chances are they wanted to keep the family's name hidden.

She decided that removing hospitals and larger therapy facilities was the next logical step. That narrowed the invoices down to around one hundred. Then, she eliminated invoices with patient names. That left forty-seven invoices. She shortened the list further by removing doctors ordering only one device.

A quick internet search of the remaining twenty-three

doctors enabled her to remove ten more. These doctors worked in physical therapy and kinesiology facilities and she felt safe to assume that only a general practitioner or pediatrician would care for the children in question.

Of the thirteen remaining general practitioners and pediatricians who'd ordered multiple Stimutheras, only three ordered them within the right window of time based on their best guess of when the children became ill.

She was about to dig deeper into the three remaining doctors when her screen flashed with a new dialogue window in the lower right corner.

Her program Ted had decoded twelve new messages.

She minimized everything she was working on and expanded Ted's window to full screen.

She clicked and typed several commands, then white text appeared on black. The messages were from January 19, 2043, one day before the last set had led them to the Jorgetsons.

IMANPOR R: Team is worried

ALKORN L: Team or you

IMANPOR R: Plz

ALKORN L: Shouldn't talk outside too dangerous

ALKORN L: And do not forget we are doing this

ALKORN L: No choice

IMANPOR R: No need to remind

SHOEMAN N: Certain no one else knows

ALKORN L: Only us for now

IMANPOR R: Assurances

ALKORN L: None

WINTHORPE S: So be it move forward

ALKORN L: We must no choice

Malina stared at the last two words, *no choice,* repeated twice in the exchange. Why did they have no choice?

If Aubrey was right and someone else really called the shots, then it would make sense; it meant they were under pressure. They sounded worried, unsure of what they were doing.

At the time the messages were written, they must have been planning the embezzlement scheme, if not BSS and the bombings as well.

The Jorgetson boy would have been ill for weeks at that point, but she and Aubrey had suspected he and the Binns-Lourdes girl were probably trial runs before the full-scale assault.

One line of text stood out: *And do not forget we are doing this.* Even without punctuation, the intent was clear. This was a command coming from Alkorn.

* * *

Aubrey returned from his meeting with Aaron Lewis, but the trip back took him quite a bit longer than the trip out.

He hired one car using an app on a burner phone and the prepaid cash card, both provided by Malina. He gave the car a random destination several miles from the hotel, got out and walked several blocks where he hired another car. He repeated the process twice, hiring a total of three cars. He exited the last car a full mile from the hotel and walked with his head bowed and hood up the entire way so as not to let his face captured by any cameras. He even altered his gait slightly, recalling his own company's software that could track and identify individuals by their mannerisms and nonverbal behavior.

Caution was a necessity, now.

Ryan Grant was dead.

Reynolds had been attacked.

Aubrey had been attacked.

There was no doubt in his mind now, they were being hunted.

19

Dead Ends

Brother Rudolfo scanned the pages of former Brother Wilcott's journal for what must have been the hundredth time since acquiring it.

The personal effects of a deceased Member of the Order of the Coppice were handled much like that of a deceased inmate—anything of value was re-appropriated and the rest incinerated.

Brother Wilcott's personal effects were sparse and mundane, but the journal was of particular interest to Rudolfo. A Member's life's work lay on the pages of their journal. Every assessment, every Sacred Task performed was in there. One could glean a Member's philosophy on their duties and the role they played in society at large.

The only way for Rudolfo to determine what, if anything, pushed Wilcott to self-select would be in his journal.

Rudolfo believed that Wilcott's choice of venue and the method of his suicide were a message of some kind. Members were free to self-select after all; suicide was common after a long tenure when the side effects of each Task became too painful to bear. No Member he knew of had ever self-selected in public, nor had they exposed so much of themselves, both literally and figuratively to the inmate population.

Most chose to do it in private with the very poison they used on the inmates, applied to the back of their neck in the same way. The end was quick and, it was thought, painless. Most chose another Member, a close friend or confidant, to perform the deed for them out of fear of botching it by themselves.

Rudolfo thought of the last Task he had performed and its aftermath. How many more Tasks did he have in him before self-selection became a desirable alternative?

He pushed the thought from his mind. There'd be time enough for that later.

Wilcott's suicide was one of two things, he thought, madness or a sign. Rudolfo would have to figure out which of the two it was if he ever wanted to rest easy again.

Staring at the pages of Brother Wilcott's journal, a case could be made for each possibility—madness or message. The entire journal was full of detailed analyses of every inmate under his charge. Each page contained thousands of words on each inmate with notes on every perceivable interaction of substance. Rudolfo read with a sense pride his colleague's assessment of one inmate:

Inmate 2587 observed standing alone in corner of the rec room behaving strangely—talking to himself under his shirt. Later it was revealed to be a baby bird hiding in his clothes. The bird died later in the day, 2587 unfazed by its passing.

In the shower room, Inmate 2587 loaned his towel to another inmate who'd lost his. The towel was never returned. 2587 became irate and berated the other inmate until the towel was returned. He demanded it be cleaned first.

Inmate 2587 stole shower shoes from one of his cellmates.

Every inmate's page mimicked the example—line after line of detailed observations.

Rudolfo wondered how often Wilcott performed the Sacred Task. He chose several random pages and scrolled to the bottom of each of the digital pages. He made a mental note every time he saw *"selected for the Sacred Task".* If his calculations were correct, Wilcott's Task frequency was no greater than his own, reserving the Task for the most heinous and irreformable of individuals.

Nearly the entire journal followed a pattern of detailed observation, thorough analysis, thoughtful conclusions, and reasonable use of the Sacred Task. There were four exceptions that broke from the norm: the last four entries.

Inmates number 7822, 3509, 7789, and 0988.

These four inmates were the last four active entries in Wilcott's journal. Each was blank. Rudolfo flipped through the four pages over and over. Each page had an inmate number written at the top and nothing else. It was a Member's prerogative how much or how little they recorded in their journal as much as it was their prerogative who they selected for the Sacred Task. If this had been any other Member, Rudolfo would have thought it unprofessional at best and derelict of duty at most. But having seen the rest of Wilcott's journal, and knowing the man, even as little as he did, he found the emptiness of these pages to be significant.

Madness or message? Rudolfo shook his head at his own question. Either could explain both the way in which Wilcott chose to die and the blank pages.

He needed to know what was behind Wilcott's suicide. He needed to investigate.

If it was madness, nothing changed and he lost only a small amount of time. If it was a message, then he'd honor the man's unnatural death by figuring it out. Wherever it led him, he'd decide what to do next once he got there.

In the corner of the room, Francesca stirred. She'd been asleep for twelve hours. The last time she woke up, she'd drank several glasses of water and fell promptly back to sleep. Forty-eight hours before that, she'd saved his life.

"Water?" she whispered.

"Nightstand." Rudolfo stood in case she needed assistance; she didn't. He sat back down in the chair and watched for signs of trouble. He'd never seen anyone go through what she had; it may not be over.

Francesca propped herself up in bed and drank the entire glass without stopping. Once she was finished, she swung her legs off the bed and sat on the edge of the mattress with her head bent low, breathing deep, hands at her side.

"Sixty hours," Rudolfo said. "Before you ask. It has been two and a half days since your foolhardy act." He stood at the foot of her bed, letting her gather herself.

"I thought I was going to die."

"Yes. The Solution has a way of taking you to a point from which you think there is no return. Then, it releases you."

He folded his hands in front of him and tilted his head.

"Had you used the Oil, the effect after your first time would have lasted minutes," he said, shrugging. "If nothing else, you should now appreciate how important it is to follow protocol. I don't think anyone else, Apprentice or full Member, could say they've felt the Solution's cruel sting the way you did.

Had it been your fiftieth Task, or maybe even your tenth, it would certainly have killed you."

She continued staring at the floor.

"I had ... dreams. Or, something like dreams. More like virtual memories. They were ... visceral. I could feel it all over again, the fear, the pain, the sadness. I could smell the air, feel the rain." She looked at Rudolfo, the features of her face tightening, wincing. "Is it like that every time?"

He adjusted himself and clasped his hands in his lap.

"Not at first, no. The more times you perform the Sacred Task the more intense they will become, however. The more ... visceral, as you put it." He paused before continuing. "When you get to the stage in your tenure where I find myself at the moment, then, yes, they will be that intense every time. And at that point, you will begin having the flashbacks in your waking hours as well."

Rudolfo picked up a plate of fruit and bread from the table beside him. He stood and walked toward her, then laid the plate on her nightstand. He refilled the empty glass from a pitcher of water next to it.

"Eat something and let me know when you're ready to talk more. I'd like your opinion on something."

* * *

An hour later, Francesca sat across from Rudolfo, who sat silent with his arms crossed. He had given her a book, clearly a Member's journal, and asked her to make an assessment of what she saw within it. He did not give her any specific instructions, just to make an assessment.

It hadn't taken long for her to discover the four blank pages at the end of the journal. She scanned the pages and swiped up with her finger to scroll, wondering if, for some reason, the owner of this journal wrote something at the bottom. There was no nothing there.

She had difficulty controlling her eyes in her weakened state. They wandered to her newly blackened appendage.

Her right index finger was black from its tip to the third knuckle. Every time she caught her eyes wandering to look at it, she chastised herself and turned another page, hoping to find something more worthy of her attention.

She knew the obsession with her new stain must be the same for every new Member. Her life was now a ticking clock, the countdown to her demise now visibly measured, every millimeter of growth a minute subtracted from her life.

"There will be plenty of time for you to examine your mark." Rudolfo seemed to be reading her thoughts. Her behavior made her inner dialogue easy to read.

The food had been an energizer for her, simple though it was. Rudolfo's description of the Solution taking her and then releasing her was apt. She felt no residual effects from it other than extreme thirst and hunger.

"I'm sorry," she said. "It looks so large; I wasn't expecting it to be so after the first Task."

"No Oil. No protection. Normally, it's no bigger than a pea after your first Task. And the aftermath is no worse than having the flu for a few moments." He pointed at the book in front of her. "Now, your assessment, please."

Francesca put her right hand under the table and forced herself to pay more attention to the assignment Rudolfo set in front of her.

"These pages are blank, which is clearly out of character for this Member judging by the rest of the journal."

She looked up to see Rudolfo nodding.

"Is the Member who owned this journal still alive?"

"No."

"So, he or she died immediately after these inmates were assigned, but ..." She flipped back to the page before the blank ones. At the top, there was the inmate number—2019. She looked below it at the first entry. She read aloud, *"entered my ward December 13, 2042."* Looking at Rudolfo, she said, "He entered their names in here the first day they arrived?"

"That or he waited and wrote the date after the fact."

Francesca looked down again at the page with 2019's observations. "No. He was too diligent. These notes are too thorough and thoughtful. He would have done it the day they arrived."

"So, why no entries for the last four inmates?" Rudolfo reached forward and turned the page back to the first blank one—inmate number 7822.

"First, a few questions."

Rudolfo's eyebrows raised. He spread his hands. "Proceed."

"Would four inmates enter his ward on the same day?" Francesca crossed her arms and stared at the book, willing answers from it.

"It would not be entirely unusual, but not common either."

"Did this Member have ... were his mental faculties intact?"

Rudolfo paused. She thought it possible that some level of sadness crossed his face. "I think so."

"My final question." Francesca uncrossed her arms and leaned forward. "A Member's journey is their own. A Member's decisions and their deeds are unquestioned."

He didn't move. He just stared back at her. "Yes."

Francesca took a deep breath. "Why are we asking these questions about this Member and his last four inmates?"

Rudolfo's gaze fell to the floor and he repositioned himself in the chair. He stared at the wall a moment. She thought there must have been some terrible inner struggle raging inside him. He wanted her help, he must or he wouldn't have brought her this book. She also felt he was wise enough not to go on a fool's errand. He must have good reason for digging into a dead Member's past, but what was it?

Her question seemed to dislodge some last vestige of uncertainty within him.

His eyes fell on hers again. "I believe Brother Wilcott wanted me to ask these questions."

Francesca's face fell. She closed her eyes, unsure what to think. The Member who self-selected on the very same morning she arrived at the Coppice. The same Member who the Principal and her Mentor had discussed.

This was his journal.

"The manner in which he self-selected and these blank entries do, in my thinking, make it worth asking a few questions," Rudolfo continued. His face now held a look a confidence. He tilted his head back. "I believe he was sending a message."

Francesca's eyes darted from the journal to her Mentor and back again. Without looking up, she said, "What if we answer these questions and find nothing?"

Rudolfo pursed his lips, shrugged. "Then, we find nothing. All we have lost is time."

"And what if we find something?" She looked at him now and he did not look away.

"I do not know what happens if we find something."

* * *

Working on the assumption that Wilcott was trying to send a message, Francesca felt the four inmates with blank pages must be connected. She concluded that even if the pages of the journal were full of the same painstaking detail as the rest, it would only inform on the lives they led while at the Coppice. A Member's journal only observed the present day, not past deeds as Rudolfo had so vehemently taught her after her arrival.

"The only way to know how these inmates were linked is to know who they were before. If we find nothing, then there is nothing."

Rudolfo nodded. "Why do you think these four are linked in some way other than being in Wilcott's ward?"

"It's like breadcrumbs. If it's all part of a message, then he would link them in here first. This would be the first breadcrumb." She pointed at the journal. "If I were trying to send a message, I put it somewhere I knew someone would look."

Rudolfo's eyebrows knitted and he nodded again. "Okay. What next?"

Francesca explained that the next logical steps were to examine their prison files then move on to police and court files. Finally, they'd look into their lives before being arrested.

Reluctantly, Rudolfo conceded that it might be the only way to determine what Wilcott was trying to communicate, if anything.

In the observation room, Francesca pulled up the prison file for each inmate and displayed them on the screen side by side. Instantly, she realized something was wrong.

"Are prisoner files generally accurate?" she asked.

"Yes, always." He answered from behind her at the table where he read from Wilcott's journal. "Those are legal records, not to mention most are medical in nature when someone dies."

Francesca checked and rechecked what she saw on the screens, comparing each file to verify the dates were correct. "And in the case that someone dies, their actual death date is recorded? Not when the record was created?"

"Yes. The actual date of death," he confirmed. "We may be takers of lives, but we respect them enough to ensure accuracy. The guards who take the bodies away record everything and they are exceedingly professional and diligent."

Once again, she rechecked the records. Each death date was accompanied by a guard's name as witness. They were all different. Nothing obviously nefarious going on unless all four of them were corrupt.

In the case of inmates selected for the Sacred Task, as these four were, the name of the Member responsible was listed as well.

"There must be some mistake," she whispered to herself.

"What is it?"

"The four inmates are … dead. All of them selected."

Rudolfo sat silent for a moment. "Not terribly concerning. Selected for the Task by Wilcott, I assume?"

"Yes."

"Again, not terribly …"

"On the same day." She turned to look at Rudolfo. Disbelief crossed his slackened face, his mouth opened and closed.

"Impossible," he muttered. "He would have ... he couldn't have ..."

She waved a hand at the screen. "If these are correct, then he did. He selected all four of them on the same day."

Rudolfo sat like a statue. Only his eyes and mouth moved, the former darting back and forth as if hearing opinions from different sides of his mind and the latter flapped like a fish taking its last breaths.

"There is something else," she said looking back at the screen. "One of the inmates was female."

* * *

In keeping with the unquestioned nature of a Member's selections, it was permissible for a Member to enter another's ward and perform the Sacred Task on an inmate there. It was, as Rudolfo explained, not uncommon for this to occur.

In times of high demand in a particular ward, or if a Member was ill, they would often call on another to perform the Task on their behalf. In rare instances, a Member would witness a heinous act by an inmate and take it upon themselves to select them for the Task.

Much like self-selection, it was in no way forbidden, but highly frowned upon without permission or invitation. Wards were more or less seen as territories not to be encroached upon.

As Francesca and Rudolfo rode the elevator up to level thirty, they hoped to discover whether it was permission, invitation, or neither that brought Brother Wilcott into an all-female ward.

When the elevator reached level thirty, the two of them stepped into a passageway identical to the one in their ward. The exception was a large number thirty painted on the wall directly ahead of them.

Turning down the curved passageway, Francesca decided to ask a question she couldn't shake.

"How could he have performed all four Tasks on the same day?"

Rudolfo continued his long strides, not looking at her. She wasn't sure if he heard her.

His silence didn't deter her curiosity. "Judging by Brother Wilcott's age and the records in his logbook, I would assume the Tai … the aftermath of a Task would be quite debilitating. In that condition, how could he have performed a second one after the first? And then go on to perform a third and a fourth in the same day?"

Rudolfo walked in silence. As before, he gave her no indication that he heard a word she said.

She continued undaunted, "I see no way he could have completed all four without some type of protection …"

She stopped cold. Rudolfo walked along for several paces before he stopped and turned toward her. His eyes were deathly cold, almost menacing.

"He used protection," she said. "He must have used a glove."

Rudolfo sighed audibly and nodded. "That is my theory as well," he said.

"But that's taboo. It goes against the essence of the Order's purpose. The sacrifice. The penance." She was flabbergasted. She held Members of the Order in such high regard that she could never have imagined one would so callously disregard the most fundamental tenant of the Order—that each Member willingly took on their responsibility and its inevitable end. They gave up their lives and their existence in the name of serving. "That's sacrilege. It's … it's tantamount to heresy."

It was like learning one of her parents had committed cold-blooded murder.

Rudolfo stared at her. His eyes softened and he approached her. "Like all things in life, the Order gets less pristine as you dig further down into its depths. Many Members, I would say almost all, serve honorably." He paused. "Some do not."

"What do we do about it?"

His eyes searched the air then settled back on her face.

"We serve honorably. So much so that our contribution will outweigh other transgressions." He paused, which allowed Francesca's mind to settle a bit. "There will be plenty of time to discuss all of this. But first, we need answers to the questions on hand." He turned on his heel and walked further down the passageway.

* * *

Everything she'd seen on the east ward of level thirty mirrored their own on level twenty-four, including the Member's quarters where they now sat. Francesca planted herself in the corner as the two Members sat opposite each other at a round table.

The conversation was brief.

"The woman was here barely a month," Sister of the Order Jocelyn said. She was a small woman, not quite five-foot-three. Her silver hair reached her shoulders and framed a face that could have been etched from a block of salt. "She exhibited no signs of hostility, malice, or violent behavior. But it had only been a month."

Rudolfo nodded. He crossed his legs and contorted his face subtly. It appeared strained. Every word seemed forced as if he only had a passive interest, as if he was here against his will on some unsavory assignment.

Sister Jocelyn continued, "Whatever Wilcott saw in her was his prerogative to see. His decision to perform the Task on her was ..." She paused and looked at the wall, then back to Rudolfo. "Well, it happened."

"Would you have Tapped her, Jocelyn?"

The woman twitched her eyebrows and inclined her head at the word "Tapped." The use of the slang term for the Sacred Task had surprised her, Francesca guessed. It was the second time Francesca had heard Rudolfo use the term. The first time had been when he was in a weakened, angry state, but now he was perfectly within his right mind. Perhaps he used it to throw Jocelyn off guard, trying to elicit some hidden truth by flaring her temper.

Jocelyn, however, remained preternaturally calm. "At that point in my observations of her, I would not have selected her for the Sacred Task." Sister Jocelyn's back stiffened. "And our long acquaintance is the only thing keeping me from asking you to leave, Rudolfo. These questions are inappropriate and unbecoming."

Rudolfo bent his head and nodded. Francesca knew the conversation had ended. They had learned all they could from Sister Jocelyn.

It was clear, however, that Wilcott had no permission and no invitation to perform the Task in Jocelyn's ward.

* * *

Back on level twenty-four in the observation room, the two of them stared at the computer screen, both dumbfounded.

They were reading the arrest records and case files for the four inmates. Leo Alkorn, Rajesh Imanpor, Stanley Winthorpe, and Natalie Shoeman had all been involved in the same crime—a scheme to rob their employer, Ventana Inc.

Francesca knew of Ventana, of course. Nearly every Member of the Order used Ventana's revolutionary Zentransa pill to take advantage of the extra hours it added to their day. Zentransa was mentioned time and again in classes at the Pupil's School as an effective weapon in a Member's arsenal.

All four inmates had arrived at the Coppice on the same day. The three men had been assigned to Wilcott's ward, the woman to Sister Jocelyn's.

"Leo Alkorn was inmate number 7822 and according to this," Francesca pointed to a file on the screen, "he managed the other three at Ventana. He was the so-called ringleader of the crime. And," she pointed her finger at a different file on another screen, "he was the first to be selected by Wilcott."

Her eyes bounced between monitors and her mind swam with ideas. These four were obviously connected on the outside and Wilcott's selecting of them for the Task could not have been random. The question was why. She could not fathom a reason why Wilcott, of all people, would want these four people dead.

She looked up at Rudolfo, hoping he would have some answers, hoping his wisdom, so much greater than hers, could shed some light on the problem. His face revealed nothing. He turned and began pacing behind her.

She spun back to the screens and searched for more information on the four prisoners. There was so much information about them on the internet it was difficult to know where to start. Their lives had been rich with accomplishments: awards in science, chairs of research departments, prizes, hundreds of scientific journal articles, and prestigious jobs one after another until the four of them coalesced at Ventana, Inc.

She scanned news articles, looking for any clues that might reveal more. She didn't know what she was looking for, but felt she'd know it when she saw it.

Nothing stood out to her for several minutes as she clicked and scrolled through page after page of search results. The article titles were clipped, but she could glean their substance by the first few words. Most of the articles dealt with the Ventana crime and the subsequent trial.

One, however, was not like the rest. The title read *Ventana Four Linked to Bom ...*

She clicked the link.

The full title read *Ventana Four Linked to Bombings Says Inside Source.* The article, dated April 30, was from a publication called The Aberdeen Bugle. She read the short article.

Insiders at the Metropolitan Police Department have revealed to the Bugle that there is suspicion of a connection between the Ventana Four and the bombings and strange poisonings plaguing the city.

The Ventana scientists, arrested and convicted recently on embezzlement charges, are now locked up in the Regional Correction Center. An insider with knowledge of the investigation and current police theories states that it is believed the scientists had a score to settle with their former employer and the city that sentenced them to an unknown length of time in the notorious prison also known as the Keep.

It is believed that their knowledge of chemistry and other sciences aided in their creation of the violent plan to dismantle the city. How they communicated with OFP to execute their deadly plan is unknown as they were locked away when the violence started.

More to come on this story.

Ventana, Inc did not respond when asked for comment.

A quick search revealed no other publication had investigated the story further. Her suspicion was that Wilcott must have researched the four inmates, as they just did, and then selected them for the Task based on what he found.

She voiced her theory to Rudolfo.

"Maybe. But why these four?" He shook his head, not looking at her as he did. "I'd like to believe he would have indicated research like that in his journal, but I did not see any. So why choose these four to do this kind of research and no others?"

"Families of blast victims could have told him," she offered. "One of the guards here could have had a loved one killed in one of the attacks."

He squinted at her with crossed arms, his chin rested in the web of his thumb and forefinger.

"That article is conjecture at best." He pointed at the monitor behind her. "Brother Wilcott would require proof."

Francesca leaned back in her chair and steepled her fingers in front of her. She stared through them toward the wall, wondering what their next steps should be; wondering if any of it was worth pursuing at all. She had no idea where all this would lead them.

She turned back to the monitors. The results of her last search were displayed. Below the Bugle story, an article from the City Sun caught her eye. *Metro Police Bring Peace, OFP Eliminated.*

Out of curiosity, she clicked the link. It was about the last police raid on the OFP stronghold that resulted in a fierce battle claiming the lives of two officers and eight combatants. In the center of the article was a photograph of an officer being lifted into an ambulance, a wound in his side.

Below the picture there was a caption.

Detective Aaron Lewis, lead investigator in the OFP manhunt, seen here being taken to the hospital after suffering wounds in the battle with the terror group.

She had not noticed Rudolfo standing behind her until he spoke.

"We need to know what they know," he said. She looked over her shoulder at him then turned back to the screen. His eyes were locked on the photo of Detective Aaron Lewis.

20

Plans

Nicholas Fox leaned against a tree, one foot propped behind him, spinning a twig between his fingers and thumb.

His first plan had failed, that much was clear. He found it unlikely that he could secure another breather as easily as the first and equally unlikely that he could convince another inmate to commit murder. The Tappers were likely suspicious already. All they had to do was dig through video footage and put the pieces together. They were probably asking questions about the breather and the weapon and the obvious trap.

Not to worry, he thought. His backup plan was well under way. He just needed a few more recruits to go along with the plan.

He closed his eyes and tried to relax, allowing his chin to rest on his chest. He imagined himself somewhere else, anywhere else.

The harsh, pungent smell of sap wafted up from a newly felled pine tree twenty feet away. He could be camping, under the trees. He could be lying on his back on a cushy sleeping bag with a young woman next to him. She'd caress his chest while he stared at the blue sky through the branches overhead. It'd been a long hike that day; time to wind down.

"Hey, Prof!"

His eyes snapped open. The daydream vanished. Bad timing, he thought. These guys always had bad timing.

Footsteps crunched through pine needles and tree bark. He looked up to see a burly man approaching, olive skinned with tattoos covering most of his neck, face and head. The tattoos were a patchwork of violent symbols, letters, and numbers connected within a network of spider webs. There was no clear motif or theme. A clear patch sat on top of his skull with the standard barcode running down its center.

With his head still bent low, he greeted the leader of the Church Street Jackals.

"Hello, friend. Enjoying your day in the great outdoors?"

The man did not appreciate the humor.

"Don't have time for this shit, Prof. You have ten seconds to tell me why I'm here before I gut you, boy."

"Easy, Ko. No need to do any gutting today." He paused to make sure Ko was listening. "I need you to execute on our plan. Soon."

Ko took a step closer to Fox, standing a foot from him. The leader of the Jackals produced a ten-inch wooden stake from under his shirt and pressed its sharpened point against Fox's belly. Ko leaned in close and snarled, his breath stank of sardines overlaid with general halitosis.

"I told you I wasn't doing that." Ko gritted his teeth and pressed the point harder into Fox's belly. "It's a bullshit plan. Ain't no getting the other shot callers to go along with it."

Fox tried his best to steady his voice, but couldn't resist a hard, noisy swallow.

"Have you talked to your mother recently?" Fox's voice wavered. With trembling fingers, he produced a tiny earpiece from his pocket. Ko's eyes shot to the earpiece then back to Fox. The earpiece was the highest form of contraband, nearly impossible to sneak in and just as difficult to keep under wraps.

Fox handed the device to Ko. "Go ahead. Speak her number. Then ask her how she's doing."

The pressure on the wooden shiv softened, but Ko held it there while he did as Fox instructed. With the earpiece inserted, he spoke a ten-digit number. After a few seconds, his face fell and the leader of the Jackals took two steps backward with the stake at his side.

Fox exhaled a breath and watched as Ko spoke into the earpiece. His hard featured softened. He even smiled a few times.

Having the earpiece made conducting and executing his scheme far simpler. His employer had risked a great deal getting it to him, which meant moving quickly must be paramount.

Still speaking into the earpiece, Ko turned to look at Fox. He spoke in Spanish and it sounded as if he were asking his mother questions. The entire time, he stared at Fox with cold, hard eyes.

Finally, he raised a hand to his ear and removed the earpiece. The call was over.

"Good news?" Fox asked.

"Yes." Ko nodded. He turned his head and handed the earpiece back to Fox. "Yes. Let me know when you want to start and we'll be ready."

Fox did his best to smile sincerely. "That's," he cleared his throat then continued, "good to hear. I'll be in touch."

Ko grunted, turned and walked away, flinging the wooden shiv into the dirt as he went.

Fox had conducted a dozen of these conversations over the last two days; he was exhausted. These tough guys all melted when their mothers or wives or favorite aunt told them the good news: that they'd miraculously found huge sums of money in their bank accounts, and all their debt had been erased. At least gang leaders held true to one stereotype—family first.

Nicholas Fox had never studied riot behavior or mob mentality. His field of study had involved the less violent sides of human psychology. Based on what he knew about the human mind, however, he estimated that he would need at least eight percent of the prison population to riot in earnest before the rest would follow suit out of peer pressure or boredom.

To be safe, he wanted at least twelve percent of inmates rioting like savages in order to kick up the fervor of the others. If all of the gang leaders he spoke to followed through and their members did what they were told, that would give him somewhere in the neighborhood of nineteen percent. Plenty of wiggle room.

Fox still had no idea why a full-on prison riot was so important to his employer. He didn't care. The only thing that mattered was what came after—his own freedom.

And he'd kill every man and woman in the Keep to get it.

21

Convergence

Martin Aubrey was sitting on the sofa again. It had been his defacto quarters since he and Malina had moved their operation to the hotel.

He laid on his back, scrolling on the tablet to read and re-read the newly decoded messages.

This string of messages was sent just five days before the Ventana four were arrested and nearly three weeks after the Jorgetson child fell ill. The timing made no sense to Aubrey. And there had been no mention of One Front for the People or anything alluding to it.

He wished Ted could work faster.

Aubrey looked over the edge of the tablet. Malina stood at the room's narrow window, peering around the curtain. She scanned the street below and the buildings across from them, her head bobbing and turning to get a better look.

When he told her about the attack on Reynolds and his hunch that it, the ambush on him, and Grant's murder were connected, she went into a frenzy of activity. She placed discreet sensors in the hallway outside their room and in the lobby on the ground floor. She installed a worm in the hotel registration system that would alert them if anyone penetrated it looking for them. Lastly, she deployed three microdrones to hover over the building as sentries.

Once she had hacked the hotel computer system to install the worm, she linked the guest registry with the drones' AI. Anyone who entered the hotel whose facial recognition did not match someone already registered triggered an alert. The worm also compared every face entering the hotel with a rough description of the woman who attacked Aubrey. That too would trigger an alert.

"All the high-end tech you've put in place for security and you can't help but look out the window."

"It makes me feel better," she said, not turning around.

"If anyone out there sees you, they're going to find it suspicious. You've been at it for nearly twenty minutes."

With an audible grunt, she turned and fell back into the desk chair.

Aubrey watched her, she watched him back.

"Thoughts?" she asked.

Aubrey tossed the tablet onto the coffee table where it spun for several turns. "I should have been an accountant."

She gave him a wry smile. "I meant about the messages."

"Other than I wish we had more?" He raised his eyebrows and pointed his chin at the desk behind her. "How much longer do you think it will take Ted?"

"For the hundredth time, I don't know. What do you make of the latest ones?"

"You're right." He sat up. "Alkorn is applying pressure and the team has cold feet. I wonder what kind of leverage he had on them?"

"Financial or professional or personal. Or a combination of all three. Who knows?" Malina shrugged and crossed her arms. She then uncrossed them and fidgeted with a pen on the desk.

They were both getting antsy. The attacks, the hotel, the stress of not knowing answers to so many questions weighed on them. Had he and Malina known each other better, they'd probably be at each other's throats.

"And the words 'no choice' repeated twice," he said. "That, once again, points to an outside actor. Someone pulling the strings."

Malina stood and moved to the couch. She sat next to Aubrey and picked up the tablet from the coffee table. "So, this 'actor' applies pressure to Alkorn who in turn applies pressure to his team. Makes sense."

Aubrey sighed. "What did you find on the doctor?"

"Oh, I almost forgot." She moved back to the computer desk. "After considerable digging through the Nebular records, I found three doctors who had ordered the Stimuthera machine inside the timeframe we needed."

She pulled them up on screen. Aubrey saw three headshots. All male doctors past middle age.

"They all had multiple orders of the machine in that window. Two of them ordered over half a dozen each. The third doctor," she clicked once and two of the photos fell away, "ordered exactly two. Both within days of each other."

Aubrey straightened, suddenly attentive. "Before or after the Binns-Lourdes ordered theirs?"

"Before." She smiled.

"That lines up." He stood and began to pace a well-worn path. "Who is the doctor?"

"Doctor Randall McCalister."

"Any other connections for him?" He rubbed his chin against the rough stubble. He needed to shave. Against his hand he caught a whiff of his own breath—disgusting. How long had it been since he'd had a shower? He was suddenly concerned about his hygiene.

"Just one." He stopped fretting over himself and looked at her. She raised her eyebrows and tilted her head.

"What is it?" he said, his hand still on his chin.

"He's only had one patient for the last three-and-a-half years."

Her penchant for relishing in suspense would be something he'd have to get used to.

"Who?"

"James Sarazin."

* * *

Malina watched him as the news sank in. She herself wasn't sure what it meant, just that it meant something.

Aubrey's stony face was crowned by bunched eyebrows. He sat on the couch and leaned back slowly, resting his head on the back of the couch.

Inwardly, she thought that in this light at a certain angle …

"Shit!"

"What?" she said, startled, her head darting around looking for intruders.

"More answers just create more questions." He shook his fists and stood, resuming his pacing.

Malina crossed her arms and turned back to her computer. A flash of paranoia made her want to get up and look out the window again. She settled for checking the feed from her drones, knowing that she wouldn't be able to distinguish friend from foe from the window anyway.

The feeds showed her nothing unusual, as far as she could tell. She pulled up the worm program she'd installed in the hotel computer system. No alerts.

She turned back around to find Aubrey on the couch with his head in his hands.

"Any ideas?" she asked.

"Sarazin has his doctor treat these kids. Why?" He pulled his head out of his hands and stared at the wall. She got the impression he was speaking more to himself than to her. She answered him anyway.

"We know they were connected, had socialized in the past, and they were significant investors in his company." She stood. Now, it was her turn to pace. "He probably just wanted to help out. Like the Jorgetsons's nanny told you, they like to keep to themselves. They don't want their business out in the open."

"He sends his doctor to treat his friends' kids. So, he probably pays for all of it. Can you confirm that?"

She nodded and took three quick steps back to her chair at the desk. Her fingers flew across the keyboard. Behind her, Aubrey audibly continued his train of thought.

"His doctor, his money, and he has no idea that it's people at his own company causing it. He has no idea his trusted business partner is poisoning these children." The room filled with the clicks and clatter of the keyboard.

She scanned the financial records of Doctor Randall McCalister. His checking account from First Trinity Bank showed rows and rows of incoming deposits from an external account. The dollar amounts varied here and there, but on the last day of every month there appeared a payment of twenty-thousand dollars. Maybe it was a retainer.

Every deposit came from the same account.

On another screen, she clicked a red icon. Up popped a red dialog box. She entered several lines of code, one of which contained the account number. She clicked the launch button and waited.

Aubrey sat silent, apparently, lost in thought.

The pages fluttered in front of her with window after window cascading in front of one another. The program had scoured the internet for any occurrence of the account number she entered according to the parameters she gave it.

After some sorting, she found the page she was looking for—the account the payments came from was owned by a company, JS Holdings, LLC. Another quick search revealed JS Holdings' one and only owner, James Sarazin.

"Yep," she said. "Sarazin was paying the doctor through an LLC."

Aubrey didn't respond. She turned only to find him standing next to her. She had been so focused on the account search, she hadn't noticed him approaching her, now leaning over the desk next to her. He leaned in toward the far-left monitor. Squinting. Reading something.

"What?" she said.

"Ted."

"He got something? Let me see." She rolled her chair over to the first monitor. Aubrey hadn't moved. He stood hunched over her shoulders, his cheek against the side of her head. "Whoa. Way to go, Ted."

On the screen appeared white text in a window with a

black background. Ted had deciphered three days' worth of messages.

Date stamps told them when each set of codes had been sent. She read the messages.

Jan 16, 2043

Alkorn L: No comm out of this chat

Winthorpe S: We know

Imanpor R: Q Are we safe

Alkorn L: Yes

Winthorpe S: Q we are doing this

Alkorn L: Yes

Winthorpe S: Q Certain

Alkorn L: Dead certain

Jan 17, 2043

Shoeman N: Q Plan

Alkorn L: Get what we need first cant move on without it

Shoeman N: Q Then

Alkorn L: do what we must no choice

Jan. 23, 2043

Alkorn L: Do nothing say nothing Families at risk

Shoeman N: What have we done

Imanpor R: Q Trust his threats

Alkorn L: Yes very much

Winthorpe S: What now

Alkorn L: Prison and wait and say nothing do nothing

"Three days' worth. Way to go, Ted," she said, pumping a fist through the air.

"Let's celebrate later," Aubrey said, placing a hand on her shoulder and standing up straight. "What are the Qs for?"

"Probably indicating they're questions. Punctuation must not count as a character in the book cipher."

She looked up at him, he nodded his understanding.

"Look at this one." He reached out and pointed at the third line from the message sent on January 16th. "'Are we safe?' The team was getting cold feet again."

"Not getting it again." She reached out and pointed at the date. "Martin, that's the first group of messages they sent. January 16. They had cold feet from the get go."

"And Alkorn is in command from the get go." He pointed again. "'We are doing this?'" He moved his finger down. "'Dead certain.'"

"A threat?" Malina asked.

"Sounds like it. Then, here," he pointed the next group of messages from January 17. "'Get what we need', 'do what we must, no choice'. There's that 'no choice' crap again. No choice my ass."

"What did they need?"

"Money, I would assume. The scheme would have been in full motion at that point. They were probably waiting for the cash to accumulate before moving ahead."

She nodded and re-read the last group of messages, the last messages any of them sent. "'Do nothing, say nothing, families at risk'. Whoever had leverage on them made sure they didn't talk to anyone once they were caught."

"That's him. Whoever started all this, that's him, right there." Aubrey leaned against the desk next to her. "Anyone who can orchestrate the murder of hundreds of innocent people and the poisoning of children could certainly keep a bunch of scientists quiet."

The thought sent chills down her arms. She rubbed the goose bumps away with her hands. The invisible force was out there, the voice as Aubrey called him, pulling strings and applying pressure. Aubrey was right, he had killed hundreds and there was no indication he would stop.

"Why is he working so fast all of a sudden?"

She snapped her head around, the question caught her off guard. "What? Who?"

"Ted." Aubrey had his hand on his chin.

"Oh. Well, he's learning." She reached out and patted the little box that held the brains of her computer and Ted. "We should get the messages faster from here on."

"Good. We're close. We're really close. Hopefully the rest of the messages will ..." Aubrey trailed off.

Malina turned to face him. He stared at his phone; his brow had furrowed in deep crevices.

* * *

Aubrey had never seen the number before. The area code was unfamiliar. Thinking it must be a crank call or telemarketer, he almost hung up. Something told him he should answer it. Aaron Lewis was the only one who had the number to Aubrey's burner phone.

"Hello," he answered.

"Mr. Aubrey?" said a man's voice on the other end, hard and steady. "Detective Aaron Lewis gave me this number." A pause. The worst possible scenario ran through Aubrey's mind—Lewis kidnapped, tortured, held captive until Aubrey gave himself up to the killer that hunted them.

Aubrey said nothing. He tried to steady his breath and calm the jackhammer in his chest.

The man continued. "I have information that may help you, Mr. Aubrey. And I believe you have information that may help me."

Aubrey placed the phone on speaker and held it out. "What kind of information?"

"I do not think it is wise to speak over the phone. We must meet in person."

He looked at Malina, who held her hands out and shrugged.

He turned back to the phone. "I'm not going anywhere if you don't tell me what this is about."

A pause, then the man continued. "Years ago, you were the lead detective on a case. A man had killed his wife, her lover and a third unfortunate soul. I believe he used a hammer. Do you remember the case?"

Aubrey knew the case. Victor Hamburg. Triple homicide. A jealous husband and a hammer. A nightmarish scene of carnage. "Of course, I remember. What does that …"

"At the trial," the man interrupted, "there was a man in the back of the courtroom. Do you remember him?"

Aubrey placed a hand to his forehead, massaging his temples. "Look, sir, I don't know what you're getting at. How would I remember one man in a courtroom from a trial six years ago?"

"This man was quite memorable, Mr. Aubrey. Surely, you remember him."

Aubrey's head shot up. He felt his eyes widen; the room blurred. His lungs refused to draw breath.

The man dressed in black. The man no person would go near.

The Tapper. Death was in the courtroom that day.

Aubrey never found out why he was there; Tappers rarely showed their faces in public and had never been seen in a courtroom. He assumed the Tapper was there to execute the defendant on the spot, but he only observed, as Aubrey did.

"You?"

"Me, yes, Mr. Aubrey. Can we meet?"

Aubrey finally took a breath.

"Yes, we can meet."

"Good. Please come to my place of business. I will ensure your passage. Come now. We'll be waiting for you and we have much to discuss."

* * *

Jacira Barretto saw her tablet flash to life from the floor in a bhujangasana pose, spine arched, head back. An adagio blasted from invisible speakers.

Standing, she moved to the bed where her tablet sat. It was an alert triggered by the trace she'd placed on Aaron Lewis's phone. Apparently, it had come in ten minutes ago, but she hadn't seen nor heard the notification.

"Shit."

She tapped her watch to silence the music. The alert told her the incoming call came from somewhere odd. She knew the number but found it exceedingly strange that it was calling Aaron Lewis.

She listened to a recording of the call. She listened to it once more. Not to hear the words, but to hear the voice. Who was that?

She closed her eyes and played it again, letting her mind absorb the cadence of the words and the pitch of the voice. The sounds penetrated the far reaches of her memory, bounced around until they landed on a match.

It made sense, now. The strange number and the voice.

"Shit," she whispered, staring at the floor, putting the pieces together in her mind.

Her tablet pinged her again, interrupting her chain of thought. She tapped the notification. Facial recognition sensors had captured the face of Aubrey's unknown female helper leaving a hotel.

Frantically, she tapped several commands on her tablet to pull up street camera footage for the location the woman had been spotted. She watched the woman leave the Silk Princess Hotel. Next to her walked Martin Aubrey.

They each had a shoulder bag and walked fast.

More pieces came together in her mind. The voice on the recorded call to Lewis, then these two headed somewhere. As unlikely as it seemed to her, she knew exactly where they were going.

"Shit," she said for the third time. She typed a short message to her employer telling him they needed to talk.

A moment later the phone rang. She answered before the first ring ended.

"He's on the move," she said without preamble.

"You found him?"

"Sort of. But I have a hunch where he's going."

"So, get there and take care of him. Why do I have to tell you this?" He sounded impatient.

"Their destination is why I wanted to speak to you. It's ... well, I don't know why they're going there, but I thought you should know."

He cleared his throat. "Where are they going?" His voice had calmed. She thought she could hear something like anxiety in it.

"They're going to the Copp- ... to the Keep." Silence on the line. "I have reason to believe they were contacted by a ... a Tapper. And I think they're on their way to meet with him at the Keep."

More silence, no noise at all. She wondered if the man was still there. She was about to confirm he was still on the phone when he broke the silence.

"Okay. Okay." He breathed into the phone. "I need you to meet me somewhere. I'll give you more instructions when you arrive."

"Meet?" She avoided meeting clients if at all possible; it was better for everyone involved—safer, cleaner. "Are you sure that's wise, sir?"

A heavy breath into the phone. "Yes, I'm sure. I will send you the location after we hang up. Be there in ten minutes."

The call ended. A second later, her phone pinged. The secure message had the location information—the address and where to meet him when she arrived at the building. She read it several times to ensure she wasn't mistaken. She knew the location, though she'd never been inside it, much less to the roof.

She changed clothes, packed a few tools for the likely job ahead and jogged out of her building.

* * *

Wise Brother and Member Principal Jacobi dialed the numbers into his phone. It was a call he dreaded. He had hoped all this was behind him and now it felt like it might explode in his face.

Jacobi had to let him know. He also wanted to be told what to do. This sort of work was not his specialty. The deception and corruption made him uneasy. He had just started to relax when Sister Jocelyn came calling, asking about why Rudolfo was investigating Wilcott's Selection of an inmate from her ward, was he under special orders from Jacobi.

Much was at stake now and he wanted more than ever for it all to end, to go away for good.

With trembling fingers, he pressed the green send button on the touchscreen. The line picked up a moment later.

"Yes," a man's voice said. A loud rustling in the receiver forced Jacobi to pull the phone away from his ear. "Yes?" the voice said louder.

"Um, yes, it's Jacobi. We may have a problem."

"What sort of problem?" the man said, near shouting. More rustling in the phone. More like wind, Jacobi thought. Wind blowing into the phone. Jacobi was surprised the man could hear him.

"Someone is asking questions. Questions about our ... our mutual friend."

A pause, more wind on the other man's end. Where was he? On a boat?

"Don't worry." The man shouted this time and Jacobi jerked the phone away from his ear again. "I'm coming to you. We can discuss further after I arrive."

Jacobi's throat tightened. He involuntarily swallowed. "What ... um, to me? You're coming here?"

"Yes. Prepare the rooftop for my arrival," the man said. The line went dead.

Jacobi stared mystified at the phone. He's coming here? Why? What could possibly bring him here?

The dread he felt before the call now intensified to a full panic inside Jacobi.

* * *

Nicholas Fox, the Professor, daydreamed.

It was Sunday, an entire day of free-time. Most inmates spent their time in one of the rec rooms, playing cards, or reading. Nicholas would usually engage in one or more of those activities, but today, with freedom so close, he dreamed about the future.

He sat on a rolled-up blanket, slouched against the wall of his cell.

In his mind he lay on a beach. His hair shoulder length like it was before prison, colored a deep chestnut. Would it still be the same color? He hadn't seen it in so many years it was probably silver by now.

A different woman laid by his side this time. They sunbathed with mojitos in sweaty glasses propped up in the white sand. Salt spray blew over them from time to time. The perfectly blue sea sang its steady song as waves collapsed against the sand.

Labored breathing invaded his brain. He opened his eyes and looked over to see Warren Samuels sitting next to him, breathing like a pug through hairy nostrils. The squatty little man squinted in concentration, totally absorbed in a paperback novel that must have been a hundred years old. Yellow pages on the verge of crumbling to dust were stuck between faded, barely recognizable covers.

He stared at his loyal henchman, wondering what was in store for him after it all started. Warren's friendship was a necessity in the Keep. On the outside, Fox had no room for him. They'd have to part ways. If either of them survived.

Leaning his head back against the wall, Fox attempted to

ignore pudgy Warren and get back to his fantasy. Then, he felt a vibration between his legs.

He nudged Warren to get his attention, then pointed his chin toward the doorway. They were alone for the moment and he needed to keep it that way for a little longer. Warren stood and moved to the doorway, leaning against one side of the frame with an arm stretched across it.

Nicholas reached into his pants and removed the earpiece from its hiding place. He pushed it into his ear opposite the door and tapped a small button on its side.

"Yes," he said, still sitting.

"Now," a voice said. "It has to be now."

Nicholas froze. This was the call he'd been waiting for. "Give me an hour."

"You have it."

"What happens after? How will you get me out?" Nicholas asked in a whisper.

"Let me worry about that," the voice said.

A beep told Fox the call had ended. He placed the phone back in his pants and stared at Warren, whose bulk filled the lower half of the door frame.

"Warren?"

"Yes, boss," Warren Samuels replied without turning around.

"Time to get started."

* * *

Jacira exited her car, which sped off into the river of automated traffic to park itself somewhere nearby. She looked up at the massive building and did her best not to look impressed.

Her philosophy was simple: always appear as though you are supposed to be wherever you are and people will usually assume as much.

She followed the instructions her employer had given her, bypassing security to an elevator off the lobby. She almost missed it; the doors were made up to blend in with the granite and glass walls.

Just as she stepped in front of it, the doors whispered open. A large man with black hair and three chins stood inside. He wore a black uniform. No badges or labels. This guy was muscle. He glared at her. She stepped in.

After a short, quick ride the doors opened onto a plain, gray walled hallway with dingy ceiling tiles overhead. She stepped out and looked around. The hallway had a door at each end.

"Go right," grunted the man behind her. She turned to look at him and he jerked a thumb to his right, then pressed a button inside the elevator closing the doors.

She walked to the door at the end of the hall on the right and opened it. She stepped out onto the roof of the one-hundred-fifteen-story building. Wind and sun assaulted her in equal measure. The former pushing the door with such force that it almost sent her tumbling backward back into the stale hallway.

Muscling the door open, she stepped out onto the roof. Gravel crunched under her black boots. She shielded her eyes from the blinding sun and scanned her surroundings.

She had come out from one corner of the building's roof. Other than the hallway behind her which protruded from the roof like an out of place block, the roof of Ventana Tower was completely flat.

On the far side, fifty feet from her, a winged aircraft sat atop a helipad platform several feet above the gravelly surface. The aircraft resembled a long white cigar with sharp ends and a flat bottom. Two long fins jutted out from its tail at ninety degrees from each other and short thin wings held large rotors inside metal rings. The rotors buffeted the ground as they idled.

She recognized the craft as one popular among the wealthy elites, but she couldn't put her finger on the make or model.

Through the craft's windows she saw several people already seated inside behind what appeared to be a pilot. A door stood open near the tail; steps trailed down to the helipad.

Taking the open door as an invitation, she jogged to the aircraft and bounded up the steps. When her head breached the door, she froze.

Seated in plush white leather seats facing her on either side of the central aisle were two people. They were both dressed in black fatigues with black gloves covering their hands. Their eyes were as cold as Jacira felt.

These were the people her employer told her about. These were the people like her.

With an air of caution, she stepped into the aisle and took a seat across from a woman about her age. Long red curls fell across her shoulders contrasted against the pale white of her skin. The curls caught the sunlight. She would have been considered beautiful were she not so obviously full of venom.

The woman looked vaguely familiar, unlike the large, barrel-chested black man across the aisle; him Jacira knew well. His black curls were thicker now, a little grayer, and his face fuller, but there was no mistaking Balthazar.

He was a man she'd known in her former life. They had traveled like paths, but Jacira hadn't realized to what degree they were similar until now.

He gave her a sideways glance, then turned his gaze forward again. A flicker of a grin crossed his face.

When it came to killers, her employer obviously had a type.

The cockpit door slid open and a man's head emerged. He sat in the pilot's seat; the rest of the cockpit was empty.

Upon seeing his face, Jacira's insides jolted. She knew this man, knew him well. Everyone in the city knew him. He was the wealthiest person in the city, one of the wealthiest people in the world. His company had changed the lives of millions, for better or worse.

His most important claim to fame, of course, was Zentransa, the sleep-eliminating pill.

"We'll be there in ten minutes," he said. The voice matched the one she'd heard on the phone so many times.

He slid the cockpit door shut and the aircraft lifted off. With James Sarazin at the controls.

22

Descent

Inside the gleaming white train, Martin Aubrey stared out across the sea of green tree tops wondering what waited for them at the end of the line.

The man from the phone, the Tapper, had kept his first promise—a pass to board the train was waiting for them when they arrived. Whether he kept the rest of his promises remained to be seen.

They brought everything they could carry in the event they'd need to share evidence or search the mountains of documents and data they already had. Ted continued working back at the hotel, wirelessly connected to the tablet in her bag. They prepaid for the entire week at the hotel so no matter where they ended up, Ted could keep working.

"You sure that thing will work inside the Keep," Aubrey asked when they left the hotel. If Ted cracked another batch of messages, he wanted to be alerted right away.

"Pretty sure," she'd said. "If anything, I can stick a repeater near a window. Then, I'd get a signal anywhere within a few thousand feet."

On the train, she monitored Ted's progress on the rest of the messages, checking and rechecking her tablet. Aubrey looked at her every time she did, hoping there was news, but every time she'd simply shake her head and slide her tablet back into her bag.

He felt sure that the next batch would contain all the remaining messages.

"What do you think they have?" she said ten minutes into the train ride.

"I don't know." Aubrey sighed. "If they have information at all."

From the corner of his eye, he saw her shocked look. She leaned in close. "Martin, if you think we're walking into a trap, you need to tell me."

"I don't know what we're walking into." He turned toward her and suddenly felt like bringing her was a mistake. "Somebody at that prison wanted those scientists dead. Then, the guy that killed them dies. And all of a sudden, we get an invitation out there to have a chat? I don't know what it is, but I do know we should meet him."

Her eyes grew wider. "Martin, I told you I'm not a field person. There is a reason, a very good one—I sit behind a screen all day. I'm not good with people and I'm certainly not good in tense situations with people."

He placed a reassuring hand on her arm. "I'll be there, don't worry. And I don't know what's going to happen, just be ready for anything."

She glanced at his hand and turned away.

"What's the plan anyway?" she said, not facing him.

"Plan?" He shrugged. "Well, we hear what they have to say. And if we feel like it, we tell them what we know." Aubrey leaned in toward Malina. "If this guy is legit, then he's been digging into this thing from his side. I have no idea what kind of investigation he's conducted, but it could be the answers we need. It could help us crack this thing wide open."

* * *

Malina's eyes traced up the dark monolith towering over them as the train entered the brightly lit archway in the prison's side. It was like a gaping wound in an otherwise perfectly symmetrical and featureless edifice.

"Is it just like you left it?" she asked.

Aubrey grunted. "Something like that. I don't think this place changes very much."

Aubrey told her about his interview with Alkorn and his team soon after they'd met, and it was one of the major reasons she agreed to help him.

Malina searched their surroundings. Receiving platforms, separated by block walls, passed on their left as the train entered the prison's hull and began to slow. The last, and largest, platform came into view, nearly empty. She assumed this was where workers embarked and disembarked everyday.

The train halted with a soft bump, the doors slid open, and passengers shuffled from their seats to the doors. Aubrey got Malina's attention and jerked his head toward the platform. For a moment, she didn't move; sitting with her hands gripping the seat in front of her. She'd convinced herself that coming to the Keep was a good idea, but now that she was here...

Aubrey stood in the aisle waiting, a hand out. She took one

deep breath, then two, grabbed her bag, stood, and together they disembarked the train.

Several shut doors stood on the back wall a hundred feet away. The rest of the passengers were milling toward the one open door on the far left.

"I just realized I have no idea where to go from here," Aubrey said.

The two of them stood in silence, then as one, they noticed a pair of forms standing against the wall far away on their right. The two Tappers wore long, form fitting black cloaks. Cassocks, she remembered they were called.

"I guess that's the welcoming committee," she said.

"Come on, let's go." Aubrey started toward the Tappers and Malina followed.

* * *

The shadowy figures did not move or speak as Aubrey and Malina approached. Ten feet from them, Aubrey stopped.

There was no mistaking the man in front of him. He was in the courtroom six years ago, frightening all in attendance. His hair had grown a good deal grayer since then, but it was him—Aubrey had no doubt. The woman next to him shocked Aubrey. He had never considered the that there might be female Tappers, but here stood one. There must be more.

She was young, no more than twenty-four or twenty-five. In any other circumstances, she would be considered quite beautiful with her platinum hair and soft features. Her youth fascinated him. How early did these people start their training? How young did they begin killing?

"My name is Rudolfo." The male Tapper spoke. His voice

matched the one Aubrey heard on the phone an hour before. "I am a Member of the Order of the Coppice and this is my Apprentice, Francesca. It was I who called you."

Aubrey nodded. "I didn't realize there would be two of you." When neither Rudolfo nor Francesca offered an apology or explanation, Aubrey continued. "Yeah, well, this is Malina Maddox." He gestured toward his partner. "She's been helping me with the investigation."

"An unsanctioned investigation." Rudolfo's face held no expression. Much like the exterior of the Keep, it gave no impression as to what exactly happened inside, only that you'd be advised to stay away.

Aubrey gave Malina a sideways glance. It was a statement of fact, less an admonishment or an accusation. It had the tone of something close to respect but well short of admiration.

"I imagine it's about as sanctioned as your investigation."

Rudolfo's face remained unchanged, but he nodded. As if the short exchange between the two men were some sort of binding treaty, Rudolfo turned and beckoned the others to follow.

He led them through a gray door and down a long hallway where the sounds of mechanical equipment thrummed behind double doors and the cold, crisp air smelled of sterilizing ions.

"How often are outsiders allowed in here?" Aubrey asked after several quiet minutes.

"Almost never." Rudolfo spoke loud enough for the others to hear but did not turn toward them when he spoke.

Aubrey knew what that meant. They weren't allowed to be here. Either a very special exception was made for them or nobody knew. He guessed nobody knew. This Tapper risked a hell of a lot to bring them here, which meant he either really cared about his investigation or he wanted Aubrey there for other reasons.

Rudolfo walked fast, even for Aubrey's six-foot frame. Glancing over his shoulder, Aubrey saw Malina nearly jogging to keep up, her sneakers slapping the painted concrete floor.

At a set of elevator doors, Rudolfo stopped. He reached for a button on the wall, when Aubrey grabbed his forearm. With a look of confusion, the first human expression Aubrey had seen the man make, Rudolfo glared at him.

"Where are we going?" Aubrey asked.

"Somewhere we can talk."

"Where?" Aubrey let go of the man's arm but continued staring back at him.

"To my ward. We will have privacy there."

"Your ward? Won't there be inmates there?"

The Tapper tilted his head. "Yes, of course there will be inmates there. This is a prison, Mr. Aubrey."

In a way, Aubrey appreciated the sarcastic tone from Rudolfo. It meant the man was human, he was flawed.

"Well, what about *us*?" Aubrey gestured covertly toward Malina, who seemed not to notice. She was still catching her breath from the long, fast walk.

Rudolfo straightened. "You will have us." He placed a hand on his own chest. "It will be more than enough protection, you'll find. And there will be guards posted along the ward." Rudolfo punched the button next to the steel doors and a second later they opened.

With a look toward Malina, Aubrey stepped inside. Malina

and the two Tappers followed.

* * *

Francesca boarded the elevator last. She had said nothing upon meeting the two visitors and now looking at their reflections in the polished metal doors, she tried to imagine what they must be thinking.

The woman with Martin Aubrey seemed confident and probably a formidable opponent when cornered. Behind the purposely disheveled hair and careless attire, she exuded a dogged determination.

Martin Aubrey carried himself like a cop through and through, whether he officially wore a badge or not. She knew he pursued this investigation without pay and without orders. Aaron Lewis had made that clear. Brother Rudolfo would have never had the notion to bring him here were he not certain the man was just as committed to finding the truth as he.

The elevator halted with a bump. Francesca led the way off and into the outer passageway.

"This is the outermost passageway," she said. She glanced at her Mentor. Rudolfo's expression told her she had his blessing to keep speaking. "There are four passageways forming concentric rings around this floor of the facility. There are four hallways, or corridors that divide the floor into symmetric quarters. Each floor is divided into two wards."

The group approached a corridor and the woman, Malina, gasped.

"What is that?" she asked, pointing down the corridor

toward the central column of open air.

"That is the Great Atrium," Francesca explained. "It runs the entire height of the prison from just above the train platform to the glass ceiling over the top floor."

As they stood gawking at the massive, open air tube in the center of the complex, a group of four inmates turned a corner from an interior passageway. One caught sight of Malina and Aubrey and turned toward them, his eyes fixed on Malina. He was pale and thin, not more than five-foot-six. He walked toward Malina and called back to his friends.

"Hey, boys! We got visitors. Let's show them around." He smoothed the front of his white prison uniform and rubbed his shaved head as if smoothing back a rich mane of hair.

The others turned to follow their mate and began quietly cat-calling toward Malina, who was visibly uneasy. She backed away toward Aubrey, who then stepped forward between her and the inmates.

Ten feet away the inmates suddenly froze, all signs of bravado melting away like wax in a hot fire. They bent their heads, some using their hands to shield their eyes, muttered apologies, and slinked away in the opposite direction.

Malina and Aubrey looked at Francesca. The inmates hadn't noticed her and Rudolfo until just that moment.

"See," Francesca said, "you have us."

Aubrey nodded and looked at Malina, still shaken. "Come on," he said to Malina, then motioned to Francesca that they could move on.

She led them further down the long passageway.

Outside the observation room, Francesca and Rudolfo stopped. She extended a hand, inviting them to enter.

Inside, she watched Malina go right to the monitors on

the long table. Aubrey pointed to a chair with a questioning look toward her and Rudolfo.

"Please," Rudolfo said and Aubrey sat.

Malina turned back to the group and the four of them sat around the wooden table. Atop the table sat Wilcott's journal.

"So," Aubrey said, crossing his arms, "what have you got for us?"

* * *

Stepping out of the aircraft onto the roof of the Coppice was a surreal experience for Jacira. Her former life had been spent, in large part, inside this damnable place. She spent years trying to leave, now her new life brought her back.

She owed a great deal to her time here. Her skills were varied and honed here. The ease with which she removed the breath from a person's body had been refined here.

Nevertheless, she didn't feel right being back here.

The others exited the craft behind her. Looking back at them, she couldn't see any of her own misgivings in their faces. Surely, they felt it too, she thought. They must. This place had been hell for all of them.

She shouldered her bag and followed James Sarazin to a nearby hatch in the roof. She had no idea the hatch existed or the helipad for that matter. Both may have been installed after her time, but then again, there would have been no reason for her to know they existed.

The helipad was off to one side of the circular roof, well clear of the glass ceiling. The aircraft idled down to a dull howl before falling silent.

Through the open hatch, thirty feet in front of them, a head emerged. The man had silver hair and pudgy cheeks; his light eyes squinted against the harsh sunlight before fixing first on Sarazin, then on Jacira and the two others.

Cold recognition peeled away the man's soft expression. His face froze between bewilderment and rage. With a stern look at Sarazin, the man disappeared down the hatchway.

After descending from the roof, the group found themselves in a room filled with mechanical equipment—air handlers, electrical boxes, cables traveling down through the floor.

Following the silver haired man dressed in the traditional black cassock, they passed through a door into a familiar space. The massive circular room with a floor and roof made of glass was a space Jacira never thought she'd see again.

Looking down into the bowels of the prison, her gut tightened. At least this time it was her choice to be here.

"Wait here," Sarazin said. "I have to speak with Jacobi."

She and the others nodded and watched Sarazin strut across the glass floor to where Member Principal Jacobi stood smoldering. When Sarazin reached him, Jacobi verbally berated the man. She couldn't make out what was said, but the nonverbal clues were indication enough. His hands flew around like serpents lashing out. Many times, he pointed back at Jacira and the others then down at the prison.

Sarazin remained stoic. He listened to the man and made no reaction, then spoke. When he finished, Jacobi seemed to melt into a more compliant state. His shoulders sagged, he stared at the glass floor and he shook his head softly.

Jacobi left Sarazin for a moment to enter a room behind

him. Shortly after, he emerged with a stack of white linens.

"Weird to be back," Balthazar said, his deep voice breaking the silence between the three of them. His hulking form looked almost too big to be held by the glass floor.

The red-haired woman said nothing.

Jacira nodded.

Sarazin rejoined them with the stack of white linens, tossing them to the floor.

"Put these on so you'll blend in," he said, turning to walk back toward Jacobi.

Jacira realized the linens were uniforms, inmate uniforms.

"I don't do white," Jacira said. Sarazin stopped and turned.

"It'll help you blend in. You'll need it," he said.

"We're going down there?" Balthazar pointed at the prison below.

"Yes."

"We have hair," Jacira said. "And no barcodes, no ID numbers. We might as well go down there like this." She gestured to her outfit. "We're never going to blend in."

Sarazin regarded the three of them and inhaled a deep breath. "Everyone will be too distracted, don't worry. But you'd be noticed like this." He waved a hand at them, indicating their clothes. "The uniforms aren't foolproof, but it'll go a long way. Trust me."

"Distracted?" Balthazar asked, but Sarazin had already turned to cross the floor once again toward Jacobi sulking on the far side.

Jacira stripped to her skivvies and protective vest. Whatever the distraction was supposed to be, she felt confident it would involve violence. Violence in prison meant blades.

She reached into her bag and pulled two rolls of thin

material ribbed with stiff panels. Unrolling each she strapped them to her upper thighs, protecting her femoral arteries. She pulled out two smaller versions and wrapped them around her biceps.

"Got any more of those?" Balthazar said, as he removed his own clothing. He also had on a protective vest.

"No."

* * *

As Member Principal Jacobi rambled on with his complaints about the three unexpected guests, James Sarazin nodded. He had to placate the man for now. He did his best to give the impression of concern for the man's objections.

"I just don't understand, James. Why them? Couldn't you find any other killers in a city with millions of people?" Jacobi gritted his teeth and pointed at the three of them across the room. "They don't belong here. Their very presence is an insult ..."

James tuned him out. He'd perfected the art of tuning people out during countless conference room meetings over the course of his career. Jacobi was just another dissatisfied partner. He would object at first, then slowly realize he had no choice in the matter. That was another skill of James's—convincing others they were stuck. That they had no choice. That they would do what must be done.

James watched the man gesticulate, reasserting his point again and again. The veins in his neck bulged, protruding so far above his skin that James thought it might be possible to kill the man by simply grabbing ahold of one and squeezing.

He'd never killed anyone in person. The notion made him

curious. Was he capable? Of course, he was capable. But much like running a business, it was best to hire others to do the dirty work.

At the end of this day, he would do what he had to do. If that meant making a personal, gruesome goodbye for his old friend Jacobi, so be it.

"I obviously recognize them. Did you think I wouldn't? Did they tell you about their time here? They must have." Jacobi shook his head. His jowls vibrated and rippled like a pond in the wind.

James nodded some more. He wondered how long he'd have to hold that vein before Jacobi would pass out, how long until brain damaged started, how long until the man would suck in his last rattling lungful of air.

He understood the man's complaints. He even empathized with him. Were James in his shoes, he'd feel the same way. It was a disrespectful intrusion. James understood. He just didn't care.

Pushing people off balance was another skill. How to get the job done while also adding a little bit of an extra advantage for yourself was the mark of efficiency. James had always been exceedingly efficient.

"I just don't understand how, of all the people you could bring here, you'd pick …" Jacobi eyes widened. His face fell. "Unless …" He stared at James slack-jawed, his face growing pale. He pointed a shaky finger at James who was tempted to bend it back on itself. "You did it on purpose," he whispered. "You knew and you brought them here for some twisted reason. Was it to spite me? I thought we were partners in all of this."

James held up a hand. That had always been his move. Stay

quiet and let the other person come to the conclusion on their own, then throw up the hand. Everyone who knew him well knew that the hand meant all discussion would now cease. It was time for James to talk and time for them to listen.

"I brought them here because they are the best at what they do. And I need the best today." True enough, he thought. "And yes, we are still partners." True for now. "I didn't bring them for any other purpose than cleaning up this mess. The rest is an unfortunate coincidence." Not true.

"Okay, okay." Jacobi's eyes fell. He nodded softly.

"I need to brief them. You don't have to talk to them if you don't want to. In fact, it might be best for you to go back to your quarters."

"Yes. Yes, good idea," Jacobi muttered.

James left Jacobi and strode across the glass floor toward the assassins; as he crossed, he looked down into the prison. It was like looking into the gullet of some foul creature. The three assassins he brought had been spit out by the beast, but now they were back. They'd been forever sullied by it, and it bound them to the place. They could leave, but it would always call them back.

James also thought about how fortuitous this day turned out to be. By the time he left, all of the loose ends would be tied up. When he boarded his plane alone later that night, he would be free of all this mess.

No one would know the truth but him. His life, his fortune, his legacy would remain secure.

A terrorist was not something he ever imagined he'd end up becoming. He only started acting like one out of necessity. Now, however, if he really thought about it, he enjoyed it.

And, like everything else he'd tried in life, he excelled at it.

23

Eruption

Brother Rudolfo slid the thick book across the table to Aubrey. The Tapper's hands remained on the book and his eyes locked on Aubrey's.

"Mr. Aubrey, no one outside our Order has ever seen what is inside one of these books. It's a journal of every assessment of every inmate that has been under a Member's charge. This is essentially a summary of a Member's life. All that he or she has done."

Aubrey's skin prickled. How many deaths were recorded in this tome? He knew the Tappers didn't execute every inmate, but he had no idea how many they left alive either.

He reached out and took the heavy book from Rudolfo. Before opening it, he said, "Why are you showing me this?"

Rudolfo asked Aubrey to examine a few random pages toward the front of the Tapper's book. He then showed Aubrey the last four entries.

It clicked for Aubrey instantly. Four pages, totally blank except for their inmate numbers. Uncharacteristic of the Tapper in question, that was obvious. Four pages for four inmates. Was it *the* four?

"What happened to these four inmates?" Aubrey bent over the book, glaring at Rudolfo through narrowed eyes.

"They were selected for the Sacred Task," Francesca replied.

"What is that?" Malina asked.

"It means they were Tapped," Aubrey continued, glaring at Rudolfo. "When?"

"April 29th," Rudolfo said.

For a moment, no one spoke. Aubrey saw Malina through the corner of his eye looking from him to Rudolfo.

"Oh, shit." She jabbed a finger at the book. "This is them. The Ventana four. This is their record."

"Was it you?" Aubrey said in a low voice.

Rudolfo shook his head.

Aubrey sat back in the chair and crossed his arms. "Where is he? Where is the Tapper that did this?" It seemed unlikely that the Tapper in question was the puppet master, merely a puppet. But if they could get to him and question him, it could lead them to the man, the voice.

"Brother Wilcott, Member of the Order, is dead," Rudolfo said with no emotion. "He self-selected weeks ago."

"Self-selected?" Malina asked. Aubrey had been thinking the same thing, but he had a hunch what it meant.

"Brother Wilcott selected himself for the Sacred Task; performing it, with some variations," Rudolfo shifted in his seat, "on himself."

"Why did he kill himself?" Aubrey asked.

"I believe Brother Wilcott wanted us to figure that out."

"What makes you say that?" Aubrey leaned forward, resting his elbows on the table.

"He self-selected in a very public manner." Rudolfo stared

at the wall. His voice had gone quiet. "He made himself a display, in front of the inmates. He looked at me just before he did it, I think, to convey some kind of request of me. I want to fulfill that request." His voice trailed off; his face grew blank.

Francesca finished his thoughts for him. "That, plus the blank pages and several more ..." She looked around, apparently searching for the right words, "irregularities led us to believe there was something more."

"Irregularities?" Aubrey and Malina asked the question in unison.

Rudolfo didn't speak as Francesca explained all they had discovered. Four inmates selected in a single day was not only unheard of, but impossible. She told them about the Taint, the effect their killing potion, as Aubrey thought of it, had on a Member's body, physically incapacitating them for a short time.

They believed he used a glove to shield himself from the solution. She went on to explain the taboo nature of this decision. This sacrilegious act would be inexcusable for any Member and would only have been done out of extreme desperation. Someone had pressured him.

Of the four scientists, one was female belonging to an all-female ward not under Wilcott's purview. Members were basically allowed to do anything they wanted, including killing inmates from another ward, but the practice was not common and not well-liked.

Finally, all three male prisoners were assigned to Wilcott's ward on the same day. The ward was already near capacity but assigned to him anyway. Wilcott would have had some degree of influence over assignments and could have prevented it.

"Once we realized their deaths were connected here, we checked on their lives out there." Francesca gestured to the walls. "We saw the stories about the bombings, the child poisonings, and that group One Front for the People. In the midst of all that we saw a picture of your friend Aaron Lewis."

"And he led us to you," Rudolfo said in a low voice. He hadn't spoken throughout Francesca's description of their investigation. Aubrey had the sense he was deeply disturbed by all of it. "And now you are here." He lowered a flat hand to the tabletop.

Aubrey cleared his throat. It was time to return the favor and share the information he had gathered while working with the police and everything he and Malina had uncovered in the weeks since he left the hospital.

First, he told them what he knew about the scientists' arrest for stealing from their company, Ventana, Inc. Despite being paid very well and most of the them having amassed considerable wealth over their careers, the entire team was somehow convinced to embezzle millions of dollars. Alkorn held lost money due to a bad gambling habit but still had plenty of cash savings and other assets. The team used a program that took fractions of pennies from various transactions throughout the company's business lines.

The last raid, when Aubrey and the police battled the OFP bombers, they found no evidence linking OFP to the scientists, but they also found no evidence linking the bombers to BSS. The police still held the belief that the OFP men killed in Aubrey's firefight were the mastermind's behind all the bombings and BSS. No expert had yet been able to explain how OFP had deployed Boarding School Syndrome to the infected children, nor how it was possible.

Next, he described finding the confusing statements from OFP detainees and how they always used "them" and "they" as words to describe the bombers, indicating a separation between the bombers and the rest of OFP. The fact that the bombers turned out to be mercenaries supported his theory that the real terrorists only highjacked the OFP name in order to pass blame.

Malina described finding the game "A Word With You" in the Ventana intranet and the messaging system therein. She described the coded messages and how she used a special program to decipher them.

"That led us to what we believe to be the first two victims of BSS," Aubrey said after Malina finished her description. "Owen Jorgetson and Polly Binns-Lourdes, both eight years old."

"And you believe Dr. Alkorn and his associates poisoned these children as well?" Rudolfo said.

Malina began nodding and Aubrey looked at her, pausing to give his answer, reconsidering all he knew until now.

"Maybe," he said. "Someone did. They're prime suspects as far as we're concerned. But it's becoming clearer and clearer that an outside actor is pulling the strings in all this."

Rudolfo nodded.

Aubrey went on, "These two kids were not claimed by OFP like the others. Maybe it was a test to see if the poison actually worked, I don't know. But the timing and how it was treated is suspicious."

He went on to explain how Dr. Randall McCalister treated the children, who were his only two patients other than James

Sarazin.

"And now, with this new information," Rudolfo waved his hand over the book in front of them, "what are your conclusions?"

Aubrey leaned forward, his elbows on the table. He rested his chin on his thumbs and took a deep breath, letting it out in an audible sigh.

"I think this confirms that this outside actor is behind all of it: the BSS poisonings, the bombings, these killings," he said laying a hand on the book, "and ultimately Wilcott's suicide."

He stood and began pacing, his hand in his pockets. "I'm almost grateful he killed himself in such a fashion or we wouldn't be here and wouldn't have confirmation."

No one spoke. The implications of the recent discoveries settled on the room like a cloud. Aubrey's mind swirled with the possibilities. It could be anyone, he thought. Who had the motivation to do all this? BSS, the bombings, these murders by proxy, and, he forgot to think about it until now, the woman hunting him and Malina—all orchestrated by someone. Who? Why?

He refused to believe it was simple terrorism or a murderous psychopath. There were too many layers for bloodlust and too many attempts to keep people quiet. Whoever this puppeteer was, something drove him. He wanted something.

Aubrey stopped pacing. Malina pulled her tablet from her bag. Her eyes went wide.

"We have incoming." She looked at him. "Ted has the last of the messages deciphered, he's sending them now."

"How long?" He rushed to her side, leaning in to view the tablet.

"Hard to say. Signal in this place is garbage."

"Can you use our connection?" Francesca looked toward the monitors behind Malina.

"No way. This has to be on a secure line. Locked down tight or ..."

A crash from somewhere outside. Muffled shouts and panicked yelling filtered through the door.

Francesca sat in front of the monitors, not moving. "Everyone," she said, "we may have a problem."

* * *

Jacira Barretto lifted her shirt and inserted the three-inch dagger into a sheath attached to her body armor. Handle down and under her left armpit made for easy reach and relatively good concealment. The rest of her tools were nearly impossible to hide. The white linen shirt and trousers were a lot like the nurse's scrubs she wore recently, loose and billowy, light and thin, betraying any foreign object under them.

She decided she'd carry her pistol and pass it off as having stolen it from a guard. Inmates were dumb for the most part, they might believe it, she thought. Her hair was a different story; it would give her away at a glance. She'd settled on a makeshift do-rag to hide it as best as she could. No way she would cut it, not for this.

She looked over her shoulder at Balthazar. He had the same idea as her on the do-rag, situating it and checking its placement in the reflection in the glass floor.

The unnamed woman, who had apparently taken a vow of silence, did nothing to hide her long curly red hair. She pulled it back in a ponytail.

Sarazin stepped into the midst of them, holding something in his hands. He handed each one of them a small cylinder about as long as Jacira's hand was wide.

She recognized it as a scroll tablet. The tech impressed her. She unrolled the thin flexible tablet and looked at it.

There were five rows of photos on the screen. Some of the photos were actually videos, moving around in their tiny squares. Each row was dedicated to one person. She scrolled to the left and right on each row; every possible angle and lighting change was captured. There could be no mistaking the people they were looking for.

"You will find these five people and kill them," Sarazin said with a blank face, his tone matter of fact. He might have been ordering a new espresso machine for his office. "All five of them must be dead before you return. Is that clear?"

Jacira and the others nodded their consent. She looked at the targets. Two she expected—Martin Aubrey and the woman working with him. A name appeared above her row of photos—Malina Maddox. How did Sarazin find out who she was? It was a testament to his resources and skills that he uncovered her identity before Jacira could.

The other three people on the kill list were a surprise. Two of them were Members of the Order, the last was an Apprentice Member. Jacira knew two of them well.

One thing was certain: they'd be killing Tappers and she wasn't sure how she felt about that.

"Okay," Balthazar said. "Do you know where they are?"

"Probably on the twenty-fourth floor. Rudolfo's ward," Jacira said, surprising herself as she did. She shrugged, "If he hasn't been reassigned."

Sarazin nodded at Jacira in confirmation. "Four of them

will be there. Jocelyn will be on the thirtieth floor."

"Let's go." Balthazar made for the elevator.

"Wait." Sarazin held a hand up, then looked down through the glass floor into the prison. "You'll know when it's time. And you'll need this." He held up a small white disk about the size of a quarter. "A gift from Member Principal Jacobi. It'll get you past the security barriers."

Jacira took the key fob from Sarazin. "Why would the emergency security barriers be activated?"

Sarazin smiled. "You'll see."

* * *

Nicholas Fox reached through the hole in the steel lattice. Holding the mirror tight, he stretched his arm as far as it would go through the jagged gap that ran along the edge of a support flange. The sharp, cold metal poked him through his shirt, pressing into his skin. Inwardly, he thanked a god he didn't believe in that he was skinny.

His hand was in space, inside the Great Atrium. If he dropped the mirror, he'd be screwed. He didn't have time to go back for another one. He must do it now.

Fox twisted his arm so the mirror faced straight up. Careful to catch the sun just right, he angled the mirror and searched the upper levels until he saw the faint white square of reflected light. Moving the mirror side to side and angling it back and forth, he watched the white square wink in and out of existence.

He repeated the flashing signal five times, ensuring every level above him could see it plainly. After the fifth flash, he stopped, counted to sixty in his head, then did it all over again. Five flashes.

With his heart pumping and his arm protesting with pain, he pulled the mirror back in from the hole. He pressed his face against the steel cage and craned his neck upward, panting to catch his breath.

Two dozen stories above him, someone lowered a white rag down through a gap in the cage. It remained there for a full ten seconds, then they pulled it back in. His signal had been received.

He pulled away from the cage. His bald head cool from sweat. His breathing slowed. He felt an awkward calm overcome him. There was no stopping it now. Once it started, he'd hole up somewhere safe and wait for the carnage to die down.

Then, he'd get out of this shithole.

A sound from high above. Was it a scream? It came from too high up, he couldn't be sure. More screaming. Coming closer. Coming fast.

Fox leapt back to the cage and pressed his face against it once more. The screaming was right on him, virtually on top of him. He was just in time to see the pale blue blur of a guard fly past him, down through the Great Atrium.

Shouts erupted around Fox.

"Did you see that shit?"

"It's starting! Let's go."

More shouts. More screams. Another body flew down through the air, a prisoner this time; some old grudge got hashed out in the commencing chaos. Doppler was in full effect as the crying man sped past Fox.

He heard the riot start like a growl, then become a roar.

The Keep came to life.

* * *

Jacira and her fellow assassins had a front row seat for the mayhem. It started quietly and soon blossomed into rage personified.

They watched through the glass floor as bodies flew down the Great Atrium like confetti, one after the other. Others lay slumped and bloodied against the catwalk's protective fencing. Prisoners ran in frenzies along the catwalk and the corridors.

The inmates wielded blades, spears, chairs, chains, and other makeshift weapons against guards and other inmates.

Members, Jacira noted, were not immune. This budding riot fueled a new confidence in the inmates. At least one person in a black cassock lay dead on the catwalk ten stories below.

A moment later, another Tapper fell, or was thrown, from a maintenance platform into the open air; a rope trailed behind. A second later, the body snapped against the noose in mid-air and swung back banging against the metal lattice, bouncing twice before it settled. The Tapper was a woman. She hung like a ragdoll, her body limp. The rope around her neck stretched taut to the its origin five floors above her.

"I'll take that as our cue to go," Jacira said, her eyes still fixed on the hanging Tapper.

She turned to find Balthazar reaching into his duffel bag on the floor. From it he pulled a three-foot long assault rifle with a snubbed scope mounted on top and two barrels, one for bullets, the other for grenades.

Jacira bunched her eyebrows at his choice of weapon. He noticed her questioning look.

"I don't think there's any point in trying too hard to be inconspicuous. And," he slapped the bottom of the magazine and flung back the charging handle, "it's going to get rough down there. I'm not letting myself get killed by such an uncivilized foe."

Suddenly, she felt the same way. At this point, camouflage was a secondary concern. Staying alive was primary and that meant more, better, and deadlier weapons.

Jacira walked to her own duffel bag and pulled out another pistol still in its holster, several magazines, and another blade. Then she withdrew a black assault rifle similar to Balthazar's and a vest packed with a dozen magazines. Donning her gear, she watched the redheaded woman remove a small pistol from her bag, which she strapped to her ankle, then a larger one she tucked into her waist band. Finally, the woman threw a satchel over her shoulder along with a black machine pistol.

Balthazar eyes went wild. With his rifle slung across his wide chest, he said, "Let's go hunting."

"Let things settle. Then, we hunt," Jacira said.

Balthazar frowned like a school child sent to his room without dessert. "Fine."

* * *

Malina watched on the monitors as chaos erupted outside. Divided into six windows, the monitor showed live video feeds from different locations in the prison. Probably just this ward, she thought.

In one window she saw a group of three men savagely kicking and beating someone curled on the floor. In another, an inmate with a knife stood over the bloodied form of another inmate. Others showed inmates fighting guards with fists, clubs, and blades. On another, on the catwalk around the Great Atrium, she saw a body fall through the open air beyond the cage.

Francesca sat at the workstation next to Malina and began pressing keys. The images on the monitor multiplied to fill the other two. She now saw feeds from eighteen cameras. Francesca toggled each to show different areas of the prison.

Violence was everywhere, spreading like a dusty wind. Every feed showed some form of it—a fight, a killing, things or people burning. Guards were rounded up on several feeds, tied up and bound. They were led by bloodied inmates, like cattle being led to slaughter. Other guards weren't as lucky—many lay dead or clutched wounds that would soon kill them.

"Oh, god," Malina said. Her hands flew to her face, covering her mouth. She felt her eyes grow to the size of saucers. "Oh my god. What the fuck is happening out there?"

"It's not just our ward. Look," Francesca said pointing to six feeds on the far-right monitor, "this is us. And all the rest are from the other floors. It's everywhere. It's a ..."

"A riot." Malina finished her sentence. "And we're stuck in the middle of it. Goddamnit." She spun to face Aubrey. Her breath had quickened and she felt like a hook had pierced her stomach and someone was pulling her into the floor. "How the hell are we going to get out of here now?"

Aubrey just stared at the screen.

"A riot?" Rudolfo's voice sounded incredulous.

"Where is that?" Aubrey pointed to a window showing a part of their ward. It was the group of inmates beating someone on the floor.

"Just outside. Central corridor." Francesca pointed toward the door and to the left.

"That's a guard." Aubrey made for the door. "Let's go."

Just as he reached the door, Malina saw the blue uniform, a large red stain spread across its front.

She darted after Aubrey and saw Rudolfo hand something to Francesca. It was small. A test tube, she guessed, but had no idea how that would be useful in their situation.

* * *

Martin Aubrey rushed through the door into the passageway and swung left, running. Ahead, the corner to the central corridor came into view.

Thudding sounds and cries of pain reached him as he rounded the corner. Three inmates stood over the unmoving body of a prison guard. His light blue uniform now crimson. From his angle, Aubrey could see the guard's face purple and bloodied, his eyes were just slits through swollen lids.

The inmates' legs swung back in short arcs then flew forward to deliver kicks to the guard's ribs, torso, and head. The guard could barely defend himself.

The inmates had their backs to Aubrey as he silently jogged toward them. If he could get one down quick, that would even the odds.

The inmate closest to him produced a ragged looking blade, red from rust, or maybe blood. The man bent, threw his hand back ready to sink the blade into the guard.

Aubrey was on him. His limbs acted on their own accord from years of hand-to-hand training. He pulled the wrist back and gripped the inmate's neck with the other hand. He wrenched the man straight upward by the neck, swept the legs, and threw his body weight into the man's downward trajectory.

The prisoner's skull collided with the concrete floor with a hollow *thunk*. Aubrey spun, blocked a blow coming at him and stepped back once, then twice, blocking another punch.

His mind and his moves sped up as he fought; muscle memory was a hell of a thing and it all came flooding back. At that moment, he could have been back in either of his uniforms from past lives, camouflaged or blue. The fight had never left him.

Another block, the inmate was thrown into an awkward, twisted position. Aubrey found his opportunity and punched hard at the man's exposed throat. The second inmate fell, choking and gasping.

The third inmate was on him. He was quick, but less skilled than the first two. Aubrey gave a swift kick to the man's sternum and he toppled.

Fiery pain shot through Aubrey's leg. Jumping back, he saw throat punch on the ground holding the knife. Blood dripped from it. Aubrey's blood.

He backed up a pace as the man got to his feet. Aubrey steadied himself. The inmate had one hand on his injured throat, the other gripped the blade. He snarled through crooked, dirty teeth. His eyes wolfish.

A crack. The man's eyes rolled. He fell.

Malina stood panting behind where the man once stood. She held a thick table leg in her hands. Still panting, her eyes were like saucers. She stared at the club, the man on the floor, then Aubrey.

"I thought you weren't a field agent," Aubrey said.

She stood silent.

"Let's get him up," he said, gesturing to the fallen guard. Together they heaved the man up onto shaky legs. Aubrey took one arm over his shoulder and Malina took the other.

Looking up he saw Francesca and Rudolfo at the corridor's intersection with the outer passageway.

"Thanks for your help." Aubrey didn't try to hide the sarcasm in his voice.

"We had issues of our own," Rudolfo said.

"They did," Malina said, looking up at Aubrey from across the guard's chest. "Some inmate grabbed me, but Francesca did something and the guy dropped." She paused. "I mean dropped." She grunted under the guard's weight. "Then another one came, saw his buddy and ran the other way. Just seeing them scared him away."

"Hmm," Aubrey grunted.

As they crossed the threshold into the outer passageway, Rudolfo swapped places with Malina. Aubrey angled toward the observation room, but Rudolfo pulled another direction.

"No," he said. "To my quarters. It's more secure."

Turning right down the passageway the group stopped dead. In front of them stood a gang of men dressed in white prison uniforms. Aubrey counted at least twelve men. They all brandished some type of weapon—shivs, clubs, or spears. They shouted obscenities and pointed their weapons at Aubrey and the others.

"Shit," Aubrey muttered. "Back the way we came. Come on."

Turning around, another gang appeared from the other end of the passageway. They numbered as many, maybe one or two more than the other group. More cursing and pointing.

The gangs ran, converging on Aubrey and the others.

"Shit," Aubrey said again. "Down here." He led the others down the corridor they'd just left. Hefting the guard's body, he set off at a trot, Rudolfo keeping pace.

Aubrey cautioned a glance behind him and watched the two gangs collide in a mass of flesh, metal, and wood. It was a blur of violence. Blood blossomed from under the white garments. Weapons swung with sickening, wet thumps against limbs, heads, and tissue. Several fell dead in the initial clash, the rest fought on wildly. Screams, shouts, and shocked yelps reached them over the ruckus of objects piercing and beating bodies.

"Keep going," Aubrey shouted, pointing to the catwalk. "They're not after us. We'll circle around and double back to Rudolfo's room."

They passed the third and second passageways without further incident. The catwalk around the Great Atrium was in front of them. Stepping from the concrete of the corridor to the metal grating of the catwalk, the immensity of the prison struck Aubrey. Something about this hollow pit at its center gave its size new meaning.

"This way," Rudolfo urged, pulling on the guard and leading Aubrey.

A blur of movement overhead. Aubrey ducked, felt the air move as something flew past his head. Metal on metal clanged near his ear as an object struck the cage. Without Aubrey's support, Rudolfo and the guard toppled sideways.

Half crouching, Aubrey turned his head to see a short, dark-skinned inmate gripping the end of a thin handled axe embedded in the cage. The weapon had a smooth shaft like an old broomstick and a rough homemade blade attached to its tip with layers of silver tape. The small man growled as he struggled to free the makeshift axe.

Aubrey punched at his open groin. He buckled and fell sideways.

Another inmate came from the same direction, something long and sharp in his hands. He reared back and heaved the spear.

Aubrey fell to his side and rolled the first inmate over as cover. The man's body jolted against Aubrey's arms as the spear impacted the man's chest.

Aubrey pushed the body off and got to his feet. The second inmate was out of weapons. He looked at his dying friend, then at Aubrey. He turned and ran back the way he'd come.

Aubrey put a foot on the dead prisoner's shoulder, gripped the homemade spear, and wrenched it upward. With a wet sucking sound, it came free.

Smoke filled Aubrey's nose. There was a fire somewhere nearby. He smelled something else too, hoping he was wrong.

"Here, take this." Aubrey handed the spear to Francesca. He hefted the guard's body once more with Rudolfo on the other side and they continued down the catwalk toward the next corridor.

Their footsteps clanged on the metal grating. Under their combined weight, the catwalk flexed and creaked. He wondered how much abuse it could take before it crumbled.

From high overhead he heard a sharp crack, then another shortly followed by a staccato, higher pitched than the first two sounds. Was it gunfire?

"Do guards here have guns? Maybe for a quick reaction force or something?" he asked Rudolfo.

"No. There are no guns here. They have lethal and nonlethal riot gear, but no guns."

"Shit," Aubrey said. "If someone has guns, we're in serious trouble."

Ten feet from the corridor a cloud of black smoke billowed from within it. It stank of burnt meat and plastic, stinging Aubrey's nostrils. A second later, a fiery form came stumbling out of the corridor.

The flaming man bounced against the cage with a muffled thud, then fell backwards onto the catwalk. The burning body writhed and twitched. His skin blackened. Patches of white cloth showing through here and there were quickly consumed.

Aubrey guessed the man must had been doused in an accelerant then set ablaze.

As Aubrey watched the burning man, Francesca muscled her way past. She stood next to the twitching burning inmate. Holding the spear with both hands she raised it in the air and drove the point into the prisoner's chest.

With a final shudder, the body went still.

Aubrey stared as she extricated the spear, regarding her with a great deal of respect, but mentally questioning whether this was the best situation for an abundance of mercy.

A crash against the cage made him jump sideways sending Rudolfo and the guard into the inner bulkhead. The three of them twisted into each other and fell. Malina ran to help, pulling on Aubrey's arm.

As he was getting up, he caught a look at Rudolfo's face. It was stone. His eyes were blank, like he'd seen a ghost over Aubrey's shoulder.

Following his gaze, Aubrey saw it. A body hung on the interior of the cage, inside the Great Atrium. It swung at odd angles, twisting and bouncing against the steel lattice.

The body was dressed in black. A cord cut deep into the neck of the body; the skin bulged out around it. The neck stretched grotesquely and unnaturally crooked. As the body settled against the cage with one last soft bounce, it spun to face them.

It was a man with short brown hair, not unlike Rudolfo's. His red bloodshot eyes were open. They bulged and were nearly bursting from their sockets.

Looking around, Aubrey noticed Francesca also fixated on the hanging Tapper.

He allowed himself another second to scan the other floors of the prison. Equal amounts of violence and bloodshed were being wrought on everywhere he looked.

Through the metal cage he could see bodies lying in various states of bloody savagery. Bodily fluids dripped like long crimson ropes. Smoke issued from corridors and rose toward the skylight above. Two floors up, an inmate stabbed the head of another who lay facedown. On the same level, three men kicked and punched another. Several floors higher, bodies thrusted and gyrated in some violent act he couldn't make out.

Looking down was no different. Men and women on every level took advantage of the chaos to deliver some long-held vendettas. Or they were simply bored. Or they were bloodthirsty madmen feasting on a moment of consequence free mindless bloodletting while they could.

The putrid stench of human waste, charred flesh, and blood drifted through the air into his nostrils. His guts turned and it was all he could do not to vomit.

Shouts in the corridor behind them shook Aubrey from his thoughts.

"We have to move, Martin." Malina shook him. She had fistfuls of his shirt in each hand. How long had he been zoned out?

"Yeah. Yeah, let's go," he said.

On his feet again, he heaved the guard and Rudolfo up at once.

"Where are your quarters?"

"Down that corridor," Rudolfo pointed to where the burning had come from. His eyes were still locked on the hanging Member. "A right at the last passageway, first door on the left. I have to scan my hand to get in." He held up his left hand still in its black glove.

"Okay, we're close. Francesca, lead the way with that spear. Malina, keep an eye on our six. Don't let anyone sneak up on us."

"Eye on our what?"

"Our six. Six o'clock. Behind us." He pointed behind them. She nodded.

With a nod, Francesca stepped forward and turned left into the corridor. With the spear in front of her and her platinum blonde braid cascading down her back, she looked like a Viking warrior on a raiding party.

The rest of the group followed her.

They found the corridor empty. An acrid smell filled the air. Crossing passageway one, a cell to their right burped black smoke. The inside of the cell appeared scorched, something in there still smoldering.

They moved silently, no one speaking.

The first two passageways were largely empty. A few lone inmates ran here and there in the distance but wanted nothing to do with their group. Most took cover or otherwise looked like they were searching for a safe place to hide. Maybe the Tappers scared them away, or maybe they had no interest in partaking in the festivities with the other inmates. Either way, Aubrey was grateful to be left alone.

How long had it been since he'd run out to help the guard? Five minutes at least, he thought, but no more than ten.

Combat, especially hand-to-hand, always felt longer than it really was. He could remember sparring with other cadets at the police academy for three minutes and it feeling like three hours.

How many people had been killed or maimed in just five to ten minutes? How much blood would spill in another ten minutes? Or by the time this riot was put down for good?

Coming level with passageway three, the group peered down it in each direction. It was empty. Ahead, down the final passageway to the right, he could see the outer edge of a door. He gave Rudolfo a questioning look who responded with a nod in the affirmative.

That was the room. Safety was thirty feet away.

Footsteps and chatter reached them from somewhere down the outer passageway. An inmate stepped into view. He had a dark olive complexion and a spiderweb tattoo on his chin. In his hand he held a long, rusty metal blade, a homemade machete.

The man with the machete stopped when he saw the group, eyeing them. They eyed him back.

Francesca stood closest to him. She bent her knees and pushed the spear in front of her, bracing for battle.

Only one, Aubrey thought, shouldn't be too bad.

As if reading Aubrey's mind, the man with the spider-webbed chin shouted over his shoulder, "Tappers up here," then turned back to Aubrey's group before continuing, "and women."

More footsteps. People running. Five more inmates barreled into view, four men and one woman. Spiderweb tattoos covered some or all of their faces. They were a gang. Each held some implement of death in the form of a blade or a club.

They all smiled and snarled at their prey. As one the gang moved toward Aubrey and the other.

"This way," Rudolfo hissed, pulling Aubrey and the guard backwards into the third passageway, on their left. "Francesca, this way."

She backed into the passageway, managing to keep the inmates at bay with her spear. The gang moved slowly but didn't stop. Apparently, two Tappers together were something to approach with caution.

Aubrey threw the guard's arm off and reached back pulling Malina in under it. To Rudolfo, he said, "Get them to safety. I'll slow these assholes down so you can get away."

Malina's eyes protested, but he ignored them. "Go," he said then he turned and stood by Francesca's side. The prisoners were still wary of her. After five more seconds, the standoff ended.

The prisoner with the machete moved first. "Killed me one Tapper today. Happy to make it three," he said as he reared back with his machete, swinging it at Francesca in a long arc. She caught it on the spear, the dull rough edge twanging against the wood of the spear. She threw it off and cracked the man in the head with one end of the spear.

Two men rushed at Aubrey, both with weapons raised. Sidestepping the nearest one, Aubrey got in close. He pushed an arm as it came down, spinning the man into the other attacker.

He grabbed the collar of the nearest inmate and pulled the body in. He found the hand holding the shiv. With a double-handed, iron grip on the wrist, he pulled inward toward himself, making a Heimlich maneuver motion. The blade punched into the man's gut. His strength immediately washed away.

Aubrey dropped him, pulling the blade from a slackened hand.

He sidestepped and backpedaled, as the second man rushed at him with an axe.

Aubrey jumped back, letting the axe blade clunk harmlessly into the hard floor. Aubrey lunged forward with a hard step onto the wooden handle, pinning it and the inmate's hands to the floor.

Aubrey didn't look as he threw his hand holding the blade forward. It sank into the man's neck and he toppled forward. Blood poured from the severed jugular, spreading across the floor in a widening circle of crimson.

The rest of the gang had been occupied by Francesca and her spear, and Rudolfo, who'd joined the fray in spite of Aubrey's order.

Just as Aubrey moved to join them, Rudolfo fell from a club strike to his head. He crashed to the floor. The inmate turned his attention to Malina.

"Now that that's out the way," he said, skulking toward her.

Aubrey raised the axe. "Hey," Aubrey shouted.

The man turned just as Aubrey swung the axe down. It landed where the man's neck joined the shoulder. He collapsed in a heap to the floor. Aubrey reclaimed his axe with a quick pull.

Ten feet away, he saw Rudolfo moving. It was a good sign.

Aubrey bent and pulled the club from the dead inmate's hand. Wielding both weapons, he strode toward the remaining four gang members. Francesca still held her own against the original spiderwebbed inmate with the machete.

Aubrey swung the axe through the air with one hand at the nearest prisoner, the female, and she ducked; the rest of them stepped back. Anticipating that the woman would duck, Aubrey kicked and his foot connected with her face. She flew back.

Swinging at her as she scurried away, Aubrey saw the other two spreading out. They were going to flank him. That would be trouble. Panting and with his arms burning, he didn't know how long he could keep up the fight.

Going for broke, he threw the axe end over end at the man to his right and jumped at the man to his left. He held the club high and brought it down on the prisoner.

The club connected but broke in two. Aubrey dropped the stump of it. He punched and thrusted, he grappled and twisted. They fell to the ground, the inmate on top of him. Fatigue soaked him like sweat.

Another inmate came near them. He kicked and yelled, at the one on top of Aubrey. "Move goddammit. I got him." He held something. The axe blade glimmered near Aubrey's head.

"He's mine, motherfucker," said a wet voice in his ear. A hand tightened around Aubrey's neck. Blackness cut into his vision. His strength had vanished.

The man on top of him grew lighter. The tightness around Aubrey's throat loosened and he looked to the side. The man with the axe lay down beside him, staring at him. Not staring, Aubrey thought, dead. Inches from him.

The man on top of Aubrey didn't move. He was dead too.

"What the hell?" Aubrey said. He pushed the dead man off.

He got to his feet. Rudolfo stood nearby, wiping a black substance from the tip of his gloved finger.

"Is that," Aubrey paused, not sure what to call it, "is that what you use to ..."

"Yes," Rudolfo said, not making eye contact with Aubrey.

Aubrey checked the two corpses now at his feet. Both had inky black splotches on their necks at the base of the skull. A chill passed from his ankles to the nape of his own neck. He rubbed it, suddenly grateful to be on Rudolfo's side in this fight.

Looking around, he saw that the skirmish had moved them back to roughly the halfway point of the passageway. Francesca stood ten feet away, pulling the spear from another inmate lying on the floor.

The female inmate ran back the way she'd came. Breathing hard and clutching his side, Aubrey watched her run.

Turning to the others, he said, "Let's get going before she comes back with more friends."

Now using the axe as a crutch, he and Rudolfo slowly hoisted the guard onto their shoulders and began making their way down the passageway. Francesca led the way once again. Her spear now a proven weapon.

At the door to Rudolfo's room, the Member raised his left hand in front of panel in the wall. The door clicked open.

"Take him," Aubrey said to Rudolfo. To Malina and Francesca, he said, "Let's go grab our gear and some of the computer equipment."

The observation room where they'd met moments earlier was a short distance down the passageway. Aubrey kept watch outside the door while Malina and Francesca gathered up the equipment. The passageway remained clear while they worked.

Minutes later, the three of them were back in Rudolfo's room. The guard lay on the bed; his chest moved lightly up and down. Aubrey walked to the bed and checked his pulse. It was weak.

"He's alive for now. But he needs a doctor." Aubrey turned to Rudolfo who stared at the guard. Something like tenderness crossed the elder Tapper's face. Maybe they were friends, Aubrey thought. It was likely they knew each other having worked alongside in the prison.

Malina dropped bags of equipment onto the floor. Francesca did the same. Aubrey moved to the door, slammed it shut, and mashed a button in the wall to activate the magnetic locking system.

He turned to Malina. "Get the video feeds back up. We need eyes on what's going on out there." As they worked, he and Rudolfo tried to make the guard as comfortable as possible. They cleaned his wounds as best they could with what they had on hand.

"We're up," Malina said behind him.

Turning around, Aubrey saw the three monitors standing upright on the floor already displaying video feeds from all over the prison.

The carnage he saw from the catwalk several minutes

ago was nothing compared to what he now saw on the monitors. Francesca sat on the floor, scanning through the feeds from dozens of cameras. Not a feed passed that didn't show evidence of the bloodshed. Bodies, pools of blood, viscera and limbs littered the hallways in every shot. Inmates running, clutching homemade weapons. A group of men mercilessly beating another on the floor. A guard lying in a pool of blood. She continued scanning, lingering mere seconds before switching to another feed, then another. Each camera showed some version of the grisly violence outside.

"If this is a random sample of what's happening out there, this entire place is now a living nightmare," Aubrey said.

"It's everywhere," she said. "Everywhere. The whole prison is rioting."

Francesca stopped on one feed that showed a passageway on level thirty-two. The pile of bodies reached almost to the ceiling. Blood seeped from the bottom of the pile, forming a slowly growing pool around it. A woman in white poured a liquid on the pile. A second later, the feed went white, then came back in focus. Aubrey watched as the pile of corpses turned into an inferno of burning flesh.

"Gangs." Rudolfo sat on the bed gently wiping the guard's face with a damp rag. "Rival gangs must be responsible for the mass violence." He rested his hands on his knees, gazing at the guard. "You saw the face tattoos of the inmates we encountered? They're the *aranas*. One of the major gangs here. Many more minor ones exist, of course, but the four major ones are especially heinous."

"So, what's the plan here? What's the protocol for a riot?" Aubrey continued watching the feeds as Francesca scrolled through them.

"Nothing on this scale has ever happened," Rudolfo said, now standing next to Aubrey, his eyes locked on the monitors. "Wards have rioted in the past, occasionally an entire level. Not the entire prison. Never anything like this."

"What are they going to do? What are the guards and administrators supposed to be doing now?" Aubrey asked.

"The guards and Members have safe rooms where they are supposed to hole up." Rudolfo pointed to the ceiling. "They're more like secure closets at various locations on each level." He sighed heavily. "For a multi-floor riot, all the guards from the other non-rioting levels are to form special quick reaction teams. Together, they clear the levels in question one by one." He pointed at the screens. "Every level is affected, so every guard will have holed up in their secure rooms if they weren't already attacked or," he turned toward the guard on the bed, "killed."

"Are we safe here?" Aubrey asked.

Rudolfo didn't respond, still gazing at the unconscious guard. After a moment, he said, "My quarters are somewhat secure, but I'd rather us be in a designated safe room."

"Okay, we'll need to move then." He gestured to the guard. "When he's feeling a little better. Who is the quick reaction force if every guard on duty is holed up or otherwise unavailable?"

"My guess is they'd call in off-duty officers. Which also means they'd start from the bottom of the prison and work their way up."

"Meaning, it'll be a while?" Aubrey rested his hands on his hips. Malina turned to look at him with a worried look.

"Yes," Rudolfo said. "I just don't understand how the rioting could have spread so fast. It's as if it all started at the same time in different parts of the prison."

Aubrey shook his head. "It must have been orchestrated by these gangs. I don't know what they were planning, but this took planning."

Francesca kept scrolling through the feeds. Large groups were congregating in the mess halls on each level. Guards that managed to survive the initial violence were being corralled there.

"Elevators?" Aubrey asked.

"The Members' elevator will still function," Rudolfo replied. "The freight and inmate elevators will be locked down. Stairs too. Security barricades will be deployed momentarily I suspect, if not already."

"Barricades?" Malina asked.

"Yes. They divide the wards into manageable sections, making securing each of them easier."

"That female inmate," Aubrey said, "how did she get up here if the place is locked down?"

"Must have arrived before the lockdown. Or ..."

"Or what?" Aubrey asked.

"Or they're using some other means of crossing between levels," Francesca said.

"Can you get us through the locked doors and the barricades?" Aubrey pointed to Rudolfo's hand.

"Yes." Rudolfo tore his gaze away from the screens.

"Okay. We need to work on a plan to get to the safe room. Where is the nearest ..." Aubrey stopped speaking, his eyes fell on one of the screens. He was confused by something he saw on the video feed. He pointed at the strange image. "What is that?"

As she scrolled through the prison's camera feeds,

Francesca had not been discriminant. Aubrey had asked her to get a general sense of the situation, so she scrolled fast. Apparently, when she saw the object, she felt it was strange enough to stop and take a closer look.

The view was on the top of the prison. The camera's fish-eye lens gave a full 180-degree view of the area surrounding the building. At the outer the edge of the panoramic scene, a white triangular shape stood in view. The object was on the roof. And it didn't belong there. It hovered several feet off the ground and whatever held it aloft was out of frame.

Rudolfo stood. "Check the opposite camera."

Francesca clicked the mouse a few times and the view changed. Now, they saw the other 180-degree view from the other side of the prison complex. On the right side of this screen sat the rest of the mysterious object. It was long and pointy with wheels below it and wings jutting from its sides.

"An aircraft." Aubrey answered for everyone else. "Is that normal?"

"No," Rudolfo said.

"Who would be ..." Malina started to ask.

"I do not know." Rudolfo interrupted Malina's question.

Rudolfo leaned forward and took the mouse from Francesca. He changed the view back to the shot of the triangular tail section of the aircraft. A series of numbers and letters were printed vertically on the tailfin.

"I can find out who its registered to." Malina began pulling out a tablet from her bag.

"Please do." Rudolfo stared at the craft, looking deeply puzzled.

Aubrey sat on the bed, overwhelmed by all that was happening.

Looking back, he concluded that immeasurably bad luck had put him in front of Tim Frass's building the day it exploded. More bad luck found him at the police station at the right time to hand them their first major clue. Now, luck led him to this prison at the same time the inmate population decided to stage a murderous riot.

No, he knew none of that was true. It wasn't luck. He wanted all of it. He'd desperately wanted to help the police in their investigation into the bombings. After the battle with the mercenaries, he could have let it all go and gone home from the hospital to resume his work with OWG Insurance.

He chose to seek out Malina. He chose to pursue the leads and evidence.

He was here now because it was where he wanted to be.

"Okay, you're not going to believe this," Malina said, staring at her tablet, transfixed. "That plane belongs ..." Her tablet pinged with an alert and Aubrey recognized it as a notification from Ted. Her eyes shifted to a corner of the screen. Her eyes scanned that section of the screen for several seconds, then her jaw dropped.

"What is it?" Aubrey asked. Malina appeared to be re-reading the same text over and over. Another moment passed and he persisted, "What is it, Malina?"

"Um, Martin." She looked up at him with wide eyes. Her face pale.

"Yeah?" Aubrey stood and approached her.

"Ted came through with the last of the messages. I just ... Well, you need to read them." With shaking hands, she extended the tablet.

He took the tablet from her as if it were the antidote to a poison about to stop his heart. Ted had decoded the last three strings of messages from the Ventana intranet game, *A Word With You*. They were listed in order by date, earliest to latest.

January 18, 2043

Alkorn L: have what we need to go to next steps
Imanpor R: Q outsiders
Alkorn L: Yes need them
Imanpor R: Who
Alkorn L: reliable passionate people
Shoeman N: What do they need
Alkorn L: Proof
Winthorpe S: How much
Alkorn L: Proof Z is cause

Aubrey paused and read the first string again. He was struck by the reference to outsiders. He looked at Malina.

"Outsiders. He must be talking about OFP. And 'proof Z is cause'? OFP thinks it's the cause of everything wrong with the world, so that fits."

He continued reading, scrolling to the next set of messages.

January 21, 2043

Winthorpe S: forty eight hours Q update
Alkorn L: asked for more time two more days
Shoeman N: have what we need move ahead
Alkorn L: two days we wait

"Giving somebody time," Aubrey spoke to himself. The rest of the room had dissolved as he was consumed by his own thoughts. "'Have what we need'. Proof of whatever Z was the cause of, I imagine."

He moved on to the last string of messages, vaguely aware

of Malina working on her other tablet and the Tappers scanning video feeds. The final string was sent two days before the scientists were arrested.

January 22, 2043

Imanpor R: What is going to happen

Alkorn L: Unknown

Shoeman N: Are we safe

Alkorn L: Unknown

Winthorpe S: People need to know

Alkorn L: They will

Winthorpe S: Kids are in danger

Winthorpe S: We must stop Z now

Alkorn L: Too late no stopping it

Imanpor R: We are demons

Alkorn L: Then Sarazin is the devil

His eyes lost focus. The white text on the tablet screen blurred. What did he just read? He went through the messages again and again. Did he read it right?

"Malina, are you sure Ted deciphered this correctly?"

"There's only one way to decipher them. The wrong way would make them totally unreadable." Her face was stone, staring back at him. Apparently, she had come to the same conclusion and wanted to believe it as little as he did.

"Malina …"

"I know," she said.

"They're saying that …"

"I know."

Francesca had turned to face them, her mouth open, but she said nothing. Rudolfo's face looked as stony as ever, placid and incomprehensible.

"Can you put them all together? All the messages together in order?" Aubrey handed Malina the tablet. He had to be sure. He had trouble recalling what the rest of the messages said exactly and he had to know. Hunches like this could be dangerous.

A moment later, she handed the tablet back and sat down on the bed next to him.

Together they read all of the deciphered messages between Dr. Leo Alkorn and his team of scientists spanning the seven days prior to their arrest.

January 16, 2043

Alkorn L: No comm out of this chat

Winthorpe S: We know

Imanpor R: Q Are we safe

Alkorn L: Yes

Winthorpe S: Q we are doing this

Alkorn L: Yes

Winthorpe S: Q Certain

Alkorn L: Dead certain

January 17, 2043

Shoeman N: Q Plan

Alkorn L: Get what we need first cannot move on without it

Shoeman N: Q Then

Alkorn L: do what we must no choice

January 18, 2043

Alkorn L: have what we need to go to next steps

Imanpor R: Q outsiders

Alkorn L: Yes need them
Imanpor R: Q Who
Alkorn L: reliable passionate people
Shoeman N: Q What do they need
Alkorn L: Proof
Winthorpe S: Q How much
Alkorn L: Proof Z is cause

January 19, 2043
Imanpor R: Team is worried
Alkorn L: Q Team or you
Imanpor R: Plz
Alkorn L: Shouldn't talk outside too dangerous
Alkorn L: And do not forget we are doing this no choice
Imanpor R: No need to remind
Shoeman N: Q Certain no one else knows
Alkorn L: Only us for now
Imanpor R: Q Assurances
Alkorn L: None
Winthorpe S: So be it move forward
Alkorn L: We must no choice

January 20, 2043
Alkorn L: He knows
Shoeman N: Q Jorgetson
Alkorn L: Yes now we wait

January 21, 2043
Winthorpe S: twenty-four hours Q update
Alkorn L: asked for more time two more days
Shoeman N: have what we need move ahead

Alkorn L: two days we wait

January 22, 2043

Imanpor R: Q What is going to happen

Alkorn L: Unknown

Shoeman N: Q Are we safe

Alkorn L: Unknown

Winthorpe S: People need to know

Alkorn L: They will

Winthorpe S: Kids are in danger

Winthorpe S: We must stop Z now

Alkorn L: Too late no stopping it

Imanpor R: We are demons

Alkorn L: Then Sarazin is the devil

January 23, 2043

Alkorn L: Do nothing say nothing families at risk

Shoeman N: Q What have we done

Imanpor R: Q Trust his threats

Alkorn L: Yes very much

Winthorpe S: Q What now

Alkorn L: Prison and wait and say nothing do nothing

As Aubrey read the last line, he could feel the others' eyes waiting for him to say something. What he had figured out was going to change everything, and their lives were already at risk in more ways than he cared to think about. What he had to say had the potential to throw the world as they knew it into total upheaval.

In a low voice, Aubrey said, "One Front for the People was right. Zentransa is poisoning society."

24

Answers and Questions

"Can you clarify what you mean by that?" Francesca sat in a chair near the bed while Rudolfo stood in the corner.

Aubrey looked up. Francesca's placid face made him wonder if it was the same expression she'd wear were she evaluating an inmate who had just caved in another man's skull.

"OFP has always claimed Zentransa was poisoning society, but in a socio-economic way. This," he waved a hand over the seven days' worth of messages, "paints a different picture. A picture with Z still front and center as the culprit, but guilty of an entirely different crime."

"Please elaborate," Rudolfo said with his arms crossed, leaning into the corner.

Malina looked at Aubrey open-mouthed. He knew they had both come to the same conclusion. He nodded and she began.

"Weeks before these messages started between Alkorn and his team," she handed Rudolfo the tablet displaying all the decoded messages, "two children never woke up from a night's sleep. They were the first two cases of what's being called Boarding School Syndrome."

Rudolfo nodded. "I know of this Syndrome." He scanned the messages then handed them to Francesca.

"Originally, we thought the scientists were behind it all: first, BSS then, the bombings. We thought they were out to harm Sarazin and his company. Now, it looks like they were a red herring for something much worse."

Aubrey stood and began pacing in the small space. "At first, we read all those messages with an assumption of the scientists' guilt and it skewed our perception." He felt that Rudolfo and Francesca could appreciate the power of bias. Their entire purpose was to judge. Judgment was the more acceptable cousin of bias.

"But," Aubrey continued, "if you read it as if they're the victims, as if they're being held hostage with threats and blackmail, things look different." He stalked over to Francesca and took the tablet from her hands. "See, here," he pointed to January 17th, "Alkorn says 'get what we need first cannot move on without it'. Initially, we assumed that referred to the money they were stealing in order to fund their reign of terror. But they weren't after money at all, they were after data."

"What kind of data?" Francesca asked.

Aubrey ignored her, speaking fast. "Then the next day they're talking about outsiders, 'reliable passionate people'. You think they're talking about OFP, but it's not. It has to be journalists. Journalists to get the word out."

"Word out about what?" Francesca asked.

"Malina, put some feelers out and see if any of your reporter buddies were contacted about this." She nodded.

Aubrey still held the tablet, pointing at it as he resumed the story.

"Then, the Ventana four are on their way to prison and can't risk exposing ..."

"What are you talking about?" Francesca said, near shouting.

Aubrey saw the entire puzzle now. Its curved, notched, misshapen pieces that had for so long taunted and frightened him now fell into place and came together as if magnetized.

"James Sarazin created Zentransa with the help of Dr. Leo Alkorn, his lead scientist." Aubrey spoke slowly and clearly, more for himself than for Francesca or Rudolfo.

They nodded.

"Boarding School Syndrome is not a weapon used by OFP to terrorize the city. It's a side-effect. It's a side-effect of Zentransa."

Francesca leaned back, her mouth fell open.

He thrust his hand at the tablet. "Look at some of the things they say: 'proof Z is cause', 'people need to know', 'kids are in danger', 'we must stop Z now', 'Sarazin is the devil'." He shrugged. "My guess is the first child, Owen Jorgetson, falls ill and Sarazin gets wind of it because he's close friends with Mr. Jorgetson. Then, maybe Sarazin has a hunch what's causing it. He's a smart guy, he could have figured it out. He brings in Alkorn to confirm it. He runs some tests and confirms Z is somehow responsible."

"'He knows'," Malina said, referencing the first message Ted decoded. "They meant that Sarazin knew about Z being the cause, not that he knew about them stealing."

"Right, because they never were stealing anything. So, Alkorn goes to Sarazin, tells him it's Zentransa making the kids sick. He pretends to care, hence the message 'two more days' sent on January 21st. Sarazin must have asked them for time to figure out what to do."

"Then, Alkorn and the team get arrested for allegedly stealing from Ventana," Malina said.

"Framed," Aubrey corrected her. "They were framed and arrested and sent here. Sarazin wanted to shut them up."

"Right. And he threatens them and their families, so they couldn't do anything about it. They wouldn't talk to you and your partners when you came here to interrogate them."

Rudolfo closed his eyes, shaking his head. After a long pause, he spoke. "Children aren't even supposed to be on Zentransa. How could it affect them?"

Aubrey sighed, he'd thought about that in the short span since their discovery and had some theories. "It must be passed down from the parents. Plenty of disorders and genetic abnormalities can be passed that way. Imagine a mother who drinks heavily while pregnant or a father who is exposed to radiation before conception. Genetic mutation passing from parents to children is common."

Francesca raised a hand and Aubrey stopped pacing. "What about all the bombings? I thought they were connected to BSS and OFP."

Aubrey looked away, staring into space for a moment. He'd almost forgotten about the bombings. The revelation about Zentransa was brought into clearer focus when the bombings were added as a variable. It was like wearing glasses and walking out of a cold room. Slowly the fog was lifting and he started to see everything perfectly.

"He knew there would be more." He spoke in a low voice, turned and started pacing for several seconds before continuing. "Alkorn probably told him Polly Binns-Lourdes and Owen Jorgetson were only the beginning. More kids would get BSS and ..."

Malina shot to her feet, startling Aubrey from his thoughts. "They were all in on Z early."

"What? Who? What do you mean?" Aubrey said confused.

"All the kids who have BSS. All of them had parents who were involved with Ventana in the early days of Z. That's what they all have in common. It must take a certain amount of time to manifest in the parents before they have kids who go on to be affected."

Aubrey froze. He stood silent, staring at Malina with a profound sense of awareness of her. Not only was she highly skilled at her chosen profession, she was also an incredibly good detective.

"Damn. You're right. And Sarazin must have put that together too. Maybe he did the math and figured more would fall sick soon." Aubrey sat on a wooden chair near the foot of the bed. Discoveries such as these had a tendency to sap his energy. It was as if his brain burned extra fuel to figure things out.

"Go on," Rudolfo said.

"He needed a distraction. He needed someone to take the blame. He hires the mercenaries to bomb the city, claim responsibility, and wait for the next case of BSS to come out. Then, they'd claim responsibility for that too." Elbows on his knees, he stared at the wall. His eyes felt heavy. He was suddenly starving.

"So, OFP had nothing to do with it?" Francesca asked.

Aubrey shook his head.

"And the scientists?"

"Not even scapegoats, just victims. Like all those killed in the blasts and all those kids who might never wake up." Aubrey felt the weight of it all now. It pressed on his back and shoulders like an existential pressure.

Malina stood with her arms crossed looking at Aubrey. "All for the sake of keeping the real cause of BSS from the public. To keep society's addiction to the Z pill firmly in place." Her hair was a mess, but it suited her, like she meant to do it. He liked that about her.

"Yeah," Aubrey said. "There's something else, though. Wilcott. How could Sarazin possibly penetrate the Order to convince him to execute the Ventana four?"

Rudolfo's chest expanded as he breathed in audibly. He clasped his hands behind his back and moved closer to Aubrey. Staring at the door, then above at the ceiling he said, "There is only one person who will know."

"Member Principal Jacobi?" Francesca asked.

Rudolfo did not respond. His silence was affirmation enough for Aubrey.

"What do we do?" Francesca asked.

"Go to the police?" Malina said, shrugging.

"No." Aubrey shook his head. "We've seen what he's capable of when no one is on to him. I'd hate to see Sarazin cornered or under pressure."

"So, what then?" Malina said.

"You two need to get to Jacobi while he's still alive." Aubrey stood and pointed to Francesca and Rudolfo. "We'll find Sarazin and ... well, I don't know what we'll do. We need to find him first."

"Shit." Malina slapped her forehead. "I completely zoned out while we were talking." Her eyes were the size of saucers.

"I know where he is."

"Sarazin? How?" Aubrey moved toward her.

"The aircraft parked up there," she said, pointing to the ceiling. "On top of the prison. I checked the registration numbers. It belongs to him. It belongs to James Sarazin."

Once again, Aubrey stood speechless. Why would Sarazin be at the prison? In the middle of a …

"Riot," Aubrey finished his thought out loud. "The riot is him. He staged it somehow."

"Impossible," Rudolfo said flatly. "How could he?"

"You've seen all he's been able to do in the past few months," Aubrey waved an arm toward the door, "and you doubt he could cause this?"

"Why would he?" Rudolfo asked incredulously.

"There are four people here who he knows are looking into BSS, the bombings, all of it. What better way to have us all killed than under the cover of a prison riot?"

"Five. Five people." Francesca was on her feet. "The Member Principal has to know too."

Everyone nodded.

"So, what do we do?" Malina asked. The four of them stood in a circle.

"The two people we need are here. And so are we," Aubrey said.

"And?" Rudolfo said, squinting.

"And we go get them," Aubrey said.

"Then what do we do once we have them? If we can even get to them," Rudolfo said.

Aubrey took a deep breath and let it out in a long smooth exhalation. "I don't know. But by the time we get there, I'll have thought of something."

"There are twenty-four floors between us and Jacobi and Sarazin." Francesca spoke in a matter of fact tone. "Twenty-four floors full of violent, unfettered inmates who have a newfound bloodlust for killing Members of the Order."

"Yeah," Aubrey said, rolling up his shirt sleeves. "But who wants to live forever."

III

Part Three

25

Beginnings

Eighteen Years Ago

Frannie sat on a thick matted rug watching her brother Hank play with wooden blocks. At eighteen months old, he was pretty good at stacking them up in a neat tower a few blocks high. His favorite part, however, was swinging his arms wildly at them, sending them crashing to the floor.

Frannie would sit with him all day like this. If she walked away, even for a moment, he cried his head off. She didn't mind his need for her. She loved him very much. She loved him as much as she missed their parents.

The beige rug was large and round. In places she could see through the shag to the woven matting beneath. Stains of various size and color dotted it.

Hank's blocks were as bad as the rug—worn and faded, adorned with teeth marks and slobber stains from who knows how many orphans like them.

Orphans. That's what they were now. The shock of the word and the feeling it brought stunned her every morning she woke up for the last six months. When she opened her eyes for the first time every day, if she slept at all, she found herself here, inside a waking nightmare. Every moment, every interaction here reminded her they were alone, forever.

At least they had each other. Hank didn't know anything about anything yet, but every now and then he'd utter a "mama" or "dada" in his garbled speech. He looked for them everywhere. So did she if she was honest with herself. She kept hoping it was all some joke, some prank her parents were pulling.

She'd just started to accept that her mom was gone. She hadn't gotten over it, but she was getting used to it. Then, her dad was killed in the mudslide six months ago. Why did they have go for a walk that day? Frannie had been in one of her bad moods and her dad thought it would help.

Around them, children of all ages milled about playing with broken toys or reading worn out books. At seven years old, Frannie was among the oldest.

Nearly every day, she and Hank spent time with people looking to adopt children. The other kids called them shoppers. Usually they came in pairs; sometimes they came alone. Every time, Frannie and her brother were passed up.

"You're too sad," Drew, a boy about her age, had told her after one meeting with two shoppers. "They don't want sad kids."

"Then why are you still here?" Frannie had bit back.

The other kids didn't like her. She had barely spoken to any of them since she and Hank arrived. Most were in similar situations as she and Hank—dead parents. Others were taken from their parents for reasons she couldn't figure out. Why would parents let them go? Her parents would never let her and Hank go. Her dad died to keep them safe.

Hank looked at her with a look of total contentment, his smile permanently plastered on his chubby face. He made her feel better. She saw her dad in him, some of her mom too.

"Frannie," called a woman's voice behind her. Frannie turned to see Ms. Elmyr walking toward her. Ms. Elmyr wore her usual costume of a knee length gray skirt and purple sweater, a bright gold locket hung around her neck. Her graying dark hair sat like a helmet of tight curls on top of her head.

Frannie couldn't figure out what the woman smelled like, but it reminded her of her dead grandfather.

"Yes, Ms. Elmyr?" Frannie replied.

"Come with me, dear."

Frannie suspected it was another pair of shoppers and reached to pick up her brother.

"No, dear. Just you."

Frannie looked back at Ms. Elmyr then at Hank, who drooled on a block stamped with a green J.

"He'll be okay, dear. The nannies are watching."

Frannie shrugged and stood. Hank started to whine and when Frannie was ten feet away, he wailed in protest. She started to turn back, but Ms. Elmyr had her by the shoulder.

"He'll be fine, dear."

Ms. Elmyr's office was down the hall from the large playroom where she and Hank spent most of their time.

Inside, a huge wooden desk took up most of the room. Behind it, Ms. Elmyr took a seat in a squeaky desk chair. She extended a hand, inviting Frannie to sit in one of two wooden chairs on the opposite side.

The office was small and the desk made it feel smaller.

Loose papers and file folders were stacked on shelves and atop metal cabinets around the room. A ceiling fan whirred overhead, wobbling as it spun, sending the pull-chain in an orbit around the lone light bulb.

"I have good news, Frannie dear." Ms. Elmyr propped her elbows on the armrests of her chair and steepled her hands in front of a wide smile. "Someone has requested to adopt you."

Surprised, Frannie blinked and looked around the room. Something on the desk caught her eye—a piece of paper with her name on it. It looked like a list. There were other names on it too.

Ms. Elmyr rearranged the top of her desk and the list disappeared among the files and papers.

"Aren't you excited, dear? Someone wants you to come live with them."

"I thought I was too sad," Frannie said. "One of the other kids told me I was too sad. No one wants sad kids."

"Oh, no no no," Ms. Elmyr clucked. "Some children like to tell stories, dear. No, you're not too sad. Not at all."

"So, who wants us?" Frannie felt brighter. She tried to picture all the faces she and Hank had met who wanted to adopt children. Who could it be?

Ms. Elmyr tilted her head back and pursed her lips. "Oh, I see I wasn't clear. So sorry, dear. I don't know where my head is today."

The woman stood and walked around to Frannie's side of the desk. She leaned against it with her hands clasped in front her. Lips still pursed, she gazed down at Frannie.

"Frannie, dear, it is very difficult for families to take in two children at the same time. It's just too much for most people.

Do you understand?"

Frannie did not understand. What kind of family didn't want two kids at the same time? Her parents seemed to manage just fine. She didn't care. She didn't want to be with any family not willing to take both of them.

"I thought you said someone is taking us home?"

"Someone is, but it will only be you, dear."

"What?" Frannie's lip quivered; she breathed faster. "What about Hank? You can't split us up. I won't go. I won't," Frannie shouted.

"Calm yourself, dear," Ms. Elmyr said in a much louder voice than Frannie had ever heard from the woman. She brushed the front of her sweater with one hand and after a pause, she continued. "As I said, it's difficult for any family to take on two new children at the same time, two new mouths to feed, two new backs to clothe, and so on."

"But ..."

"But," Ms. Elmyr said, raising a finger, "a baby, especially one so cute and adorable as little baby Hank, is highly sought after. Many, many people want to take Hank. They'd snap him up like that." Ms. Elmyr snapped her fingers. "But with the two of you together," she shrugged and looked away, "I don't think Hank would ever be adopted. You two would end up permanent members of our little home here." She spread her arms and looked back at Frannie.

A fat tear ran down Frannie's cheek and splashed against her T-shirt. Staying at the orphanage forever sounded terrible, but at least they'd be together. She and Hank could make it work. They could have fun here as long as they were together.

Frannie shook her head and wiped the tears away. No.

Hank needed a home. Hank deserved a home.

"So, if I leave, Hank will go to a nice home?"

"Oh, dear, little Hanky will go to a very nice home. I'm sure of it." Ms. Elmyr clapped her hands together.

"Who wants me then?" Frannie said. "Where am I going?" Frannie realized Ms. Elmyr never used the word family when she said someone wanted her.

"Do you remember the woman and man you spoke with earlier today? In the dark clothing?"

Frannie remembered them. A dark-skinned woman and a very pale man dressed in the same tight black clothes that looked like dresses with long sleeves. Frannie did not get the feeling they were married or even a family. Their questions felt more like a test than anything else. They wrote down a lot of things while they asked her their strange questions.

Frannie nodded.

"They're going to take you to a wonderful place. A lot like a school, really. You'll live there and there will be other kids just like you." Ms. Elmyr leaned forward and gripped Frannie's chin in her claw-like fingers. "They will be your new family."

* * *

Member Principal Amadi of the Order of the Coppice and her associate waited in Gilda Elmyr's office. It was late in the afternoon and after a day full of interviewing children, she was ready to get back to their hotel for a drink.

The door behind them flew open and Ms. Elmyr scurried in. She greeted the two members by name as she flopped into her creaking chair across the desk from them.

"Good day to you both. I see your interviews went well." Her smile stretched in an elongated U shape from temple to temple, compressing her eyelids to slits. She leaned forward, her elbows on the desk and her hands clasped in front of her.

Member Principal Amadi nodded. "You have spoken with all of the children?" She pointed at the list of names on Ms. Elmyr's desk. The list she'd given Ms. Elmyr hours earlier.

"I have. But I'm afraid there is one I cannot give you." Ms. Elmyr's smile faded to a grimace.

This again, Amadi thought. Every visit it was the same and Amadi thanked the heavens that she only had to come here once a year.

Amadi took a deep breath. "Oh? Which child would that be?"

Ms. Elmyr looked down at the list in front of her, as if searching for a name. "This Miss Frannie. Such a dear, but I'm afraid she and her brother Hank are highly sought after. Many lovely families are hoping to bring them home." She shrugged and leaned back. "We don't want to separate them, you see. I'm afraid she simply cannot go with you." She gave the two Members a grim smile.

What will it take this time? Amadi wondered.

"I see. We particularly liked her. She is the perfect age. High aptitude. Very astute." After another deep breath, she continued, "If she were included, there could be additional compensation on top of the normal state funding. This compensation would be," Amadi paused so she understood, "in the usual amount and delivered with its usual discretion."

"Madame Amadi, you know the protocols." Ms. Elmyr shook her head in what Amadi took to be an attempt to appear affronted and bewildered. "You are only allowed to take a child if he or she is passed up for adoption and seemingly *unadoptable*. If a child is sought after by would-be parents, they cannot go with you to your," she cleared her throat, "facility. Besides, what am I to tell all those nice people who would give Frannie and little Hank a home? I simply can't."

Ms. Elmyr leaned back and turned her chair to face the wall, showing Amadi and the younger Member her profile.

Amadi hated these games.

"Gilda, we could double the usual amount of additional compensation if Frannie were allowed to come with us." Amadi just wanted to get the charade over with.

Ms. Elmyr frowned and shook her head. "No, I just don't think I could do it. It's not just illegal but immoral—that's the thing. No, I just can't, Amadi. I am sorry."

Amadi closed her eyes, closed her mind to the greed wafting across the desk. After a brief, internal meditation, she opened her eyes and said, "Triple."

Ms. Elmyr's head tilted back and a flicker of a smile flitted across her face. She inhaled deeply as if breathing in the steam from a hearty stew. Turning in her chair, she began shuffling papers on her desk.

Not looking up, Ms. Elmyr said, "You will be here in the morning at your usual time, I suppose? I shall have them all cleaned and dressed for you when you arrive."

Amadi and the man next to her looked at each other for a moment then stood. "Very well. Good day to you, Ms. Elmyr." Amadi bowed slightly before turning to leave.

Behind her, Amadi could hear Ms. Elmyr humming as she quietly rearranged the mass of paperwork covering her desk.

* * *

That night, after bedtime, Frannie snuck out of the girl's wing. In the silent stillness she crept through the orphanage to the toddlers' wing. Weaving through the cribs, careful not to make a sound, she found Hank.

He lay on his back. His sleep sack hung loosely around his body; his arms splayed limply at his sides. She climbed into his crib and laid down beside him. She rested a hand on his chest, watching it rise and fall with his breaths.

In the months after her mother died, Frannie and her dad would lay on either side of Hank, each resting a hand on his chest, watching their hands rise and fall with each breath. Now, next to her brother, in the middle of dozens of other orphans, she closed her eyes and imagined both her dad and her mom were there with her. Three hands on baby Hank. A family connection she'd never had a chance to know.

* * *

"Oh, dear, I thought I'd find you here."

Frannie opened her eyes. Ms. Elmyr stood over her and Hank. He was still asleep. Glancing toward the window, Frannie saw that it was still dark out.

"Come now, dear. Your new home is waiting."

Tears spilled down her cheeks. She wiped them away as quick as they came. Her dad would want her to be brave; she knew that.

Bending low, she kissed her brother on the head.

"I love you, Hank. Be good for whoever you end up with. I love you."

Ms. Elmyr lifted her from the crib and set her on the floor. "Good girl. Now, it's time to go."

Frannie turned as she was pulled away, trying to catch a glimpse of Hank, but she lost sight of him as they turned through the maze of cribs.

* * *

Outside on the sidewalk, Frannie stood in a line next to a dozen other children about her age. Each of them had a small bag next to their feet. Somewhere in the orphanage behind them, her brother still slept. He'd be looking for her when he woke.

Frannie shivered in the cold, damp air. Sunlight peeked over the horizon.

The sound of a vehicle crept through the dim light of morning. Soon, a large black van pulled from around the side of the building and stopped next to the sidewalk where she stood.

Out of the van stepped three people. Two of them she recognized as the woman and man who asked her all the strange questions the day before. The third person was a young woman, taller than Frannie with long dark hair and brown skin. Maybe a teenager. She wore an outfit similar to the other two, only it was gray instead of black.

The older woman in black, the one who'd asked her all the questions, opened the side door of the van and began welcoming the children as they stepped forward to enter.

Frannie, at the end of the line, hesitated. Would she ever be able to get back here? Would she ever see her brother again? Where were they being taken anyway?

The pale man stepped in front of her. He bent down and looked her in the eyes with a kind face.

"Sweetie, are you coming with us?"

"Where?" She looked down at her feet, trying to hold back the tears. "Where are you taking us?"

"To a very special place." He rested a hand on her shoulder. "A special place for special people."

She looked up. Her dad had always called her special. The tears slowed.

"You think I'm special?"

"I know you're special," he said, smiling. "And we can teach you how to be even more special. How does that sound?"

She nodded.

"We met yesterday, didn't we? I'm Frannie."

"I know, honey." The man placed a gloved hand to his chest. "You can call me Brother Jacobi."

"Hi, Brother Jacobi."

"Hi, Frannie." Brother Jacobi pursed his lips. "Why don't I introduce you to someone who can be your buddy for today? Someone who could help you settle in at your new home. Would you like that?"

Frannie nodded and for the first time in a long time, the hint of a grin crossed her face. She hadn't had a buddy in a very long time.

Brother Jacobi stood, his hand still on Frannie's shoulder. With his other hand he waved for the young woman in gray to come over. With warm eyes she approached the two of them.

"This is my friend Frannie," Brother Jacobi said to the young woman. "Would you please be her buddy for the day and help her get settled in? Answer any questions she might have. Could you do that?"

"Certainly," said the young woman.

As Brother Jacobi walked back toward the van, the young woman gave Frannie a broad smile.

Frannie turned away, searching the high windows, wondering where Hank might be.

"Leaving someone behind?" the young woman in gray said.

Frannie's head whipped around. How could she know?

"Yeah, me too." She looked down at Frannie.

"What was his name?" Frannie asked.

"It was a she, actually. My twin. Why don't you join me in the van and I'll tell you all about her." She extended a hand to Frannie. "It's Frannie, right?"

"Yeah. It's short for Francesca."

The young woman shook Frannie's hand. "I'm very pleased to meet you, Frannie. My name is Jacira."

26

Old Friends

Jacira Barretto leaned an ear close to the security barrier between the east and west wards on the thirtieth floor. The riot put the entire prison into lockdown, activating solid steel emergency barriers along the meridian of each circular level and thus, blocking every concentric passageway. These, combined with the always locked stairwell doors, effectively contained each ward in a half-circle steel box. Using the key fob given to them by Member Principal Jacobi, Jacira, Balthazar, and the unnamed redheaded woman could open the barriers, but they had to be careful to make sure no one waited for them on the other side. They'd decided to avoid groups, large and small, as the weapons the three of them carried made them attractive targets. While they could easily defend themselves, they wanted to avoid the attention if at all possible.

The three former Members of the Order of the Coppice had worked their way down the west stairwell from the top level of the Keep without major incident. They'd waited almost an hour after the riot started before setting out. Jacira figured the time gave the thrust of the worst violence time to fizzle out and enough time for their quarries to get to their quarters and settle in. They'd be easier to find and easier to kill.

Having donned impromptu ponchos made from prison blankets, the three assassins and their weapons had attracted little attention. The seven inmates they encountered in the stairwell had been dispatched easily and silently with blades. They used scroll tablets to tap into video feeds from all over the prison. The extra eyes allowed them to avoid trouble where possible, but it also gave them an idea of what was happening in the prison. Most of the inmates had gathered in the mess halls on each floor. The seating areas and kitchens had been divided by the security barriers along with the rest of the floor, but plenty of food could still be found there and it provided an open area for rioters to gather.

It was clear that factions of gangs controlled each floor. In some cases, summary executions were carried out on rivals—their bodies tossed down the Great Atrium or hung from homemade ropes to dangle in the open air as a warning. In spite of the lockdown, however, inmates were managing to traverse between levels. The stairwells were used by some who, Jacira assumed, had kidnapped a guard or a Tapper and used their access chips. Others used makeshift rope ladders thrown down and strung across the Great Atrium. One view from a higher floor showed the Great Atrium growing into a multi-tiered spider web of cordage, sheets, and cables of various types.

She couldn't speak for Balthazar and the redhead, but Jacira was anxious to finish this job and leave the Keep behind forever. Once upon a time, she thought she'd done just that

... only to be proved wrong by fate ... and James Sarazin.

In the outermost passageway, in the west ward of the thirtieth floor, Jacira listened with her ear an inch away from the metal barricade. After a moment, she looked at her partners and shrugged.

"I think we're good, but ..." She shook her head and scanned the video feed on her scroll tablet. The view from the other side of the barrier showed nothing but blackness. The camera lens had been obstructed, which meant they could be walking into an ambush.

Jacira reached out with the key fob, about to swipe it across a panel in the bricks, when she stopped cold. Leaning forward again, her ear grazing the cold metal of the barrier, she squinted in concentration. A soft thud from the other side and she pulled back.

"Let's ..." She was interrupted by a shower of sparks overhead. They rained down with a loud crackling and popping. Everyone spun in place, weapons at the ready, searching frantically for the threat. The sparks continued for five more seconds then stopped. Acrid smoke filled the space.

"Shit," Balthazar shouted and jumped backwards, kicking and stomping on the toes of his right boot.

Jacira looked at the barrier and immediately saw the source of all the commotion. A quarter-inch wide gash, roughly eighteen inches long, had appeared in the barrier. It stretched from the top of the barrier straight down. The metal around the cut glowed bright red with heat. She looked back at Balthazar's boot. A wisp of smoke rose from a hole above his big toe. He cursed and sneered at the fresh cut in the steel.

Voices reached Jacira's ears. Another soft thud against the

steel barrier and the sparks resumed. She jerked her head in the opposite direction and the three killers raced stealthily down the corridor. She and Balthazar took point with the other woman in the rear.

"Where did they get a cutting torch?" Balthazar said. The sound of fire melting through metal faded as they jogged.

"No idea." She pointed down a corridor to the right. The others' footsteps padded behind her as she then turned another corner into the next passageway. Another steel barricade stood across the curving hallway; four open cell doors lined the right-hand side. Random items had been wedged in the jambs and under the doors to keep them open. The prison lockdown would have sealed all cell doors that were already closed. To her, it looked like none in this passageway had been closed.

A quick check of her scroll tablet and Jacira could see the other side of the barrier. Empty. The hallway onscreen was a replica of the one they stood in now with the exception of one cell door sealed shut.

"It's clear," Jacira said. She reached into her pocket and grasped the key fob.

"What we got here?" said a voice behind them.

The three assassins turned. Two cell doors away a wiry man leaned against the doorframe.

"Hey, boys, y'all didn't tell me it was time for visitation?" he said toward the interior of the cell. He stepped away from the door and four more men emerged from inside the cell.

Jacira faced the redheaded woman. "I thought you cleared the cells."

With a shrug, the woman smirked, looking amused.

The five inmates lined themselves up in a rough line across

the passageway. Each held a weapon of some type. Some stained, caked with dried blood. Two of the men bore the crimson stains of a recent fight on their white uniforms. All looked thirsty for violence.

"I could tell you was a lady even with that bullshit do-rag you got there," the lanky man said from the center of the line. "And ole red there ain't even tryin'. I mean what the fuck? You must want to bed down with one of these here lunatics."

The redheaded woman laughed. Jacira looked at her again and became convinced that she was genuinely amused.

"Big fella is mine," a massively built black inmate at the end of the line said. "The rest of you can fight over the split tail."

"To each his own, Lentwood." The lanky inmate grinned. Looking back toward Jacira and the others, he said, "Y'all make this easy and nobody has to die. Can't guarantee it won't hurt, but you won't die." He held up his hands. "You probably won't die. Let's just say that."

The three assassins didn't speak. They silently spread themselves across the hallway. Hands disappearing under their ponchos.

"Either way," the lanky prisoner continued, "this is happenin'." The five inmates moved forward as one. Smiles grew. Eyeballs darted between Jacira and the redhead, except for Lentwood, he only had eyes for Balthazar. "What did you plan to do about that steel wall behind you anyway? You got some secrets under them get ups?"

Jacira tightened the fingers of her right hand around the grip of the knife attached to her body armor. Her left hand found the pistol with its attached suppressor in her rear holster.

"Let's do this quietly," Jacira said.

The lanky man threw his head back in a gut busting laugh. "That all depends on you, hon. We can be as loud or as quiet as you want."

The nearest man was three feet away. Jacira's hands whipped from under the poncho. The pistol fired into the center mass of the man on her right; the bark of the pistol gave a muffled *pop* from the suppressor. He fell back. She fired at the man on her left, red mist puffed from his shoulder; the shot was off target. The man staggered but kept coming toward her raising his club high, swinging at her head before she could adjust her aim and fire again.

She fell to one knee, ducking the blow.

The knife in her left hand swung in a short arc across the man's inner thigh. Bright red arterial blood shot like a fountain from the wound. He fell back.

Leaping forward, Jacira swung her knife across the throats of the two inmates laying side by side. They clawed at the gaping slashes as pools of blood spilled from between their fingers.

Standing over her kills, she surveyed the rest of the fight. Balthazar had dispatched his two foes in a similar fashion as Jacira. Four men were dead on the ground. The fifth, the lanky ring-leader, squirmed and moaned on the ground as the redheaded woman, with a blade in each hand, made cut after cut across his face, legs, arms, torso, and groin. She laughed through bared teeth, barely containing her mirth.

The lanky man whimpered, "Stop. Please. Stop," while he pushed with one good leg trying, but failing, to escape her wrath.

The blades flew for another minute until finally, Jacira said, "Okay. We get it. End it already so we can move on."

With a final thrust, the redhead drove her blade into the man's eye socket, twisted the knife, then withdrew it. She then proceeded to clean her blades on the clothing of the dead man with what little fabric there was left free of blood.

The trio made their way through the barrier into the east ward, down the hall, and then backtracked in the outermost passageway. Soon, they stood several feet from the steel barrier they'd initially encountered. It stood with a gaping hole in its center. Eighteen-inch cut lines zig-zagged their way around the large square opening; the cut away section lay flat on the tile floor in the west ward. Bits of plastic attached to thin wires littered the floor.

Balthazar reached down and picked up a thin bar of what looked like silver clay roughly eighteen inches long. He turned it over in his hands and Jacira examined it. The brick's edges were smooth, a plastic circle hung from a thin wire off one end. The wire ran down the clay bar's centerline. "I think that's a welding strip," Jacira said. "Used to cut and weld metal. Pull the tab and it lights up. That's what they're using to cut through the barriers. Where did it come from?"

"Found it on the floor," he shoved the welding strip into an unseen pocket under his poncho, "and I'm keeping it."

Jacira nodded toward the door they'd gathered around. "Who wants dibs on this one?" She jerked a thumb toward the door. The redheaded woman patted herself on the chest, to which Jacira said, "You want it, you got it." She reached out with the key fob and unlocked the door to Sister Jocelyn's quarters.

Inside the Member's room, Jacira stood with her back to the door. Balthazar crossed to one corner and the redhead stood in the center, near the foot of the bed. Jocelyn was sleeping when they entered, fully clothed in her long black cassock on top of her made bed.

Jacira watched the redheaded woman, wondering when she'd strike, but the woman just stood there staring at the sleeping Member.

Suddenly, Sister Jocelyn's eyes shot open. With unnerving calm, she studied the three intruders. Then, as if this was something she completely expected, she sat up and swung her legs over the edge of the bed. Her eyes settled on the redhead, looked her up and down several times.

"I guess I knew you'd come for me at some point," Sister Jocelyn said to the woman. She spoke slowly, deliberately. Waving a hand toward the door, she asked, "Was this all your doing, just so you could get to me?"

The redhead said nothing in reply.

"And who are these two you've brought with you?" Sister Jocelyn eyed Jacira and Balthazar. "But wait," she said, squinting at them, "I recognize you two. Aha, I see now. You've found ... others ... like you. Others who were ... cast out. Others who weren't worthy of the responsibility of being a Member of the Order."

"No, Jocelyn," said the redheaded former-Tapper, speaking for the first time since Jacira had met her. "The Order wasn't worthy of me." Her hand slipped from under the poncho, revealing a red stained knife.

The old Member blinked slowly and took a deep breath. A bead of sweat dripped from her temple. "No, Oona. No, I'm afraid you're very wrong." Sister Jocelyn eyed the murderous blade. "But I'm truly glad you've found a profession suited to your ... skills and disposition."

"You should be," Oona said. "It was you who gave me my

first taste."

To Jacira, Jocelyn looked ill. She didn't notice when they first entered the room, but the woman now looked frail and sickly. Her face was pale and her skin clammy. Maybe it was a good thing she was about to die, she thought. Put her out of her misery.

It was only then that she noticed Sister Jocelyn's shimmering right index finger.

"I'm afraid," Jocelyn said, reaching her right, ungloved hand to the back of her own neck, "I can't oblige you with another taste just now."

"No!" Oona reached out for Jocelyn's arm, but it was too late. The old Member's body stiffened, and with a feeble wheeze, she fell forward onto the floor.

Oona stood glaring down at her old Mentor's corpse, her face unreadable.

"Job's done, Oona. Let's go," Jacira said.

Oona stood there, not moving, staring down at the dead Sister Jocelyn. She dropped to her knees beside Jocelyn with what Jacira thought was a look of grief. Instead, Oona raised her knife in both hands, and with a cry of rage, stabbed Jocelyn's lifeless body. She lifted the knife again and stabbed once more. Then again. And again. And again. She spent the better part of two minutes mutilating the corpse of Sister Jocelyn before Balthazar physically removed her, kicking and screaming, from the bloody scene.

27

Ascent

On the twenty-fourth floor of the Keep, Martin Aubrey twisted his hands around the wooden handle of his axe. He stopped at the corner of the central corridor and glanced back at Malina who was scanning a tablet hanging from a lanyard around her neck. A machete hung at her side. Francesca and Rudolfo stood silently behind her, both holding spears with blackened tips.

Malina held up a flat hand, seemed to watch something move across the screen, then pointed forward.

The four of them crossed the opening of the north corridor and continued down the passageway. Aubrey glanced toward the Great Atrium as they passed the corridor. Bodies, at least half a dozen, strewn about on the floor. Blood covered the floor, the walls. The air smelled of burnt metal, plastic, and flesh.

They knew this section of the ward was relatively clear, having seen most of the prisoners gathering in the mess hall, but Malina kept an eye on things using her hacked feed of the Keep's security cameras. Once again, Aubrey found himself immensely grateful to have found her.

They passed offices, the rec room, the Members' observation room. All stood empty. Patches of blood-stains dotted the floor of the passageway but it was nothing like the north corridor behind them. No one spoke as they skulked along. Shouting could be heard coming from other parts of the Keep, some from their floor. The Great Atrium played tricks on the ear as it carried sounds up and down the tube of air.

It had been roughly an hour since the start of the riot. Aubrey had debated with the others on whether they should wait for things to settle before venturing out. His hunch was that Sarazin, having somehow started or at least facilitated the start of the riot, wanted to accomplish some objective in the midst of the chaos. He'd use the riot to cover his true plans and vanish once he'd accomplished what he came to do. Frequent checks of the video feeds showed them his plane was still parked on top of the Keep, which meant he was most likely still there.

They'd escorted the injured guard to a safe room, which Rudolfo could access with his implanted chip. Several other guards were in the small space already and quickly saw to caring for their co-worker.

Aubrey found the Tappers to be ideal companions, perfect for their present circumstances. They moved nearly silently, showed no fear, and, most importantly, seemed totally unflappable. Francesca especially impressed him. She was ruthless, lethal, and surprisingly powerful. She'd mentioned that future Members underwent some physical training and self-defense and it was obvious she'd excelled.

Aubrey stopped shy of the intersection with the central corridor and turned back to Malina once again. She swiped the screen, moved her fingers deftly across it, appeared to zoom in and out, then, finally, gave Aubrey the signal to move ahead.

Their destination lay on the other side of the central corridor thirty feet away. Once they reached the elevators, Rudolfo would use his chip to gain access and they'd shoot to the top floor and confront both Sarazin and Jacobi.

Crossing the central corridor, Aubrey heard more shouting. Where was it coming from? Closer this time?

As if in response to his thoughts, Malina whispered, "We're good all the way to the elevator. A hundred feet beyond it, though, is the cafeteria where we are most definitely not clear. So, let's not go that way."

At the elevator, as planned, Aubrey and Francesca took up defensive positions while Rudolfo moved forward to call the elevator.

Aubrey faced down the passageway toward the mess hall trying to determine if the faint voices bouncing off the walls around him were close by.

"Something is wrong," Rudolfo said behind him.

Aubrey turned. Rudolfo ran the back of his left hand over a square panel next to the elevator. No lights flashed above the elevator or on the panel itself. Aubrey moved to the shiny steel doors and pressed his ear against them. No sounds came from behind them. Nothing could be seen or heard to indicate the elevator had been called.

"Is it usually this quiet?" Aubrey asked Rudolfo.

"No." Rudolfo passed his hand over the panel again and again. He removed his glove and tried again, finally pressing his hand against the panel and scraping it across. Nothing happened.

"It's dead," Aubrey said. "The lockdown killed it."

"No, the elevators are supposed to remain on during a lockdown." Rudolfo looked down, apparently lost in thought. "Only one person could shut down the Members' elevator."

"Jacobi?" Francesca answered the question for everyone else.

Rudolfo nodded.

"Fuck." Aubrey spun to check the passageways. The voices were closer, he was sure of it. He could make out individual words now. "Options?"

"Stairs," Rudolfo replied. "Our only option."

The rest of the company followed Brother Rudolfo twenty feet further down the passageway toward the mess hall. Aubrey could hear footsteps and feet scuffling as they reached the locked door to the west stairwell. Once again, Rudolfo passed the back of his left hand across a square panel. This time, a loud *clunk* sounded from inside the door.

Rudolfo swung the door open and Aubrey held it as Malina and Francesca filed past. As Rudolfo walked through, figures came into view down the passageway. The three inmates rounded the gentle curve of the hallway and saw Aubrey holding the door open.

"What the fuck?" one of the inmates shouted. They ran.

Aubrey pivoted. He rounded the door and pulled it shut just as the men came within spitting distance. They pounded the outside of the windowless door.

"How the hell did he open it?" one voice shouted.

Aubrey and the others climbed the stairs, carefully peering around each corner to the floor above. Malina's tablet couldn't pick up a signal inside the thick concrete and steel of the stairwell, so they were forced to take it slow. No one should have had access to the stairs except Members of the Order and prison guards, but they had no idea if any Members or guards had been compromised. They also heard unmistakable screams of pain from high above soon after entering the stairs. Someone else was using the stairs.

"Does that chip require the hand to be attached to a living person?" Aubrey asked as they reached the twenty-ninth floor.

"It does," Rudolfo replied.

"Good."

A moment later, Aubrey threw up a fist and the group halted behind him. A thud on the floor above. A door slamming shut. He looked back at the group. Francesca pointed her spear forward and began to creep ahead, but Aubrey stopped her, shaking his head. When no other sounds reached them, he let go and together they traversed the remaining stairs up to the thirtieth floor. They were alone. Indiscernible noises could be heard from far above them, but in the immediate vicinity, it was just the four of them.

On they climbed, meeting no one else along the way. On the thirty-fourth floor, they encountered the first physical evidence that others had been there. An inmate lay on his stomach, head pointed down the stairs. The sides of his uniform top were soaked red and blood cascaded from his neck and torso, down the steps like a macabre waterfall.

"The blood is only just starting to dry," Francesca pointed out, touching the toe of her shoe to the edge of the mess. Sticky crimson tendrils stuck to the bottom of her sole, stretching as she pulled it away.

A slam jerked Aubrey's eyes from the corpse. He scanned the area but saw nothing.

"Up there," Malina said, pointing directly overhead.

"That's where we need to go," Aubrey said, following her finger up. "You can still go hole up in one of the panic rooms and wait for the cavalry. You don't need to come with us."

Her gaze fell for a moment, then she locked eyes with him. "No. I feel safer with ... the group."

An awkward moment passed while he and Malina stared at one another.

"We should move on." Rudolfo broke the silence.

"Yeah," Aubrey said, looking away. "Let's get going."

They climbed four more flights and discovered six more dead inmates killed in a similar fashion as the first—knife wounds.

"These weren't your standard inmate-on-inmate kills." Aubrey bent to inspect the body. He rolled the head of the last victim to view the slash across the man's jugular. "This was a good, sharp blade and the cut was precise. Professionally done." He pointed down the stairs. "But I think they were going down, not up. See the way the bodies fell?" He gestured to the corpse laying with its feet on the landing, torso and head on the stairs below. "Looks like we must have just missed them."

This seemed to give Rudolfo pause, who backed away and glared down the stairs, the way they'd come.

"You think it's her?" Malina asked Aubrey.

He knew exactly who she meant. The woman who tried to kill him on the road back from the Jorgetsons' home.

"Why would she be here?" he asked, still kneeling beside the dead inmate. "How could she be here?"

"I know we haven't talked about it since the revelation about Zentransa and Sarazin and all that, but isn't it obvious?

He hired her to kill you because you were too close to the truth. He staged this riot somehow to cover up Wilcott Tapping the Ventana four. And now there is a professional killer roaming the halls of the Keep. That's not a coincidence, Martin."

Aubrey cocked his head to the side. "The Keep is full of professional killers."

Malina threw her hands in the air. "Not assassins, Martin. Professional killers avoid getting caught. This has to be her."

Rudolfo inserted himself between them. "Who are you talking about? Did you see this person? Describe them to me."

Aubrey did so, quickly recounting the story of the ambush, what the woman looked like, how she acted, her style of movement. When he finished, all the blood seemed to leave Rudolfo's face. His eyes were saucers and he stared into space.

"You're absolutely positive your description is accurate?" Rudolfo looked to be beside himself.

"Yes. You don't forget someone like her."

"No, I imagine not." Rudolfo stepped away from the group, seemingly lost in thought.

"Sir? What is it? Who is she?" Francesca asked.

"I … I don't know. Probably nothing." He took a visibly deep breath and said, "we should …"

A noise from below cut him off. To Aubrey, it sounded like rushing air mixed with quick popping noises. The smell of hot, burning metal also reached him. He knew what it was—someone was welding.

"That's how they're getting inside the stairwell," he said. "They have a welder or cutting torch."

"No." Rudolfo bent down and rolled over the dead inmate Aubrey had been inspecting. "That is how." He pointed to a backpack that had been partially hidden under the body. It was unzipped; long rectangular bars sticking out from inside it.

Aubrey pulled out one of the bars. It felt like heavy clay, thin, and about a foot and a half long. A round plastic tab hung from one end connected to a thin wire that looked to be pressed into a seam in the bar.

"What is it?" Aubrey asked.

"Welding strips." Rudolfo picked one up and held it out. "Made of highly combustible malleable material with a thin rod of magnesium alloy down its center. Pull the tab's wire from top to bottom and a chemical agent is released that ignites the bar." He placed the strip in the backpack and zipped it. "Maintenance crews use them here quite a bit. Prisoners work on some of those crews, which is probably why a few know how to use them. Here," he handed the bag to Aubrey, "take it. We may need them."

"Where are we now?" Malina asked.

"We just passed thirty-eight," Francesca answered.

A loud boom echoed several floors below them.

"We need to go. Up now. Let's go." Aubrey ushered the others up the stairs and pushed the small of Malina's back urging her forward. "Hurry, we're almost to the top."

Aubrey soon cursed himself for saying those words. On the forty-second floor, their ascent ended abruptly as a mountain of debris, from floor to ceiling, confronted them. The barricade was a mixture of metal desks, plastic chairs, wire, and sharpened sticks fashioned from broom and mop handles. It stretched from one corner of the landing to the other, completely blocking both the door to the forty-second floor and the staircase to the next level up.

"Shit," Malina said.

Aubrey looked back down the way they'd come, then back at the barricade. "There's no getting past it anytime soon." Below them, the sound of cutting stopped, quickly followed by an enormous slam of a metal slab falling to meet concrete. Cursing and cheers reached them—gruff, coarse voices celebrating the felled door.

"Forty-one and then to the east stairwell. That's our only chance," Rudolfo said, already descending the stairs in that direction. "We must hurry."

The four of them leapt down the flight of stairs to forty-one. They paused only briefly to listen at the door before leaving the stairs. Below them, footsteps pounded the stairs accompanied by the loud chatter of dangerous sounding voices.

"Go," Aubrey said to Rudolfo who passed his left hand over a square panel. The door unlocked and they barreled through it.

Aubrey slammed the door shut behind him and swung around toward the others.

"The next stairwell." Rudolfo pointed. "This way."

They raced after the Member of the Order past empty offices and bloodied corpses. Rudolfo was running past the central corridor when his head flew violently back and he crashed to the floor, flat on his back.

Aubrey raised his axe and rushed past Malina and Francesca, who'd slid to a stop.

"If there's too many of them, just run. Get somewhere safe," he shouted to them.

He rounded the corner into the corridor and was faced with a half dozen inmates, all armed similarly to him—long sharp implements of death. A fat headed black man in the middle smiled wide, patting his palm with the shaft of a mean looking club. Aubrey stepped forward. He could hold them off while Francesca and Malina got to safety, he thought.

A woman's scream brought him up short. He doubled back into the passageway.

Aubrey never saw what hit him. There was a swift blur across his vision, a hard impact against the back of his head, then he was lying on the ground.

His vision began to fade, a dark circle collapsing. Before all went black, in the middle of the ever-receding sphere of light, a dark, puffy face came into view.

"Look at this Hollywood lookin' motherfucker."

28

Barter

Aubrey's head pounded. Pain pulsed from the back of his skull and radiated down his neck and shoulders. He opened his eyes and blinked the world into focus. He was seated on the floor of a cell, hands bound behind him. He straightened his aching neck and relief flooded him when he saw Malina across from him. She too sat with her hands tied behind her. She leaned against the wall looking back at him from the opposite corner, looking relatively unharmed. Her gear sat in a pile on one of the lower beds.

They were alone in the cell, but the door was open. Angry voices spoke outside.

"I told you, motherfucker. She needs to be clean when we go to Rasta. Don't fucking touch her."

"She'll be clean, man. I won't mess her up, I swear on my mama's ..."

"You gonna swear on your mother's life while you talking about force fucking a woman. Motherfucker, get the fuck out of my face. Go wait for Landers."

"Why'd you send Landers, man? That dude can't talk for

shit and he gonna negotiate for us?"

"'Cause I needed somebody who won't fuck me. Somebody who do what the fuck I say."

Mumbled protests came from the other inmate as his voice drifted down the hall away from the cell where Aubrey and Malina sat.

"You okay?" Aubrey whispered.

Half a smile creased Malina's face. "Yeah, I'm fine. You?"

"My head is killing me, but otherwise, I guess I'm okay. What happened to Rudolfo and Francesca?"

"The gang out there herded them into a closet or something. They were all too afraid to touch them." She looked suddenly at the open door. The fat headed man entered the cell and looked at Aubrey. He lingered for a moment then left.

"Why didn't they kill us?" Aubrey asked. "What's going on?"

"From what I can gather," her voice faltered, barely audible in a harsh whisper tinged with what Aubrey could only think was fear, "they're trying to make a trade with a larger gang. In exchange for protection." Her chin quivered. "I guess they're buying their way into some sort of alliance." She shut her eyes tight, her shoulders shook.

Aubrey didn't ask what the gang outside their cell was going to trade in exchange for the other gang's protection. It was clear. Malina was the item up for bid. And to some degree Aubrey was being bartered too, or he'd already be dead.

* * *

Francesca felt around the dark space, looking for something, anything she could use to get them out of the situation.

"It's a maintenance closet," Rudolfo's voice came from the dark, somewhere nearby. "There is nothing in here but mops and cleaning chemicals."

"How do you know where we are? When did you wake up?" She'd had to drag him into the closet while he was unconscious. The inmates had threatened to do unspeakable things to Malina and Martin if she didn't comply.

"I was half awake as you dragged me in here. In addition, the smell is fairly recognizable."

She continued searching with her hands. She felt metal shelves holding plastic bottles of various sizes, further down a rack on the wall holding wooden handled mops and brooms. A deep sink basin. Buckets full of unknown substances on the floor. A low, four-wheeled cart. A chest-high plastic barrel with a tube and pump protruding from a hole in its lid.

A sliver of light shined from under the door. Shadows passed it and she could hear footsteps outside.

"They're going to kill them," she said. "We have to do something."

"What did you have in mind? We can unlock the door with my chip, but it is barricaded from outside with a large object of some kind. It is probably quite heavy."

"It's a giant plastic barrel filled with some kind of cleaning fluid. I watched them pull it out before they made us come in here." She stopped her search of the small space and stood in front of the door. "Please unlock the door."

She heard his feet shuffling, something fell over on the floor. Some movement by the door, then a soft beep and an accompanying *thunk.* She imagined where the door handle might be, and kicked it.

The door didn't budge. A deep *thrum* came from the other side.

"That would be the barrel," Rudolfo said.

* * *

"Looks like we have a deal," said the fat-headed inmate as he entered the cell. "On your feet, motherfucker. Let's go." He grabbed Aubrey under the arm and dragged him upright.

"Martin," Malina said, struggling against the two men lifting her. "Martin?"

* * *

Francesca kicked the door again. Three more cycles of Rudolfo unlocking the door and her kicking it with no results. The door hadn't moved a millimeter.

"The barrel must be exceedingly heavy," Rudolfo said.

"It took three of them to drag it out of here." Francesca began a new search of the closet. A woman's scream from outside the door made her freeze. "Malina."

Sounds of a struggle, a man's painful grunts, and more cries from Malina, then they were gone.

Francesca began her search more frantically now. How could they open the door and move the barrel? Her hands shoved objects out of the way, threw things to the floor, hoping that she'd feel something that might be of use. She had no idea what it might be, what she was looking for; she'd know it once she found it.

"Francesca."

Her hands flew in the darkness, touching everything, finding nothing. Handles, bottles, shelving, hoses, rags. Nothing. Nothing. Nothing.

"Francesca."

There must be something, she thought. She refused to believe the situation was hopeless. Refused to believe there was nothing, amongst all the objects and materials in the closet, that she couldn't find something to extricate herself from this closet and help Martin and Malina.

"Francesca."

"What?" she shouted, surprising herself with the curt reply.

"The barrel is too heavy to move."

"I realize that, sir. But there is nothing in here to get enough leverage ..."

"It's too heavy. So ... make it lighter."

"Make it ..."

"Lighter."

She slapped her forehead, cursing herself for not thinking of it on her own. Feeling her way back to the corner with the rack of mop handles, she searched for a moment, then found what she was looking for. Removing the mop handle from the rack, she then wedged it between the floor and the first shelf. She wrenched it upward, snapping the metal cradle of the mophead. It left a short, sharp point.

On her knees, she forced the pointed end of the mop handle under the door, through the narrow gap. She pushed on it, twisted it. The metal point barely made it through the gap. She moved the handle back and forth trying to get a feel for metal hitting plastic. After several attempts, she realized it wasn't going to work. The sharp tip was too short.

"Not what I had in mind," Rudolfo said behind her. He

placed one hand on her shoulder; the other placed something in her palm—a small, glass vial. "This ... will melt plastic."

Francesca held the vial between her thumb and forefinger. She couldn't see it, but she knew exactly what it was. "This will ..."

"Yes. Now, hurry."

* * *

Aubrey was thrown down. The cold floor pressed against his cheek. Malina forced to her knees beside him. The crowd of several hundred inmates buzzed around them with excitement. In front of him sat the largest man Aubrey had ever seen. The arms of his prison uniform had been torn away to show off biceps the size of small trees, bristling with popping veins. A flat forehead and slits for eyes made him look reptilian. The way he sat on the edge of the mess hall table, moving his head back and forth, made Aubrey picture one thing—a snake.

Aubrey's body hurt all over. He'd been badly beaten after a failed attempt to fight off their kidnappers.

"Like I said, we just want to be part of your crew. We want to work for you." The fat headed inmate who'd attacked Aubrey spoke for his gang. "Who knows how long we'll all be here. I think it's best we work together, fight together. When the cops or army comes, we'll ..."

"Da fuck I need you for?" The gang leader spoke in a low gravelly voice. It sounded like his vocal cords had been replaced by rocks and sand. "Look around you, minnow. Plenty of fish her on my side. So, again, da fuck I need you for?"

"Look, Rasta. I can give you six good fightin' men. Plus, this bitch." Malina fell forward from a kick to her back. "She's yours. Just let us work for you."

A deep throated moan resonated from Rasta's throat. "Her I could use." He smiled with a mouthful of broken teeth.

Aubrey thrashed and screamed. "Don't you fucking dare, you goddamn ..." A blow to the back sent him flying forward. His skull collided with the floor producing dancing white lights across his vision.

Raucous laughter and then silence. Footsteps near Aubrey's head and then two titanic black boots on either side of his head. "Somebody here'll use him too," Rasta said above him.

"That mean you accept our offer?" Fat head asked.

"Welcome to the family," Rasta said.

The crowd roared and converged on the group in the center of the mess hall.

Aubrey, still on his stomach, rolled to his side and watched as Rasta lifted Malina off the ground by her shoulders. She stood, shivering in the clutches of the man's ham hock sized hands. Rasta reached with one meaty paw and caressed her trembling cheek. He whispered something inaudible.

Aubrey's stomach lurched. His skin grew hot and some unknown mammalian sound issued from his mouth. Hands still bound, he twisted around and shot his legs out toward Rasta, catching him in the side of the knee.

Rasta's elephantile limb didn't move. He looked down as Aubrey got to his knees and threw himself at the mountain man's midsection. Rasta stumbled back several paces with Aubrey's shoulder buried in his gut. Then, Aubrey felt two huge hands take hold of both sides of his ribs. Rasta's hands squeezed like anacondas. Aubrey felt several pops. The pain sent a shockwave through his body. Knees buckling, he fell to the floor.

Rasta lifted a gigantic foot and planted it on Aubrey's back, leaning into it with all of his weight, compressing Aubrey's chest and ribs. More ribs popped, his breath escaped and wouldn't return.

"For that," Rasta said, "I'm not going to keep her all to myself. I'm going to share her with all my boys." This brought cheers, lewd gestures, and snarling faces from the crowd around them. The weight lifted from Aubrey's back, but was quickly followed by a battering ram of a kick to Aubrey's kidney. He couldn't breathe, could barely think. His hands were still bound, his body in knots of pain.

But he had to do something. He wriggled like a worm in the sun, trying desperately to right himself. Rasta had Malina by the hair now, turned to drag her somewhere, then after two steps he stopped. A commotion at the front of the mess hall made Rasta turn.

The crowd split and Aubrey saw it too. A black cloaked figure holding a spear—Francesca.

"Ain't gonna happen, Tapper," Rasta shouted. He gestured to some of his men nearest the female Member of the Order. "Tear her apart."

Five men advanced and Francesca backed away through the doors into the passageway. She, and then the men, disappeared from view. The mess hall went silent. Aubrey used the distraction to slide his tied hands under him and stood on wobbly legs. His hands were still tied but at least they were in front of him.

Rasta watched the double door entry to the mess hall.

Nothing happened for several seconds, then a man in white fell across the threshold. A second later, Francesca, and her spear, reappeared. Someone was with her this time—Rudolfo, but he was pushing some kind of cart.

"Get that cunt and her fucking friend," Rasta shouted. A few men stepped tentatively from the crowd but stopped when Francesca lowered her spear toward them. Its bloodied tip glistened in the white lights from overhead.

While Francesca held off the crowd, Rudolfo lifted two buckets off the cart and set them on the floor. He went back to the cart and lifted two more off, placing them behind the first two buckets. Francesca took a step back behind the first row of buckets. Then, she and Rudolfo kicked over the first two buckets spilling their contents which pooled in an oblong oval stretching into the center of the mess hall.

The smell was immediately recognizable—bleach. What were these two doing?

Francesca and Rudolfo kicked over the next two buckets and it became clear when the smell of ammonia wafted toward him. Bleach and ammonia. Together, they make a deadly combination—chlorine gas.

A white haze rose as twenty gallons of bleach and ammonia mixed in the middle of three hundred crowded inmates. Everyone looked on in apparent confusion for a moment. The coughing started; panic quickly followed. Those closest to the gas fell to their knees gasping, clawing at their chests.

The crowd fled in every direction—some out the doors past Francesca and Rudolfo, others back further into the kitchens.

Aubrey didn't hesitate any longer. He bolted for Rasta, who ran with Malina held in a loose grip. He continued yelling at his men to get the Tappers, cursing and gesticulating while coughing violently.

Rasta rushed through the doors into the passageway. Francesca attempted a jab with her spear, but Rasta dodged it. The big man was too quick.

Aubrey followed him, ignoring the pain in his body as best he could. He ran down the passageway, into a corridor, and soon found himself on the catwalk around the Great Atrium. Twenty feet ahead, Rasta had stopped, doubled over coughing. Malina lay on the ground kicking at him, her hands still tied behind her. Behind Rasta was a large, jagged hole in the catwalk. A rope lay near the hole.

On weak, barely functioning legs, Aubrey rushed Rasta, grabbing the rope in his hands before laying a shoulder into the giant. Rasta fell to his knee, weakened by the gas but still ox strong. He flung one huge arm at Aubrey and knocked him back for a moment. Aubrey threw himself forward onto Rasta's back, wrapped a loop of the rope around the big man's neck, and pulled back with all his remaining strength.

Rasta wheezed and flailed his arms, reaching for some part of Aubrey to squeeze and break. Aubrey twisted the rope tighter around Rasta's neck and pulled with every bit of himself he could muster. Rasta arched his back, stood, and threw himself and Aubrey into the metal catwalk. Aubrey was half-hanging out of the hole in the fencing, when Rasta reached for his ace in the hole. With what must have been a Herculean effort, Rasta bent down and wrapped a hand around Malina's leg. In one motion, he snatched her up into the air and gripped her neck with the other hand.

Rasta was going to kill her.

Aubrey pulled back on the rope with everything he had.

He'd have to kill the man before Rasta could squeeze the life out of Malina. But Rasta wasn't going down. Malina was already going purple in the face. She'd die before Aubrey could kill Rasta.

There was nothing Aubrey could do to stop it.

It was then Aubrey realized where he was. He was *inside* the Great Atrium, leaning through the ragged hole into open air. He'd applied so much leverage to pull on the rope around Rasta's neck that he pushed himself further into the hole in the catwalk's fencing. All that was left inside the catwalk were his legs below the knees.

He loosened his grip on the rope slightly and Rasta did exactly what Aubrey wanted, the man instinctively leaned forward.

Aubrey's legs were loose.

Like a SCUBA diver taking an ocean plunge, Aubrey leaned back and let himself go. The freefall lasted a half second. A jerk and the rope went tight, hanging from Rasta's neck. Aubrey swung in open air; his hands tightly gripping the rope anchored by Rasta's mass.

Weak as he was, Aubrey managed a quick glance back up at the gang leader. The unnatural angle of the man's neck and head told Aubrey what he needed to know. Rasta was dead.

He held on for another second, unsure how long he could hang there. He'd have to let go soon. He just didn't have much left in him to keep at it.

The thought that Malina was safe, for the moment, comforted him. Rudolfo and Francesca could get her out. She'd be all right. That was something.

A tug on the rope. Fearful Rasta may have miraculously

revived himself, Aubrey wearily looked up.

It wasn't Rasta.

The faces of Francesca, Rudolfo, and Malina looked down at him. Each had a hand on the rope and together they pulled Aubrey up.

29

Reunion

“Shit.” Jacira paced the empty quarters of Brother Rudolfo angry at herself for not being more diligent about keeping an eye on their targets. On the way down from Jocelyn’s they hadn’t checked on their location more than a couple of times. This proved to be foolish as Rudolfo and the others had apparently abandoned this room since the last check.

The three killers had burst into the small dormitory with guns at the ready, expecting to encounter the remaining four of their five targets. Instead, they found an empty room.

“We all assumed they’d be here,” Balthazar said. “We couldn’t possibly keep an eye on them and the rest of the prison the whole time and expect to get down here in one piece.”

Jacira continued pacing, scanning every inch of the room, hoping to find some scrap of a clue that would tell her where they might have gone. The bed, bookshelf, bathroom, nightstand, showed her nothing. The computer monitors seemed out of place. Rudolfo wouldn’t have had those in his room under normal circumstances, but …

"I think it's obvious where they went." Balthazar interrupted her train of thought. "They would have gone down, toward the only way out of this prison. The wisest move would have been to stay here and wait for the riot to be put down, but they were too stupid to do that. So, we just need to use the cameras to search the floors between here and the train depot."

Jacira thought about it, and yes, it did make sense that they would have gone down to try and escape the riot. But Balthazar's comment about them being stupid made her think otherwise. She didn't know about the two women, but Jacira knew Martin Aubrey pretty well since she began surveilling him. And she certainly knew Rudolfo quite well. Neither man was stupid. They were both highly capable and clever. If staying in the Member's quarters was the smart move, they would have done just that.

Jacira stood, thinking over all the possibilities. If they didn't stay in Rudolfo's room, and they didn't go down toward a possible exit, then that only left going up. Why? She couldn't think of a single reason for them to go up instead of down.

Oona cleared her throat. Any sound from the selectively mute woman got Jacira's attention. Her eyes moved to Oona who stood in front of the computer monitor that sat on the ground. She'd forgotten it was there for a moment. Oona turned to her and lazily pointed a finger at the screen. Jacira moved closer to it and bent low to view it properly.

In one corner of the large monitor, a window displayed an exterior view from the roof of the Keep. Jutting out from the left edge of the camera's viewpoint was the white tail of an aircraft. The aircraft they had ridden in just a few hours ago with James Sarazin in the pilot's chair.

"Shit." Jacira stood and threw off her poncho. "I know where they're going."

Oona followed suit and tossed her own poncho to the floor.

Balthazar looked confused. "What am I missing?"

"Whatever Sarazin has on these people, they know about it and they're going after him."

"So, no more trying to hide our goodies?" Balthazar asked as he removed his blanket turned poncho.

Jacira began removing the suppressors from the muzzles of her pistols and rifle. "No. We move quick and make as much noise as possible. Maybe we can scare the shit out of everyone enough to leave us alone."

"Should we call Sarazin? Let him know they're coming for him."

Jacira had considered it. "Yes. We'll do it on the way. After all, if he dies, we don't get paid."

She strode to the door and flung it open. A tall prisoner with a large nose and broad shoulders stood in the passageway. For a split second, they both just stood there waiting for the other to flinch.

A shot from over Jacira's shoulder, she flinched sideways and spun around. Balthazar held his rifle high, a hot brass casing spun on the floor.

"No time for this," he said. "Let's go."

Leaving Rudolfo's quarters, she glanced down at the inmate now lying on the floor, his hands clenched over a spot on the left side of his chest. His white uniform soaked up the blood now spewing from the fresh hole in his breast.

* * *

Nicholas Fox, the Professor, hadn't expected it to end with him getting shot. He didn't believe in fate or destiny, and openly chastised those that did. But he'd truly felt in his heart of hearts that he'd make it out of the Keep alive.

In a few weeks, he'd predicted, he'd be sipping cold drinks on a hot beach with a beautiful woman.

Instead, he lay on a cold floor watching his own blood pour from his chest. His feeble attempt to stem the flow by pressing his hands against the wound was hopeless. The deep red pool under his shoulder widened with every second.

The pain, at least, had passed. Now, he just felt numb.

Who would have guns like that in a prison? Who would have let them in? Then, he remembered who had started all this—Sarazin. Of course, Sarazin.

Watching the life leak out of him, he was struck by the irony of it all. He, Nicholas Fox, had made this riot happen. He'd coordinated it all. Gone to great lengths to do so and was ultimately killed by it.

Life, he thought, was nothing if not comical.

He laughed quietly as his eyelids grew heavy.

* * *

Brother Jacobi, Member Principal of the Order of the Coppice, paced the edge of the glass floor on the forty-eighth floor of the Keep. He alternated the outlet for his nervous energy between rubbing the edge of his pockets and pulling at the fringe of his lapel. The violence he watched unfold below him made his blood run cold.

He was used to death, of course. His Order dealt in death like others dealt in marketable goods. They provided that service to humanity. The symbolism of the Coppice was to cut down one thing so others could flourish and he took pride in that. His life had been in service of the Order's purpose, which was, fundamentally, that of killing.

What he watched taking place on the floors of the prison was beyond just death. It was carnage. It was a bloodletting.

Members hung from nooses up and down the Great Atrium. Bodies burned on every level. Blood and viscera painted the walls. And that was only what he could see from where he stood. If it was an accurate representation of the true violence in the Keep, it was on a nearly inconceivable level.

And he couldn't help but feel somewhat responsible.

Wilcott had done what was necessary and self-selected. That was the right thing to do from Jacobi's perspective, putting aside the manner in which Wilcott did it. Then Rudolfo and his little upstart Apprentice had to get involved. They had to get curious. Jocelyn was dead now because of them, of that he was convinced. A five-minute conversation with her and they'd condemned Jocelyn to death.

Jocelyn had come to speak with Jacobi about something else entirely and mentioned her conversation with Rudolfo in passing. And that was all it took to mark her down for assassination. Sarazin was clear—no one can know anything or he'd expose the Order and all their misdeeds at the orphanages. It would all come back to Jacobi. He'd made that clear too.

"Enjoying the show?"

Jacobi jumped with a start, his hand flying to his chest. "Good god, Sarazin. Don't sneak up on a man like that."

"Sorry." Sarazin squinted at the scene below. "You know, I

never actually killed anyone. With my own hands, I mean. And, until this moment, I've never seen anyone die with my own eyes. Now that I see it, I'm acutely aware of … how much it doesn't bother me."

"That it doesn't bother you should bother you, Sarazin." Jacobi gave him a sideways glance. The look on the CEO's face was of placid enjoyment.

"Maybe."

"I can't believe all this. Just to kill five people? Did we need all this?" Jacobi spread his arms at the display of mayhem below them.

"Jacobi, I didn't get to where I am in my life by not planning ahead. This riot was always in my back pocket if I needed it. And it wasn't just to kill five people. It was meant to kill as many as I needed to make sure the job was done."

Jacobi's face grew hot. He stared down through the glass. "You'd planned to murder Members of the Order all along?"

"I had to get rid of Alkorn and his cronies and the Keep is as good a place as any. Killing them out in the civilian world, all at the same time, would have been too suspicious. But no one questions a Tapper, which was pretty convenient for me." Sarazin could have been discussing financial reports at Ventana, Inc. "Since they were here, there was no way to know who they might have spoken to. Had they not feared me killing their families, they might have divulged potentially damaging information to our friend Aubrey when he was here just a few weeks ago."

Jacobi could feel Sarazin staring daggers at the side of his head. "I never knew he was coming. It didn't go through me. And as soon as I heard they were here, Wilcott was sent to intervene. As a result, the prisoners said nothing at all, much less anything potentially damaging."

The CEO laughed. "I bet our boy Aubrey gleaned enough from their saying nothing to do us plenty of harm." Sarazin continued, "So when he and his sidekick were invited to come visit the Keep by your esteemed colleague, I extricated the riot plan from my back pocket and put it into motion."

"All this was just some sort of backup plan?" Jacobi gestured again to the scene beneath them. As if on cue, a scream reached them from below. Both men looked to find its source. Five levels down, a naked woman ran along the catwalk, her bald head dripping lines of blood, more crimson oozing from gashes in her back and from between her legs. As quickly as she appeared, she vanished into a corridor. Three men entered the catwalk carrying metal hooks and shivs and disappeared down the same corridor as the terrified woman. A shiver coursed up the back of Jacobi's arms and legs.

"You are certainly a strategist, Sarazin, I'll give you that but this seems a little excessive. I think there was more to this than just a contingency plan." Jacobi locked eyes with Sarazin, who said nothing and made no visible reaction to the accusation. The Member shook his head in consternation. "But you won't tell me what that is, even if I'm right. Do me the courtesy of answering one question though, will you Sarazin? Why did you have to bring those assassins here? They're outcasts of the Order. Why did you have to use them? Couldn't you find other killers to do your bidding?"

"They're very efficient and highly effective." Sarazin's cold eyes stared back into Jacobi's. "And I always knew I'd probably end up here, so I needed people who knew this place inside and out. I needed people who didn't possess that all too common and ridiculous fear of you and your people. They were more difficult to find than your average bloody-minded hitman. I had to scrape the dregs of the underworld, but I knew they were out there, so I kept looking—not an easy thing to do without exposing myself, but I managed to turn them up." Sarazin's eyes narrowed and he jammed a finger into Jacobi's chest. "I needed a very specific type of job done, and you'll have to forgive me for not giving a fuck about your precious sensibilities."

Jacobi felt his face go slack. The look in Sarazin's eyes was one he'd seen before in Members of the Order. The ones who'd enjoyed the act of killing a little too much. It was an obsession. An addiction. A compulsive, relentless attachment.

"How many Members of my Order were you prepared to murder? Where's the line? What if fifty had known something about your little scheme? Would you have destroyed the Order and with it the entire system of justice we uphold?" Jacobi could feel his knees shaking and his lip quivering with a mix of anger and fear.

Sarazin visibly relaxed and placed a hand on Jacobi's shoulder. "Let's not trouble ourselves with hypotheticals." The CEO brushed unseen dust from Jacobi's chest and straightened the front of his cassock as if he were adjusting a necktie. "We'll get through this, old friend. Don't worry." He released Jacobi and reached into his own pocket. Pulling out his phone, he read the screen then looked back at Jacobi with a huge grin. "Excuse me a minute. Ventana business doesn't stop churning just because I turn on my out-of-office. Know what I mean?"

Jacobi watched Sarazin walk away typing messages into

his phone. The Member Principal returned to the scene below. It was like a bad movie he couldn't turn away from. As much as he hated it, he had to watch. If nothing else, to get a sense how many Members may have been killed by inmates. He was already thinking about the impact on recruiting neophytes for the Pupil's School of the Order.

A strange scraping sound got his attention. He spun around to find Sarazin approaching, ten feet away, staring down into the Great Atrium. Jacobi turned his attention there too. They watched in silence.

"Jacobi, you're right, actually," Sarazin said. "This was more than a back up plan. I had no idea how widespread Alkorn's stories might go. I had no idea who Wilcott might talk to or who else might turn against me. I had to have something in place to eradicate any and all possible loose ends."

Ice ran down Jacobi's spine. He stood frozen to the floor.

Sarazin continued, "And to answer your question from a moment ago: how many Members was I prepared to kill?"

Jacobi turned to face the man. Sarazin shrugged and his hand slid from behind his back revealing a short red fire extinguisher.

"I was prepared to murder all of them, and you."

Jacobi flinched just as the red metal cylinder swung toward his head. His face met the glass floor and a veil of black smothered his vision.

* * *

As soon as Member Principal Jacobi woke up, he knew he was not in his top floor chambers any longer. The smell wasn't right. The light wasn't right. The temperature wasn't right. The sounds reaching his ears weren't right.

For a moment, he thought it was a trick of the brain as he emerged from the fog of unconsciousness. The image of a red metal cylinder hurdling toward his head swam to the front of his mind.

That bastard.

Jacobi lifted his aching head. He was in a passageway. Gray walls. White tube lighting overhead. The wall to his left was painted with a stenciled *47.* He was one floor below his quarters and exposed.

A throbbing in his left hand got his attention. He lifted it. Examined it and his mouth dropped. A long slit down the back of his hand oozed blood.

"No."

He struggled to his feet only to immediately fall to all fours. The world spun around him. His stomach doubled over on itself and he vomited. He kept vomiting until he had nothing left but dry heaves.

Finally, after several minutes, he was able to stand. He stumbled to the stairwell door. Leaning his right hand on the wall to steady himself, he lifted his bloodied left hand and dragged it across the square panel leaving a bloody trail like a morbid slug.

The panel did not change.

The door locks did not disengage.

He tugged on the door handle, but it didn't move.

"Sarazin, you goddamned bastard."

He slammed a bloody fist against into the wall. His chip had been removed. He was trapped out in the open.

* * *

From the forty-first floor, Aubrey, Malina, Francesca, and Rudolfo climbed up the east stairwell toward the top of the Keep. They'd avoided further trouble since leaving forty-one. Francesca and Rudolfo's chemical weapon attack in the mess hall had the effect of renewing, if not escalating, the fear Members inspired in the inmate population. The stairwell had been clear all the way to the landing on forty-seven where the stairs ended.

"Other than the elevator, the west stairwell is the only access to level forty-eight." Rudolfo pressed an ear to the door while he spoke.

On the way up, Aubrey had listened to Francesca recount how they broke out of the maintenance closet, found the drums of bleach and ammonia, and concocted the plan to gas the gang members in the mess hall. He was impressed to learn that the gas attack had been Francesca's idea and judging by the look on the old Tapper's face, Rudolfo was as well.

"We'll have to cross the ward to get there, right?" asked Aubrey. He'd had enough of this prison and the murderous inmates that inhabited it. The idea of traversing the deadly ground in his current state of exhaustion and pain did not appeal to him in the slightest.

"Yes." Rudolfo ran his hand across the square panel next to the door and opened it slowly, peering through the crack as he did so.

The two Members and Aubrey stepped out first, setting up a rough defensive perimeter. Francesca and Rudolfo had their spears and Aubrey his axe; it had been recovered along with Malina's gear after the battle on forty-one. Malina followed them, scanning her equipment for possible threats.

"This floor is pretty clear. If we stick to the outer passageway and avoid the mess hall, we should be okay."

"We can go through the barrier on the opposite end of the ward from the mess hall," Francesca said.

"Yeah, that should be ..." A staccato of gunfire interrupted her. They all exchanged looks of concern.

"Wherever it's coming from," Aubrey said, "I think it's below us. We should be okay for the moment."

"Okay, let's just go," Malina said.

The group moved at a jogging pace, careful to consult Malina with her tablet each time they crossed a corridor. Before long, they reached the barrier; a black wall stretching across the gray floor. Rudolfo lifted his hand to open it, but stopped and glanced at Malina. She searched her tablet, squinted and said, "We're good, but ..." She paused mid-sentence.

"But what?" Aubrey asked, moving toward her. She pointed to a man in a white prison uniform running down a corridor in the east ward; his right arm was wrapped in some sort of sling. "What? Just an inmate. What's wrong?"

"He has hair," Malina said. She gave Aubrey a look of profound confusion.

Francesca approached and scrutinized the tablet. Her eyes narrowed. "Sir, you need to take a look at this."

Rudolfo stepped toward them, a wary expression on his face. Once he saw the tablet and the man on screen, he cursed. Everyone looked at him in surprise. "Jacobi," he said. "The Member Principal."

Realization dawned on Aubrey. "You and Francesca go get him. We'll get Sarazin."

Rudolfo opened the barrier for Malina and Aubrey then

stopped. "You'll need me to get through the stairwell door."

Aubrey patted his backpack filled with a dozen welding strips. "I've got a master key. We're good."

"The hinges have actuators to close them. You must cut the hinges and the lock." With a nod, Rudolfo set off toward the corridor where they last saw Jacobi.

Francesca stood there for a moment, watching her Mentor go. She turned to Aubrey and Malina and said, "Good luck." Then turned to set off after Rudolfo.

* * *

Jacira, Balthazar, and Oona tore through the stairwells on their way to run down their quarry. Thwarted by the impromptu barrier on level forty-two, they took a path around level forty-one to the east stairwell.

Level forty-one had been a hornet's nest of activity when they entered it. In a show of force, they wasted every living soul that presented itself, threat or not. They took turns at point and watching their rear, rotating like a deadly clock every few paces. Crossing forty-one was slower than Jacira had wanted, but they made it with only a few dozen rounds expended between them.

She knew level forty-seven would be a dead end when they reached it. To reach Jacobi's floor on forty-eight, they'd have to cross again. They'd sent Sarazin a message shortly after setting out, so she felt comfortable that he would be somewhat prepared. She'd told him of a few items in the bags they left behind that he could use if a fight came to him. They hadn't left any guns, but there were plenty of useful toys.

In the outer passageway of level forty-seven, she stopped and checked her scroll tablet. Then she rechecked it. The feeds from forty-seven showed her something she wasn't prepared for.

"Shit."

"What?" Balthazar stood with hands on his hips catching his breath after their quick run up twenty-three floors.

"They split up. Tappers went one way. The civilians went another." Jacira took the opportunity to catch her breath also.

"Where did the civvies go?" he asked.

"Toward Sarazin, I think." She gazed down the passageway to her left, toward Aubrey and the girl.

"And the Tappers?"

She pointed her chin in the opposite direction. "That way. Not sure what they're after."

"Well," Balthazar said, turning his head in either direction, "who do we hit first?"

* * *

Francesca saw Jacobi turn the corner into passageway two. She didn't know how he'd ended up in an open ward or why he was alone, but she thought his attempt to disguise himself in an inmate's uniform was a wise choice. Why he hadn't used his chip to open the stairwells or even the elevator, assuming he had special access, was a question she couldn't answer. Somehow, he'd managed to get himself into quite a bit of trouble and she intended to find out why.

Several inmates walked alone in the corridors and passageways but bolted the minute they saw her or Rudolfo. Thus, they tracked Member Principal Jacobi unmolested.

She peeked around a corner and watched Jacobi dart into an open cell about halfway down the passageway. She motioned to Rudolfo and together they moved toward the cell.

Ten feet short of the door to Jacobi's cell, Rudolfo placed a hand on her shoulder, stopping her.

He leaned in close. "Let me go in first. You can listen from the door, but … I need to hear this from him. I need his confession without coercion." He eyed her spear.

She nodded quickly and watched Rudolfo enter the cell.

Francesca stood just outside the door with her back against the wall, listening to the two men talk.

* * *

Jacira watched the young Apprentice Member in a small window on her scroll tablet. "What the hell is she doing?"

Balthazar looked over her shoulder. "Where is the old man?"

She searched the camera feeds until she found a view from inside the cell the Apprentice stood next to. Rudolfo stood in the center of the cell speaking to an elderly inmate who sat on the edge of a bed. Something was off about the prisoner. Puzzled, Jacira zoomed in tight on the inmate and realized what was wrong—the inmate had a full head of white hair. She recognized the Member Principal instantly.

"That's Jacobi," she said. Both Oona and Balthazar craned their necks to see the camera feed. "What is he doing in there?"

"Audio," Oona said.

Jacira had forgotten about the audio. With a quick tap, sound emanated from the tablet.

" … everything. I had no choice, Rudie," Jacobi said. "It was never supposed to get to this point. I could never have imagined it would have become …"

"Many Members have died today." Rudolfo's voice came through the tablet in an even, almost monotonous, tone. "Many more prisoners."

"Lest you forget, Rudie, our job is to kill prisoners. If they didn't die today, they'd die later." Jacobi stared at the floor. "I care deeply about the lost Members, however. I take their deaths heavily. But we will rebuild, of that I am certain." He scratched his chin and looked off into space.

"How did it come to this, Jacobi? I've never been so naïve as to think the Order was infallible or without corruption in the rank and file. This, however," Rudolfo gestured to the prison outside, "is an otherworldly level of deceit."

"You always had a way with words, Rudie."

"Tell me why."

"I told you. He was going to expose everything if I didn't comply." Jacobi pointed skyward.

"Who was? And what is everything?" Rudolfo inched closer. "Tell me."

"I thought you weren't naïve." Jacobi smiled at Rudolfo and let out a slight chuckle. "Just know that it wasn't ever about me. If I got in trouble, so what. But he … he could have brought down the entire system. The entire Order would have crumbled. Imagine the implications, Rudie!"

"Who? Who would bring it down?" Rudolfo's voice elevated for the first time, surprising even Jacira.

"Sarazin, of course. James Sarazin. The man behind the

magic pill. If he takes down the Order, the ripple effects would be felt through all levels of society in ways we could not claw back from. Believe me, old friend. I had no choice."

"Sarazin." Rudolfo paused. "Ventana, Inc. The four scientists … and … Brother Wilcott. That was him?" He paused again. "No, that was you."

Jacobi faced Rudolfo open mouthed. His eyes drooped. "Yes. Wilcott. He did not have to self-select. I did not order that of him."

"Tapping the scientists, though. That was you. You made him do that."

Jacobi physically recoiled at Rudolfo's words. "Rudie, please don't use that term. So crude."

"You don't deny it?" Rudolfo took a step toward Jacobi, who eyed him warily.

"No. No, I don't deny it. Had to be done. I tell you, Rudie, if Sarazin had gone public it would have been catastrophic to our way of life."

Rudolfo took another step toward Jacobi. "Tell me everything. What would have been made public?"

Jacobi stared at Rudolfo for a moment then looked away, shaking his head. "Common practice. It was common for all Members Principal for decades. I never thought anything of it, but …"

Rudolfo moved closer still, his voice became louder. "Tell me everything."

Jacobi closed his eyes. "The orphans. All Members were once orphans. Myself included." He pointed at Rudolfo. "You included, Rudie."

"Yes. That is the way. Orphans no one else claims, no one else can care for are taken into the Order."

"Yes, that is the way. Do you really think we get the best orphans?" Jacobi looked up with a knowing smile. "Or, I should ask, do you think we would have got the best orphans?"

"I don't ..."

"Rudie, you're being naïve again." Jacobi touched his own chin. "Imagine some smart, kind, well-rounded kid is at the orphanage. Been there a little while, seen a lot of potential parents, but no one wants them. How could that be? How could a great kid like that get passed up? Not given a home?" Jacobi paused as if waiting for an answer. "They don't, Rudie. They don't get passed up. We intervene. We bribe. We make deals. We cajole."

The confession seemed to animate Jacobi, who gesticulated wildly as he spoke. "It's been done for decades and for good reason. We need the best people possible to do this job. We need the brightest, most even-keeled, sharpest thinkers we can get. Imagine, Rudie, if we took only the children no one wanted? What would we do with the dregs? The Order couldn't function. It couldn't provide the ..."

"Those children could have had homes," Rudolfo said in a quiet voice. "Who knows what their lives would have been like?" He looked away for a moment, then said, "Was I one of these children? One of the lives you stole? Could ... could I have had a family?"

Jacobi exhaled a lengthy sigh; his shoulders slumped. "I honestly don't know, my friend. That was before my time. But if I had to guess ..."

"My brother." Someone entered the frame on Jacira's tablet. It was the Apprentice. She stormed toward Jacobi, shouting at the man. "They said my brother would be stuck there at that awful place if I didn't go with the Order. Was that true? Did you snatch me away from him? If I had stayed, would I have been given a chance at a real family?"

Jacobi stood, a look of defiance across his face. "Are you implying the Pupil's School didn't provide you with a family? I know for a fact that they treated you with every kindness." He jabbed a finger. "You had friends. You had teachers, counselors. You learned more there than in any other educational institution in this hemisphere. It was a home to you whether you want to believe it or not."

"Answer her question," Rudolfo said. His voice sucked the fervor out of the Member Principal.

Jacobi's eyes shot between the Apprentice and her Mentor. "I have no idea. It doesn't work like that. We just give them names and they provide." He shrugged deeply and held out his hands. "Sometimes it requires a little more incentive than usual. A little more compensation than the state will pay out. How the facility goes about meeting the request is up to them." Jacobi straightened.

On Jacira's tablet screen, it appeared that the confession had taken physical weight off his shoulders.

"You see," Jacobi continued as he sat back down, sounding and looking calmer than before, "I couldn't let it get out. Imagine the implications, Rudie. Imagine the repercussions. We'd never recover from it." Jacobi buried his head in his hands.

"Perhaps we shouldn't recover from it. Maybe the Order has reached the end of its usefulness to the world. Perhaps the Order should wither just as we do." Rudolfo held up his right hand and removed the leather glove to reveal the deeply stained purple-black flesh. "Ours was meant to be a divine purpose. Serving the world by upholding the purity of our duties. Judging and selecting without bias, without corruption, without deceit or dishonor." He pulled back the sleeve of his cassock revealing his equally blackened forearm. "We Members take on the stains of our terrible responsibilities so the Order itself stays clean."

Rudolfo reached into his pocket and removed a small glass object.

"I have judged you, Jacobi." He opened the vial in his left hand. "You have been selected for the Sacred Task."

Jacobi glanced up as Rudolfo dipped his finger into the vial. The Member Principal's face solidified. His eyes burned with fear, never leaving the vial. Rudolfo did not relent, moving forward with his deadly finger held in front of him. Jacobi watched as the man stepped closer, his eyes locked on the Member's finger. Then, the Member Principal's features relaxed. He let a held breath escape and closed his eyes. As if resigning himself to the inevitable, he let his head hang, exposing the back of his neck.

Jacobi offered no resistance.

Rudolfo reached out with the finger that had spelled the end for so many. Now, it judged and condemned a man Rudolfo had known most of his life. A man he'd looked to for wisdom. A man he considered a friend, a brother.

Rudolfo touched a spot at the base of Jacobi's skull.

Jacira and the other outcasts couldn't see it, but they knew what happened next. The solution slid from the end of Rudolfo's finger, pooling for the briefest of seconds on the man's skin, like mercury on a nonmetallic surface. Then, it was absorbed by the body, deep into the tissue, the muscle, and the membrane surrounding the brain stem. All body and brain functions immediately shut off, like a light bulb winking out.

Member Principal Jacobi, the leader of the Order of the Coppice, fell face first into the concrete floor.

* * *

"Damn," Balthazar said, audibly exhaling. "Quite a show. Well, let's go waste those two while they're distracted." He stalked off down the corridor toward Francesca and Rudolfo. Jacira and Oona stayed put.

"Did you know?" Jacira asked. "Did either of you know about the orphanages and what the Order was doing?" Balthazar stopped and turned to face Jacira.

Oona, standing beside Jacira, shook her head. "No."

Balthazar's eyes darted between the two women. "I heard rumors and gossip, but nothing ever definitive." He spread his arms wide. "Honestly, I don't care. People end up where they end up. My parents died in a fire and now I'm here. Fate is fate. Destiny is destiny. I'm here now because I'm here now. We can't change the past." With one arm he pointed his rifle down the corridor. "I'm going to go shoot these assholes so we can get paid. I suggest you come with me or I'll have to tell Sarazin to increase my share for ..."

A red crater blossomed on Balthazar's forehead and his body fell limply to the floor. Jacira held her pistol up, still eyeing down the sights of the barrel. A movement to her right and she spun on her heel. Her weapon trained directly at Oona's face. Oona's gun pointed back at Jacira's face.

The two women stood there in an uncertain standoff for a moment. Steady hands holding weapons that, with the slightest twitch of the finger, could deliver a brain liquefying ball of lead, copper, and steel. Neither lowered their weapon. Neither fired.

"I had a sister," Jacira said, breaking the silence. Still holding her pistol level with Oona's head, she continued. "A twin actually. We looked identical, but we were total opposites. That head bitch at the orphanage told me that my sister would be better off if I left with the Order. She wouldn't want to leave with a family if I was still around."

Oona seemed to consider Jacira. Her eyelids twitched almost imperceptibly. "I had two brothers. Much younger. It seems we took similar paths."

In a show of good faith, Jacira took her finger off the trigger. She figured that Oona would have shot her by now if she really wanted to kill her.

"I don't care about the money at this point. I just want to leave this fucking prison. Forever." She lowered her pistol a few inches.

Oona followed suit. "I have enough money." She looked at Balthazar's corpse, then down the corridor toward their targets. "Fuck this place. Fuck Jacobi and fuck Sarazin."

"Go to the roof and wait for me. We'll take Sarazin's plane back to the city." Jacira started walking toward Rudolfo and Francesca's cell.

"Where are you going?" Oona called out after her.

"To see an old friend."

* * *

Rudolfo shivered on the floor, shaking bodily. Sweat dripped in rivulets from his scalp. Francesca could feel the heat radiating through his thick cassock. His face had gone gray, his eyes bloodshot.

"You didn't use the Sacred Oil, did you?" Francesca knelt beside him on the floor of the cell. Jacobi's body lay several feet away.

"D-Didn't think about it." He smiled up at her. His hands clenched on his chest.

"Will this kill you?" Francesca asked in as calm a voice as she could muster.

"M-might wish it w-would soon," Rudolfo stammered. "My t-time anyway. Better this w-way." His eyes shut tight. She could tell he was fighting to hold it together. When he opened them, they looked different, more determined than before. "F-Francesca, please. You m-must. Please." His eyes spelled out the request. Pleading with her.

With a nod and watery eyes, she reached into Rudolfo's front pocket and removed two glass vials. She pressed both into his left palm until their lids shot open with a *slink.* After gently rolling her Mentor onto his stomach, she dipped the tip of her right index finger in the Sacred Oil, coating it up to the second knuckle. Then, she dipped the same finger into the viscous, black Solution.

* * *

Jacira stepped into the cell but stopped just beyond the threshold. Her former Mentor lay dead on the floor next to the Member Principal who had excommunicated her. On the edge of a bed, staring blankly at the wall, sat a young woman she knew from her life at the Pupil's School.

Francesca didn't notice her at first, then with a start, she scooped up a spear on the floor and shot to her feet. Jacira didn't move. Her old friend was fighting mad for a moment, ready, it seemed, to run Jacira through. And judging by the black stain on the spear's point, Jacira knew it wouldn't take much more than a scratch to do the job.

Recognition crossed Francesca's face. A moment later, confusion.

"It was you?" Francesca asked. "The one hunting Aubrey and Malina."

"Yes, and you and him." Jacira pointed to Rudolfo. "But not anymore. I've … grown in the past few hours. Hell, in the last few minutes."

"Are you here to kill me or not?" Francesca held the spear firmly, her lead hand blanching white at the knuckles. A black discoloring on her fingertip drew Jacira's attention.

"Already selecting? Pretty early for an Apprentice. It took me almost a year …"

"Are you?" Francesca spat. "Are you going to try and kill me? If so, let's get it over with." The spear shook. Not out of fear, Jacira guessed, but out of anger.

"No, Frannie. I'm not going to try and kill you. I heard the old men talking and let's just say that it's … changed my perspective." Jacira turned her gaze to Brother Rudolfo lying on his back, lifeless on the floor. His hands at his sides. Eyes closed.

She moved into the cell and knelt beside him. "I've only come to pay my respects."

A pause hung in the air. "He was your Mentor?" Francesca knelt. Jacira noticed she still had one hand on the spear.

"Yes. He was good to me. Taught me a lot and tried to help me quell my … tendencies." Her eyes fell on Jacobi. "He was the real bastard. The reason I'm no longer welcome in the Order. Good riddance."

"Yet you were going to kill Rudolfo," Francesca said.

Jacira raised her eyes to Francesca's. "I wasn't sure what I was going to do, actually. Without hearing Jacobi's confession first, I might have. Then again, I might not have." Jacira stood. "But I did hear it. And now, I choose not to kill you. And even if I wanted to kill Rudolfo, you've beat me to it."

"He was suffering." Francesca stared at Rudolfo's body with a tight face.

"I'm sure he was." Jacira moved to the door. "It was good seeing you, Frannie. Truly, it was."

Francesca sat silent as Jacira left the cell and headed toward the west stairwell.

30

The Long Fall

Aubrey and Malina jogged down the curving outer passageway toward the west stairwell. At every intersection, he waited for the all clear from Malina, but only briefly. They reached the stairwell door in the west ward. To their surprise, it was already open. Stepping into the door's threshold, it was clear some inmates had employed welding strips to cut the door off its hinges because it laid flat on the landing in front of them.

Straight ahead, the stairs descended to the forty-sixth floor. To their right, they went up to the forty-eighth.

"And we don't have any shots of the forty-eighth floor's interior?" he asked.

"That's right. But I may have a trick up my hoodie." She tapped and scrolled on her tablet for a moment. "Got it." She showed him the screen. "No feeds from the interior of forty-eight, but the floor is mostly glass, so I can see some of it from below."

Examining the tablet screen, Aubrey saw an upward view from a lower floor from the inside of the Great Atrium.

Through the glass, he could make out odd shapes of what looked like luggage or duffel bags. No movement and no people, however.

"Looks clear from there."

"Yes, but there are rooms all around the perimeter." She motioned to the area around the outer edge of the glass. "He could be in any of them."

They climbed the steps to the last door in the stairwell. Aubrey set down his axe and swung the bag off his shoulder, removing four welding strips. He began pressing one over each hinge, which were, conveniently, on their side of the door.

He handed the last strip to Malina. "Push this into the gap between the door and the jamb right over where the deadbolt should be."

Once all the strips were in place, Aubrey looked at Malina who gave him a thumbs up. At the same time, she pulled the tab on the strip over the lock and he pulled the tab on the strip over the top hinge. They ran down the stairs and waited.

A second of silence passed followed by a loud hissing intermixed with popping and crackling. The noise lasted thirty seconds. Aubrey bounded up the stairs once more, pulled the tabs on the remaining strips and ran down to wait with Malina.

Once the hissing stopped, another second of silence passed. A loud scraping sound, and an angry groan echoed through the cavernous stairwell. A rush of air and a deafening boom washed over them as several hundred pounds of steel crashed flat with the concrete landing.

"Stay here," Aubrey said. "Better yet, go find an empty cell and lock yourself in there."

"Fuck you, Martin."

He feigned a confused grin. "I thought you weren't a field operative?"

"Can we just go catch this asshole? We can discuss the division of labor after we get out of this." She started up the stairs, Aubrey leapt to follow.

Each hugged the edge of the flight of steps then rushed to each side of the open door. Aubrey made eye contact with her across the opening and held up a finger. He pointed at his eyes then to the tablet around her neck. She looked down, scanned the screen, then gave him a thumbs up.

Aubrey peeked his head around the door jamb and quickly pulled his head back, blinking away the bright spots on his retinas. The room he'd just seen was incredibly bright, the light compounded by his eyes having adjusted to the dark stairwell. He squinted and peered back into the bright space.

Every surface reflected sunlight. If it wasn't the glass floor acting like a mirror, it was the glossy white surfaces of the surrounding floor and walls. Soon, however, he could visually confirm what Malina had seen with the camera feed. The space was empty. Three duffel bags lay open on the floor. Articles of black clothing near the bags, but otherwise the space was empty.

He crept through the door, axe in hand. To Malina, he held a finger to his lips. No sound.

Down both white, shiny walls were more doors set flush. Ensuring the space was clear of threats, Aubrey raced across the white floor path and out onto the glass where the duffel bags lay. He searched them quickly but found only spare clothing, empty pistol magazines, and boxes of various sized bullets. Nothing he could use beyond a short folding knife.

Aubrey stood and jogged back to Malina, who stood with her back toward the wall. She stared down at the glass with wide eyes.

"I hate heights," she said.

"Don't worry. That glass is strong. See those support struts? And anyway," he handed her the knife, "I don't plan on being out there too much." Aubrey pointed to the first door to the right of the stairs. "Let's start here and work our way around."

They took opposite sides of the door. Aubrey reached for the knob, his back pressed against the wall. He turned the knob and the door swung open toward them. He waited, listening. When he heard no sounds from inside, he peeked around the jamb. The large room was set up as living quarters. With a wide bed, several bookshelves, and even a television, it was far and away more lavish than Rudolfo's tiny hovel.

Two doors led off the bedroom. After a quick search of the room turned up nothing, Aubrey tried the first door which led to a lavish bathroom with standup shower, clawfoot tub, and a vanity at least fifteen feet long.

The second door led into a long wide library unlike anything Aubrey had ever seen. He made sure the room was safe then invited Malina in to see it. They both stood in mild awe. The books covered every wall and were sorted by color. Dark brown books at the far end melted into yellows, oranges, reds and blues as they circled the room. It was like a wave of color washing over the walls.

"This dude has too much time on his hands," Malina said.

Aubrey ran to the far side of the library where a door stood amidst a sea of brown books. He opened it slowly, peered inside. It was some sort of anteroom with a table and chairs. Walls inside were as white and bright as those in the circle room. He waved to Malina to follow him.

The only door off the anteroom led back outside to the circle room. From there they continued their search, door to door around the floor of glass. The rooms ranged from closets of different sizes to conference rooms. They found a set of stairs leading to the roof and a large kitchen with a formal eating area.

"His plane is still here," Malina said, checking her tablet. "He's here somewhere."

The door they came to next looked identical to the others. As they did at every one before it, Aubrey stood on one side and Malina on the other. He reached for the knob, expecting it to turn like the others, and it did. He pulled it open a few inches and turkey-peeked around the jamb. It was a long dark room with no windows, and no lights on inside. The space was dimly lit by the light of several screens along the right-hand wall; a console with a myriad of buttons and touch pads stood below them. An empty rolling chair was tucked under the console.

"Control room," Aubrey whispered. He continued scanning the room. "This is the only exit. And ... it looks empty." He pulled the door open all the way, waited briefly, then stepped inside. "Let's check it out. Maybe we can use the console for some recon."

The room was indeed empty with nothing large enough for anyone to hide behind. The two of them entered and after a quick search of the space settled their view on the screens. Four large monitors filled the wall. Each screen displayed four windows with different views from around the prison. Malina tapped on the control console and quickly began scanning through the feeds.

"Looks like things have settled a bit," she said. She was right, the prison had settled into some sort of mundane existence. Most of the violence had occurred in the first few hours. Now, a majority of the prisoners looked ... bored.

Inmates were still gathered in the mess halls and some in the social areas. Overall, it looked as if they were waiting out the interim until the authorities retook the prison.

"Check on progress to retake the prison," Aubrey said, momentarily distracted from the search. "Try the lower levels."

She clicked the control pad and punched a few keys. The screen showed half a dozen views of a single level. "This is level one," Malina said. "It's empty." She tried more camera feeds. "No one is there."

"Try the cells."

She changed the feed to the inside of a cell on level one. "There they are," she said. Inmates lay on beds or the floor in each feed from inside the cells. Some were bruised and bandaged, others appeared fine. It looked as if their numbers had thinned. Many beds stood empty.

"Try each level until you see one that is not cleared yet." Aubrey glanced toward the door of the control room. A feeling that they should hurry settled over him.

Malina rapidly scanned feeds from each level until she found it. "Here," she said, pointing. On screen, officers stretched across a corridor clad in body armor, face masks, and carrying clear curved shields stalked the corridors and passageways. Prisoners were surrendering to them. Others tried to fight, but the officers, numbering in the hundreds from what Aubrey could tell, and their tight phalanx style formations quickly overwhelmed them.

"What level is that?" Aubrey asked.

"Sixteen."

"Shit," he sighed. "It's going to be a while before they make it all the way up here."

"Here's something new," she said. "I can see into the Tappers' quarters." She typed commands and manipulated a touch pad. "I couldn't see those feeds on the connection I hacked into from Rudolfo's room."

"Try this floor," Aubrey said.

Malina typed a few more commands and brought up several feeds on one screen, each with a location stamp in the lower corner that read *48.* Every view from the forty-eighth floor was blank. She kept cycling through the various feeds as if to confirm.

"What the hell happened to the feeds from …" A sound made Aubrey turned on his heel. Something moved past the door to the control room behind him. An object rolled in. A metallic *tink tink* from the floor. No, he thought, it was thrown in. A flash of light burst from it. So bright, Aubrey was blinded momentarily.

Shielding his face from further flashes, he felt around for Malina. He found her shoulder and forced her to the ground, shoving her under the console.

"Get down!"

Smoke filled his mouth and nose. Another *tink tink*. Then another. Two more flashes visible through his eyelids. A second later, more smoke. The light from outside cut off as the door was slammed shut.

"We have to get out," Aubrey coughed into Malina's ear.

"It's a trap, Martin."

"I know. But we have no choice." The flash bangs and smoke grenades had been brilliantly deployed into the confined space with no way out but the way they came in. Whoever was out there, was waiting for them just outside the door.

He deduced they had no guns or they would have used them already. He needed to shield them from attack for about half a second. He looked around the narrow room, but there was too much smoke. He tried to remember what was inside the space. A small plastic trash can. A flimsy, cumbersome desk chair. Nothing else not bolted down. He needed a literal shield.

Then he realized they were staring him in the face. Through the thickening smoke rising from the floor, shone the video monitors. Large, flat, and lightweight, they'd make a pretty decent emergency shield.

He handed Malina his axe. "Hold this," he said and reached up, grabbed the nearest monitor by the bezel, and lifted it off its mounting hardware. Malina yanked the cables from its backside and the warm screen that pressed against Aubrey's cheek went dark.

The door opened to the right, which meant the attack would most likely come from their left. He held the monitor lengthwise vertically on that side and turned to Malina.

"Stay on my right," he said through wheezing breaths.

She gripped his shirt, coughing violently near his shoulder. Her hands trembled.

"Now."

They sprinted toward the door. Aubrey lifted his foot

and kicked the door in midstride. It flew from its casing in a splintering crash. They kept running. Aubrey stiffened, tightened his grip, braced himself for an attack from the left side. The shield side.

The impact he expected never came. What came instead was a muscle clenching, heart stopping, unmistakable shock of thousands of volts of electricity pumping through him. The surge paralyzed his body and he fell like a deadweight to the hard, glossy floor. He landed flat on his back. The monitor turned shield crashed into his face, his nose and teeth crunching against the plastic.

Malina screamed somewhere near him, maybe a few feet away.

His paralysis left him as quickly as it came. He threw the monitor to the side in time to see blue sparks coming right at him. They hit him in the chest, seizing his muscles, paralyzing him again. His body froze as pain coursed through every muscle and joint. All he could do was stare straight ahead at the man on the other end of the stun baton.

James Sarazin glared with eyes in slits, like a predator. A snarl crossed his face.

"You thought you could just sabotage everything I've created. My life! My legacy!" He screamed into Aubrey's immovable face.

Sarazin pressed the baton harder into Aubrey's chest, leaning with what must have been his full weight into it, just over Aubrey's heart. Tremors coursed through him along with a tight, binding pain he'd never felt. The smell of burnt flesh filled the air. He tasted copper in his mouth. His breath had stopped completely. He continued seizing from head to toe, small high frequency jitters so fast and so violent he thought his bones might snap. No matter how much he concentrated, he could not resist.

He knew that in a few seconds, his heart would stop.

All he could do was watch Sarazin murder him.

"Who the fuck do you think you are? You're not even a goddamn cop, Martin Aubrey," Sarazin said. "You just a fucking ..."

Sarazin flew to the side within a blur of green hoodie.

The seizing in Aubrey's body stopped instantly.

A shout came followed by a woman's scream. Aubrey couldn't look up. His body had relaxed slightly, but the residual effect of the baton lingered in his muscles. With considerable effort, he rolled to his side and curved his neck. Slowly, Sarazin and Malina's struggle came into view.

She was on top of him with her knife out, her arms held at bay by Sarazin. He bled from a cut on his face. His baton had been knocked away. Malina, though small, was wickedly quick. Several times she twisted out of Sarazin's grip and cut him on the chest, neck, and face—only superficial cuts but it kept Sarazin busy. Aubrey used the time to focus on regaining control of his limbs.

A second passed and he was able to bend his legs. It was like breaking dried clay from a mold. His arms were immensely sore. His chest burned.

He rolled onto all fours, got one leg under him just as he saw Sarazin connect a right hook with Malina's jaw. She wavered backward, stunned. Sarazin's leg shot out, landing a powerful kick to her chest. Her body collapsed in on itself and she flew back, unconscious.

The Ventana CEO twisted toward Aubrey. "You've got quite the fucking crew, Aubrey."

Aubrey's muscles were still in shock, refusing his commands. Sarazin got to his feet and took two long strides toward him delivering a swift, unfettered kick to Aubrey's abdomen.

He folded onto the floor once again. His head smashed into the glass floor for the second time in as many minutes. Aubrey's limbs, however, were coming back under his control. He got back to his hands and knees, quicker this time, then onto two wobbly legs.

Sarazin had walked back to the control room door and picked up Aubrey's axe. He hefted it over his shoulder as he walked casually toward Aubrey. His shirt had been slashed open by Malina's knife. Through the slashed fabric, Aubrey could see black body armor.

"I was just telling someone earlier," Sarazin said in a conversational tone, "I've never actually killed anyone with my own hands. Shit, what I did there," he pointed at Malina laying unconscious on the ground, "was the first time I'd ever hit anyone. I mean like, flesh on flesh and not during some jujitsu workout or something. You know what I mean." He held up a fist and looked at it like he just learned of its existence.

Sarazin rambled on while Aubrey slowly backed away farther out onto the glass floor. "Even when I was kid, I would just convince someone else to beat up bullies for me. I wasn't rich back then, but I've always been exceedingly persuasive." He stopped and placed a hand on his hip, surveying a spot in space with a triumphant expression. "I like it, Aubrey. I like the intimate, visceral nature of hand-to-hand combat. So much better than hurting someone through a computer, phone, or a ... proxy."

"Like OFP," Aubrey said. "Or should I say the mercenaries who pretended to be OFP. They did your dirty work for you."

"Such a smart boy, Martin." Sarazin smiled and pointed a finger at Aubrey.

"All those innocent people died just to cover up your lie." Aubrey continued moving backward, regaining strength with each step. "To hide what Zentransa does to the children of longtime users."

Sarazin's eyebrows shot up. "Figured that out too, did you? I had a feeling you did when you found not only the kids, Jorgetson and the other one, but *how* you found them! The game *A Word With You.* That really made me laugh. After I found her," he pointed at Malina with the axe head, "poking around in our servers, I knew it was only a matter of time. I didn't know exactly what Alkorn and his cronies were saying to each other in that game, but I knew it wasn't good and I knew where it would lead."

"And the Tapper? Wilcott? You got him to kill Alkorn and his team. Someone else doing your work for you."

"A story for another time." Sarazin swung the axe off his shoulder, the wood slapping into his open palm. "This isn't a goddamn movie, Martin. I'm not going to spend the next several minutes divulging my entire plan." The CEO took a step forward. "But I will say this: if you were to succeed here today, if you were to bring the problems with Zentransa to light, it would throw our whole way of life into a downward spiral. Civilization is not just addicted to Zentransa and what it can do for them, it's now a part of them. It's connected to them as much as they are to it. It's symbiotic. Remove it now, and society will wither."

Aubrey stopped backing up. He was weak, slow, and

injured in more places than he could count. But Sarazin was an inexperienced fighter and the axe was top heavy and unwieldy. If Aubrey could bring him in close, he might have a shot.

He exaggerated his very real exhaustion by bending slightly, blinking rapidly and taking deep, stuttered breaths. With eyelids half closed, he waited for Sarazin to strike.

"Now, I've already been here longer than I planned." Sarazin stepped forward holding the axe like a baseball bat. "So, let's get on with it."

With a growl and an expression that was a mix of exertion and rage, Sarazin swung the axe at Aubrey's head.

Aubrey snapped himself fully upright and arched his back. He watched the red and silver axe head pass two inches in front of his face. He saw Sarazin's eyes go wide with surprise as the axe's momentum carried him around.

Aubrey pounced. He threw his full weight behind a kick to Sarazin's exposed rib cage. The man tumbled away but managed to stay on his feet. Aubrey closed the gap, wrapped Sarazin's neck in a rear naked chokehold. The man scrambled to his full height, thrusting his shoulders back. Aubrey steadied himself. The axe head came up, Sarazin punched at him with it but Aubrey dodged it.

He tightened his chokehold. Sarazin's face went gray, then a shade of blue. He fell to his hands and knees, Aubrey still tight on his back. The CEO crawled, pulling both men along for a few feet. Aubrey risked a glance around at Sarazin. His hand was wrapped around the baton; blue sparks flew from its sharp chrome tips.

A second later, Aubrey felt the familiar jolt of electricity in his thigh. The waves of pain coursed through him again, incapacitating him. Sarazin flipped, crashing down on Aubrey in his weakened state. The chokehold released.

The man stood over Aubrey, the axe held high over his head. The blade flashed down toward Aubrey's head.

He rolled just as the head of the axe collided with the glass floor in a spray of glimmering shards. He rolled back and reached for the wooden handle only to find Sarazin struggling to extricate it from the floor. The blade had cracked the glass and knocked away a chunk, burying itself into the alloy support strut running beneath them and under the floor.

Aubrey kicked Sarazin away from the weapon. He rocked the axe back and forth, yanking it free just as the man was nearly on him again. The blade swung away, off the floor, the blunt end of it smashing into Sarazin's orbital socket. The CEO fell to the side but was back on Aubrey with surprising quickness.

He held the baton again, aiming it at Aubrey's chest. Dropping the axe, Aubrey grabbed the wrist holding the stun baton with one hand and gripped Sarazin's neck with the other. The baton grazed Aubrey's left arm, sending a tremor down his forearm and bicep. His left arm went slack for one heartbeat and the baton sank toward his chest. He released the hand on Sarazin's throat and slapped the baton away, gripping it as he did.

He rolled slightly, pushing the tip with its fiery blue sparks into the glass floor.

Aubrey had never believed in luck or coincidence, but the next two seconds would make him question that belief.

As the baton's tip hit the floor, still in both men's steely grip, it landed squarely in the crater left by Sarazin's axe swing.

There it found the alloy support strut. Thousands of volts traveled through the strut, instantly heating and expanding it. A crack formed, growing with lightning speed, shooting across the floor and splintering into a thousand strands of a massive spiderweb.

Sarazin fled, turning and dashing across the still intact glass behind him toward the walking path.

Aubrey scrambled into a crawling position and followed him, his feet slipping on the glass. Behind him, crunching and buckling echoed off the curved walls. He felt the floor wrench violently. Malina lay ahead of him, her upper half on the walking path, her lower half on the glass. With a burst of energy, he didn't know he possessed, he pumped his legs and stretched out toward Malina grasping her ankle as he dove for safety.

He reached the path just as the floor fell away, sliding Malina's entire body onto the smooth white floor. He watched several tons of glass fall into the open air of the Great Atrium. Like the throat of a terrible beast that swallowed all things, it devoured the downpour of glass.

Movement to his right, but Aubrey reacted too slowly. A red flash in the corner of his eye and something hard slammed into his head. Blackness washed over his field of vision. Someone pulled on him, propping him up. Aubrey's hands felt around; looking for a weapon. Looking for anything he could use to fight. His right hand felt a back pack. Long rods of what felt like clay.

Sarazin's hot breath in his face.

Eyesight returned in waves of color reminiscent of the unusual library from moments ago.

"Like I said, Martin," Sarazin sneered, "this is not a fucking movie. The good guy doesn't win in real life. I'm going to throw you down that convenient hole that just opened up. And you're going to die. Then, I'm going to throw your little girlfriend into the hole and she's going to die."

Aubrey pushed against Sarazin. Pressed his hands into Sarazin's chest, against his body armor. Sarazin didn't budge. Aubrey's arms were so weak. Dizziness flooded his brain. His head lolled to the side.

Sarazin didn't even attempt to fight him off, Aubrey's resistance was so feeble.

He closed his eyes. Felt himself being lifted up. On his feet, then dragged. Cold wind rushed across his face. His hands feeling, searching for something he knew was there.

His heels over the edge. Fingers finding it. Finding the tab, the small plastic circle. Clutching it with desperate little strength he could summon.

"Good bye, Martin," the man hissed into his ear.

And Sarazin released him.

Aubrey fell back and only then opened his eyes. He saw his own hand, outstretched, still holding the small plastic circle tab. Saw the wire attached to the tab pulling away from the welding strip. Saw Sarazin look down in confusion then shock. Saw sparks come to life on the man's chest. Saw the strip give birth to smoke and fire. Watched as Sarazin's upper half disappeared in a fireworks display of white and yellow light.

A heartbeat of time passed and Aubrey's body began a slow mid-air turn. The last thing he saw was the flaming, smoking mass of Sarazin's body falling into the Great Atrium, toward Aubrey.

The ground came quicker than Aubrey had expected. And

he felt it. Felt himself impact the hard floor of the bottom of the Great Atrium.

He could still feel it, seconds later. He could feel the ground but knew that it couldn't be right. He shouldn't feel anything at all. He didn't know what death meant, but it wasn't what he felt after falling from the forty-eighth floor of the Keep.

Pain, a great deal of it, all over. He also felt his own weight pressing against his chest and ... air ... in his lungs ... going in and out involuntarily.

He could think of nothing else to do except open his eyes. He blinked the world into a blurry funhouse map of mixed colors and indiscernible shapes. Then, something close to focused.

Soon, he saw emptiness, literal emptiness. The yawning emptiness of the Great Atrium below him. He was floating in the center of the great cylinder of air.

Was he still falling? Was time arrested for him as his death raced toward him? Would he spend eternity watching his end come frame by frame?

Something against his face convinced him he was no longer falling. He managed to twist his head and felt a scratch against his cheek. With all the will he could muster he lifted his neck and head. He was laying in the middle of a nest. No. A rope ladder. Some patchwork of white and green material stretched across the atrium and somehow, Aubrey had managed to find it.

His body was stuck like a fly in a web. And like a fly, he couldn't move if he wanted to. And he was fine with not moving. He was happy to wait for help and in the meantime, he'd get a little rest.

31

Rest for the Weary

Aubrey didn't know how long he'd been unconscious. When he opened his eyes, he was on his back staring at a gray ceiling. White tubes of light rushed by overhead. His eyelids were heavy. The world winked in and out of view as he strained to stay awake and alert.

A voice next to him spoke, "We'll get him stabilized for travel. Then, he'll get in a drone and fly back to the city for further treatment."

His head rolled toward the voice. A man in a white lab coat, a doctor's coat, walked along beside him.

Another voice. "Thank you, doctor," said a woman from somewhere over his shoulder.

"Will you be meeting him there? I can have a passenger drone sent to take you," said the doctor.

"No. Too much to do here."

Aubrey knew the voice. He tried to raise his hand to get their attention, but all his energy was only sufficient enough to lift one finger. It did the trick.

"He's waking." The woman came into view. Platinum hair,

black cloak. Francesca. "Hello, Martin. They're going to take care of you and get you back to a hospital in the city."

He tried to speak. He had a question about someone. Someone he'd been thinking about. His lips moved but the words were stubborn, refusing to leave his throat.

Francesca's head bent closer, turning her ear toward him.

"Malina," he said in barely in a whisper.

"She's going to be fine. She'll be on her way to the city also."

"R-ru-ru ..."

Francesca's face fell. Her eyes filled with sadness. She shook her head.

Aubrey felt his finger fall. He couldn't keep his eyes open any longer and the light vanished.

* * *

June 17, 2043—One week after the riot

Malina Maddox sat at a table in the back corner of *Le Grind Coffee*. Her hoodie pulled over her head, she watched the entrance of the coffee shop. It was late in the day so customer traffic was light. The baristas busied themselves cleaning tables, restocking the pastry display, and surfing their devices.

She was one of four customers seated in the long narrow shop. While the other customers' heads were buried in their computers or tablets, Malina's was stock still, waiting and watching. The sound of ceramic cups clinked against a granite countertop. An espresso machine hissed. The faint sound of easy listening music bled through speakers somewhere overhead. She heard all this, but her focus was singular—the door.

When Desmond Varela's face appeared in the oval window of *Le Grind's* front door, she tensed. Would he do it?

Desmond stepped inside, looked around for a moment, then spotted her. His face was blank when he sat down across from her, adjusting his tweed jacket as he did.

He cleared his throat.

"I have to admit, I was surprised to hear from you." He scanned the shop as if checking for anyone in earshot. "I'm the one who seeks you out. Usually, I'm the one who needs something from you. Now, it seems you need me."

"Yes, well, we all need people, don't we?" She slid a small square of paper across the table. He took it. "Memorize these. You're not leaving here with them." On the scrap of paper, she'd written a pass code for access to a digital dead drop on the web.

Desmond nodded slowly as his eyes took in the numbers. Folding the paper and passing it back to Malina, he said, "What will I find there and what am I supposed to do with it?"

Ignoring the first question, she said, "I need you to write a story."

* * *

"Do you think he'll do it?" Martin Aubrey asked Malina as she handed him a coffee in a paper cup. He removed the lid and blew on the surface of the hot liquid.

She looked back in the direction of *Le Grind*, two blocks from the street corner where they stood. Squinting against the sun of late day, she said, "This story will define his legacy.

He'll do it."

"And he'll leave us out of it?"

She smiled. "I left a little Easter egg in the dead drop so he knows what will happen if he reveals his sources. A little something to remind him of what we can dig up when properly motivated."

Aubrey sipped his coffee, savoring the bitter, earthy flavor.

"Did you see the news this morning?" she asked.

He nodded. Three more children had been found with BSS. Triplets whose mother had been Vice President of product development at Ventana, Inc.

"This will help," she said, pointing a thumb back toward the coffee shop. "People will know what's really happening, they can stop taking Zentransa, and the doctors can finally look into the real cause instead of flying blind looking for cures in all the wrong places."

"Yeah." Aubrey was unsure of how to feel. What he and Malina had uncovered would certainly make a difference, but was it enough? Or was it too late?

"So, why don't you want credit for any of this?" She punched his arm playfully. "None of this would be possible without you. Even if they can't cure BSS, they can prevent it now. Why don't you want people to know it was you?"

He smiled at her. "Why don't you want credit?"

She smiled back. "I'm off the grid and want to keep it that way."

He tilted his head back and looked at the sky. "If I don't take credit for it, who do you think people will suspect was the source? Based on all the evidence we gave Desmond?"

She pushed her hood back and brushed her fingers through her hair. Her forehead creased for a moment. "Naturally, they'll think it was Alkorn and his team. People will assume they had some deal with Desmond to release the story if something happened to them."

Aubrey raised his eyebrows and cocked his head.

"And ..." she started, but when she saw his expression, she appeared to change tack, "and that's exactly what you want. You want them to be the heroes." She shook her head. "I should have seen that coming."

"You're going to make a great detective, Miss Maddox." He turned and the two of them began the short walk back to his apartment. "I can't wait to do this again."

"Less violence next time, please," Malina said.

"Sure thing," Aubrey said. "I'll make sure the bad guys know that in advance."

Epilogue

July 5, 2043

Gilda Elmyr clutched her purse under one arm and with the other she dragged the two-wheeled wire frame cart packed with bags of groceries. She still liked to shop the old-fashioned way. Delivery to her building was available, her doormen were trustworthy, and she could certainly afford the concierge service where they would even put the food away for her, but it was best not to trust others to do something so important. Who knows where those delivery people had been before touching her food. No. She trusted one person to do her food shopping—herself.

Besides all that, it was good to get out. Living alone was hard on a woman, but she was used to it. Had been alone her entire life so she knew how crucial it was to get out and move around a little each day. This had been especially true in the five years since her retirement.

She reached her building and began climbing the gratuitously wide marble steps to the front entrance. As if waiting for her, a smiling doorman rushed down the stairs.

"Let me, Ms. Elmyr," he said, gently lifting the cart with two hands.

"Thank you, Riley." Gilda let the man take the cart up the stairs without complaint. He was dressed in the usual forest green uniform the men wore in the summers. As long as he didn't touch anything in the cart, she was okay with letting him help.

When she reached the front entrance, Riley held the wide, brass-trimmed doors open for her. Her cart was already inside where another door man scurried over to take it the rest of the way to the elevators.

She chose this building for these little niceties—the attentive doormen, the in-house dry cleaning, and the exquisitely decorated lobby that made her feel like she was walking into a palatial luxury hotel every time she entered. She also loved the spacious apartments and, of course, the privacy. She had an entire floor to herself and if she so desired, and she did so often, Gilda could altogether avoid seeing any of the other thirty-five residents in the building.

Her neighbors probably thought Gilda was a wealthy widow or a benefactor of an inheritance from a moneyed family. She let them think that. Friends from her old life probably considered her choices opulent or luxurious. She let them think that too.

She deserved everything she had. She'd devoted her life to helping others. To helping children. So many had better lives because of her. So many had families because of her.

Gilda retired from the Maryland Department of Human Services one day after turning sixty-five. Having worked twenty-three years for the department as Director of the East Region Orphanage on New Aberdeen's southside, she'd built up quite a bit of equity in the state's pension fund. The pension itself provided her with enough to live off if she had chosen a different lifestyle. But she'd wanted this lifestyle. So, along the way in her career, she had to make different choices regarding her income streams.

Her choices had reaped benefits beyond anything she could have imagined. Most former directors from Human Services couldn't boast her cash savings. She knew of a few other directors who could come close, four exactly, but no others.

Gilda stood at the elevator door waiting for it to open. Her face reflected back at her in the gleaming golden doors. Her white hair was in short curls. Lines stretched from the corners of her eyes to her temples. The bags under her eyes were heavy, drooping lower than normal. Her lips pursed in their usual look of dissatisfaction.

She gripped the handle of her cart when the light above the elevator illuminated.

Of course, there had been questions about her choices as Director of the Orphanage. There had been investigations. And she still ended up here. Still made it to retirement.

Gilda had been helping the Order of the Coppice, after all, and she'd never known of any investigations into the Order to have any teeth. If she had been exposed, the Order would have been exposed. Simple as that.

But she always had to remind herself, she had done it all to help the children. "Mustn't forget that," she told herself aloud. "I was helping the children."

* * *

The birds sang overhead and the breeze rustled his hair. Martin Aubrey wondered if he'd ever paid attention to the sounds of birds before. He found himself noticing things like this lately. He stopped on the street to pet a cat two days ago. He used to hate cats. The strangest thing, he hadn't thought about returning to the police force at all since the Keep.

Aubrey talked to police while he was still in the hospital and had visited the station several times to answer questions. But not once did he feel the old familiar sting of regret and emptiness. He missed the people he had worked with, but he wasn't filled with the overwhelming longing to have his badge back.

He sat on a park bench across the street from a luxury apartment building. The forty-story building looked like something out of the Victorian era supplanted into the ultra-modern architectural landscape of the city. The park around him bustled with activity. Children played, adults ran and exercised, old men battled across chessboards. On the street in front of him, the cars buzzed past, pedestrians walked to work, school, or to do their shopping.

Life around him looked normal. It was as if no one had heard the news released days ago—Zentransa was poisoning children through gene mutations in their parents. Production of the pill had been halted until further notice by a federal judge and upheld by an emergency session of the U.S. Supreme Court. Pharmacies, however, were permitted to continue selling the Z they had on hand until the investigations into Boarding School Syndrome and its causes were complete.

Ventana Inc., was busy doing damage control after their stock plunged as a result of not only the temporary death of their most popular product but also the very permanent death of their CEO, Chairman, and founder James Sarazin.

Aubrey had expected a monumental shift in the socio-economic fabric of society. The toppling of long held beliefs, traditions, and societal mainstays had a knack for throwing things into chaos. Instead, it appeared as if most people intended on carrying on with life as usual. It reminded him of the stories he'd read about revelations about cigarettes in the twentieth century. Even when everyone knew it was bad for them and those around them, people still smoked.

Everything, at the moment, felt normal, like it always had. There were signs of things to come, however. According to his sources on the Metro Police Department, there had been an uptick in the manufacture and sale of *street Z*.

Almost as soon as Zentransa was released to the masses, some enterprising street chemists reverse engineered its chemical makeup, giving birth to what was referred to as *street Z*, *dirty Z*, or just *dirt*. Some *street Z* was a legitimate clone of commercial Zentransa, chemically identical. But like all drugs, the higher quality meant a higher price tag. High end *street Z* often cost more than real stuff.

If there were no real Z, however, *street Z* would suddenly become infinitely more desirable and more expensive. Even the real dirty stuff.

Aubrey was in the process of weaning himself off Zentransa altogether. He and Malina both felt like the consequences of long-term use weren't worth the gains. He wanted kids, eventually, and he thought that quitting sooner rather than later was probably better. Even weaning off Z slowly was a huge adjustment for him. Suddenly sixteen hours seemed like not nearly enough time to fit in a whole day of work.

And, he thought, if it had been a difficult adjustment for him and Malina to slowly get off Zentransa, then he hated to imagine the ripple effect of millions of people forced to go cold turkey.

Another breeze rushed over Aubrey. A child pushed a

scooter down the sidewalk across the street. The silent river of cars all flowing in one direction.

Movement at the front of the luxury apartment building caught his attention. The doorman in his green uniform darted from the door and down the wide white steps. He disappeared momentarily behind a passing crowd and when he reappeared, the man in the green suit was bending to lift a small two-wheeled grocery cart from the hands of a white-haired woman in a gray cardigan and navy-blue skirt that stretched down past her knees.

Aubrey tapped his watch and a phone rang inside his earpiece. As it rang, he watched the woman climb the steps, no worse for wear after seventy years, he thought to himself. He raised his phone and snapped several pictures of the woman.

"Yeah?" Malina's voice said in his ear.

"Yeah? That's no way to talk to your boss, Maddox." He kept his eyes on the old woman as she entered the building's tall doors.

She huffed on the other end of the line. "I don't work for you, man. We're partners, remember?"

"Oh, right, I keep forgetting."

"So ... do you have her?" She asked in his ear. "If you do, I need to inform our client."

"Yes. I have her," Aubrey said. "Tell Francesca we found Gilda Elmyr. She is alive and well and will be here when Francesca decides to pay her a visit."

Before you go

Just a couple of things before you move on.

Martin Aubrey and Malina Maddox are going to continue kicking ass in future thrillers! Stay up to date on new releases by joining Justin's mailing list. Just go to justinrishel.com to sign up.

Also, did you know that reviews are a book's lifeblood? Good reviews, middle-of-the-road reviews, and even bad reviews tell a potential reader whether or not that particular book is meant for them. How many products have you ordered or not ordered based on the number and quality of reviews? Probably a lot and the same goes for me!

Do your fellow readers a favor and leave a review for the books you read. Maybe start with this one? Amazon, Goodreads, Bookbub, or wherever you like to find and discuss books would be a great place for leaving reviews.

You can leave an Amazon review for this book by returning to the book's product page. If you decide to write a few honest words on what you thought about *Executioner's Lament*, you would make this author's day.

About the Author

Justin is an author of thrillers, science fiction, and technothrillers like the Martin Aubrey Series.

Before becoming a writer, Justin was a U.S. Marine, a high school history teacher, a woodworker, and a corporate schmuck. Born and raised in Long Beach, Mississippi, Justin now lives in Tennessee with his wife, three kids, and the family dog.

You can connect with me on:

- https://www.justinrishel.com
- https://www.twitter.com/jrishelauthor
- https://www.facebook.com/justinrishelauthor

Made in the USA
San Bernardino, CA
11 August 2020

76654868R00275